Also from Bluestone Press

T.K. O'Neill (ebook)
Fly in the Milk

Thomas Sparrow's Northwoods Noir Trilogy
Northwoods Pulp:
four tales of crime and weirdness

Fatally Flawed

Northwoods Standoff

ISBN 978-0-9672006-6-8

Cover design by Joe Gunderson

Jackpine Savages

A Carter Brown Novel

T.K. O'NEILL

Bluestone Press

Chapter

1

I had wanted to be a private eye ever since I was a kid. Got the bug from watching detective shows on television. We had Mike Hammer and Michael Shayne, two trench-coat-wearing tough guys quick with the fists and the gunplay, and Peter Gunn, tough as railroad spikes but still cool, handsome and sophisticated.

These programs had a lot of things a kid could get behind. Hammer and Shayne never took guff from anyone and seemed to find a willing woman in every dive bar or lowball diner. Peter Gunn hung out in upscale nightclubs while the glamorous Julie London sang him torch songs. And he always looked like a million bucks at the end of a case. Their world was exciting and dangerous, and these guys had it all handled.

In my teen years, I discovered the paperback detectives: Marlowe, Archer, Spade, Spenser and the rest. I was still hooked on the dream. But like it is for most of us, I suspect, the future turned out unlike anything I'd imagined in my youth.

Never did become the detective. Ended up getting married and divorced and married and divorced again. Went through a heavy drug thing in the late eighties and lost my longtime job at the county highway department. Drifted from there, with stints on the railroad, bartending, dealing blackjack at the Indian casinos and house painting.

And those were the legal jobs.

Everything changed when my wealthy uncle Carl died last year at the age of ninety-seven. The resulting inheritance—twenty-five grand in a lump sum and a guaranteed two thousand monthly for the next ten years—was truly manna from heaven. Carl was one of the precious few fortunates who'd purchased 3M Stock at twenty-five cents a share. His lifelong business was used cars (always drove a late-model Cadillac)
but he'd made his big score in the stock market.

The money came as a pleasant shock, as Uncle Carl and I hadn't communicated in any way since the late sixties. It was then, while arguing politics at a family reunion, that Carl had icily offered his belief that Abby Hoffman and I were ruining the country. And I'd never even met Abby. But, although younger, I did have long curly black hair like his and had read his literary masterpiece, Steal this Book. I actually paid for it.

Upon learning of my windfall, I immediately assumed my uncle had acquired some wisdom before his death and finally accepted the truth in what I'd been saying back then, although, to be perfectly honest, I no longer remembered what it was.

I found out later that Uncle Carl was suffering from Alzheimer's at the end.

With these incoming shekels from such an unexpected source, it seemed like the right time to pursue my dream of private eyedom. Then one winter morning, the path became clearer. It was a snowy Sunday and I was fantasizing about the future while browsing the morning paper. I opened the sports section of the Minneapolis Star Tribune and a card dropped from the fold and fluttered into my lap. I immediately felt the stars align, the planets jog into concurrence and Jupiter enter the seventh house. It truly was a message from above:

50 exciting careers to choose from!
Choose your CAREER DIPLOMA stamp,
affix it to the postcard, and MAIL IN TODAY.

Sure enough, there it was in row four, column two, next to Psychology/Social Work DIPLOMA and directly above Interior Decorating DIPLOMA.

Private Investigator DIPLOMA.

Could the message be any clearer?

All I had to do was pop out my CAREER DIPLOMA stamp, paste it in the little box on the reply card and drop it in the nearest mailbox (no postage necessary). In a few short weeks the Drake Career Institute would have me on the way to a "brighter future."

Sam Spade and Lew Archer would have nothing on me.

Now don't misinterpret here, I held no illusions that being a private dick in Duluth, Minnesota, would entail much besides spying on cheating spouses or tracking down deadbeats. That was all good with me. Creaky knees and a balky back made a lack of violent adventure a positive.

I mailed the card.

Six months later, after a June graduation from the Drake Career Institute for which there was no ceremony and no cap and gown, I put down the first and last months' rent and a security deposit on a long, narrow one-bedroom apartment in Canal Park above a tony outdoor clothing shop.

My office.

I bought some used furniture: desk, chairs, file cabinet and a computer, splurged on a flat screen TV and started keeping regular hours like a genuine shamus. My office was a block away from the Savannah Gentlemen's Club and I took frequent advantage of this proximity, as they had a good lunch buffet. Which is, I suppose, like saying you buy Penthouse or Playboy for the articles.

The days rolled by.

As the vernal rapture of August came on I had yet to have a case. This wasn't exactly surprising, considering that I hadn't done any advertising. Except for my second ex-wife and a few close friends, the only people who knew I'd graduated from private eye school were fellow afternoon inebriates at the Savannah. I was beginning to get bored, thinking a few marriage cheaters or a landlord skip might be just the ticket for me.

One hot summer day I was standing in front of an open window in my office hoping to catch a breeze off Lake Superior, acutely aware that in a similar situation, Philip Marlowe would likely be drinking from the office bottle trying to ease the pain from losing the femme fatale on his last case. As I gazed out the window at the tourist traffic and contemplated happy hour at the Savannah Club—coming up in thirty minutes—I saw a brown Ford van pulling into the handicapped zone in front of my building, sun glaring off its smooth, polished roof.

I started to get annoyed. No way somebody driving that humongous vehicle could be handicapped. I wanted the space to be open for my own personal use, should the need arise in the course of the business day—or if I was tired.

I watched a man climb out of the passenger door of the van. The thick potbellied body and curly thinning gray hair were familiar, belonging to an old associate of mine name of Dick Sacowski. A resident of Taconite Bay, a small company town on the northern shore of Lake Superior, Dick was one of the few privileged souls who knew I was in the private eye business, as he'd been at the Savannah one afternoon when I'd been blabbing about my new occupation.

Sun glinted off the bald spot on top of Sacowski's head as he slid open the side door of the van and leaned inside. A ramp with a wheelchair on it oozed out of the van and moved slowly down to ground level. Sacowski rolled the wheelchair off the ramp and again reached into the van. The ramp smoothly returned to the interior of the vehicle. Dick then wheeled the chair around to the driver's door, opened it and helped a skinny loosely put together man with a slightly disoriented look slide out. Sacowski held him firmly under the arms and eased him down into the wheelchair.

Seeing them approaching my door brought to mind a story Dick had told me about a friend he occasionally did errands for, taking him to the doctor and the Ford dealership and other things. I recalled that it was a couple years back, during a blizzard, when the poor guy was T-boned by a Rourke Mining Company truck and sent catapulting off the highway into an unforgiving ancient pine tree, crushing the man's lower spine. The resulting insurance settlement was allegedly gargantuan. Set the guy up in a fabulous cliff-side house overlooking Lake Superior equipped with all the fancy devices needed by a paraplegic, such as elevators and lifts and remote control everything. Including, according to Dick, a custom-made, specially equipped boat, which the man could operate with just his hands. Hardly a fair price for one's spine but better than nothing, I suppose.

I craned my neck as Sacowski bumped the wheelchair onto the sidewalk and started toward the stairway leading up to my office. Dick's large tanned biceps rippled out of a lemon yellow strap undershirt. He swung the chair around, opened the door, held it there with his work boot and started up backwards.

I heard the thumping and clumping on the wooden stairs and wondered if I should help. I quickly rationalized that the stairwell was too narrow for all of us together—and my back wasn't right for lifting. Any guilt over this quickly faded away as I recalled Dick Sacowski handling one end of my first wife's newly purchased upright piano—all by himself—as three of us struggled at the opposite end while attempting to traverse the front steps of my old apartment.

Dick was one sneaky-strong son of a bitch.

I was excited for my first possible case. I wanted to look right, like a real private eye. I wished I had a cute-but-not-beautiful secretary/receptionist to greet my prospective clients.

I couldn't decide if I should wait calmly inside the office or go to the door and show them in. Before I could make up my mind, my brand new frosted-glass door, recently installed by one of the many former-hippies-turned-carpenters in the area, slid open.

Sweat rolled from Sacowski's back and shoulders like spring runoff on a North Shore stream as he swung the wheelchair around, faced me and wiped his palms on his jeans. The dude in the chair was grinning up at me, his eyes kind of floating off to the side. I was wondering what drugs they had to feed the guy just to keep him going. Must've been one hell of a cocktail.

"Dick, come on in, man, good to see you," I said, smiling at both of them in turn, and gesturing towards the interior of the office, the former living room.

Dick Sacowski gasped for breath, tried to speak but started coughing. He put his fist to his mouth, doubled over and retched for thirty seconds.

"Richard smokes too much," said the guy in the wheelchair, his voice unsteady and weak.

Dick gave out one last hack and smiled sheepishly.

"You going to be all right, Richie?" the guy in the wheelchair said. "Think you can get me to the desk?"

I heard the sarcasm in his voice but I didn't think Sacowski noticed. Or he didn't care. Or he was used to it. He just shook his head, laughed nervously and wheeled the chair across the scuffed hardwood floor to the front of my oak desk.

"Gentlemen," I said, going around to my side of the desk and taking a seat in the wheeled, cloth-covered gray chair. "How can I be of service to you today?"

"Billy here's got woman problems," Sacowski said, finally regaining his wind.

Of course he's got woman problems, the business end of his body is fucking paralyzed.

"We haven't been formerly introduced," I said, getting up and going around the desk. I extended my hand as the dude twitched in the wheelchair. "Carter Brown."

"Billy Talbot, Mr. Brown," he said, his voice steadier and stronger as he extended a slightly bent hand on the end of a wiry, thin arm.

I shook it. It was cold on a hot day. Surprisingly strong grip.

"Exactly what kind of woman problems are we talking here?" I said, going back to my chair.

Sacowski walked over to the open window and bent down to receive the breeze while Talbot straightened his torso as best he could. "It's my wife, Mr. Brown," Talbot said. "Since I've come into some money, she's becoming—shall we say—a little difficult."

"By difficult, you mean you think she's having an affair and you want me to tail her?"

"I haven't jumped to those conclusions yet. But there is some unexplained time—and some financial difficulties, as well. Ritchie tells me you're perceptive when it comes to women."

I tried to keep a straight face. "I'm sure my two ex-wives would agree," I said. "But I'm still not clear on what it is you want me to do."

"His wife is robbing him blind, Carter," Sacowski interjected, pacing back and forth in front of the window. "She takes the mail and applies for all the credit card offers that come in, then maxes them out and sticks Billy with the tab. Any time he says something, she threatens to turn him in for smoking pot. Now and then he gets a slap on the back of the head."

"This true, Billy?"

"My wife is from peasant stock, like most of us in this neck of the woods, Mr. Brown. Occasionally, she lets her frustrations get the best of her. I think if she is made to see the error of her ways, her behavior will change for the better."

"I still don't get it. Can't you discuss this with her? Or have your mail routed to a post office box? Maybe a divorce? I mean, it's not like I can stop her from driving to the post office."

"He's tried all that," Sacowski said, depositing himself in the curved-back wooden chair next to Talbot. "She laughs at him. And if one of his friends says anything—well…what the fuck can we do about it?"

"Divorces are pretty cheap these days," I offered.

"This one wouldn't be, at least not at this point," Talbot said, his face twisted and reddening. "No, divorce is out of the question at the moment. What I want is to get something on her. Adultery, or some violation of the law—anything to hold over her head that will help her, ah, toe the line."

"I think I'm beginning to get the idea." I was picturing a rough-hewn, Eastern European-type broad in a faded red babushka cuffing poor Billy with her paw-like hands. I didn't like it. "So when do you want me to start?" I said, sensing my opportunity to be a real white knight of the streets.

"As soon as possible," Billy said, attempting a smile that didn't quite get there. "Tomorrow morning Ritchie and I will be in Two Harbors getting a part for my boat. Then we'll be stopping at Sky Blue Waters Lodge for brunch. If you could meet us at say, eleven o'clock in the restaurant, I can fill you in on the particulars and put down a cash advance for any expenses you might incur in getting started."

Talbot glanced over at Sacowski. Dick stood up. "That way you can see where she goes after the mail comes," Dick said. "Damn near every fucking day one of those credit card offers comes in the mail, Cart. I'd follow her myself, if she didn't know my car."

"Or if your car was running, Ritchie," Talbot said, with a crooked grin. Then his eyes darted impatiently and Dick grabbed the handles of the wheelchair.

"Yeah, okay," I said as they moved toward the door. "But don't you want to talk about my rates and stuff like that?"

"Charge what you need to, Mr. Brown," Talbot said, not looking back. "Money is not a problem. As long as you're successful, I'm sure the price will be right. Ritchie assures me that you're

an honorable man. Be sure to bring along any contracts you
need signed."

                              *   *   *

The wind was coming hard out of the southeast as I eased my
Subaru Forester onto scenic Highway 61, a winding, predomi-
nantly two-lane strip of asphalt that traces the northern shore
of Lake Superior all the way to Canada. It was the kind of day
a travel magazine might claim we're famous for around here.
The lake was emerald green and churning with thin whitecaps. Seagulls circled in the air-conditioned winds that held the
coastal area at a pleasant seventy-four degrees while the inland
sweated in the nineties. The type of day that attracted the tourists, the throngs who'd changed the region from the remote and
isolated area it once was to the RV and SUV magnet of the present. The old motor lodges and commercial fishing shacks were
pretty much gone, replaced by rustic-look condo developments,
trophy homes and upscale lodges.

Sky Blue Waters Lodge, where I was to meet Talbot and Sacowski for brunch, was part of the "New North Shore." Freshly
milled log structure, flowery name and all. But I didn't care. It's not
as if it was ever going to become like Florida up here, every inch
of coastline filled with development. No, it was still winter half the
year this far north and that simple fact was a time-proven natural
ceiling on high-end growth. Or so it had always been.

Traffic was heavy through Two Harbors even at ten-thirty in
the morning. Farther north, up past Crow Creek, a paved bike
path meandered along parallel to the highway. Thing had fancy
wrought-iron bridges that seemed to have yuppie bait written
all over them. I was exceeding the speed limit because I didn't
want to be late for my first client, especially one who seemed to
be generous with the filthy lucre. A private eye has to be punctual unless danger has somehow detained him. The only danger

I sensed at this point was the pop-up camper directly in front of me dancing on the back end of a Chevy pickup like a johnboat in a hurricane. The shock absorbers on the trailer were obviously shot, and the ones on the truck not much better. It brought to mind a past incident on this same highway. A horrific incident that occurred when just such a trailer broke loose from its moorings on one of the very same curves we were approaching. The wayward trailer then flew across into oncoming traffic, severing the heads of a young couple on a motorcycle.

Death by trailer was not the way I wanted to go out. Especially not when my fortunes seemed to be on the upswing. But I knew the Forester was a real safe vehicle because the ads on TV had told me so. Also a symbol of earth-friendly progressive thought and an adventurous spirit. Fortunately, I saw the Sky Blue Waters Lodge sign coming up on the right. I took a deep breath and flipped on the blinker, found myself wondering what a wealthy paraplegic eats for brunch. Told myself it was a stupid question and not worthy of one such as I. But that's the way it is for me, the thoughts just come flying through, quality control non-existent.

Shortly I found out that a paraplegic—Billy Talbot anyway— eats scrambled eggs and a pile of bacon for brunch. Just like nearly everybody else in the nearly full restaurant. Myself, I had the eggs, American fries and coffee. I don't usually drink coffee these days; stuff gets me too edgy, but I wanted to at least create the illusion of alertness.

We had a pleasant meal and Talbot agreed to my terms and fees, all of which I'd obtained from *The Private Eye Handbook,* a handy tome purchased on the Internet.

And now I'm going to be perfectly honest. I need to tell you that my Drake Career Institute Private Detective diploma was about as worthless as a paper shirt in a windstorm. As if you didn't know. Maybe it could have been helpful if I had actually studied; but in fact, I had cribbed the answers to the final exam off the Internet. You can find anything on the Internet these days.

Leaving the restaurant, I was feeling pretty good. I had to thank Sacowski for lining me up with a sweet gig. Even sweeter when you consider it was the maiden voyage on my sea of cases, if you don't mind a little purple prose.

Talbot had it all mapped out. Had me follow his van back to a wayside rest just down the highway from the entrance to his cliff-side home. I was to wait there until Rose Marie Talbot came bouncing out in her red Ford Focus. Then I was to follow her.

Surveillance. Put on a tail and make it stay. A simple and basic act that all fictional private eyes from Race Williams to Patrick Kensey depended upon. If I had known the situation in advance, I might have brought in an assistant. That way we could change vehicles if Rose somehow got hip to the tail. Then again, maybe I wouldn't need any help. Most women, the only thing they see in the rearview mirror is their hair and makeup.

It was nice in that wayside, even a little chilly at times with the lake breeze coming in the car window. I had the sky blue water on my right and the brilliant, sun-speckled green of the hillside on my left. After an hour or so of waiting, just as my client had predicted, the postal truck rolled to a stop across the road from me. A short, squat guy in blue Postal Service shorts got out and stuck a handful of mail in the unpainted metal box mounted on a post at the side of Talbot's steep driveway. Fifteen minutes after the truck drove away, a small red car came bouncing down the asphalt and pulled up next to the mailbox. I'd been trying to imagine what Rose might look like, narrowing it down to either a burly bowling broad type in a red and black lumberjack shirt or a gum-chewing nymphet in hair curlers with the IQ of a snow hare.

As she exited the car, I could see she landed somewhere in between. I put the binoculars on her—an indispensable P.I. tool— and found her to be cute, but not beautiful, with short brown hair and a few freckles. Tall, wide in the shoulders and hips but with a nice little teacup tush inside cut-off jeans that showed off strong and nicely shaped, tan legs.

She pulled a stack of mail out of the box and jumped back in the Ford, jerked onto the highway and headed north towards Taconite Bay. I gave her a little head start and followed, feeling confident she'd never notice me, at least until we got into town, if in fact that was where we were headed.

According to Billy Talbot, who'd been quite talkative at brunch with a load of coffee running through him, Rose was the daughter of a former Rourke Mining executive. Rourke Mining being the company that had essentially built the town of Taconite Bay. This seemed to contradict Billy's earlier "peasant stock" comment but with the kind and quantity of drugs he was taking I'm surprised he could even string a sentence together.

Gamely continuing, Billy sadly recalled how Rose's father had resigned from Rourke and taken his family to Minneapolis, shortly after the asbestos-like taconite residue the company was routinely discharging into Lake Superior caused a huge environmental scare and forced the state to shut down the entire operation. Taconite Bay had gone from boom to bust in no time at all but was currently on a slight rebound, as Rourke was back in operation on a limited scale.

Our sweet Rose, whose marriage to Billy had been against her parents' wishes, had defiantly stayed behind in the dying town. Now it seemed she was nurturing some regret. After the accident had left her man only half there, she had allegedly begun to communicate more frequently with mumsy and dadsy. And, Billy said, was growing more receptive to her parents' familiar refrain: *Leave your husband and return to civilization.*

Billy was obviously hurt, confused and suspicious. It was hard for me not to hate this woman without even having met her.

I swung the Subaru onto the asphalt and got the red Ford in my sights, staying comfortably behind until she drew alongside the Rourke plant, a looming, rust-brown industrial monstrosity with the aura of a Third Reich munitions plant, lines of belching smokestacks on the roof pointing to the sky like anti-aircraft guns.

The warning light at the railroad crossing was flashing red. Rose came to a stop and I had no choice but to roll in behind her. An ore-filled train was crossing the highway and chugging up the incline to our left, throwing out dust that was undoubtedly toxic. Rose fussed with her hair in the rearview. I turned my head toward the plant and pulled my Guinness cap down over my eyes.

Staring up at the gargantuan Rourke building, I recalled fondly how, in the middle of the aforementioned taconite tailings fiasco, my first wife had freely and frequently expressed a strong desire to blow this hulking polluter of the last clean Great Lake to shreds. Recyclable shreds, of course. Ah, for the good old days and dreams of social activism. Talk like that today and you get a visit from the friendly folks at Homeland Security.

The train passed, the red light went off and Rose sped away. A half-mile ahead another stoplight stood at the turn to Taconite Bay. I saw the left turn signal on the Ford Focus start to blink. I kept my distance. Although it had been a while since I'd been here, I knew everything in the tiny town of Taconite Bay was either on or very close to the main drag.

I followed the path of the little red car into town and found it in the parking lot of the municipal liquor store and lounge. It was 3:45 by my dashboard clock. I debated going inside for happy hour, thought better of it and instead parked at the edge of the lot where I could see both the front door of the tavern and the Focus.

Forty minutes later, my mouth was dry as a cob as Rose spilled out of the muni and flounced back into her car. She was alone, no men following. That was good. At least for Billy. I started the Forester and watched her pull out and head back toward the highway.

She wasn't screwing around this time; blowing through town at fifty miles an hour with her arm lolling out the window, thumb flicking at a cigarette. She flew through the intersection just as the light turned red, made a left and headed north.

I got stuck at the red light.

Just as I was contemplating running the light, having deduced that local law enforcement was scarce, a sheriff's department SUV appeared in my rearview. He must not have seen Rose's turn because he stopped behind me and we both waited like good citizens for the light to change color.

The copper turned right and I went left. I put the pedal down and ran up the shore for thirty minutes, vainly searching every driveway and side road for red-red Rosey.

No luck. No sign of the Ford. I'd lost my pigeon. Failure in my first day on the job. I wanted to hit a bar and get hammered. Instead I got out my cell phone to call Talbot and tell him the bad news.

Goddamn cell phones.

Billy chuckled at my tale of woe. I felt my face warming and it wasn't from the sun. My insides squirmed like leeches on a hot sidewalk.

"No problem, Carter," Billy said. "My little Rose is a slippery one."

"I don't think she was hip to me, Billy," I insisted. But I wasn't so sure.

"You'll just have to try again tomorrow, Carter," he said dryly. "I think you should be there at ten tomorrow morning. I'm sure you'll do better on your second day."

The condescension iced my brain and made my temples throb.

The next day dawned like the kind of day the locals would say we're famous for: gray and rainy skies with a wind off the lake keeping the coastal area in the low fifties. I drove up in the morning and had to put the car heater on—in August.

I sat in the wayside by Talbot's road and listened to KUMD FM while the North Shore began to wake up. Nothing moved down the Talbot Road until after two in the afternoon. It was the same deal, the mail truck came and went and shortly thereafter the red Ford bounced down the hill and stopped at the mailbox.

This time she was dressed in a blue jeans and a blue flannel shirt with the first three buttons open. I caught her full frontal in the binocs and I thought she smiled at me, if only for a second.

I kept her in sight all the way to the municipal, where she pulled in to the same spot as the day before. I swung into my familiar space and threw the shifter in Park. I turned up the radio and the fan on the defogger. The college radio station faded and I punched the search button.

After half an hour of mind-numbing hackneyed classic rock from the likes of Styx and Rush and ELO, I was getting restless. This aspect of private eye work plain flat sucked.

I watched water droplets collect on my windshield. Again I pushed the search button. Pine trees bobbed and weaved on the hill across the road. A Canadian talk show came on the FM.

Is back bacon good for you?

I shut off the ignition and went in the bar.

It was a generic barroom, two-thirds full of guys in flannel or denim shirts and Carhartt overalls, the weather having evidently cut the day's labors short. Rose was sitting in a high-backed chair at the brightly polished bar, a tall coke drink of some kind sweating on the counter between her and the bartender, a forty-something guy wearing an orange T-shirt with *Ask Me For a Slow Screw* printed across the front. He was leaning in close with his hands on the bar top.

He ignored me as I sat down.

I shuffled nervously and took a good look at Rose. She was cuter than I'd thought. Looked younger than her years, which I guessed to be mid-to-late thirties. She had a kind of athletic grace in her movements that more than compensated for her wide shoulders and hips. Old Billy must have been quite a stud back in the day to corral this sexy beast. But I was getting carried away. I was here to find out if she was having an affair, not entice her into one.

"Bartender, can I get a Budweiser please?"

The tender shot me a slightly annoyed glance, straightened up and sighed. He turned around and bent over, opened the cooler door and wearily dragged out a Bud. Without making eye contact, he twisted the top, set the bottle in front of me and continued down to the end of the bar where a wrinkled elderly couple was drinking Miller Lite and watching the wall-mounted television.

I put down a five, took a swallow of beer and snuck a look at Rose. She was smiling at me like a flower in the desert. Always a sucker for a pretty face, I felt like saying something to her. Instead I grabbed my beer and moved down to where I could catch the live poker action on the tube.

I saw Rose turn toward the front door as a blond wearing a blue denim jacket and jeans and sporting red lips and scary black fingernails sashayed in.

The pony-tailed blond sat next to Rose and the two women started talking excitedly, shutting the bartender out. I tried to listen but I had my weaker ear towards them and the TV was turned up high for the old couple. The bits and pieces of the conversation I could catch didn't sound like much of anything. Nothing important or relevant to the case.

During a tense, quiet moment in the ESPN Texas Hold'em game, I heard Rose say: "God, I wish you could smoke in here. I can't get used to not smoking in a bar."

Another positive reaction to the statewide smoking ban.

The blond said, "Wanna go outside?"

Rose: "It's shitty out."

Blond: "Ain't that bad."

Rose: "All right then. You want a drink first?"

"I can wait."

"A Bud Light for Gloria, Pete, on my tab." Rose said. "We're going out for a smoke."

The two women both glanced at me at the same time. Quick, darting glances. Then they stood up and went outside. I took advantage of the opportunity and hit the men's room. Came back out and got another Bud. Gloria's Bud Light was still sweating on the bar top. I looked up at the TV. The poker game was in the final hand. High stakes. High tension. A bald guy wearing sunglasses eventually won. Had a full boat, queens over fives.

A few minutes went by and I started wondering how long it took to smoke a cigarette these days. But you know how it is with chicks: they talk a lot. Ten minutes later, I got a jumpy feeling in my gut and headed for the door. Once outside, I looked slowly around and saw no one, only mist rising from the gravel. I walked toward my vehicle. The red Ford was nowhere to be seen.

Rose had beaten me again.

I had to swallow a lot of shit to tell Talbot of my latest error in judgment. He took it well, and just said, "Try it again tomorrow," while I struggled to reassure him that his wife didn't know she was being shadowed.

I knew this was just bad luck. I'd find my P.I. chops real soon.

Back in Duluth, I went directly to my apartment, a nicely designed basement one-bedroom in the elegant East End home of an elderly retired couple. I grabbed a beer from the fridge and got on the telephone. I was going to need help with this case.

* * *

The next morning there were two of us heading up Highway 61. I was behind the wheel of the Subaru. Following closely behind in his GROAT (Grossly Oversized American Truck) was my old pal Dan Burton. We had attended college together (when we actually chose to attend) at the University of Minnesota Duluth, and partied together for a long time after that. Dan was now one year sober and unemployed, which made him perfectly suited to be my sidekick. Not only, was he grateful for the work, but now I wouldn't have to buy him drinks, something that could have amounted to a small fortune in the past. About six-two and over two hundred pounds, Burton was handy to have around should trouble start up, something I had learned a few times over the years.

I set Burton and his truck in the wayside near Talbot's driveway. I parked on the shoulder about a half-mile south of him in case Rosie decided to alter her previous pattern. Burton and I had in our possession Motorola Walkie-talkies with a seven-mile range, recently purchased at a local Best Buy with some of the retainer money.

Just as before, I passed the morning playing tourist mesmerized by the beauty of the lake. It wasn't difficult on a sunny and cool day with a clean northwest wind wrinkling the surface of the steel-blue water. Dan would occasionally pop on the airwaves just to fight his boredom and I'd have to tell him to stay off until necessary. I think it was hard for him to take the situation seriously. After all, it was Carter Brown he was working for. That fact alone was strange enough to him, I was sure.

The world slowly turned to early afternoon.

I was thinking about food when the walkie-talkie crackled.

"She's got the mail and she's headed your way," Dan said hoarsely.

I snapped up the binoculars and homed in on a blinding sunspot on the hood of the Focus. Little blue spots erupted in my vision. I scrunched down in the seat and turned my head toward the lake as Rose hissed by.

"Get after her, Dan," I said into the little black and yellow box, "I'll follow you."

Seconds later the big gray pickup roared by, Dan waving like an idiot.

We followed Rose to Two Harbors where she drove up to the small, brick post office building. I parked a block away where I could still see her car. Dan drove down past the post office and parked facing me.

It wasn't long before she came through the double glass doors and strutted down the steps, got in her vehicle and left the lot. I was guessing she was heading for Duluth to do some shopping, as she was wearing a green, short-sleeved cotton dress. Exactly why the dress made me think she was going shopping, I really don't know.

She quickly proved me wrong by turning north on 61 and moving away at high speed.

Burton and I gave chase and again the strange caravan began weaving its way along the scenic North Shore Drive. I was a little worried Rose might recognize the Subaru so I stayed back as far as I could while still keeping her in sight. The fact that these small SUVs were nearly as prevalent up here as the black flies, worked in my favor.

Rose was passing everything on the road and making it difficult to keep up. At one point, I had to hurtle past an RV and a UPS delivery van in rapid succession and cut back into my lane at the last instant, narrowly avoiding a speeding semi while the little Subaru "boxer engine" roared like a sewing machine about to blow. Up ahead of me, Rose's Focus was making a left on Highway 1 and shooting off into the forest primeval.

I gave chase.

I rode the bumper of the Suburban in front of me, pushed down the turn signal and checked the rearview. Dan was hopelessly mired behind three other vehicles. I got on the squawk box and filled him in.

Minnesota State Highway 1, along which Rose was rapidly racing, flows north from Lake Superior to Ely, gateway to the Boundary Waters Canoe Area, a destination where thousands of tourists arrive yearly to paddle around in pristine, un-crowded waters and be harassed and shot at by drunken local youths.

Soon Dan's big truck was right behind me as we sped along between the pines. I got on the walkie-talkie and told him to turn around and head home, I'd pay him tomorrow.

It seemed I didn't want to share Rose.

I watched in the mirror as Burton pulled off at a forest road and turned back toward the lake. I sped on, came to the crest of a hill and caught sight of the Focus about a mile ahead, approaching a bridge construction site, flagman standing in the road. I felt my heart drop into my gut. I hit the gas and watched with growing frustration as the flagman (actually an aging blond woman with leathery, sun-baked skin) waved Rose through.

I had to hit the brakes when the flag bearer spun her little orange sign on its axis, showing me the STOP. I was forced to wait as the traffic from the far side trickled across the bridge in the only open lane, my gut like the inside of a beehive.

Again I had blown it.

Five minutes later, after ten or fifteen vehicles had gone past, the chesty blond spun the sign to SLOW—CAUTION. I raced ahead recklessly but Rose was nowhere to be seen. I drove all the way to Ely, futilely searched up and down the town for the Rosemobile before turning around and making the long drive back to the lakeshore.

First bar I could find with a view of the lake, I ordered a double-vodka on the rocks and called Talbot, told him the sorry state of affairs. The edgy tone of his voice let me know he was losing his patience. But the words he spoke were again understanding and sympathetic, ending with: "Tomorrow is Friday. What say you have one more try at it?"

Of course I agreed. The money was too good to quit. As long as Billy wanted me on the job, I'd be there for him.

* * *

Later that night I was collapsed on my couch drinking from a cold bottle of Molson Canadian and watching the Twins getting pounded by the Yankees. The phone jangled on the end table. I picked it up. "Hello," I said.

"That you, Carter?"

I recognized Dick Sacowski's voice. "Yeah, Dick. What's up?"

"That fucking cunt smacked Billy again tonight, man. This shit has got to stop, Carter. He'd just come home from fishing with me—he's sitting in his chair looking out the window—when she comes up behind him and snakes his bag of pot out of his jacket pocket. He grabs at it and she slaps him in the goddamn head, says she'll call the fucking sheriff if he raises a stink. That's the second time she's done that shit."

"Not good, man," I said. "Not good at all. I tell you what; I got an idea. A change of tactics." Inspiration had come to me just a few minutes prior while watching a TV replay of a stand-up triple by Twins first baseman Justin Morneau. "I got a friend here in town that's pretty good with video. I was thinking we could get inside Billy's house and set up some hidden cameras and micro-phones and stuff. Then if she pulls anything, Billy will have his bargaining chip."

"Great idea," Sacowski said. "I'll tell Billy. How long you gonna need inside?"

"I dunno, couple hours at least, more if possible. Can we get away with that?"

"I think so. Rose usually hits the Safe Harbor Bar in Bea-ver Bay on Fridays for happy hour. They run a special on them Long Island ice teas. Bitch can really throw'em down. Usually stays a while."

"Great. Tell Billy that my assistant and I will be up there tomor-row around one. I'll call him when I get close."

"Gotcha. See you then."

After the connection severed and the line buzzed in my ear, the first thing that came to me was a question: Why didn't somebody think of the hidden-camera bit a long time ago? Just about any-body who ever saw a reality TV show could have come up with it. But what the hell, that's what I was getting paid for, coming up with clever plans to trick the evildoers. The kind of shit we dicks do.

By six o'clock Friday afternoon, my electronics-wizard friend Tommy Basilio had tiny cameras and voice bugs set up in strategic areas of Talbot's house: kitchen, living room, carport entrance and Billy's bedroom. I stressed to Billy that if he was going to confront Rose or accuse her of anything, it was best done in one of these areas. I was feeling pretty good as Tommy and I left that fabulous house on the cliff. Besides being blown away by the view, I felt we had gone a long way toward solving my client's dilemma. Billy Talbot must have felt the same, because he'd written out a nice large check and told me my services would no longer be needed, at least, until further notice.

I could have taken this as a rude dismissal but chose instead to look at it as an acknowledgement of a job completed satisfactorily.

I took it easy for the next few days and tried to enjoy the fruits of my unlikely success. But I couldn't shake the lingering feeling that the job was unfinished. That there was something more I could do to help Billy.

And then one day I got the chance.

I was at my office researching possible forms of advertising, idleness having proved to be not as fun now as it had been at age thirty or forty. The only marketing plan I'd come up with was an ad in the yellow pages of the phone book. I was nearly finished with the Brown Investigations ad copy, having rejected *What Can Brown Do for You?* and *Brown Gets Down*, in favor of the straightforward *Brown Gets It Done*.

My desk phone sounded.

It was Talbot, croaking in a weak, hoarse voice: "Brown? This is Billy Talbot. I need your help again. Things here are getting out of hand."

Seemed to me they'd been out of hand for a long while. "What can I do to help, Billy?"

"Today I got three credit card bills for a total of thirty-seven thousand dollars. Cash advances at the maximum rate of interest the bloodsuckers can charge." His voice trembled.

"Jesus fucking Christ—that's a lot of scratch. Have you thought of communicating directly with the companies that issue the credit cards? Get Rose on some list or something?"

Suddenly there was strength in his voice: "You think I should start contacting every fucking banking conglomerate that might issue credit cards? Not to mention the retail outlets and other financial institutions and whoever the fuck else…"

"It's not like I can pull her over and confiscate her wallet or anything, Billy. My hands are pretty much tied. I can't mug her at the steps of the post office. You'd think the recent state of the economy would limit the number of offers out there."

"Maybe you could do a better job of surveillance, Mr. Brown. She's gotta be doing something with all the cash. And she's also become more violent, as of late."

"Are you getting it on tape?"

"I'm afraid Rose discovered the cameras and broke them. Took out the tapes and destroyed them, as well."

"Are you shitting me? That's some expensive equipment."

"Tell me something I don't know. I've already contacted Mr. Basilio and informed him. I called the number on the business card he left with me when the two of you were here."

"Oh. I see."

"Got any other bright ideas, Brown? Things are worse now than before you set out to *help* me."

"All right, Billy, I get the hint. Do you want me to put a tail on her again? I can find another vehicle and bring a partner. I'm sure we can stay with her this time."

"If that's the best you can come up with, I suppose it will have to do. Excuse me if I don't jump for joy."

Dude and his sarcasm were beginning to get on my nerves, disabled or not. Then inspiration hit me and washed the annoyance away. All private eyes had their little group of assistants and confidantes. I just needed to gather my own gang of cohorts together for a bit of subterfuge.

"You know what, Billy?" I said. "You're right. I was piss-poor at surveillance. But now I've got a plan that will solve all your problems with your wife. All you need to do is have her home and in the house at a prearranged time and date. I'll have some friends of mine pay her a visit with a message she'll find hard to deny."

"My ravaged heart is fluttering with anticipation."

"That's a start. I'll get back to you as soon as I can."

I clicked off, relieved to sever the connection with Talbot, who seemed to have the power to suck out my energy through the phone line.

It took ten minutes of deep breathing before I could call around about renting a Ford Crown Victoria, preferably in black. I settled for a maroon one. Found it in the West End at the rental agency that used to try harder. I figured it would suffice, maroon being one of the Minnesota state colors. Rah, Rah for the old Maroon and Gold and all that.

With transportation taken care of, I began recruiting players for my upcoming theatrical production of "Scare the Hell out of the Misbehaving Wife." I delved deeply into a mixed bag of old associates—burnouts, recovering alcoholics, head cases and general refugees from the past. I already had Dan Burton and Tommy Basilio on board and needed one more willing participant.

The spinning wheel stopped at the image of Jeff Tormoen—local actor, radio DJ and barroom brawler with the size, authoritative voice and upright bearing needed for the role I had in mind.

Being somewhat "between gigs," Torm was more than willing to jump on for the ride.

The next step was ordering phony badges and blank identification cards off the Internet. After that, I assembled the cast of characters for a morning photo shoot with Tommy Basilio. We spent the afternoon going over our roles. Three days later, the ID cards arrived in the mail. We were well rehearsed and ready.

On the morning previously arranged with Talbot, Dan Burton, clean-shaven and dressed in a cheap brown suit and brown wing-tips, and Jeff Tormoen, similarly clad in a navy blue suit and scuffed black oxfords, motored up the North Shore in the big maroon Crown Vic. I followed close behind in the Subaru, staying in voice contact through the police-style radio system Tommy had installed in the Ford for the sake of realism.

It was another beautiful day in northern Minnesota: baby blue sky, white puffs of clouds, not a breath of wind and temps in the mid-seventies. The lake was flat and glassy—the kind of day you wanted to bottle and save, not waste on a cheesy deal like this. But everybody knows that a P.I. must be steadfast and finish what he starts. A case must be seen through to its rightful conclusion for the good of all.

I pulled into the roadside rest as Burton wheeled the Crown Vic up the hill towards Billy Talbot's castle made from heartbreak. My gut was jumping and I sensed something haywire, like the proverbial monkey wrench dropping into the gears. I tried to reassure myself. I'd spoken to Talbot and he had seemed confident and positive. I dropped the windows down and soaked up the lake air, trying to clear my head, shake the doubt and fear. Then the two-way radio crackled: "Here we are, Brownie," Tormoen said in his powerful baritone. "We're going in."

"Break a leg," I said.

All that was left to do was wait. I kept an eye on the road. My neck was in knots. Thirty minutes went by and then time stood still.

I thought something terrible was probably going down, but I also knew how windy Tormoen could get when enjoying a role. I could almost feel sorry for Rose, with the big Norwegian hounding her in his cop voice about forged signatures on credit card applications and the dire consequences this type of behavior can lead to.

Yessiree, Mr. Tom Higgins, Assistant Director of the State Bureau of Fraud and Financial Crimes, could be a hard and unforgiving man. Relentlessly, he could hammer away at you, holding possible punishments over your head like the blade of a guillotine. But Torm could also bring out his soothing good-cop voice to reassure Rose that her husband had only her best interests at heart. Hadn't Billy firmly refused to press charges as long as no further credit lines were opened? Surely only the most foolish and churlish among us would refuse an offer such as this. The presence of one in such a high position of authority as Mr. Higgins spoke volumes on both the severity and sensitivity of this situation.

Despite my anxieties, the boys eventually came down the hill and turned toward Duluth. I gave them a few minutes start and followed, joining them down the road at a predetermined wayside.

I climbed into the huge backseat of the Crown Vic. Burton had a grin like a lemon wedge. Tormoen's chest was puffed out, his face flushed. They were sharing a joint and laughing at the memory of Rose's deer-in-the-headlights look after being told she could go to jail for ten years. How the tears running down her suddenly pale cheeks and the shudders in her torso were indeed a sad sight.

"I was the Barrymore of Bullshit," Tormoen said proudly. "Olivier would've given me a standing ovation. I had the wench writhing in agony and begging for mercy."

"A gifted performance indeed," Burton said, blowing out smoke and grinning like a leprechaun.

Later that night when I walked into my apartment carrying a slight celebratory buzz, I couldn't shake a vague sense of uneasiness, possibly from a residue of unfamiliar scents picked up at a primitive level. Simply put, I had the feeling that someone had been there while I was gone. Because we all have atavistic instincts buried beneath the many layers of complacency civilization has piled upon us, I took the feeling seriously.

I searched through the place but found nothing obvious missing. Told myself I was just paranoid. Could have been Mrs. Swanson from upstairs checking to see if I was building a meth lab. But something still nagged at me. I went around the front of the house and knocked on the Swanson's door. It was a little late and I was a little tipsy but Mrs. Swanson smiled knowingly and told me that two workers had come that afternoon to install new water meters.

There was my answer. I was in too good a mood to question it.

* * *

A couple days after the performance, I was at the office, staring out the window at the seagulls circling manically in the hovering exhaust of a nearby Burger King. The phone rang. It was Billy Talbot, informing me that he and Rose had begun marriage and financial counseling sessions and that Dick Sacowski was on his way to Duluth with a sizeable bonus for me. After I cradled the receiver, I couldn't help but smile with satisfaction at a job well done.

Sacowski arrived an hour later with Billy's check for fifteen grand. My career as a private investigator was off and running on all cylinders. And if the business suffered a seasonal slowdown (summer had quietly turned to fall), I had more than enough money to get through the winter. And in the downtime between gigs, I would certainly be entertaining many at the Savannah with the colorful tale of my first case.

During the early days of autumn, I savored my recent success and basked in the beauty of an Indian summer. Then one mild and starry night my joy became somewhat tempered as I emerged from a late-night session at the Savannah to discover that someone had sideswiped my trusty Subaru, damaging the front end and passenger side. Liquored as I was, I shrugged it off and assured myself that this was just another opportunity for profit. I would bring the car to my friend Jack Running for repair and old Jack would kickback some of the insurance money my way. Things were still coming up roses.

But everything changed towards the end of October, just before Halloween.

I remember the day as damp and foggy, pea soup rolling in off the lake. I was at the Savannah Club for happy hour, elbows on the bar and eyes on the television, two beers already down. It was a slow day at the club; the evening news was droning on. They were showing footage of a wrecked car at the bottom of a ravine along the north shore of Lake Superior. The ground glistened with dead, wet leaves and the hazy air was popping with blue and reds from the lightbars of law-enforcement vehicles.

It took me a while before I realized what I was looking at.

A red Ford Focus all crushed to shit.

The footage had been shot the previous night. It was foggy and wet but it sure looked like Rose Talbot's vehicle. My ears began to burn and ring. The room swayed; I thought I was going to puke. I sucked in a breath of beer-scented air, stood up and listened to the reporter's words.

Young woman killed in late-night crash... signs of impact with another vehicle... possible hit and run... airbags failed to activate... no witnesses have come forth... investigation continues...

Then the tube blinked and a commercial for Ryan Ford of Two Harbors came on the screen. Stunned, I walked out of the bar—not saying anything to anybody—and drove home in a brain fog that matched the soup in the air. I stumbled into my apartment and flopped down face-first on the bed, passed out for three hours and woke up in the dark, my brain racing in circles like an Indy car on a short track.

I didn't sleep much that night and got up at dawn to wait for the morning paper. My suspicions were confirmed. An article on page one, *Taconite Bay woman dies in hit-and-run*, told the sad story of the tragic accident that caused the untimely death of Rose Marie Engwar Talbot, thirty-seven years of age.

Anger, confusion, guilt and fear cycled through me and put me off my feed. I showered and dressed and left for the office in the hope that something there would distract me from my thoughts. The carpenters were scheduled to finish work that morning on a small reception area, where, someday, hopefully, a good-hearted and pretty-in-a down-to-earth-way secretary would greet my perspective clients.

Moving slowly up the stairs to the office and wrestling with my emotions, I passed one of the carpenters coming down, power saw in hand. We nodded a greeting and continued on our separate ways. I could smell sawdust and new wood and wood stain. It was clean and responsible and good. All the things I wasn't.

The crew was putting the finishing touches on my new addition. I'd spent a lot of time convincing the landlord of its necessity. I guess I just wore him down. And now, there it was in front of me, smooth and glistening like a new penny. I walked through to my desk, sat down on the wheeled chair and wondered if there wasn't somebody I should call to say something about Rose. Billy Talbot for one. It seemed I should call but I couldn't pick up the phone. All I could do was waffle. Sit there and vacillate. Not what a private eye is supposed to do. Something had been taken out of me and I couldn't dodge the thought that this was just the beginning of my troubles.

My fears were validated an hour later when, as I sat numbly, gazing out the window at the thick gray clouds and unwillingly focusing on the churning in my gut, there was a knocking at my shiny new door.

With nobody there to greet them, the deputy sheriffs and the plainclothes cop just walked right on through.

They identified themselves as members of the Creek County Sheriff's Department and the Duluth Police Department. Badges were waved but I was too dizzy to really see them. They informed me of my rights and that I was being charged with the murder of Rose Marie Engwar Talbot. As well as working as a private investigator without the proper license.

Lead fell into my feet and I stammered incoherently as they pulled my wrists behind my back, put the cuffs on and brought me down the steps to a waiting cruiser, engine running.

The ride up the lakeshore was a blur of feverish silence broken only by the barking of the police radio. I didn't even have a lawyer. Every goddamn P.I. has a slick lawyer. I was shit. Toast. Cannon fodder. Life handed me lemons and fate had made lemonade out of my ass.

They brought me to the Creek County lockup and put me in an interrogation room, a narrow windowless space with puke-green paint on the walls. Reminded me of a detention room in an old high school.

I had no alibi for the night in question. I'd been at the Savannah Club but I couldn't prove it. A new bartender was working that day and I had left after only a couple of beers. I couldn't recall seeing anyone I knew by name. Surely the cops would check. Wouldn't they?

Gradually, the shock of arrest began to fade. I started to get my dander up. Embers of anger and righteous indignation began to smolder within me. I hadn't done this. What could they possibly have on me?

I found out in one hell of a hurry. About as long as it takes for the other shoe to drop.

They had traces of blue paint obtained from the rear bumper and driver's side of the crushed Focus. They were going to test my Subaru. To go with the paint scrapings, they'd also found a vaguely threatening note in Rose's purse, written on my business stationery. With a signature that looked enough like mine to make my intestines bleed.

The final straw on the camel was a video turned over to them by the deceased's husband, showing two men in suits getting out of a Ford Crown Victoria in front of the Talbot residence, a vehicle rented in Duluth with a credit card issued to one Carter Brown.

To accompany the video of the Crown Vic and the boys getting in and out, they possessed a copy of perhaps Jeff Tormoen's greatest performance, Dan Burton providing the supporting role. A performance the sheriff claimed was a crime in itself. But more importantly, a demonstration of my willingness to resort to "extreme means" to achieve a desired end.

I wanted to explain, but I knew it wouldn't come out sounding right.

They also had my bank statements. They focused on what they called my recent "abnormally large" deposit. I thought I had them there. Why would I kill her if I'd already been paid?

They had an answer for that.

Billy Talbot told them I'd offered to "dispose of his wife" for five thousand dollars. After which, he allegedly became so terrified that he paid me fifteen K to lay off and forget I ever knew his sweet Rose. Talbot dutifully added that I was a loser who had failed on numerous occasions to do even basic surveillance successfully, and that I probably killed Rose to prove I was a man.

I figured it was all cop talk. But the fight went out of me when they said a witness had come forth claiming to have seen a small, blue SUV playing bumper cars with the red Ford Focus on the night in question.

When they got through, my inner Mike Hammer had become a quivering hunk of Fletch. Gelatinous and weak, I had all I could do to keep from ratting out Jeff and Dan, wanting desperately to believe that it would go easier on me if I did, but knowing all too well that it wouldn't. I was being set up for a long fall with no net and I knew it.

I refused to speak and asked for a public defender.

They put me in a cell. The air smelled of stale sweat and old urine with an overlay of cheap pine cleaner. Time slowly ticked away.

The court appointed a public defender.

Sam Frederickson was about my age, with curly salt-and-pepper hair, thick glasses and chronic garlic breath. Close quarters with Sam was a little like being in a barn stall with a scampi-eating plow horse, snorting and all. But the guy had energy and enthusiasm and was a lot smarter than he looked.

I quickly discovered the courts didn't allow Sam the same level of respect as I did. Murder One in Minnesota requires a grand jury indictment. Nobody except me seemed in a hurry to proceed. I was remanded back to a cell in the county lockup as the gales of November came knocking.

Gray cloudy day after gray cloudy day rolled by my tiny window. I began to lose hope. I was almost beginning to believe I had actually done the murder while in a fugue state or blackout, like in a bad TV show. I began to search for ways to end it all. My life seemed over, all because I'd wanted to be a private eye.

In the days approaching Thanksgiving, my despair became unbearable. An opportunity for relief appeared to me one dreary afternoon in the form of some loose plaster on the ceiling of my cell. I discovered the slightly discolored soft spot, probably the result of a small leak in the roof, while lying on the bed staring at the ceiling, lost in torment.

I stood up on the bed, pushed on the ceiling with my fingertips and a chunk of plaster fell easily into my hand. I could see a thick overhead support beam through the resultant hole. *More than adequate to hang yourself from,* I thought, feeling an immediate sense of release.

I removed my orange jailhouse jumpsuit and tied the torso around the beam. I stood on the edge of the bed and carefully knotted one of the legs around my throat.

As I stood on my toes, ready to step off into sweet oblivion, I remembered reading that you had an orgasm when you hung yourself. I also recalled that a few kids had died trying to get off that way, back in the days when it was a fad. Maybe it was still a fad. Look what happened to David Carradine.

As I jumped off the bed and felt the cloth tighten around my throat, I couldn't help but wonder:

Would I be going—or coming?

Chapter
2

You really had to hand it to the architect of the jail, I guess. Or whoever it was that designed the cells with just enough room for my toes to hit the floor while hanging from the overhead beam. A welcome discovery, since my attitude about dying had changed the moment my feet left the safety of the cot.

Feeling even more depressed and self-loathing than before my failed attempt at suicide—and now with a sore neck—I slipped out of the thick knot. I took the orange jail suit off the beam and sullenly pulled it back on.

I realized I was going to have to stay and fight this thing. Slog through the dreary court proceedings and the unrelenting fear. Stand up to the bully cops and the automaton officers of the court. Something wouldn't let me give up. Even though resignation seemed the path of least resistance, I had to struggle.

Maybe I had the true private eye spirit.

I lay back down on the cot, stared up at the damaged ceiling. Now they would at least have to move me to another cell. A different view, anyway. The weight of being held in captivity like a dangerous animal was sitting on my chest like a Volkswagen. And although the Creek County Jail certainly wasn't as bad as Riker's Island or San Quentin or even the state pen down in Stillwater, it still had a ways to go to make the Top Ten Minnesota Destinations list.

The order of the day became *Get out of here.*

I sat on the edge of the bed and rubbed my eyes. In spite of my pressing need for freedom, thoughts of my ex-wife came to the forefront of my troubled mind. That being my second ex-wife, Jan, the sexy blond who'd left me for a slick lawyer with a Mercedes, a big house and a sizable bank account. Jan liked clichés. And fortunately, she still liked me. For some reason, she had stayed in touch since the split. Something I'd fought against at first. But lately, I had begun to look forward to her calls and the occasional meetings for gin and tonic at the Boat Club.

Sometimes I entertained the illusion she'd kept in contact out of guilt for the way she'd dumped me. Although it was more likely she did it to piss off her new husband Rick, who seemed to be having little success in controlling his wife. Welcome to the club.

Occasionally, if I was feeling particularly good that day, I convinced myself there was a chance of getting Jan back in the sack again. So far it hadn't happened. Maybe my subconscious was trying to tell me something. Maybe thinking of Jan was a sign. Maybe it was Jan who could help me beat this thing. Or maybe it was my long-suppressed libido forcing its way to the surface in order to keep me sane.

I fell back on the metal cot and stared at the hole in the ceiling, got lost in a reverie of past sexual escapades with Jan. Getting lost in reverie is a good thing when you're in jail. I flashed back to a time on Brighton Beach in the middle of warm August afternoon. We were just starting to get it on, pulling some clothes off, when we caught sight of this old guy about a quarter-mile down the beach. He was standing there in plaid Bermuda shorts and a white strap undershirt, enjoying our performance through binoculars. He continued staring through the glasses even after it was clear we were aware of his presence.

The peeping Tom had ruined the mood way back then and was having the same effect on me this time around. My dream bubble evaporated, leaving behind only the starkness of a prison cell. I heard a mumbling at the cell door and glanced over to see Deputy Monty Marshall standing there looking overweight and overbearing, as usual.

"Ya got some visitors, loser, should you choose to see them," Monty said, thumbs hooked under his belt. "Although looking like you do, ya might be doing them a favor by not seeing them."

"Been taking a Carnegie course or something, Monty?"

His puzzled look turned quickly rigid.

"What's that supposed to mean, dickface?"

"Nothing Monty, I just thought you were finally warming to me. Who's here to see me?"

"Your dipshit lawyer with the asshole breath and some hot-looking older chick."

"A blond in expensive clothes?"

"Sounds like this one."

"Great. And as long as you're here, you can verify that my ceiling is falling in and I need some new digs." I pointed a finger up at the hole.

Monty gave me one of those cocky what're-ya-tryin'-ta-pull looks that unqualified authority figures are noted for. Then he looked up at the hole in the ceiling and frowned like an adolescent school kid.

I've heard it said that if you start thinking about someone you haven't seen for a while, chances are they are somewhere close by. I'm not sure if that's true but I do know it was good to see Jan sitting in the visiting area next to the disheveled, corduroy countenance of Sam Frederickson. Even his craggy, wide-eyed face looked good to me.

Jan peered at me with a mixture of concern and uncertainty like maybe she was wondering if I actually killed the woman. I was seeing a lot of that lately—a removed and surveying look as folks passed their judgment on me.

Jan stood and gave me a hug and a kiss on the cheek.

Frederickson was filled with his usual doggy confidence. He'd been busy.

We had a nice little talk.

Sam had learned that the man who'd reportedly seen a blue SUV bouncing off of Rose's Focus on the night of her death had recently been busted for possession of methamphetamine and thus been deemed invalid and unreliable as a witness by the Creek County Attorney. Along with that, a couple of the regulars at the Savannah Club were insisting they'd seen me at the bar on the night of the crash. I wasn't sure if they were telling the truth but I didn't care. I got warm and fuzzy after hearing that Jan had discovered my predicament from the TV news and immediately called Sam Frederickson with an offer to bankroll a "more thorough" investigation.

We were chatting away like three drunks at a high school re-union when Sheriff John Daugherty pressed his former All-Con-ference linebacker's body into our space. Many years removed from his glory days, he'd developed a case of dresser disease—chest falling into his drawers. His round, puffy face wore the lost and angry look of a man who'd outlived his usefulness but was trying to pretend differently. Who knew how much brain dam-age he'd suffered playing football?

"It looks like you're free to go, Brown." Daugherty frowned until his bushy gray eyebrows joined together as one. "You got lucky this time, hotshot," he said, squaring his wide shoulders, "but don't go too far away. We're still considering other charges, and as far as I'm concerned you are still the most likely suspect. You can be sure we are doing our best to prove me right."

"I'm not so sure County Attorney Burnside agrees with you, Sheriff," Frederickson said, followed by a garlic-heavy belch.

"We still got the letter, smart guy, and the lab is going to be sending us more info on the paint match any day now. And I'm thinking either one of those things might be enough to light a fire under Burnside's butt."

"That letter's a fake, Daugherty," I said. "And you know it. Or at least you should. Why don't you go after Billy Talbot? He's the one who's lying. I never offered to kill Rose—he's obviously pulling something. You think he couldn't find some local hangdown to run her off the road? A case of beer and a gram of crank still buys a lot around here, you know what I'm saying?"

The sheriff's blotchy face got even redder. He snapped his head back, shot me an icy smirk and walked away, a .44 Magnum bouncing in a black leather holster on his large hip. His creased tan trousers were shiny at the butt.

Sam had already taken care of the paperwork.

Sign my name a few times and I was free to go.

At least for a while, said an unwanted voice in my head.

Sam and Jan and I went outside. Fresh air on my face was life affirming. Cold, but it didn't seem bad because I was free. The leaves were gone from the trees and rattling around on the asphalt. It was nearly dark at five o'clock in the afternoon. Exhaust swirled and dived behind a black Cadillac Escalade idling in the far corner of the parking lot alongside two sheriff's department SUVs. It was too dark to make out the face of the driver in the Caddy.

I gave Sam a hug and thanked him for all his good work. He aw-shucksed it and said to call him in the morning, got into his dirty green Honda and drove off.

I rode back to Duluth with Jan in her silver Audi, a birthday present from Rick the Prick. It was an awkward sixty minutes. I tried to convey my appreciation for her help. The more I tried the less she respected me. Or so it seemed. You had to be hard with Jan. In every way. If there was going to be any kindness shared, she had to initiate it. Otherwise she lost the element of control, I guess. At least that's what our ineffective marriage counselor had told us, some years back.

Pulling alongside my apartment, I was hoping she'd come in

for a condolence fuck. I wasn't that lucky. But I was lucky to still have a place to sleep. Sam had talked to my landlords, and since I had yet to be convicted of anything, they didn't terminate my lease.

Jan sent me away with a brushing kiss on my lips and a little pout on hers. Said she'd call me in the morning and not to worry about the money she'd spent because Rick was filthy rich.

I watched her taillights fade and went inside, settled into the couch and pondered my next move. Obviously, I was someone's patsy. Billy Talbot was more than likely filling the role of Someone. It sure looked like Talbot and his pal Dick Sacowski had conspired to kill Rose and frame me for the crime. A classic sucker's gambit and I was the classic sucker.

It sucked.

But what was the entirety of the motive? Isn't it always money, power, sex or vengeance? Or maybe in the odd case, love? Didn't seem like power was in the mix this time. I couldn't grasp what Talbot had to gain other than getting rid of his problem wife. Maybe that was enough. It would definitely save him a large stack of Benjamins.

I went to the fridge and found one remaining beer. There's no place like home. I asked myself what Mike Hammer would do in this situation. *More than likely maim or kill someone.* Name wasn't Hammer for nothing. But that wasn't going to work for me—for obvious reasons.

I elected to ponder the situation further and fell asleep sitting on the couch. Sometime later, I jerked awake when my snoring reached the intensity of a chainsaw about to cut my nose off. My neck snapped backwards and my lower back went into spasms.

I hobbled to the bed and collapsed on it, hoping to escape to unconsciousness before my mind figured out I was trying to trick it.

It knew me too well.

I spent the night tossing and turning and getting up to drain the lizard. My mind was flying with images of wrecked cars, dead Roses, jail cells, big ugly cops, hanging victims and naked, blond ex-wives wearing expensive jewelry. I tried to hold onto that last picture, but as soon as I focused, the channel changed and there was a stainless-steel toilet staring at me like the eye of a giant Cyclops.

I gave up the battle with consciousness around five a.m., took a shower and dressed in jeans and a long-sleeved black tee shirt, a black fleece pullover on top. I went to the tiny kitchen and filled the coffee maker. It was still dark outside and the indoor/outdoor thermometer on the window showed twenty-seven degrees. Late November and the livin' was sleazy. Ten hours of daylight and most of the time the sky was gray. North winds were usually biting.

But anything was better than jail.

The Forester was in the Creek County impound lot so I had to take a DTA bus to my office. Fortunately, I had paid up the lease for a year.

A private eye needs an office.

I drank tea and stared out the window until it got light over Lake Superior. There weren't many gulls around this time of year. Traffic was sparse now that tourist season was over. Christmas lights and decorations hung expectantly from the storefronts and the streetlights. I wasn't feeling much joy. In its place was a vise squeezing my temples and an icy wind blowing in my gut.

Around nine o'clock I started rounding up the boys.

I found Tommy Basilio at his shop *(Hi-tech Tommy's)*. He gave me a phone number for Dan Burton and told me that Tormoen was hiding out at a farm in Poplar, a small town just outside of Superior, Wisconsin. Superior, or Souptown, as many around here refer to it, is linked with Duluth by the Blatnik Interstate Bridge in the middle of town and the Richard Bong Memorial Bridge on the west side. Traversing St. Louis Bay, these bridges are the only direct land routes between the two port cities.

I reached Burton. He had a phone number for Jeff Tormoen at what Dan referred to as "Maggie's Farm." Jeff was there when I rang. He chewed me out for getting him into this mess. I reminded him it was I who'd faced a murder rap, and all they could possibly pin on him was impersonating a state official. I assured him it was only a misdemeanor but really had no idea. Chances were good he could do serious time but I figured what he didn't know couldn't hurt him.

Then I did what I did best—apply guilt. A skill you sometimes learn in a marriage. I insisted that my old plan, and by association his participation in said plan, had played a part in Rose's death; albeit a small one, but enough that he—we—owed Rose something. We owed her at least an effort to find her killer. I called upon his sense of humanity.

He laughed at that one but came around anyway. Said he'd do whatever I needed.

*   *   *

Three o'clock in the afternoon at the Hideaway Lounge in Superior is usually pretty slow. Always a comedian, Torm had chosen the location. We were drinking beer in a dark wooden booth in the dimness of the backroom. Except for Dan, who sipped a Diet Coke.

I did some pleading. Pleading for help. Pleading with these guys to help me prove who the real killer was. I hoped for more success than O.J Simpson had found.

Tommy Basilio's cousin Tony, a Duluth cop, had told Tommy that the authorities were still unsure of the identities of the phony State Fraud and Financial Bureau agents who'd visited Rose prior to her death. At this point, there were no warrants or identified "persons of interest." This was proof that I hadn't ratted on anybody. Reason enough for the boys to return the favor with their loyalty and assistance, the way I saw it.

They didn't argue that but balked when I said I wanted the team back together for another run at Taconite Bay. An all-out blitz for information or innuendo or anything we could find. The boys were understandably nervous about going back to the scene of the crime. I tried to convince them of the viability of this approach, pointing out that Dan Burton resembled a thousand other guys in the area and thus would be hard to pin down. On the other hand, Tormoen had wavy blond hair to go with his good looks and booming baritone voice—characteristics that made him hard to forget. But the only ones to see him in the Taconite Bay area had been Rose and Billy Talbot, and it was highly unlikely he'd encounter either of them.

"We have to go back up the shore and work the area for information," I announced solemnly after the third beer. "There has got to be somebody who saw something or knows something about what really went down that night. I mean, if you guys believe I didn't kill Rose."

"No, ah… I'm cool with that," Tommy said.

Dan nodded and raised his Diet Coke in acknowledgement.

Tormoen put his hand in front of his mouth and raised his eyebrows disapprovingly. "I'm not that sure about you," he said, pausing. Then he burst into a laugh and punched me in the shoulder.

"You realize I have a business to run, don't you, Carter?" Basilio whined.

"Yeah, Tommy, I know," I said. "And I also know that the cops have already spoken to you. You told them you installed a video system in Billy Talbot's house with his knowledge and permission. And that you were merely doing a job, much like the dudes who stuffed the ovens at Auschwitz."

"I never said anything about Auschwitz."

"Yeah, Tommy, I know, I know," I said, "just trying to lighten things up."

"You have a knack for lightness, Brownie," Tormoen said.

"I hear that," I said.

"Why don't we all go out to the farm, boys?" Tormoen said, his eyes unnaturally bright. "We can light a fire in the garage stove and plan and scheme to our hearts' content. My boy Pike grew some dynamite shit this year and he loves to get you high and talk about it."

"Instead of that, why don't we grab a case of beer and head to my office?" I said.

"You got any of that weed with you, Jeff?" Burton said. "This diet pop is just not cutting it."

I went with Tommy in his shop van. Dan and Jeff rode in Dan's truck. It was nearly five o'clock and close to dark as we rolled across the peak of the Blatnik Bridge. The industrial blight to the west was a blur against the darkening sky. To the east, little yellow lights dimpled along Minnesota Point as it spread itself like a giant finger across the black water. Below us, huge grain elevators loomed like floating space stations, their lights dancing on the satiny bay. Things looked better at night than in the daytime this time of year. The gray that seeped into your head like a fungus was replaced by inky blackness and artificial light. No shades of gray. I liked it that way. Maybe because I couldn't shake the feeling I was still in jail. Locked up in the Gray Rock Hotel of my mind.

There were plenty of empty parking spaces in front of my office; we didn't have to use the handicapped slot. Tormoen lifted a case of Leinenkugel's out of the truck bed and followed me to the stairs. Dan Burton looked happier now with his illegal smile on. Tommy Basilio just looked pained, although he was the only one of us who didn't seem pale in the frosty light.

We didn't get much done.

Burton and Tormoen were stoned. After a couple of beers Tommy ordered a pizza. I was just glad to have the company. The sleepless nights had scrambled my brain and made my body sore. But the electricity running through me spoke of the necessity for haste. People in the North Country were beginning to hole up and hunker down. How much time did I have before memories faded and interest in the case died out?

I wanted to get going the following day.

Tommy Basilio wore a look of pity as he calmly informed me that Thanksgiving was in two days. I had lost track. I was embarrassed. The others looked at me kindly for a change. I didn't like it.

"Look you guys," I said gravely. "I don't want to ruin your holiday or rain on your parade or piss in your beer, but this is my ass on the line. There was a murder charge hanging over my head, in case you forgot. And they could still come back at me. The only reason you guys aren't facing charges is because I kept my mouth shut, and I expect something in return."

"I won't say anything bad about you, Carter," Tormoen said from his chair, eyebrows rising, "Pinky swear." He crooked the little finger of his large right hand.

Dan Burton snickered. Tommy covered his mouth with his hand. I looked at Tormoen's cherubic face stuck in childlike innocence and sincerity and I started to laugh. The laugh had a life of its own. Took over my belly and then I was shaking with it.

"Much better Mr. Brown," Tormoen boomed in his rich basso as he stood up and spread his hands benevolently. "We are behind you all the way, honorable private dick, but one must not forget the mirth of the universe. We are—all of us here—caught up in a conundrum of inter-galactic proportions. The only way we can possibly succeed is by embracing the madness and riding the comet like interstellar cowboys."

"Well said, Jeff," Tommy said. "But I'm still going to have Thanksgiving with my family."

"If that is what the universe demands, my son," Tormoen said. "Or your ol' lady."

"Indeed," I said. "What about Friday? A holiday weekend could be a good time to reach a lot of people. I want to hit the bars up there, hear the whispers and the shouts. Buy a few drinks and bring up Rosie's demise, see what comes back at us."

"Here-here, and I'll drink to that," Tormoen said tipping a beer bottle to his lips. "Let's all vow to return on said Friday to begin our crusade for freedom. Freedom for Carter and for the whole world. But the question I feel most taxing—the nagging doubt of which torments me like a droning mosquito—manifests itself as a plaintiff inquiry as to who will be paying for the liquid enticements we must use to ply the tongues of the natives? I'm afraid that I find myself in a position of temporary financial embarrassment."

"All expenses will be taken care of by Carter Brown Investigations," I said.

"I'll second that," Burton said, standing.

We all stood. I felt like a puppet on a string as we clinked bottles (and one aluminum can) together and solemnly pledged to meet at two o'clock on Friday to begin our quest.

My assistants made their way out and emptiness came in to fill their spots. I turned on all the lights and gathered up the small pile of mail waiting for me in my still immaculate reception area, hoping something there would change the dangerous direction of my thoughts.

I sat at the desk and distractedly shuffled through the utility bills and junk mail and weapons catalogs. One distinctly different envelope caught my eye. A small hand-written white envelope addressed to Carter Brown. No return listed. The seven in the address had a line through it like Europeans use.

I got a funny feeling in my chest—a lightness. Then a twinge in my solar plexus. I tore open the envelope and slid out a carefully folded piece of stationery. The paper was heavy bond and the piece was shorter than normal size, as it had been cut neatly across the top, possibly to remove a logo or business name.

It was a brief note. Brief and to the point, handwritten in ink.

If you seek answers about death of Rose Talbot,
see Petr at Sky Blue Waters Lodge.

My first thought was that it was a ruse. But the juice buzzing through my chest told me something else. It could've been nerves kicking up, the fear and anxiety of a rank amateur out of his league and out of his mind, but what the hell else did I have?

Not much.

The way the name was spelled—Petr—without the second *e,* indicatedß he was either European or there was a spelling error on the note. Maybe Petr was one of those guys who pretend they're from somewhere exotic and foreign in order to impress people. Kind of like a guy who becomes a private detective to impress people. Maybe Petr and I had something in common other than Rose Talbot. Maybe Petr didn't even write the note. Maybe I was crazy.

Chapter

3

Thanksgiving arrived. I ate a can of sardines and a bag of chips, drank beer and watched football—alone. The games were boring. The Lions got waxed by Tennessee and the Cowboys stomped the Redskins. I concluded it was time to change the traditional Turkey day games around, move them to different cities.

After the games were over the apartment felt like a cell. The local cable company didn't carry the NFL Network so the night game was not available to me. In a state of abject boredom and growing desperation, I picked up the phone and punched out Jan's number, but shut it down after two rings. Picked it up again but didn't do anything except stare at the receiver and drop it back in the cradle.

Surrendering to indifference, I drank more beer and passed out on the couch. Popped awake at four a.m., stomach churning. I showered and shaved and walked down to Perkins on London Road for breakfast. After steak and eggs and hash browns I grabbed a morning paper and caught a cab downtown.

I walked the four blocks from Superior Street to my office to try and clear my head. The air was cold and damp and windy.

I was shivering by the time I got to my building. My head hadn't cleared. The sky was black and I could hear the waves crashing against the rocks a block to the east. The store below my office was dark except for a sign in the window blinking *Northern Woods and Waters*. Old-time-y streetlights strung with plastic candy canes glowed weakly like sad clowns trapped in cement.

I let myself in and creaked slowly up the stairs. At the threshold of my office, I was fumbling with the keys in the dim light of the lone fluorescent bulb when the door burst open, slammed into my toe and forehead and sent me staggering back against the wall. I struggled back upright but a dark figure shot out of the shadows and threw a shoulder into my chest with more force than the Lions had shown against Tennessee.

Again I toppled backwards. My head slammed the wall and I slid to the floor in a confused and startled heap. Stars circled around the edge of my fuzzy vision as the dark figure flew down the stairs three at a time and hit the street running.

By the time I made the sidewalk, the taillights of a Mopar muscle car were mocking me as it squealed away, exhaust pipes blaring. I couldn't get a read on the plate. I thought I saw two shadows in the front seat as it blew up the avenue and veered onto the northbound lane of the freeway.

I struggled and wheezed my way back up the stairs and into the office. It had been tossed and tossed well. The mail was scattered on the floor and the contents of the desk drawers were turned over on the desktop. All containers had been gone through. But my flat-screen TV was still on the wall and that eased my burden some. The note from Petr was still in the inside pocket of my jacket.

It seemed the only thing they could have been looking for was the letter. Judging by the speed and power the intruder had shown, I could conclude that it was a young man. One who the Detroit Lions should try signing. The getaway vehicle definitely seemed like a young man's car. I wondered if Petr had been trying to retrieve his mistake.

Or maybe someone else was trying to retrieve Petr's mistake.

I needed to make another stop at Sky Blue Waters Lodge.

*   *   *

We were supposed to hit the road on Friday morning. Tommy Basilio had called in and copped a plea about having to stay in Duluth and tend his store. Said he'd given his brother-in-law the day off because Tommy's sister, who was "unlucky enough to be married to the bastard" had hammered away at him during Thanksgiving dinner, insisting Tommy took advantage of her husband by making the poor bastard watch the store while Tommy "ran off to play." Basilio believed the best solution to this ultimately ridiculous situation was to give old Bob the Friday off so he and sister Jane could drink themselves stupid and fight like drunken fools for the entire day. That way she might think twice before bitching about time off for her no-good husband.

I wasn't sure about the wisdom of that or even if Tommy's story was actually true, but I had to at least give him credit for creativity.

That left Dan Burton, Jeff Tormoen and me, the private dick. I admit to being surprised when Jeff and Dan actually showed up. They were nothing close to bright eyed and shiny and ready to go—but at least they were there. Torm was wearing a white fisherman's sweater under a short, soft, brown leather jacket along with faded blue jeans, Burton had on a tan Carhartt jacket over a red chamois shirt and thick, khaki hunting pants held up by brown suspenders.

The ride up the North Shore was just as dismal and depressing as I had imagined it. The sky was full of coiling dark clouds, the lake the color of old steel. Whitecaps broke and raced with the whistling wind before exploding against the rocky shore and sending plumes of pale spray into the colorless air.

At least it wasn't snowing.

I was alone in a brown Ford Taurus rental (not from Avis). Burton and Tormoen followed close behind in Dan's pickup. I was thinking the weather might be exciting if the situation was different. If I wasn't looking for a killer and trying to save my own skin at the same time, maybe I could enjoy the drive. Our destination was Sky Blue Waters Lodge for the cocktail hour and an early dinner on my dime. These were all the enticements I could afford. I think Burton came along out of some old-school sense of duty and responsibility. Tormoen was just tickled to be paid for drinking and talking—things he usually did at his own expense. I doubted whether either of them thought much of my plan.

The dining room at the lodge was nearly empty. Quiet as a church on a weekday afternoon. Our footsteps echoed off the polished cathedral ceiling. We took a table by the windows and gazed out at the unruly lake, ordered libations and watched the light dying in the sky.

I tried to keep an eye on the wait staff. The busboys were young and had haircuts that reminded me of those I'd seen in downtown Duluth on crewmen from foreign ships. Our waitress was a pretty girl in her twenties with the edge of an accent, *Greta* printed on a little card pinned to her white blouse. Possibly eastern European, but I'm no expert. Tormoen thought it might be Romanian or something close to that. Whatever close to that might be.

Burton, ever the romantic, thought the waitress had soulful eyes. Besides a great rack and a nice tush, Tormoen added. Burton tried chatting her up. Finally broke through sometime between his second and third Diet Coke when his banter gave her a laugh. We all knew the deal was sealed when she put her hand on his shoulder.

After dinner, as Greta was filling the coffee cups, Burton kept up the chatter. Girl agreed to meet him outside for a smoke during her break, which was coming up as soon as our table was cleared. Blushing slightly as Burton smiled up at her, the waitress stopped a dark, good-looking busboy as he passed. "Petr," she said, "Can you finish this table so I can take my break?"

He frowned and shrugged and started taking our plates. I studied him closely as he made his way around the table. Could he have been the one to run over me? He was big enough but I couldn't be sure. Maybe if I smelled him. The guy who bowled me over had carried an unusual scent, aftershave or cologne or deodorant unfamiliar to me. Was it one of those body washes that seem to have replaced soap among the younger set?

You ever get down to Duluth, Petr?" I said, startling him a little.

He stared blankly and forced a mechanical grin. "Not much, sir," he said in a thick accent. "Too much work." He reached in to scoop up Tormoen's plate.

"If you do, you should drive down to the Waterfront District at night. It's nice down there."

"I will," he said, nodding, the blank look still there.

I couldn't detect a thing in his demeanor indicating either guilt or the knowledge of what I was trying to get at. He walked off with dishes and silverware cradled in his arms. I watched him put the stuff on a cart and wheel it into the kitchen.

"Dollars to doughnuts that's my letter writer, boys," I said. "He's got the right name, anyway. And the right kind of accent for a guy who crosses his sevens."

"I sometimes cross my sevens," Tormoen said, sipping coffee.

"And you're in theater, Jeff." I said.

He flipped me the bird.

"Hey look, you guys," Burton said. "I'm going outside for a smoke. I think she likes me. And I haven't been laid in so long I'm afraid to look between my legs."

"That explains the smell in the truck," Tormoen said, deadpan.

"You need to work the conversation around to asking her about Petr," I said.

"How am I supposed to do that at the same time I'm trying to convince her to meet me later for a little of the horizontal boogie?"

"You'll just have to use your great intellect and slimy reptilian nature," I said. "I've borne witness to you performing more miraculous tasks than that when it came to chicks."

"That was when I was drinking. I'm not like that anymore."

"You'll just have to resurrect old Barfly Burton for the sake of the job. We are supposed to be working here, you know."

"Yeah, I know," he said gloomily. "Forgive me for allowing the sin of lust to cloud my mind."

"You are forgiven, my son," Tormoen said, fluttering his hand downward from his chest like a rajah. "Asmodeus, the demon of lust, is a difficult beast to overcome."

"As if I would want to overcome him," Burton said.

"Hear, hear," Tormoen said.

Then Greta glided up to the table with the check and gave Burton a come hither look of sorts. They put their heads together while I grabbed the leather folder, left some bills for the tip and walked to the cash register by the entrance arch. Torm stretched and followed me.

I was putting the receipt in my wallet when I noticed Petr lingering in the hallway to my left. Torm was busy working a toothpick in his mouth as I stepped quickly down the hall and slid over next to Petr.

He looked like he was expecting me.

"My name is Carter Brown," I said, looking into a pair of dark, impassive eyes. "I think you wrote me a letter. You want to tell me why?" He was about even with my six-foot frame and he looked like he carried about one-seventy. Hell of a lot younger than me, probably around twenty.

"I knew Rosemarie Talbot very well," he said, emphasizing the very well.

Something flickered in his eye and for a moment I thought it was anger. Like maybe he thought I'd killed her and was now going to attempt revenge of some sort. But then he glanced nervously down the hallway. Then back to me with a hint of anxiety or fear. "I cannot talk here," he said softly. "Meet me at Palisade Head at eleven tonight. I know things."

Then a large man wearing a tan sport coat and a pushy managerial demeanor emerged from the bend in the hallway and locked his eyes on Petr, who went immediately into the men's room.

Tormoen came up next to me. I said something clever: "I suppose we should go to the car and wait for Dan."

As we moved away, the guy in the sport coat stared at us for a moment before following Petr into the men's room. I heard the snap of an angry male voice from behind the door.

"You know, Torm," I said. "My dad always told me to go to the bathroom before I got in the car for a drive. I think I'm going back and follow his advice."

Jeff nodded. "I'll wait here for you," he said. "Unless you need some moral support."

"I'm good. I'll yell if I need you."

I got back to the restroom in time to see Petr coming out the door with a red face, a cowed look, and the guy in the jacket following behind him like a drover for a cattle herd.

Petr avoided my eyes and shuffled down the hall toward the kitchen. The manager dude shot me an indifferent look and strutted down after the boy. I watched them disappear around the corner.

Tormoen was standing by the entrance with his back to me, gazing through the thick glass at the darkened parking lot.

"Our boy, show up yet?" I said.

"Nope. Probably trying to do her in the janitor's closet."

"And she looked like such a nice girl."

"Nice girl, shit," Torm said. "Europeans take a different view of sex than Americans do. Euro chicks are like guys when it comes to fucking."

"You think Burton's that good? Seems like they run a tight ship around here, if that managerial type at the restaurant was any indication."

Tormoen, more than likely wishing he was the one rendezvous-ing with the sexy waitress, said, "He doesn't need to be that good. She's probably spread open like a pussy buffet, as we speak."

Trying not to visualize, I pulled my car keys from my leather jacket and went outside. The sky was dark and starless and a nasty wind swirled around me like a rabid lynx. I headed for the car. Tormoen ambled along behind me. We both turned at the same time as Burton appeared at the edge of the lodge and stepped into the amber glow of the sodium light mounted on the building.

"It's the lady killer himself," Tormoen said loudly.

"Jesus Christ," I said. "Watch what you fucking say around here. Let's not forget that a lady did get killed—and I went to jail for it."

"Point taken," Tormoen said, suppressing a smirk.

Burton had a wide grin and seemed to be walking with great-er confidence. "Well, Dan," I said, "You accomplish anything?"

"She's going to meet me tonight after she gets off work."

"And how about something about Petr or Rose Talbot? Or anything that might actually be worth paying you for."

"Petr and Greta and ninety percent of the staff are foreign citizens," Burton said. "If that's anything. This place must be working some kind of scam—something to get cheap labor or something. Greta says the boys all sleep in the basement of the building on cots. It's like a barracks. And the kids have to pay rent. Greta says they try to keep'em broke and hungry and de-pendent."

"Who are *they*?" I said.

"Barnes is the guy in charge. Some out-of-town bigshot, prob-ably with a hefty loan payment."

"Where does Greta live?" Tormoen asked.

"She said the girls all stay at this motel down the highway that Barnes also owns, some old relic from the motor court era."

"Could be a sex-slave ranch," Tormoen said.

"Is that where you're meeting her?" I said, frowning.

"Nah. A bunch of them are getting together at Palisade Head after work. I'm s'posed to meet her there at eleven. I was hoping you two could ride together so she could be with me in the truck."

"No problem, Dan boy," I said. "We all sympathize. I'll be in the area myse—"

"And listen to this, Cart," he interrupted excitedly, obviously giddy with the prospect of actual sex with an actual human female. "She says there's a rumor that Petr and Rose Talbot were lovers. Flat out slamming-the-pork-to-the-pussy fucking lovers."

"Your graphic language makes me blush, Burto," Tormoen said. "Your subconscious is obviously being overrun by prurient images."

"That rumor puts a different hue on things altogether," I said. "Very interesting, indeed."

They shook their heads in agreement.

Back out on the darkened highway, my watch said 7:30. A little early for the prime drinking crowd in more civilized environs but not necessarily the case up here, as there were not exactly a plethora of nightspots available this far north. I'd pared my list down to a select few establishments: The ski resort at Lutsen Mountain and the Safe Harbor Bar, both of which had bands on weekends. For dedicated drinkers, the municipal lounge in Taconite Bay always did a brisk business, and a few roadside supper clubs in the hinterlands also attracted many of the locals.

Since we were free to roam until eleven, I hoped we'd have time to check them all. I wanted to find Gloria, Rose's blond friend from that rainy afternoon I'd first arrived on the scene.

A poster on the wall of the Safe Harbor Bar advertised a band called "Azure Du Jour." Burton and Tormoen and I went inside and ordered drinks. Not that we needed any more alcohol but it seemed like the right thing to do. I surveyed the half-full bar as the band set up their equipment.

No Gloria.

I knocked back a beer and gave instructions to Burton to hold tight at the Safe Harbor until Tormoen and I returned from our search. He could strike up conversations and buy drinks and dig for information. All the good things a private eye's assistant should do.

As Tormoen and I cruised up Highway 61 toward Taconite Bay, I was feeling a little guilty about having left a recovering alcoholic alone in a bar. Tormoen would've been a better choice but it was too late for that. I was also a little nervous about going inside the muni, the probability of Dick Sacowski being there slightly higher than the chance of snow in December. And if I sent Tormoen into the lounge to look for the brassy blond, there was no telling what complications might arise. Torm had never set eyes on Gloria before, and would more than likely start up a conversation with any woman remotely resembling my description. This would, of course, lead to a loss of valuable time and expense money at the very least. Not to mention the numerous other more painful possibilities buzzing ensemble in the back of my brain like a swarm of angry wasps.

As we swung into the lot, I vowed to myself that I was going to take charge. I parked and got out of the Taurus. Tormoen followed suit and we walked together to the lounge. A quick look around the strangely smokeless barroom revealed no Gloria or Sacowski, only two reasonably good-looking women who might have occupied Jeff's interest for a considerable length of time had I not been there to keep him in line.

We exited quickly and started across the gravel. A red Malibu crunched by us and pulled in next to the Taurus. I got a couple steps closer and saw blond hair emerging from the driver's door. By god if it wasn't old G-L-O-R-I-A. Talk about falling into it.

She squinted at me as I stood there squinting at her. I smiled. "Hello," I said.

She looked at me again, puzzling over who I was. What I was doing there. Did she recognize me?

"I know you," she snarled, her face tightening and her eyes flaring with heat. "You're the sick fuck who killed Rose. What the hell, are you doing here, you cocksucker? I should go inside and tell some of the boys that you're out here."

My ears were burning from the tongue-lashing. "There's no need to do that," I said defensively. "The charges against me have been dropped."

"Yeah, like the cops around here could find their ass with two hands and a flashlight," she said, looking at the ground before letting her gaze go up and down Tormoen's impressive frame.

I could tell she was softening, undressing Tormoen with her eyes. "I guess I'd agree with you on that one," I said. "And I think you know I didn't kill Rose. I'm trying to find the real killer and I think you can help me achieve that goal."

"You and OJ, eh? The private dick and the big dick—both with the same gallant goal."

"The similarities have crossed my mind," I said. "But I think Rose had other problems besides me. And I think, as her friend, you'd want to enlighten me about those things. Or have you gotten close with Billy Talbot since the funeral."

A look of disgust crossed her face like she'd just smelled something foul. "That shrunken little rodent? You got to be kidding, man. All I can say is that Talbot has a lot of friends. Tough and mean friends, if you know what I'm saying."

"Is that all you're going to give me? I thought Rose was your friend. I hoped there was more to you. I thought friendship meant something around here."

Her eyes turned soft and sad for a moment and then went flat. She shifted from one foot to the other and looked around the parking lot. Her hair looked silver in the light. Tormoen was smiling charmingly.

"Listen," she said, opening her white purse and pulling out a pack of Marlboro Lights. She put one in her mouth and rummaged in her purse for fire. On cue, Tormoen reached out and flicked a plastic lighter, cupping it against the breeze.

Gloria leaned into the flame, looked up into Jeff's blue eyes, inhaled and snapped the smoke into the air with pursed lips.

"You got a way with the guilt trips don't you, asshole," she said, giving me the hard eye and folding her arms across the front of her bird's-egg-blue-and-silver silken jacket. "Listen, what's your fuck—Brown—that your name?"

"Carter Brown," I said, nodding.

"Listen, Mr. Carter Brown, I'd like to help you but I can't do it here. I'm sorry I called you a cocksucker. You and your friend seem like nice guys. You guys should come to the bar at the ski hill tonight around ten."

Her eyes went up and down the studly Norwegian one more time before she flipped her cigarette to the ground and started toward the bar.

"The name's Jeff," Tormoen said to her back. "Hope to see you later."

She stopped and turned her head slightly back to him. "Ask yourselves this question boys," she said. "Why do you think there was no autopsy done on Rose?" Then she disappeared into the lounge, a block of light slowly vanishing after her as the door swung shut.

I shook my head. "Were you really flirting with her, Torm?"

"Just doing my job, boss. Trying to be the best I can be. I'd do her if I had to—in the name of duty, you understand."

"That's good to know, Jeff. Real good."

Chapter

4

With two hours to kill and plenty to think about, Jeff and I took a county road into the forest, searching for the Red Pine Supper Club. Tormoen had a road map open on his lap as we plowed along with our headlights cutting a wedge through the darkness.

"So, why do you think there wasn't any autopsy on Rose?" Tormoen asked, pulling a joint from his inside jacket pocket.

"I don't know," I said. "Don't they usually perform an autopsy on someone who dies in a car wreck? Seems like they always do. And we don't actually know there wasn't one."

"Are you doubting the veracity of the lovely Gloria?"

"Wouldn't dream of it."

"If it is true," he said, "it does sound a little odd. With all the emphasis on drugs and alcohol these days, you'd think an autopsy in a car-wreck death would be pretty common. They'd want to know if she was buzzed when she hit the tree. Got to keep the statistics up to date."

"You've got a point there," I said. "Maybe my lawyer can get some insider information, like who made the decision not to cut her open and why."

Tormoen flicked his green plastic lighter and touched the yellow flame to the tip of the joint.

"You going to smoke that thing now?"

"That was my plan," he said with a high voice as he held in the smoke.

"This is probably a pretty redneck place we're going to."

"These boys up here like their weed, same as anywhere," Torm said, letting out the smoke in a slow billow.

"Yeah, but I'm not sure if they'll like us—strangers coming into their territory and asking questions about a dead person."

"You're probably right, but what does getting high have to do with anything?"

"I don't think it's professional. We're private operatives on a case. Not two stoners out to get loaded."

"I really don't see the difference, Cart," Tormoen said. He took another hit and began looking around the cockpit. "Don't they even have a fucking ashtray in this car?"

"Evidently not. And you're violating my rental agreement by smoking in the car."

"Oh-oh." He popped his window a crack and pinched off the coal, put the roach in his jacket pocket.

We drove on through the darkness, the forest closing in on us. Ten minutes later, Tormoen was pointing at a sign on the side of the road.

Red Pine Supper Club—Two Miles.

Tormoen refolded the roadmap with remarkable ease and slid it in the glove compartment.

The parking area at the Red Pine was filled with large pickups and SUVs of all sizes. A battered yellow dump truck sat in the back corner. This part of the world is a tough place to scratch out a living, and those who do, are a hard-working bunch that like their trucks. These men (and a few women) bring new dimension to the term stolid. Even former NFL linemen like Howie Long wouldn't dare question the masculinity of the "man step" on one of *their* trucks.

The supper club was painted red. It might have been pine but it wasn't made of logs, just an ordinary one-story wood framed building with a slightly pitched, green-shingled roof and numerous beer signs blinking and glowing. We stepped through the heavy wooden door into a dimly lit room with faux-log paneling on the walls, a polished bar and a crowd of mostly large people eating, drinking and talking loud.

Tormoen and I walked slowly to the bar, every eye in the club riveted on us. I picked a barstool and briefly wondered what the hell I was doing here. What had I expected to accomplish in a place like this? Was I going to trip around the room like a gay accordionist and instead of playing "The Flight of the Bumble Bee," ask the folks if they'd known Rose Talbot?

I became depressed and filled with self-hatred, wished I had smoked some of the joint.

We ordered drinks from the square-jawed, wide-shouldered bartender. The noise in the room rose around us to a crescendo of cacophony about to break my skull. Thankfully, the drinks came fast. I dropped a twenty on the bar, swept up my drink and sucked down half of the Bacardi-Coke in one smooth motion.

I leaned back, trying to stretch the kinks out of my back and overheard Tormoen telling a guy next to him that we were reporters from Minneapolis researching a story on Rose Talbot's death.

I turned toward them, my mood lightening.

The guy looked like a logger: washed-out long-underwear shirt under his blue-checked flannel. Scruffy beard, curly dirty-blond mullet and smudges of dirt on his neck and hands and jeans. I watched his eyes get large in response to Jeff's elaborate lie. I watched him smile a kind of sinister, gap-toothed smile that reminded me of a dog baring its teeth.

"Watcha wanna do a story on a rotten skank like that for?" he said in a voice that could wrinkle steel.

I saw Jeff's body recoil slightly and I felt a sensation in my chest like the prick of an invisible needle. I turned away and gazed at the bottles behind the bar, all of them glowing nicely in soft orange light.

Tormoen rebounded smoothly. "Would you be interested in sharing your views on Ms. Talbot with the reading public, Mister, ah…" He extended his hand. "I didn't catch your name…"

"Johnson," the guy said. "Scott Johnson. Just what the hell is the 'reading public' exactly?"

"I think there must be at least two hundred people left in the state who still read newspapers," I said, turning toward them and smiling.

Nobody smiled back.

"What paper you guys work for?" Johnson said, looking Jeff in the eye.

Minneapolis Star Tribune, Tormoen said.

"Shit, I know some people who read that. I can't go talking shit to you guys. My ass would be grass."

"How about if we identified you as an informed source who wishes to remain anonymous?" Tormoen said.

Johnson's eyes hazed over and he looked down at his drink glass, empty and forlorn in his hand.

"Bartender," I said, "get us another round." I gestured to include the three of us then threw down the rest of my first drink.

When our glasses were again full, Johnson took a hefty swig of his Windsor and Coke and gave us both a bleary-eyed once-over. "The only thing I'm gonna say to you guys is what everybody around here already knows. Rose Talbot fucked anything that moved."

With that, he picked up his drink, gave us a look of bored dismissal and walked crookedly over to a pinball machine blinking beneath a wall-mounted moose head.

"Think he says that about every chick that won't fuck him?" I said.

"I wouldn't doubt it, but at least I was doing my job. Right, boss?"

"No doubt, Jeff. I spent twenty-five bucks on drinks so we could find out that a woman with an impotent husband fucks around. And that bit of enlightenment likely the words of one of the rejected homeboys."

"The night is still young, boss."

I looked at my Bacardi and flat Coke and was suddenly sorry it was there. "But *I'm* getting old fast," I said, taking a long pull.

The barkeep was down at the far end of the bar tending to Johnson, who was getting more quarters for the pinball. Jeff and I were the only remaining customers sitting at the bar.

"You know," I said, resting my arms on the bar top. "I'm still thinking about that autopsy shit. It had to be someone with money and influence who pulled that one off."

"Either that or someone in the law enforcement circle around here. Someone with a personal axe to grind." Tormoen said.

"Which makes it all point back to Billy Talbot," I said. "You think it might be some kind of town conspiracy thing? You know, where the victim was hated by enough of the locals that they all turn against the idea of truth and justice and stonewall any investigation."

"Like in one of those detective stories you read, Carter?"

"Yeah… like that, I guess. More like a made-for-TV movie."

"If that kind of thing is possible at all, this might be the place," Tormoen said, turning to look at the diners. "Judging by the recurring glances we're getting from the dinner crowd, I'd say this is a rather closed environment. One not given to entertaining newcomers gladly."

"Well said."

I watched Johnson return to the pinball machine. The bartender started back in our direction but stopped halfway to lift up the receiver of a phone mounted on the wall behind the bar. He mumbled a few words and re-hung the phone. A moment later a hulking ape of a man emerged from a doorway to the left of the bar wearing a grease-spattered white apron over a white shirt, sleeves rolled up tight around Popeye forearms.

I turned to get a better look at the pumped-up monster. Face was vaguely familiar. Then it hit me. It was Dave Sacowski, Dick's younger brother, a notorious brawler and steroid abuser who'd been at my house once years ago, when he and Dick were on the way back home after a Sunday-morning beer run to Superior.

It all came rushing back to me like a dormant virus: Dick's stories about his little brother's violent shenanigans and how the boy was putting himself back together as a chef.

At the Red Pine Supper Club, just north of town.

I tried to turn away but it was too late, he was stepping to us. A bee-stung baboon with massive, hairy forearms like two twisted trunks of swamp spruce. He bellied up to the back of the bar and gave Torm the evil eye, his barrel chest a foot from Jeff's face. I could smell the sweat and cooking grease. I leaned back to get away from the stink.

Little Sac, as he was known around here, zeroed in on Tormoen. "I hear yer a reporter," he growled. "That true?"

Tormoen didn't seem impressed by the hulk pressing in on him. "It is," he said, feigning surprise that the monster was there. "Would you care to contribute to the story?"

Either Tormoen had a huge set of balls for an actor or he truly was acting, in an attempt to save his balls from a crushing. I was leaning toward the latter.

"How about I contribute to your death," the giant said softly like the hiss of a snake.

"That might prove costly," Jeff said, rising from his stool and squinting at his tormentor like Dirty Harry. "But it would make a good story."

"Look," I said, turning to the bartender who was hovering nearby, hands on hips. "We don't want any trouble here. We were just leaving."

Little Sac looked at me and a flicker of recognition swam through his red-veined eyes. "I know you," he said, dark flashes chasing after the recognition. His voice rose to a dull roar.

"You're the faggot who killed Rose Talbot."

He stretched his paw across the bar for me but I jerked backwards. He snatched up my drink and tossed the contents in my face. I jumped off the stool, rum and Coke stinging my eyes and dripping from my hair.

"These guys are faggots from Duluth," Little Sac bellowed like a circus bear. "Rose Talbot's fag friends."

I saw the dinner crowd rise almost imperceptibly in their chairs and lean in our direction, faces sour and feral. Then, inexplicably, Tormoen launched a straight right hand to Little Sac's face that sounded like a boot hitting the side of a rock cliff. With just about as much effect.

The monster started to struggle his huge body over the bar. Jeff and I gave each other knowing looks before sprinting ensemble toward the door. We hit the parking lot running, jumped in the Taurus and tore out of there with dust flying out behind us like a dirt-track race at the county fair.

It was miles down the road before my heart slowed. I had some Kleenex in the glove compartment (it was cold season) and used it to blot at the wetness in my hair. I tried to spike up the remaining sticky spots to make it appear like a planned look—ungracefully aging hipster.

Eventually I realized I'd been driving in the wrong direction, going deeper into the woods and farther away from the ski lodge where we were to meet Gloria. I pulled to the shoulder and whipped an Alaskan-Highway turn, backing the Taurus across the pavement until we were facing the correct way.

"Maybe that Coke will darken some of the gray hair on the top of your head, Carter," Tormoen said. "Seems to work good as mousse, anyway."

"Fuck you," I said, feeling inarticulate and ineffectual.

I accelerated down the lonely asphalt and headed back toward Lake Superior, harboring the hope that even the minimal civilization existing along the North Shore would offer some safe haven for a private eye and his assistant.

Tormoen took the joint from his pocket and lit it with his plastic lighter before flexing his right hand in the dashboard lights. "My hand feels like I punched a tree," he said, toking on the funny cigarette.

"Yeah, what the fuck came over you anyway? I know that guy. Heard some stories about him. One dude you don't want to sucker punch. In the future, you should probably follow my lead and stop striking out on your own, excuse the pun."

"And your plan was what? Talk the behemoth into submission? Seemed to me like he was about to wipe the bar with your face. Seems to me, if I hadn't swung on the geek, he'd have played wishbone with your legs and you'd be shitting in a bag for the rest of your days. I was just acting in the time-honored tradition of sidekicks everywhere. You should thank me for it."

He hit the joint again and I watched the crown flare orange. Smoke drifted to my face and annoyed me even more. "Yeah well, thanks," I said. "Next time, just don't be so quick to strike. I can be a silver-tongued devil if I need to be. Have some faith in my abilities."

He kept himself from laughing outright but continued smirking. I wrote it off to the effects of marijuana and kept my eyes on the road.

"You got that map handy?" I said. "I don't want to drive past the Red Pine again, if I can help it."

Jeff dutifully got the map from the glove box and studied it. "I'm afraid we'll have to go back the way we came," he said. "The nearest crossroads is, like ten, twelve miles north—back that way," he shot his thumb towards the back of the car.

Not wanting to turn around again, I clenched my teeth and drove on. When we got close enough to see the glow of the Red Pine's roof lights seeping onto the road, I shut off the headlights and pulled my foot off the gas, coasting into a shadow that was darker than I'd anticipated.

"You sure this is necessary, Carter?" Jeff said tensing up and leaning forward to the edge of his seat, eyes peering through the windshield into the murk.

"You can't be too careful, I always say. I remember once in high school—" I tightened my grip on the wheel and strained to see the road, still trying to act cool. "A buddy of mine sucker punched a kid from Morgan Park in the parking lot of the London Inn. It was much like your shot tonight only my friend kept punching the guy until the dude's face was a bloody mess. After that, we left the place and drove around for a while. At some point, against my better judgment, my friend decides to tool back to the London Inn and take a victory lap. We go in and the Morgan Park kids are waiting for us, along with carload of fresh allies. They chased us all over fucking town. Eventually, we had to escape into the driver's parents house like a bunch of chickenshits."

"So history repeats itself," he said, teeth gritted.

As we rolled out of the soft glow from the Red Pine, the road disappeared completely. Pitch black would not say enough. I waited as long as I could stand it (not very long) and flipped on the headlights.

Just in time to freeze a big black moose in its tracks, twenty yards dead ahead. The startled look in its big oval eyes was like—well—a deer in the headlights.

I hit the brakes and swerved hard to the left. Tires howled. The moose jumped. As we careened by, huge hooves flapped through the arc of the headlights and disappeared into the black. The Taurus slid onto the far shoulder. I jerked the wheel hard right. The tires grabbed, wiggled a bit but held the road.

Torm shook his head and let out a long toxic breath. "I think you may have overplayed that one just a tad, Carter," he said. "Think we can stay on the road with the lights on from now on?"

"I'll try, Jeff. But I was just being cautious. You can't be too careful out here in the wilderness."

"Your idea of careful is too damn dangerous, my man. You actually think someone might have been waiting for us back there at the Red Neck Supper Club? It seems unlikely, if you ask me. And a moose in the road is a very *real* danger up here. Every year some poor unfortunate inebriate punches his ticket hitting a moose. The bulky part of the moose lines up perfectly with the level of your head in cars like this. The fetid beasts come crashing through the windshield and snap your neck like a dry twig."

"I don't remember asking your opinion," I said. "And like I said, you can't be—"

"Too careful," he said sarcastically, relighting the now pinched-flat roach. He stared at me. I ignored him. He blew out the smoke in a cloud that dispersed at the windshield and drifted in little wisps to the back seat.

"Caution is the haven of the mediocre and the timid, Carter. And don't forget it."

I couldn't decide who's thinking was the most off kilter.

The rest of the ride went by without incident. The radio spit out "Riders on the Storm," the Stones doing "Oh Carole," and Led Zep's "No Quarter." Perfect tunes for cold dark nights. Before you knew it, we were rolling down the final hill to the scenic North Shore Drive.

They call some of the hills, mountains, up here. But if you've ever seen a real mountain range like the Rockies or the Cascades or the Himalayas, even the Smokies—you'd know that mountains in Minnesota are really just bumps. The highest point in the state, Eagle Mountain, is right here in the neighborhood, with an elevation of 2,301 feet above sea level. The Lutsen Mountains, where the ski lodge is located and where I hoped to meet Gloria, has four peaks, the highest being Moose Mountain at 1,913 feet above sea level. In contrast, Mount Everest is 29, 035 feet above sea level.

"We've got to find out what Rose was doing with all the money she was charging up," I said abruptly, as Jeff leaned back in his seat and looked out at nothing.

He turned toward me with the beatific smile of the stoner. I was envious. He was in his element: high and playing a role that involved women and booze and just enough danger to keep the adrenaline flowing smoothly and evenly like a morphine drip.

"That's what we need to find out from Gloria," I said, "should she show up. That's got to be the main focus. Follow the money is private eye rule number one."

"I will play follow the pussy," Tormoen said, "So you can play follow the money."

Again I ignored him. "I wonder if Rose had a life insurance policy?" I said.

"I should think the cops would know."

"I'm sure they do. I'm just not sure you can trust them to do the right thing with it. If Billy Talbot is collecting a large settlement, there's another strike against him. We can only hope Gloria has some answers for us."

"Ah, Gloria… my Nordic *fraulein*," Tormoen said dreamily, going back to staring out the window.

I slowed for the stop sign at the intersection of Highway 61, turned onto the two-lane asphalt and headed north. It was about a thirty-minute drive to the ski resort, which would put us there with enough time to check out the area prior to entering the club. In this era of cell phones and email and texting and tweating, the word on us could easily arrive before we did.

You can't be too careful.

Traffic was sparse to nonexistent. I couldn't see the moon. Pairs of glowing, disembodied eyes roamed the edge of the woods like tiny Chinese lanterns. When the song "Gloria" by the Shadows of Night came on, it seemed to be a sign of some sort. Like maybe this was where Jeff and I were meant to be. What we were meant to be doing. The universe was confirming the fact by playing the song. Either that or I'd gotten a contact high from the reefer smoke in the car.

About twenty minutes into the drive there came a buzzing from inside the console.

My cell phone.

I don't like the things. Call me what you will but when you get brain cancer don't call me on the cellular to tell me about it. Once you give out your number the mobile phone becomes just another inroad on your privacy and your ability to control your environment. Those dudes with the Star Trek units on their ears drive me nuts. Same with the geeks that wear a phone holster on their belts as if they're looking for a duel. Like maybe the Verizon guy is out searching for *mano a mano* phone battles. And who hasn't been in the middle of a good coversation or a fine meal and had someone's cell go off and break the mood?

"Grab that for me, man, it's my cell phone."

Tormoen opened the console and lifted out the phone.

"You got a text message," he said.

"Better than having to talk in the thing. Who's it from?"

"Your ex-wife."

"Jan? You shitting me?"

"No, man. It says '*Hi Cart, r u fine? Hubby is here so can't talk. Meet me at the Blue Star at 11 for marts if u can.*'"

"You're lying to me, you Norwegian prick."

"I swear to God on my last piece of lutefisk that that is what it says here."

"You know how to work those things—send a message?"

"Yeah. Pike's kids showed me how."

"Then tell her I'm out of town working on a case. That will go over well. I don't want to blow it, if I'm getting a second chance with her."

"What about Rockin' Richard the high-rollin' solicitor?"

"Rick—rhymes very nicely with prick. I'll leave it at that."

Torm tapped away on the phone.

"What did you say to her?" I said.

"Just what you told me to," he said.

"How did you word it?"

"My dearest darling Jan. My heart breaks that I cannot join you. I regret I'm out of town working on case. But my work finishes a distant second to your charms and beauty. My dick grows hard at the memories."

"I should be in good with her after that."

"What I really said was: 'Out of town—working. Can't make it—bitch. And don't you think it's time to end your cock-teasing ways?'"

"Exactly what I would have said."

And then I was turning into the lot at the ski resort. You could see the well-lit chairlift peeking above the pine trees.

Over at the log lounge building, spotlights under the eaves made it all seem cheery. A cluster of folks stood around the doorway smoking.

They didn't have a brass band in the bar to welcome us but by the way the gazes lingered a little longer than normal, it seemed many of the inhabitants were well aware of who we were. The Taconite Telegraph had evidently sounded the alarm of our imminent arrival. Either that or my rum-and-Coke spiked hair was drawing all the attention.

We took a table near the door to facilitate a quick exit should the need arise. You can't be too careful. A reggae band from Minneapolis was rocking out from a small, elevated stage in the far corner of the rustic-themed room. The good-sized crowd looked to be about half tourists and half locals. The season for visitors was nearing its end.

I spied Gloria at the bar standing next to another woman, a small semi-circle of guys ebbing and flowing around them. I signaled to a waitress. Before she reached the table, Jeff was up and gone. I watched him maneuver through the cadre of suitors and squeeze his way skillfully between Gloria and her female friend, a brunette of medium height and weight wearing a black silken jacket with *Diamonds Inc.* across the back in silver script.

The blond waitress asked could she take my order, saying it with an accent, like it was ordah. I asked for a Budweiser and a Bacardi Coke in my Minnesota accent.

Tormoen beat the drinks back to the table.

"She shoot you down already, Torm?"

"In a way. She says she can't talk to us in here because the place is buzzing with the tale of our escapades at the Red Pine. The word is out that we're here to put Billy Talbot behind bars. No one is supposed to cooperate with us. A couple dudes up there were giving me the evil eye."

"So we're dead in the water before we even started," I said dejectedly.

"Not so fast, Eeyore. She gave me her phone number and I gave her yours." He waved a matchbook at me. "She says she'll text me as soon as she goes to the can."

"Saints preserve us, the wonders of technology," I said and took a long pull of my drink. I put the glass down on the square table and saw Dan Burton and Greta coming through the door.

They joined us. Greta looked chic and wasted and Euro-trash, dressed in black from head to toe.

I beckoned for the waitress and watched Gloria walk from the bar to the back of the room where I assumed the bathrooms were. Sure enough, a little bit later the phone was vibrating in my pocket.

The message: *Ths place is no good. Meet me at palisade hed at 11. Answer to earlier question: Rose was pg*

Rose was pregnant? Was that one of the reasons for no autopsy? Who would want that covered up? Just about anybody who had anything to do with her. This was indeed interesting news but I didn't know what it meant. Was Petr the father? Would the father's identity make any difference? No matter the sire, the kid was dead, along with mom. And none of it would look very good for Billy Talbot. Just one more reason he'd have for wanting her dead.

I looked up from the phone and everybody at the table was staring at me. "Everything okay, Carter," Dan Burton asked.

"Yeah, sure, Dan, no problem. I was just thinking how wonderful these phones are today. And how has your evening been so far?"

"Great. Greta surprised me at the Safe Harbor. She got off early. The band there was good, but I ah, kinda like the reggae music, mon, so we came on down, you know."

The band was bobbing through a Bob Marley medley and in the middle of "No Woman, No Cry." I needed to discuss the case but was reluctant to with Greta in our midst.

"You still planning on going to Palisade Head tonight, Dan?" I said. "Now that Greta has found you or you've found each other or whatever it is you're calling it?"

"Bitchin' party at Palisade Head," Greta said, dark eyes wide.

"We're goin'," Dan said.

"Looks like we're all gonna be there," I said.

"Why don't you take our picture on your phone, man," Burton said. "Commemorate the moment."

"Your talking evidence, Dan. Besides, I don't know how to work the thing."

Tormoen showed me how to operate the camera portion of my phone. I took a nice shot of the three of them sitting cheek-to-cheek and smiling like tourists. Then Tormoen took one of me alone in the frame. Was this a statement of some kind?

We all had a few drinks. The band took a break and then came back on stage again and before I knew it, it was nearly eleven o'clock. Time to go.

I stood up. "We need to have a meeting outside," I said. "Just the three of us. Excuse us, Greta, but this is agency business. I won't keep Dan long, I promise."

Greta smiled awkwardly and looked at her beer bottle, a very nice German one at that. Mirth lit up the eyes of Burton and Tormoen but they both got dutifully up and followed me outside.

We stood in the dark by the Taurus. Burton brought out a pack of Marlboros. Tormoen bummed one and snapped out his lighter.

"Have you been able to learn anything from Greta?" I said, looking at Burton.

"Other than that your dick still works?" Tormoen added, blowing out smoke.

Burton shot Tormoen a sharp glance then turned back to me. "She said Rose came to the parties at Palisade Head sometimes. Said Rose and Petr and a couple of his friends used to hang out once in a while."

"Did she confirm or deny the rumor of their low-rent romance?"

"She made no comment on that. But I didn't press her. I figured eventually she'd get drunk enough and I could ask her anything and get an answer."

"Spoken like a true recovering alcoholic," Tormoen said.

Burton took another deep drag off his Marly before flicking the butt on the pavement where it bounced and sparked and rolled with the wind. He blew out smoke in a thin stream. "Well, I do know the territory rather well," he said, rubbing his hands together in front of him. "It's not like I'm going to use anything she says against her."

"Depends on what she says, Burt," I said. "Let's not forget who's paying for all this. One thing I'd like to know is why all the servers are foreigners. And what the manager at the restaurant is like. What's his game?"

"Yeah, Burt," Tormoen said. "If you act like you're actually interested in what she's saying—instead of just what's inside her jeans—she might tell you something important to the case."

"I'll keep that at the forefront of my mind, Jeff. Expert manipulator that you are."

"Fuckin' A," Tormoen said.

Chapter

5

The dashboard clock showed 11:12 when I turned in at the Palisade Head sign. The road is a paved but narrow job starting with a gradual uphill grade that gets steeper about halfway up, where several cutbacks begin looping around to the overlook, three hundred forty-eight feet above Lake Superior. According to the tourist brochures, the eighty-three acre precipice consists of igneous rhyolite overlaying soft basalt, and is a popular spot for rock climbers and vista viewers. I also knew it as the plateau of choice for suicide leapers and, evidently, partying restaurant workers. It is part of Tettegouche State Park, which takes its name from a logging camp established by eastern Canadians in the late 1800's.

A rusty pickup, a faded, black Bronco, a blue VW Golf of indeterminate age and Gloria's red Chevy Malibu were grouped together at the eastern edge of the parking area.

Jeff and I climbed out of the Taurus and walked onto the blacktop overlook that currently overlooked oily darkness, the lake being something you could only hear and smell. To our right, in front of a two-foot high stone retaining wall, a wood fire crackled, flames dancing and twisting in the breeze. A boom box sitting on the wall kicked out KQDS FM while a group of stylishly clad young people stood around the fire passing a joint. Gloria and her lady friend were just joining the group. I watched Gloria's friend slide a pint bottle of some kind of liquor into the mix.

"Well here we are, Jeff," I said. "The big part-ay. You got anymore weed? Anything we can offer the group? If I'd been thinking, I'd have brought some booze to share."

"Some private eye you're turning out to be."

I tried to hide from the sting of his words. The sound of an engine laboring up the hill behind us gave me an out. I turned my head in time to see Burton's truck coming around the final bend.

Dan and Greta emerged from the pickup and the four of us walked over to the fire. The wood smoke was sweet in my nostrils and the reefer smelled pretty good, too. Gloria was watching us, biting a fingernail and roaming her eyes on Tormoen. The brunette with her flashed me a come-on look. Greta said hello to the group around the fire. Petr was there in a brown suede jacket, jeans and a black ski hat pulled tight around his head. The other kids greeted us with foreign-accented salutations with emphasis on the wrong syllables. In the background, Neil Young belted out "Rockin' in the Free World." Shadows shifted and shook in the firelight like festive specters as one of the waiters grabbed a twelve-pack of Bud from the top of the retaining wall and offered it around. A few minutes later, Tormoen fired up a joint and the whole scene changed.

With their heads now riding the high winds, Tormoen went off to the Malibu with Gloria and her friend. Greta and Dan returned to the truck. A few of the waiters huddled around the fire holding hands. Gay waiters, it seemed. And not one of them had shoulders the size of the burglar who'd knocked me down outside my office.

I stood there awkwardly for a long moment and then reintro-
duced myself to Petr. He was shuffling around trying to avoid the
smoke from the fire. I showed him the plasticized Photostat of
my P.I. license Tommy Basilio had created for me.

Petr verified that he'd indeed sent the letter. He agreed to walk
away from the group and discuss it. I didn't waste much time. I
looked him in the eye and hoped he would take me seriously.
"What was it you were trying to say to me when you wrote that
letter, Petr?"

"I want to tell you Rose was pregnant when she died. And I
think my boss at restaurant was father. Rose told me about her
husband hiring you and how she always beat the tail you put on
her. She called you 'Private Dick she liked to shake.'"

This was real compelling stuff.

"Why do you suspect your boss was the baby's father? Sure
you're not the daddy? I could see her going after something like
you." He had soft brown eyes with long lashes and a choirboy
face that could have the chicks swooning from coast to coast.

He snickered. "I'm flattered, Mr. Brown. But... I don't like girls
in that way. I'm gay."

"That would be a convenient way to escape suspicion," I said.

"Oh, I assure you it is true. Just ask any one of the boys by the
fire. They can vouch for my authenticity." He gave a fey wave of
his hand in their direction as if to confirm his statement.

"Yeah, and David Geffen has kids."

"Who is this David Geffen?"

"Never mind. I was just saying..."

He gave me a puzzled look and sighed like he was dealing
with a difficult child. "Rose would come to the restaurant often. Barnes would often disappear right after she left. Rose liked
to party. And anyway, she told me this. Rose and I were good
friends. I want you to catch who killed her."

I was trying to read his intense look. It was dark away from
the fire and not that easy to see. I was trying to get a feel for
things when a bouncing bright light hit my eyes and the roar of

an internal combustion engine hit my ears. A large pickup with its high beams on came slamming to a stop in the middle of the entrance road.

Petr turned toward the truck, tensed up and walked away from me. A cloud of exhaust washed through the bright arc of the truck lights; the cab doors flew open and two familiar shapes jumped out. Large shapes with simian overtones moving toward us.

Little Sac and Big Sac—the brothers Sacowski. Only Little Sac was twice as big as Big Sac.

My heartbeat accelerated as Big Sac (aka Dick Sacowski) glared at me. I stood there wondering what the fuck was going down. Tormoen popped out of the Malibu, stepped between the brothers and me.

"You shouldn't be up here messsing around with shit, Carter," Big Sac, my old friend, said. "I thought you were a smart enough to know when you're not wanted."

"I guess I just don't accept rejection easily, Dick."

"Maybe if I throw you over the cliff, you'll accept it," Little Sac growled, sending my heart pummeling down to my bowel.

"Maybe you should go fuck a tree, you hair-shirted freak," Tormoen said.

Without warning, Little Sac attacked, moving in and launching a right hand the size of a Christmas ham at Tormoen's head. Jeff jerked away at the last instant and backpedaled. All the way backward into Gloria, who was coming up to investigate, a can of Bud in one hand and a cigarette in the other.

The beer can hit the ground. White foam pooled on the asphalt.

"Goddamn it," Gloria yelled. "Now look what you guys did. Can't you just chill, Little Sac? We're just partying down. No harm, no foul."

"Shut the fuck up, Gloria," Big Sac said. "You know what I told you. You got any brains at all in your skanky head; you'll get your ass out of here right fucking now."

"You don't scare me, Ritchie," Gloria said. "And how can I leave when your truck is blocking the road?"

A thin smile on his lips, Little Sac took a couple of surprisingly quick steps and shot a roundhouse right at Tormoen. Torm tried to backpedal but took the punch on the chest and nearly toppled over backward.

"Why don't you pick on someone your own size?" Dan Burton said, emerging from the shadows to steady his pal Tormoen, who was coughing badly.

The logical answer: there was nobody around anywhere near the size of Little Sac. Burton went about six-two and maybe two-thirty but the young Sacowski had to be carrying at least two-seventy on a six-seven frame.

"What the hell's the deal, Dick?" I said. "What are you so afraid of? Afraid I might find out you were fucking Rosemary under Billy's nose?"

I stared as Little Sac let out a laugh that started out insane and hit a crescendo of dangerous. Then Big Sac's body coiled and I was too slow to catch it. He loosed a right hand to my cheekbone that sent me staggering. Stars and blue obelisks flooded my vision as he moved in for the kill. I threw a left jab I thought caught him pretty good but he shook it off like a bear shooing flies and kept coming. The only thing I could do was duck and charge. Dick launched another right that caught me on the top of the head. I rammed my shoulder into his chest and attempted to pull him to the ground.

He didn't go down.

I held on and we wrestled feverishly until he slammed his knee (it felt like he was wearing steel kneepads) into the area of my reproductive organs. I buckled and coughed and my hands fell. He put me down and out on the cold cold ground with a bolo punch to the chin.

The following, was told to me by Jeff Tormoen:

After the gray-haired geezer put you down, crazy fuck came after me. I was holding my own against him, y'know, keeping him at bay with stinging jabs, when Burton and the roid freak start rumbling. Sounded like two rhinos going at it—like trees snapping. So anyway, I'm dancing away from Big Sac—I can tell he's tiring—when out of the corner of my eye I see Danny stumble and the monster charge. The Gorgon scoops Burton up like a rag doll. He's screaming, "You're dead, motherfucker, you're dead. You're going over the fuckin' cliff." Danny is twisting and flopping like a fish on a pitchfork but he can't do a thing against the Beast. I'm watching the ungodly flailing twosome getting closer to the edge and I'm freaking out, not paying attention to the geezer. He sneaks in and smacks me in the jaw and I go down. He's kicking me in the back with steel-toed boots when two cop cars come roaring up the hill, roof lights whirling.

This big sheriff jumps out with a shotgun and yells for Little Sac to stop or he'll shoot him. Monster boy drops Burto to the ground like a sack of shit and starts laughing that crazy laugh of his. Then he says, "We was only playin', John. Sumbitch thought he could out wrestle me. I was just scarin' him a little." Then he laughs again and comes over to the sheriff, all docile, like a pet grizzly. Over by the fire, the blue boys are tossing pills and pipes and shit over the cliff.

At that point, I was conscious again and getting shakily to my feet.

Sheriff Daugherty greeted me with his long black flashlight shining in my face. "Goddamn it, Brown, what the hell are you doing here? Don't you know when to leave things well enough alone? You see what happens? I should throw you back in jail for interfering with a police investigation."

"I'm just up here partying, Sheriff. My friends brought me here to meet some women. My social life in Duluth has been on a downswing lately."

"I can't imagine why. Being a murder suspect ought to be a real chick magnet, I'd think."

"You see, Sheriff, you and I do think alike."

"Yeah well, get over there with your playmates and we'll see about that."

My old pal Deputy Monty Marshall gathered us all up in the headlights and started asking questions.

Big Sac went along with my story of a party out of control, while Little brother kept repeating, "We was just playin', John. We was just playin'."

Burton confirmed our story with a nod and a scowl.

Gloria said, "Yeah, Big John, why don't you just chill. Maybe you should go home and jerk off or something. Release some tension."

All eyes turned to the sheriff. Instead of righteous indignation, I saw something resembling fatherly understanding wash across his face. It surprised me, but then it was gone and Daugherty began stoically writing us tickets for being in a state park past the posted closing time, as if nothing had been said.

After we had our individual citations clutched in our sweaty hands, Daugherty instructed his deputy to search all persons in violation, as well as their vehicles.

He found nothing in the Sacowski brothers' pockets and only a few flattened beer cans in their truck. He let them leave. They were laughing out the windows as their taillights disappeared down the hill.

None of the restaurant workers were found holding anything illegal, ditto Dan Burton and Greta, and they were all set free. Gloria and Kathy were released next. After my main man Tormoen was found to be clean, having stashed his weed in his underwear, he jumped in Burton's truck, telling me later that he was worried about being identified as one of the bogus state agents who'd conned Rose Talbot. Fair enough.

My two assistants and Greta vacated hurriedly, exiting just before Monty Marshall rose out of the Taurus rental with Torm's roach pinched between his fingers like it was the key to a lost fortune.

"All right, Brown," the Daugherty said, looking at me distastefully, having established that I was the driver of the Taurus, "you're under arrest for possession of a controlled substance in a motor vehicle."

He slapped the cuffs on me none too gently, in spite of my protestations that the roach didn't belong to me, and put me in the back of the SUV.

Chapter

6

The sheriff turned his vehicle around and slowly drove down the hill with me handcuffed and bruised in the backseat behind the steel mesh screen.

"You do realize, don't you, Sheriff, that you'll never make that possession charge stick, don't you?" I said, as we reached the bottom of the hill.

"How's that, Brown? You gonna demand a DNA test?"

"That's not a bad idea. But all I need to do is establish that other people at the party were using my rental car to smoke pot. I'm sure Sam Fredrickson would have a field day with that one. We'd have, like eight witnesses saying that all the vehicles were unlocked and everyone had free access. You sure you want to go to court with this one? For a misdemeanor possession bust?"

"Possession is nine-tenths of the law, Brown. But let's say for the sake of argument that you're right and I don't want to spend the time in court answering questions from that horse-faced lawyer of yours. What's to stop me from running a field sobriety test on you right now? A DWI might look nice on your record.

And you can be damn sure I'll notify the rental agency that you've been smoking in their vehicle."

"First of all, any test would probably come out below the legal limit. And then it might be curious to some why I was the only one of the partiers to be so tested. And now that I think of it, a courtroom might be just the right venue to interject something about Rose Talbot's pregnancy and its connection to the lack of an autopsy on her body. If we get lucky enough, we might drop a bucket of shit on your whole department. Sure you want to take that chance?"

"Goddamn it Brown, what the hell are you talking about? Been listening to that bunch of drunks and dopers? You should know how the rumors fly around here. Develop a life of their own, y'know."

"I'm saying whoever drove Rose off the road also killed her unborn child. And you and I both know it wasn't me. Whoever is behind the cancellation of the autopsy wants to keep the information from coming to light—which makes the whole county look suspect."

"But there was an autopsy. Has to be in deaths from trauma. So that's just another B.S. rumor. I've heard the whispers about pregnancy, too. And that, I can say for sure, was not in the autopsy results."

"Could it have been omitted?"

He scratched his chin thoughtfully. "It's possible. The girl's father still has a lot of clout around here. He used to be an exec at the plant and he still keeps a place on the lake. The old connections are still in existence, I 'magine."

"Is that how it works? The average ordinary wealthy influential citizen can have information withheld? I get the feeling you aren't too happy with the coroner's decision."

There was a long silence. I could almost feel him frowning.

"You'd be right, I guess," he said, finally. "If, in fact, Rose was actually knocked up. And that, like I said, is just another unsubstantiated rumor. The women around here get bored and start up talk just to entertain each other. You wouldn't believe the level of bullshit I've heard over the years. On the other hand, the coroner and Rose's father are old deer hunting buddies. And old man Engwar is one of them assholes thinks he can buy anything or anyone he wants. But who the hell can blame him if he doesn't want it known that his daughter was pregnant at the time of her death? Having a husband whose thing don't work and everything…."

"Kind of hampers the investigation, don't you think?"

"Ain't been established as fact, far as I've heard."

"You check her medical records?"

"Of course. Nothing turned up."

"She could have used a fictitious name or gone to another county. Maybe the Community Health Center in Duluth. Could've given any name she chose and paid cash."

"That's a possibility. But it's all speculation."

"Seems to me the guy who knocked her up might have a possible motive for murder."

He tightened his grip on the wheel and stared straight ahead, saying nothing. I could see his jaw muscles working in the glow of the dashboard lights. My own jaw was hurting in a couple of spots and my right elbow and hip throbbed from smacking into the pavement. I was handcuffed in the back of a cop car with cuts and bruises from taking a good beating, and, in spite of it, I was thinking maybe Daugherty wasn't really that bad of a guy. If he hadn't shown up at Palisade Head, who knows what would have happened?

This was some authentic private eye shit I was going through.

And then the late November night seeped in through the windows and a black cloud of gloom filled the vehicle. Silence took over, except for the occasional fuzz on the squawk box and the hum of the tires. The minutes crawled slowly by. I counted them on the dashboard clock as the cuffs ate into my wrists and my lower back throbbed in pain. I guess my mind weakened finally, did a flip-flop like a debating politician. Found myself thinking maybe this private eye shit wasn't so hot, after all.

Then Daugherty surprised me.

"You know, Brown," he said, tilting his head and eyeing me in the rearview mirror. "A guy like you can ask questions around here that I can't, y'know what I mean? Someone who's got their job to think about and a family to support… in a town like this… well, there are things a guy can't do. Another thing is that people—those who live up north here, especially—don't like to talk to cops. A guy like you could possibly learn more in the bars in one night than I could in a month. I've been around long enough to know about the word on the street. It ain't gospel, but sometimes it can point you in the right direction."

"Exactly what are you trying to say, Sheriff?"

"I'm saying that the lab tests on the paint residue on Rose's Ford have come back and they don't match up with your vehicle. Similar color but different paint. Came from another vehicle. Looks like you were right about being set up. What I'm trying to say is—I think we can work together on this."

"Pardon me while I shake my head in disbelief. When did the paint results arrive?"

"This morning."

"And you were planning on notifying me when?"

"Your lawyer has been notified as of this morning."

"So I can get my car back?"

"Not until Monday. The wheels of government don't turn on weekends."

"Are you kidding me?"

"I never kid a kidder."

"What about that phony letter that was supposedly in my handwriting?"

"The handwriting expert thinks it's close, but he won't go to court and swear it's your writing. Professional ethics."

"Then why are you dragging me in?"

"You forget about that *cucaracha*?"

"You really going through with that? Come on."

"No. But we need to make it look good for the Sacowskis, don't we?"

"Why worry about the Sacowskis? Or are they *your* hunting buddies?"

"Listen, Brown. I've had them in my jail more times than I can count. For everything from drug possession to destroying public property. They know the system inside and out. The more they think I'm on their side, the more I'm gonna learn from them."

"Kind of like the arrangement between you and me, Sheriff?"

"A little different. One thing I can tell you, though—get rid of that phony P. I. license you got. Thing might get you arrested. In fact, the State may still decide to prosecute you."

"Are you shitting me?"

"I never shit a shitter. And by the way, just a little piece of info for you: If you are an investigator working for a lawyer on a case, you don't need a P.I. license. You follow me?"

"I think I do. So now that I'm officially on the case working for Sam Fredrickson, what can you tell me about the manager of Sky Blue Waters Lodge?"

"Barnes? Where does he fit into this thing?"

"I'm not exactly sure. But it has been said that he was the father of Rose's unborn child."

"I knew the son of a bitch was a horndog—and he has been seen running with Rose and her friends—maybe it's possible. Where'd you pick up on that bit of dirt?"

"Confidential."

"Yeah, right. This thing has got to work both ways, Brown."

"And you'll have to trust me. If I find out anything substantial, you'll hear it. But every little bird I talk to isn't necessarily your concern."

"All right then. But don't step on your dick and decide to blame me."

I didn't know what to say to that. "This Barnes a local boy?" I said in lieu of a direct response.

"Nah, Chicago. Moved up here six years ago when they built the damn lodge. He's one of four investors who own the thing. They all show up here, eventually, mostly in the summer and short visits in the off-season. One of them likes to hunt, was up here chasing birds just a little while ago. Italian name. They say his shotguns were all Italian-made and top of the line stuff. *Berelli* or *Benelli* or something like that. The shotguns, I mean."

"Think he's organized crime?"

Daugherty snorted. "Come on. Get off it. Just because he's an Italian from Chicago doesn't make him a mob guy. Get your feet back down to earth, Brown. Stop smoking that dope."

"I don't smoke it anymore."

"Uh-huh. Just the same, maybe Barnes is someone to look at. He was up at the casino with a group of revelers—Rose among them— the night she died. I had him into the office to give a statement. A bunch of them were up there partying together, and every one of them swears that Rose left early by herself. The security tape verifies that Barnes was still in the casino at the approximate time of her death. But I couldn't shake the feeling that he knew something he wasn't telling me."

And then we were turning in the parking lot of my old home away from home, the Creek County Jail. Upon first sight of its hallowed walls, I felt myself falling back down into the sinkhole of depression and despair that had marked my days here. A sick, shaky feeling, like the swine flu, spread through me.

The sheriff took me out of the backseat none too gently, grabbing my jacket and jerking outward and upward. Once upright, the frigid wind jabbed at the flesh of my neck like a warning shot from Old Man Winter.

And I'd been thinking John and I were becoming buds.

"Sorry, Brown," he said when we were safely inside the wretched building. "Gotta keep up appearances, you know. Never know who might be watching."

The tiny sparkle in his eye told me there was a bit more to it than that.

He unlocked the cuffs and then he was Good Cop again. "Tell you what," he said. "Let's go in my office where we can talk privately, in case anyone walks in. You're lucky I was on duty tonight, that's all I can say. If a deputy had been handling the shift, you'd be up Shit Creek without a paddle."

As we walked down the hall, I felt uneasy, caught between Good Sheriff and Bad Sheriff. "Where *did* ol' Monty get off to?" I said.

"I 'spect he's out keeping it safe for the citizens. Either that or up in the woods banging his squaw."

"Squaw?"

"Excuse me, Native American princess." He shot me a dart with his vague brown eyes.

"Shacking up on duty?"

"The term is actually appropriate in this situation. Girl lives in a shack in the woods. But don't you worry; Monty always leaves his radio on. Something happens, he'll be on it. Don't take that boy very long to saw off a piece, anyhow. Not much happens up here this time of year, y'know—when you get right down to it. Maybe someone shining deer or smackin' the old lady around— maybe a bar fight..."

"Or Rose Talbot getting murdered," I said.

The sheriff's body stiffened slightly but then he shrugged and sat down behind his desk, his chair squeaking as he leaned back. I slouched down in the middle chair of three curved-back wooden numbers facing the oak desk and didn't say anything, just looked around the office.

"Is it just the two of you for the whole county?" I said. "Wasn't there another deputy here? I remember a younger guy—had a buzz cut."

"Bobby Atwood. Iraq war veteran. Real hardliner. If it was up to him, guys like you would be strung up by your pectoral muscles until you admitted your guilt—like the Indians used to do it."

"Like in the movie *A Man Called Horse*?"

"Just like that. Kid owns a well-worn tape of that flick. But I'll tell ya one thing for sure; I wouldn't trade him for anybody. We had a Vietnam vet as a deputy when I first started back in '85. He believed that any halfway-decent-looking woman he stopped for speeding could avoid a ticket by getting him off. Who knows how many blowjobs he got before one of them filed a complaint? But one finally did and the feces really hit the ventilator. This Iraq War guy, Atwood, he don't screw around like that. With him, you get caught, you're gonna be arrested, blow job or no."

Daugherty smiled like a pastor at a church supper. Framed photos of his wife and two daughters smiled together with him. One of the daughters had her old man's face. I felt sorry for her. The other one resembled her mother, except for a wise-ass mouth that I could picture on a teenage version of her father. There was also a stapler, a phone, a couple stacks of papers and a china mug containing pencils and pens, imprinted with the image of three soldiers in 1800's-era uniforms. There was a freestanding fan in one corner of the room and an American flag on a wooden pole in another. Against the wall behind the sheriff's chair, a gray metal six-drawer file cabinet sat next to a glossy oak table on which rested a police-band radio and a computer.

Without saying anything, Daugherty rose and went to the file cabinet, opened a drawer and pulled out a folder. He plopped the folder down on the desk and sunk slowly back into his chair. "This is the whole of our investigation, Brown. Including a statement from Billy Talbot saying you offered to kill his wife for money." He paused and tried to burrow his eyes into my head. "Why'dya think little Billy would say a thing like that, if it wasn't true? The man is well liked around here, I'll tell you that. Lived here all his life and ain't got an enemy to be found. Got any good reasons I shouldn't believe his statement?"

Bad Sheriff was back.

"Other than it's not true? I don't know—for Christ sake. All those drugs he has to take could screw up anyone's head. Not to mention being in a wheelchair. Wouldn't be the first guy, driven crazy by a nutso wife. Crazy enough to be involved in the death of said wife and try to cover it up by blaming me."

"I hear ya, but that's a tough nut for me to chew. Ain't no one around here gonna believe you over Billy Talbot."

"Then I'd say they didn't know the Billy Talbot that I've experienced."

"Okay. All right." He stood up, arched his back and rubbed his protruding gut with both hands. "I'm going for some coffee—take a dump, if I'm lucky. Now don't you look at that file when I'm gone." He winked and then sauntered out of the room.

I slid my chair up to the desk, spun the file around and opened it.

He was gone for nearly an hour.

By the time he strutted back through the door rubbing his eyes, I had read the whole report. It was pretty thorough: toxicology reports, several photos and a few signed statements, including one from a traffic-accident expert confirming that Rose's vehicle had been hit along one side and from behind. The accompanying pictures showed dents and scratches on the driver's side and rear end of the red Focus and what appeared to be blue paint in the impressions. Paint allegedly matching that of a forlorn-looking Subaru Forester displayed in other photos. The recent lab test results had yet to be added to the file.

Along with some of Daugherty's own notes—which mostly dealt with my involvement in the case—the file also contained signed statements from several locals, including the meth-head witness who had come forth to implicate my vehicle, a local loner by the name of Ned Fifield. Even though he had subsequently been discredited, he was still a person of interest to me. I wanted to get to him before he went on trial on the meth charge.

The autopsy report contained nothing about an unborn fetus but did reveal other facts about the state of Rose's body at the time of death. Her blood-alcohol level was listed at .075, slightly under the legal limit for driving and low enough to avoid an

Impaired-driver-dies-in-crash headline in the morning papers. Or at least that's the way it had played out.

"If you want to sleep, Brown," Daugherty said, looking down at the file with a look of all-knowing benevolence on his hangdog face, "I'll open a cell for you so you can lie down."

"No thanks, Sheriff, I'm a little wired. I usually get like this when I've been arrested. And even as luxurious as those cells are, I find it difficult to relax in them."

"Suit yourself. Maybe you and Monty can play some cribbage when he comes in."

"I never learned the game."

That was pretty much the end of communication for the evening. Big John D stayed in his office and I went out front to the citizens' area, where I drank enough coffee to strangle up my intestines. Was like I'd swallowed a basket of snakes. I paced around, trying to stretch the kinks out of my back. I made numerous visits to the can. I tried to call Burton on the cell but couldn't get a signal.

Monty Marshall came in just before dawn and gave me the evil eye. I thought for a second he was going to draw his gun. Then the sheriff called him into his office and I heard voices rise and Monty say, "You're making a mistake," to which there was no discernable response except a low murmuring that seemed to end the discussion.

And then it wasn't long before the first blue-gray light was seeping through the windows and my faithful assistant Burton was walking through the door to help me fly these prison walls.

Chapter

7

I was glad to see Burton but I didn't take time to exchange pleasantries, just said, "Let's go," and walked past him to the door. I was afraid if I stood there explaining the situation, Daugherty would come running out of his office and throw me back behind the steel curtain. And who could've blamed him?

The air was cold and the wind was blowing a gale out of the northeast. The kind of day that ships sank to the icy bottom of Lake Superior with all hands on board. You could almost hear the ghosts of drowned seamen moaning in the searing wind. A good day for very little, except being someplace warm with a drink in your hand watching the waves explode on the rocky shoreline. But absolutely anything was a hell of a lot better than being in jail.

The bite of the air briefly invigorated me. But as soon as I put my butt on the vinyl seat and smelled the old sweat and stale tobacco smoke in the cab of Burton's truck, the life seemed to rush out of me like the juice of an old car battery left on a concrete floor. My head ached and my jaw felt like I had a permanent case of TMJ syndrome. I was nauseous and there was a pounding in my ears like drums at a funeral procession. The cue cards in my brain were displaying the same old lines: *Delusional loser. Cares nothing about those who love him. Drags them into his flights from reality. In way over his head, trying to be something he's not. Sad. Clownish. Fool.*

"How'd you manage this one, man?" Burton said, turning the ignition key.

I stared out the window at the bent-over trees. My wounds from last night's fight throbbed. The mental cue cards began mocking my skills of self-defense and questioning my courage. I tried to speak but excess coffee consumption had turned the ligaments in my jaw to steel wire. Nothing came out but a kind of rasp. I guess I'm caffeine sensitive.

Burton looked questioningly over at me for an instant before throwing the shift lever down and hitting the gas. We jerked out of the lot and away from the grey rock hotel. It took me a few miles of deep breathing and relaxation techniques before I could begin to verbalize the weird tale of the sheriff and the phony private eye. When the telling was completed, I felt strangely guilty. Daugherty had confided in me and agreed to work together and here I was talking shit about him behind his back.

And I also felt guilt for my very existence, thinking Rose might still be alive if I hadn't butted into her life while fueling my ego trip. Guilt was having its way with me, spreading like heat rash in the jungle. Before I could stop myself, I was apologizing to Burton for dragging him into the whole lame situation.

"Hey man," I said. "I really want to thank you for going along with me on this case. But I'm beginning to realize that this whole private eye thing is just a drawn out attempt at justifying my fucked-up life. I've been a fool and I hope you'll forgive me for bringing you into my own personal, depressing, low-ball night-mare. I wouldn't blame you at all if you never had anything more to do with me."

"Whoa, Carter, ease off yourself. Take the knife out of your gut, dude. Believe it or not, I'm having fun on this case. Haven't had this much fun since I quit drinking. And I think you have the makings of a good detective. All of us think so. This shit we're doing up here—it kinda reminds me of the old days. Back when I was partying all the time. My days of swine and hosers, if you will. Only now I don't wake up with bees in my head and the taste of moose dung in my mouth."

"Moose dung?"

"I think the Canadians put it in the whiskey."

"I guess. You're saying you're enjoying this?"

"I wouldn't say enjoying it. More like tolerating it for the vast amounts of money you're paying me."

"Aha. I see. You're brain damaged."

"That's pretty much it."

"That always helps. At least your color came back. Last night you were beyond white to a deathly gray—after the Monster got through with you."

"I think it was an inner ear problem," Burton said, a serious look on his face.

We continued to roll along the empty asphalt. I watched the whitecaps chasing each other across the steely water. A crow pecking at a flattened rabbit on the shoulder flew up as we blew past. The sun was creeping above the horizon on the southern shore and sending out a weak light. My stomach was churning and I felt shaky.

"You had any breakfast?" I said.

"Nah," Burton said. "I haven't really even slept much, either. Greta and I took your room at the motel—since you weren't going to be there—and I just now dropped her off at her motel."

"Congratulations, Burt. The drought has ended."

"Indeed."

"Should we pick up Tormoen?"

"I don't see why not."

"Then we can get my rental car."

"At the impound lot?"

"Probably. Shit, the lot is closed until Monday. Maybe it's still at Palisade Head."

"You think they'd leave it there over night?"

"You never can tell what these bozos will do. Daugherty didn't say anything about it."

We fell silent again and I tried hard to find the beauty of my surroundings. I couldn't. My mind was racing. "So, ah, did Torm and Gloria hook up last night?" I asked.

"Nah. Gloria and her friend Kathy stopped by for a while after we left you, but by then the party spirit had deserted them. I think she's more scared of the Sacowski boys than she lets on. As much as she milks the ballsy-chick act, I think she's a little freaked at the thought of what those boys might do to her. I saw a different side of her: scared and vulnerable and struggling to keep her chin up. She's got her share of issues."

"She's got good reason to be scared of the Sacowskis, as we can both attest. Her being scared might mean she knows something she ain't telling. You didn't by any chance ask her if she knew what Rose was doing with all the cash from the credit cards?"

"I didn't. But I want you to know that I'm not scared of the Sacowskis." Sounded like he was trying to convince himself. "The old one sure put the hurt on you, though," he continued. "Your face looks a bit rough this morning. Sure you're okay?"

"Fuck you. I just need some eggs."

Burton gave me a snaky grin and punched in the dashboard lighter, reached in his jacket for his cigarette pack.

"The sheriff let me read the whole report on Rose's case," I said, trying to get back on task and away from thoughts of my pugilistic shortcomings.

"They gonna jam you up for that roach?"

"Nah. Dropped the charges."

"What'd you do, blow him?"

"Twice. But now he insists he really wants our help. And for some reason, I believe him. I think he senses something peculiar about the whole deal."

"Such as?"

"Rose's rich parents still have influence in the area, for one. The Sacowskis' interest in the case, for another. And I don't think Daugherty thinks too much of the guys who own Sky Blue Waters Lodge, either."

"Greta said the owners are assholes," he cranked down his window a crack to let the smoke out. "She said one of the out-of-town dudes dresses like a movie mobster and is always hitting on her, and Barnes just acts like it's funny." He hit the cigarette one more time before tossing it out the window. "Find anything else of interest in that report?"

"A few things. They got an expert says Rose's vehicle actually was hit. Like they need to pay an expert for that. I saw the photos."

"No doubt she was run off the road?"

"Maybe some. Rose had a blood-alcohol level of .075 when she died. Who knows what else she had in her system? Seems possible she went off the road because she was loaded. Her car could've been sideswiped in a parking lot somewhere."

"Not likely, the way I see it. I used to work up here—remember? Back when they were building the pellet plant."

"Yeah, I remember. You used to come into the Paul Bunyan with the cash from your paycheck burning a hole in your pocket and buy the whole place a round. Any dope dealer happened to be in there jumped on you like a priest on an altar boy."

"What I was trying to say was," he said, eyes darting, "point-oh-seven-five is like home base for these people up here. They get to that level in a heartbeat and then pour whatever else they've got on top of that. Acid, speed, coke, Xanax... you name it. That was probably and easy night for Rose— I mean, *only* .075."

"Maybe. Not to change the subject, but I can't help but noticing that you seem to be quite chipper and alert this morning, considering your night. What's your secret?"

"Chipper? That, like a chipmunk or a squirrel, all energetic and bushy-tailed?"

"Pretty much. I thought the term would appeal to your British blood."

"Ah, my father's DNA. The wellspring of my alcoholism gene and my stiff upper lip."

"I'm just saying, you seem pretty alert for someone who's been smoking weed and fucking his brains out all night long."

"Maybe sex is a stimulant for me."

"Uh-huh. But I detect a chemical edge. I'm pretty good at detecting a chemical edge, having been married to an alcoholic and being a former drug addict myself."

"The detective deduces correctly. I'm taking a neuro-enhancer called Adderol—doctor prescribed—to counteract any temporary sluggishness or lethargy from past alcohol abuse."

"Neuro-enhancer? That what they're calling speed these days?"

"Highly refined speed. Not like the old days," he said, reaching for another cigarette. "Just makes your mind sharp, perfect for private eye work."

"I feel inspired."

Tormoen didn't look or act very inspired when we came through the door of Room 12 of the Flood Bay Motel and rousted him from the tangle of sheet, blanket and quilted green bedspread molded around him like a polyester python.

I turned on the small television. Burton hooked up the electric coffeemaker on the blond veneer dresser and poured in the packet of free coffee. Tormoen cursed and bitched but the promise of breakfast on my dime got him into the shower.

A little later, the three of us climbed in Dan's giant truck. I was in the backseat. "Before we get breakfast," I said, "I want to thank you for leaving that roach in the car last night, Torm. Added a little excitement to my dull, soft-boiled life."

"So that's what happened to it," he said. "Sorry, man."

"No problem. Without that bust I never would've seen Rose's case file. Sheriff dropped the charge, besides. Luck was on our side."

"Think it was divine intervention?" Torm said.

"Doubt it," I said. "But you never can tell."

"Whatever it was, once again you fell into a shit hole and came out smelling—"

"Like a rose," Burton interjected, shaking his head in mock disgust.

We drove to the Sunshine Café in Taconite Bay. Torm and I both had the Lumberjack Special while Burton ordered three poached eggs with sliced tomatoes and English Breakfast Tea. Evidently my previous comments had brought out the Limey in him.

Sufficiently fueled, we got back in the pickup and rolled slowly through the small, modest town. Tormoen let out a long sigh and lit a cigarette, turned down his window a sliver, leaned back and exhaled smoke into the chilled air. "A small town is a vast Hell," he said dramatically, a look of great despair on his chiseled features. "That's an old Argentine proverb. It seems particularly appropriate for this burg. Rose Talbot could have driven into that tree on purpose, given the nature of her existence in this town."

"I think she was planning to get out," I said. "I think she was trying to put together a stash of cash to facilitate her escape from said Hell."

"What about mommy and daddy?" Burton said. "Aren't they supposed to be rolling in it?"

"Yeah," I said, "but parent's money can be the proverbial gilded cage. From what I saw of Rose, she wasn't the type to accept a set of manacles, golden or not."

The sky was noticeably brighter as we popped through the trees at the top of Palisade Head. The sun was beaming through a hole in the clouds and putting a beatific shaft of light on the wreck that had once been a nice, new, Ford Taurus.

All four tires were totally gone, empty hubs resting on the blacktop. The front bumper cowling was hanging down like a drooping lower lip and the rear bumper assembly was in the same position. Symmetry. The roof was caved in as if someone had dropped a Grizzly bear on it from a helicopter. All the windows were smashed out and a pile of feces sat on the middle of the hood.

I walked around to the driver's door and discovered four bullet holes, all arranged in a nice tight square. *Welcome to the North Woods, Carter Brown,* they seemed to be saying.

A vast Hell, indeed.

"You're gonna have to take this one to the carwash, I'm afraid," Tormoen said.

"Going to need a little detailing," Burton added.

"Thank God I signed up for the extra insurance," I said.

Chapter

8

I got the distinct impression that the guy at the car rental desk wanted to make a vast Hell out of my face. But being a civilized middle manager, he let me slide and chose instead to raise holy Hell with the Creek County Sheriff's Department for letting the Taurus sit unattended overnight.

Maybe the bald little nebbish just hated cops, had some traumatic experience in his past. Or maybe he knew I was an accused murderer and was afraid of me. I didn't know the reason he was going easy on me but as long as no charges were filed, it didn't matter. I was placed on the "Don't-rent-to" list, of course, but that was the least of my worries.

I was slipping out the door as the manager began a terse alto harangue into the phone: something about suing Creek County for damages.

Upon returning home, I discovered an envelope wedged in the door of my apartment containing a thirty-day eviction notice from the landlords. They expected me out before January 1.

My luck was at least consistent in its badness.

I went to the fridge and grabbed a beer.

Instead of making arrangements to collect the Subaru, I stayed in my apartment for a day and a half, sleeping, drinking beer and doing some heavy thinking about the case, my life and my new career.

The private eye thing suddenly seemed like such a joke. A sham. The fantasy of a deranged man. But I knew had to see this particular case through to the end. It sounds corny and clichéd but Rose's soul did seem to be crying out to me.

My next working morning, I called my faithful assistants and set up a meeting for the afternoon. After a light breakfast I walked to the health club and worked out for two hours. The key to mental health starts with physical health, they say. As afternoon rolled around, I sat at my desk in the office waiting for the boys to show and admiring the new, allegedly unpickable, industrial-strength lock I'd had installed on the door.

The pains in my body were telling me I would never become a lean, mean fighting machine. My shortcomings in self-defense would have to be overcome with guile. Guile led me to a method used by those masters of corporeal violence—outlaw bikers. I'd seen it on cable TV. The Harley-riding hooligans tie a bandana to a heavy padlock and stick it in the back pocket of their jeans so that only the top of the bandana shows above the pocket, creating one of the most effective close-range surprise weapons you can find. Snap that baby out and swing it into some douchebag's skull and you've got something. Dented douchebag. Put that together with one of those long flashlights the cops use or maybe a ball-peen hammer, to create the ultimate one-two punch. A cop can hardly confiscate your padlock or your hammer or your flashlight, and you won't have to punch a heavy bag until your knuckles bleed.

Burton was the first to arrive for the meet. He strolled in the office at five minutes to four in his usual brown Carhartt jacket, red flannel shirt and easy-fit jeans. I knew the exact time because I'd been checking the clock every few minutes for an hour. It was an oppressively gray day and I was craving light. I'd been gazing out the window at the steel-blue lake and turning to look back at the clock.

Dan and I exchanged greetings and he sat down across from my desk. I moved my chair closer to the desk, wondered if he was getting sick of this gig. I was thinking if I cut him a check for his services, he'd probably take it and disappear.

"I want to go back up to Taconite Bay," he said before I had a chance to get my checkbook out. "I think Greta knows more than she's letting on. Maybe if I go back up there and earn her trust, she'll help us out."

I thought I was catching his drift.

"Help us out? Or help you out with your E.D.D.?"

"E.D.D.?"

"Erection Deficit Disorder."

"That supposed to be a joke?" Burton said, a confused look crossing his face.

"Yes, Dan. A joke. Not a good one, I guess. I was just going to cut you a check for all you've done so far. If you want to go back there, that's good. But I won't be able to pay you for a while. At least until that check from Talbot is freed up. Provided the cocksucker doesn't cancel payment."

"You still picking Talbot for the murder?"

"He seems to have the best motive, as far as I can see. Unless there's something to the pregnancy thing. But when you get right down to it, I don't feel sure of anything."

"I suspect the guy who runs the lodge is involved in some of this. Greta gets a funny look on her face when he's mentioned."

"He's her boss. She's bound to have a funny look. But we do need more info on the owners. Whether they got wives, where-they list as home on their tax returns, any other holdings they might have—shit like that. Tommy can get a lot of it off the Web, but you may be able to find another angle on it from Greta. So if you promise to spend at least as much time grilling her as you do drilling her, I'll authorize expense vouchers."

"You benevolent dick."

I grinned and started writing the check as Tormoen popped through the door carrying a brown paper bag under the crook of one arm. I looked at the bag and then at him. Mirth danced in his eyes.

"Greetings, gents," he said with his usual flourish before lifting a six-pack of Budweiser cans and two cans of Diet Coke from the bag and setting them down on my desk. He smiled and nodded, dropped the sack in the wastebasket beside the desk, took off his brown leather bomber's jacket and hung it over the back of a chair. He sat and popped the top of a beer. He was wearing blue jeans and a turtleneck fisherman's sweater, this one in beige.

"You writing checks, Carter?" he asked, smiling brightly, if a little blurred.

"Like my fancy new three-ring checkbook?" I said.

"Lotta checks in there, must be one for me." Tormoen said.

"Got your receipts?"

"Receipts? I don't need no stinking receipts. It was all on your cash, boss, case you forgot. Only receipt I got is the cherished memories."

"Then for what exactly are you expecting payment?"

"Wasn't the agreement for fifty a day plus expenses? And I thought perhaps we would be returning to the area for more detecting. Or would that be detectifying?"

I looked at Burton. "Every time I go up there, something bad happens. Maybe if I send you two up there without me, something good will happen."

"That's good logic," Tormoen said. "Danny and I are getting a feel for this private eyein' stuff."

"And I applaud your enthusiasm and dedication. Both of you. Your attitude would make me proud as pancakes if I didn't know you were both pretty much broke and motivated more by money than any sense of responsibility or high-minded thinking. But there's no shame in that. God knows I've been there a few hundred times myself. But just what exactly do you hope to find out?"

"Like, duh—who killed Rose Talbot, of course," Tormoen said, going Charley Sheen on me.

"And banging Gloria is going to lead to that?"

"Mos def, *mein herr*. You don't know the way women are after they've had the Tormoen experience. They get so they'd tell you if they wore men's underwear to church."

"That would be valuable information," Burton said.

I felt something wriggling in my gut.

"Okay boys, enough of the wholesome family fun. Jeff, tell me seriously what you think you can learn from Gloria. Seems obvious that Billy Talbot or the Sacowskis are behind setting me up. If that's true, then it follows that Billy had her killed. And I make the Sacs for sociopaths capable of killing someone, given the right motivation."

"Where's Tommy?" Burton asked, as if I hadn't spoken.

"Said he was coming after he closed the shop. Should be here any minute."

Tormoen drained the last of his beer, crushed the can in his hands and belched. "All is not always as it seems, Carter. You know that. I got the feeling Gloria was holding onto something. And it wasn't my cock." He set the crushed can on the desk and grabbed a full one. "And it was obvious the Sac boys didn't want her hanging with us. That in itself tells me she's worth getting closer to."

An involuntary sigh slid out of me. I looked at the little drops of beer dripping from the crushed can to the desktop. "Okay you guys, you can go back up there. On salary. I'll even kick in some cash for drinks—I mean expenses. But this time see if you can find out what Rose was doing with the money. When Tommy gets here we can nail down the proper division of labor."

I grabbed a can of beer. Burton took one of the Diet Cokes and popped the top. "Can I smoke in here," he said.

"No tobacco use allowed."

"How about weed?" Tormoen said.

"Not while the store downstairs is still open."

There were a coupleß of raps on the door and Tommy Basilio walked in, the collar on his gray wool jacket turned up. He wore skinny black jeans and pointy black boots, probably Italian leather. He went about five-ten, one-sixty and his combed-back hair was still black. He grinned at us. "Hard at work I see," he said, his gaze falling on the beer.

"Don't hard line us, Tommy," Tormoen said. "Grab a brew and sit down, learn how creative people work."

"Isn't that a contradiction of terms?" Tommy asked, grabbing a beer. "Hey Burt, how's it going?"

Dan stood and they shook hands. "Can't complain, Tommy," Burton said. "Missed you up in the *Bay du Taconite* last weekend."

"Tommy's got a business to run," I said. "Can't be bothered with the trivial pursuits of perennial adolescents. Even when it puts money in his pocket. Ain't that right, Tommy?"

"Or when it gets his expensive equipment broken." Tommy said.

"You have insurance on that stuff, Tom?" I asked.

"Yeah," he said, softening.

"You collect on it?"

"Yeah."

"You take the money and buy better equipment then the shit you lost?"

"Yes." He popped the beer and sat down next to Torm, took a pull, wiped his mouth with the back of his hand and smiled. "But it took a long time to get it all together."

"And for that, I apologize," I said. "I understand the great hardship you've been made to suffer on my account. And now that you've recovered from the ordeal, are you ready to get back on board? Because I got some things that are right up your alley, no fieldwork necessary."

"Do I have to break any laws?"

"Probably. But then I'm not yet an expert on the law. Especially when it comes to shit you can do on the Internet."

He took another good swallow of beer and glanced over at Dan and Jeff. "These two are still walking around free so I guess you're doing something right. Whattaya got?"

"I need to find out if Rose Talbot was pregnant at the time of her death. Medical records, any payments to clinics or doctors, things like that. Anything that can confirm the rumored pregnancy. Also some personal info on some out-of-state guys whose names we haven't determined yet. When you're done with that you can run a check on all vehicles in Creek County registered to the name Sacowski. See if there are any blue SUVs."

"I'll have to do it on your unit," he said gesturing toward the blue iMac on my desk "This the only one you got?"

"What you see is what we got, yes."

"I'll have to beef her up a bit. Y'know, you can get almost everything on the Web these days—personal info, private info, sealed records… we'll just need a little more mojo. Think I've got what we need at the shop. And if I may ask, what were you planning on paying me for these deeds?"

"You can bill me for what you think it's worth and I'll add you to the list of people I'm stiffing."

"Business as usual, Tommy," Tormoen said and the two of them clinked beer cans.

I sank deeper into my chair.

"Pitch-fucking dark at five o'clock," Burton said, nodding towards the windows. He shook his head. "Let me get this straight, Carter. You want Torm and I to go back up there and dig up dirt on the lodge owners and just generally continue what we were doing the other night, is that correct?"

"Yeah. And that meth head that tried to nail the frame on me… his name is Ned Fifield. He didn't make that story up without a reason, somebody had to be giving him something or threatening him or whatever, you know? And then there's Petr, the allegedly gay waiter. There's got to be more to his story. Maybe Greta can help you with that one, Burt. And maybe Gloria can put Jeff onto the tweaker or add more depth to Rose's personal liaisons. Other than that, use your own creativity. I have faith in you. I'll give you two days and two nights. Text or call with any pertinent info as soon as you get it. I'll ride up with you in the morning to get my car out of impound but then I'm coming back here where I can stay out of trouble. Definitely some hostile vibes up there. I'll alert Daugherty that you're going to be in the area. If things should get too hairy, you can always call him.

"Any questions?"

"Yeah," Tormoen said. "Is it alright to smoke weed yet?"

"No," I said. "But it is Happy Hour at the Savannah."

Fun was in short supply at the Savannah Club. The draught beer was flat and tasteless and the lights had an odd, harsh glow to them. The dancers, sitting at tables in their civilian clothes, looked even rougher than usual. It was one of those days when the cleaning fluid smell sticks in your nose and the bad memories stick to your soul. But at least my band was back together. This band of low-rent adventurers now known as Carter Brown Investigations.

It had a ring to it.

My cell phone also had a ring to it. It went off in my jacket pocket in the middle of my third piss-water beer. Jan was on the other end with her I'm-in-trouble-please-help-me voice working its ol' black magic.

I was always a sucker for that voice. I knew better but it didn't matter. I didn't need much pulling to leave the club and the boys. My heart wasn't in the hi-jinks anymore. A boss-and-employees divide was starting to grow between us. Ridiculous, but there, nonetheless.

I bought another round for the boys and left to meet Jan at the restaurant on Barker's Island in Superior, wondering if there was any significance to her choice of location. Across the bridge... out of the way... someplace where we were unlikely to be recognized... maybe she was coming around. Coming around to see me in a romantic light again—or at least a sexual light.

But her pathos-laden voice had told a different tale, one I didn't want to hear. It was the same old story, really. She'd come on all submissive and sad and I'd eat it up in shovelfuls until she got what she wanted. Then the need would leave her and she'd turn cold and distant and I'd be on the outside looking in through smeared glass.

I was thinking this time might be different. That's the way my mind works. Like an addict. Repeating the same act and expecting a different result. Einstein's definition of insanity.

Chapter

9

She was in the bar at a table by a window; shoulders slumped, staring out wistfully at the shimmering black bay. A short, squat glass sat in front of her on the dark table, lime wedge swimming with ice cubes in a clear liquid. Shards of light from the Whale-back Ship Museum next door filtered through the darkened window, framing Jan in her white sweater and tight designer jeans.

Like a blond Madonna, I thought to myself. And not the one who had once been married to Sean Penn.

Just as I had expected—and feared— she looked vulnerable and wounded and irresistible. I felt a twinge in my groin. I couldn't decide if coming here was doing the right thing or just follow-ing the hunger of my loins. It was too late for second thoughts, though, because I was sitting down and putting my palm on the top of her delicate white hand, looking soulfully into her eyes and asking What's wrong, dispensing with the small talk and get-ting right down to it.

What would Sam Spade do here?

Her eyes were moist and I found myself hoping that Rick had gotten physically abusive. Then I'd have an excuse to kick his ass and release all the frustrations that I've been feeling since she dumped me.

Her scent drifted over and I got hard as a flagpole. I tried to ignore the voice in my head reminding me that Rick was a lawyer and any assault on his person would do more damage to me than him. I needed a drink to deaden the voice. Nothing like alcohol to tamp down your good sense. As well as any wisdom you may have accidentally acquired on your way through life.

She didn't say anything, just looked at me like a little girl who'd lost her daddy. With her hair cut short the way she wore it now, curling around her ear and feathering out from the smooth, white skin on her neck, she reminded me of someone. Maybe a movie actress or someone on TV. Possibly a porn star. Was this a role she was playing?

"I needed someone to talk to," she finally said, the dark blue in her eyes luminous. Large black pupils shielded her soul like tiny masks.

"What, Rick lost his hearing? Developed a speech impediment, did he?"

Her expression hardened, just for an instant, but then the meekness returned.

"Rick doesn't talk, he lectures or pontificates."

"Isn't that what you used to say to me?"

"Maybe, I don't know. But you're different now. Sweeter. Smarter. Stronger."

And much harder. Getting better with every accolade.

"You got me there, I said." She did have me. My equilibrium and control were flying away on gossamer wings. "What's that you're drinking?" I could feel sweat forming on my hairline.

"*Absolut* rocks, twist of lime."

"Said it just like you used to when you waitressed. Back when we met."

Did that really slip out? Nostalgia before midnight? I was sinking fast. I took my eyes from Jan and searched the room for a waitress. Seemed like the temperature was rising.

"These days," she said, touching her finger to her upper lip, "I appreciate those times better than I did then. We had fun."

"Young and drunk and full of spunk." *But really—what the hell do you want? I thought. What's with the angel-of-the-morning-in-the-evening routine?* "You have a battle with Rick?"

"Yes," she said, biting her lip like a brave little soldier.

"He didn't hit you or anything like that, did he?"

"No. A smart lawyer knows every smack could cost him serious money. But he did scare me. He broke all of our crystal stemware and threw an antique china tea set against the wall. Made his usual tantrums seem tame. So I walked out on him."

A gong went off in my head. "Have anything to do with the money you spent on me? I've been wondering why Rick would agree to bankroll me out of jail."

"He claims it's not the money but the fact that I went out on a limb for you. He thinks I'm torching for you."

And are you? I almost said. "Shit, that's not cool," I did say, as the waitress appeared at my shoulder. "Two more of those, please," pointing at Jan's glass. The waitress left. I looked at Jan. She averted her eyes. "You were fighting over me? Come on. I find it hard to believe Rick feels at all threatened by me. I mean, he took you away from me before, so what's different now? You know, I still remember sitting in a bar the night you dumped me, thinking the whole deal was just like a Tom Petty song. The one he sings about the guy with his *money and his cocaine* trying to steal his girl away. Not that Rick was way into coke or anything—but you get the idea. In the song, Petty gets the girl. I don't like that song anymore."

I searched her eyes for some kind of tell, saw none. I could've pointed out that in the song, the girl listened to her heart. That was the name of the song: "Listen to her Heart." But I knew if I did, the night would be over.

Jan took a good hit off her cocktail, eyes crinkling, a kind of sad smile on her full, fleshy, highly enticing lips.

"There's something you're not telling me, Jan. I know it because I know you." Her familiar patterns were emerging. It hadn't been that long ago and I remembered only too well. "So what is it? Tell me now or I get up and walk out of here."

She glanced at her drink, took another swallow and blotted her mouth with a cocktail nap. "It is about money," she said, a peculiar smirk/frown shaping her face. "But not what I spent on you. It's that I've maxed out all my credit cards and it's beginning to affect things at home. Financially. Gets any worse and I'm toast, for damn sure. Big life insurance policy on me, you know."

"Jesus fucking Christ. Is there some kind of epidemic of credit card abuse going around? Some growing malady in a malignant world? Almost the same kind of thing that got Rose Talbot killed. And why a big insurance policy on you? With all due respect, you don't even have an income."

"Rick's golfing buddy Dave Baheim sells insurance. One night he and his wife were over for dinner—she's a real stuck-up bitch—and Dave and Rick got drunk and somehow decided to take out this big policy on me at the same time Rick upgraded his own policy, like there's a discount for two policies or something. They were shitfaced and acting like it was good times. I couldn't stop thinking they'd just put a bet out on my death. I die and Rick will be able to fly to Thailand and fuck thirteen-year-old prostitutes every weekend until his dick falls off."

"Rick does that?"

"No, but he would, if I died. I mean, who else could replace me but a thirteen-year-old Thai prostitute." The flicker of a smile wrinkled her lips.

"There's truth in that." I leaned back in my chair and sighed, only partly for effect, as the waitress set down our drinks on little napkins and picked up Jan's empty. I put a ten down and told her to keep it.

"That'll be twelve dollars, sir," the short, dark-haired girl said.

Jesus. I dug in my pockets and came out with a five, gave it to her. She left and I grabbed the vodka rocks, squeezed the lime in it and slammed half the drink. I glanced over at Jan and in spite of everything, she was smiling.

"You're cute," she said. "Like always."

"That's just what an old man wants to hear—that he's cute. But maybe it's not so bad." I knocked back the rest of the drink. "So now we're here talking, like you wanted. Let's fast forward to the action, the gist of things." *Or the sex scene,* a little voice in my head was saying.

"What do you mean?"

"What is it you want from me? Other than someone to talk to, I mean. You know I haven't got any money. At least the kind that could help you out. Same as always, right?"

"I'd never ask you for money, Carter. Do you really think that's all I care about? I asked you here because I know you still care about me. And I care about you."

"A real care fest."

"Stop it, Carter. I need a place to stay tonight, okay? I thought you could help me. I did get you out of jail."

"Of course, Jan. I'm sorry. You can't go to a motel?"

"Rick took all my credit cards."

"Sweet. Well then, you can stay at my place. I don't remember when I changed the sheets the last time, but—"

"I hoped you could get me a hotel room for the night. Right here on Barker's Island, so I won't have to drive. At least not very far."

"I got a better idea. I took a cab over here, so I need a ride back to Duluth. I can drive your car to my place and you can have the bed—I promise I'll change the sheets—and I'll take the couch."

"Why don't you just stay in the hotel with me? It's not like we're strangers."

"Methinks that is part of the problem, my dear." I don't know what was coming over me. The white-knight-of-the-streets bullshit must've been softening my brain. But it was more than that. I suddenly wanted nothing to do with cheating or affairs or illicit romance. Having already been through more than my share, I was acutely aware of the pain and rancor that sleeping around can cause. "I can get you a room here on my credit card, but then there would be a record of what could be construed as proof of extra-marital sexual congress. Your hubby is a lawyer, after all."

"But I'm not sharing a room with the whole congress."

I smiled thinly. "No. But Rick's lawyering ways could make it look like you did." I searched for the waitress. "You haven't even got a checkbook?"

"I have a checkbook. But there's nothing in the account. I drained it making payments on the cards before Rick discovered my secret. Now he's totally cut me off. It won't last long, week or so at the most—then he'll come around. But until then, it's gonna be hand to mouth."

Jan had been and obviously continued to be, a spending addict. Hand to mouth for her was a different thing altogether. Her needs had needs and her desires had desires. My mind replayed again how she'd jettisoned me when I lacked enough chips for the game she was playing. But I could still picture her sleek, lithe body, the feel of her sultry smooth skin and the way she moved in bed. I pushed back the images.

"Tell you what," I said. "How about we go back to my office. I'll pull out the daybed for you then take a cab to my apartment. There's TV at the office, and you can check out my brand new reception area. It's clean. Only thing missing is a secretary. Ever consider being a private eye's secretary? Sounds like you might be needing a job real soon. Economy's tough these days—this might be just the thing for you." I was enjoying the opportunity to make her squirm.

Her eyes went flat. "You're serious?"

"Only half-serious. No more than half. I'm serious about you sleeping at my office and I'm half-serious about you working there. You would definitely class the place up. I could only pay minimum wage, though."

"I don't believe this shit," she said, anxiously signaling for the waitress.

"And one more thing," I said.

"What?"

"How much did you charge on the cards?"

"Around a hundred and forty thousand."

"Jesus fucking Christ. Are you shitting me? Isn't that about what Rick makes per client?"

"That's just what I said to him, but he didn't see it quite the same way."

"I s'pose not."

Chapter

10

The bay window of my soon-to-be-vacated apartment rattled as the rumbling exhaust pipes on Burton's truck entered my driveway at ten-thirty the next morning. My muscles were a little sore from my attempts at strength training and my head was fuzzy from the time spent with Jan. She could do it to you every time.

I was proud of myself for sticking to my resolve and staying out of bed with my dear second ex-wife, as good as it might've been. She'd finally acquiesced and agreed to sleep on the pullout couch in my office. When I called her earlier this morning, she said she was busy sorting my mail and arranging my desk. Had to take her all of five minutes. Maybe she was warming up to my offer of employment, although she made no mention of it.

But now I needed to get back to the matter of Rose Talbot. I was impatient for something to happen. As much as I wanted to help the boys in their canvassing, I remained convinced that the best plan was for me to keep my distance until I was actually needed. I knew I'd have to contact Daugherty sooner or later and bring him up to speed on the investigation but I was having a hard time facing it.

Sometimes it all seemed hopeless. I was a blind man groping in the dark for light. The thing with Jan was sapping my will. All the promises I'd made to myself and here I was, still getting sucked in.

I went out the door. The air was surprisingly mild. A hazy sunlight brightened up the pine branches stretching over the roof of the idling pickup truck. I slid into the backseat and said good morning to Jeff and Dan. Grunts and the oily, fetid odor of Coney dogs drifted back from the front seat.

"You guys eat breakfast yet?" I said.

"Torm made me stop for sliders," Burton said, looking back at me in the rearview, cheeks bulging with Coney dog.

"Best thing for a hangover," Tormoen said, smacking his lips.

"Thought I smelled something extra rude. That stink'll linger in your clothes and hair for hours. The cab of this truck is now permanently damaged."

Tormoen turned around and swung a grease-laden white paper bag in front of me. "Want one?" he said, sucking his teeth.

I figured I could wait to eat.

We discussed the case during the ride.

I was hoping we could get the crankhead to implicate someone for paying him to come forth with his phony story. We could get it on tape and bring it to the sheriff, something to get the ball rolling. If the Sacowskis were behind it, they could unravel under pressure and rat each other out.

Burton informed me in clear, concise diction that if the Creek County Attorney wouldn't use Fifield's story against me, he sure as hell wasn't going to allow the tweaker's tales to be used against the Sacs.

He was right, I suppose, but we had to do something. If there was another direction to go in, I wasn't seeing it.

All Burton had to offer besides criticism was his usual saw about Greta and Petr and the guy who ran the restaurant. Nothing I hadn't heard before. Tormoen voiced his familiar refrain about Gloria somehow revealing some key bit of information when her defenses were down.

Same old same old.

We drove on. The truck tires hummed. The lake was gentle, wrinkled like blue corduroy. No snow on the ground yet. The more we talked, the less it seemed we knew.

Burton rambled on with his theory that the father of Rose's alleged unborn child could be the murderer, postulating that the killer had heard of my failed attempts at tailing Rose (Greta had said it was all over town) and begun to build a frame for the incompetent private eye. Guy might even own a small SUV.

Burton's theory made me want to strangle him. But I had to admit it was possible. Obviously I was new at this shit.

My final words to the two yahoos as they dropped me off at the Creek County impound lot: "It has got to be about money. It's always about money. Follow the money and you'll find the killer." I was saying anything just to say something.

It felt good to be behind the wheel of the Subaru again. I was on my way to Duluth but couldn't shake the feeling that I should be staying around and doing something to help. I kicked up the speed, trying to put some distance between me and Taconite Bay, hoping my head would clear. I was coming up on Talbot's cliff-side manor. I craned my neck to see what I could see. When I first heard the whoop of the siren, my heart jumped. I checked the mirror. Sure enough, flashing red lights filled the glass like sores on a leper.

I eased off the gas and swung to the shoulder. Talbot's mailbox was fifty yards ahead. The cop SUV pulled in a few yards behind me. I could see the deputy talking in his microphone as my mind created possible scenarios.

*How fast had I been going? Does this cop think I stole the For-
ester from the impound lot? Did they plant drugs in the car? Are
they selling tickets to the Fisherman's Picnic?*

I watched the deputy sheriff approach: a young guy, somewhere in his twenties, about six-foot with the carriage of a West
Point cadet. Square face with red hair cut short and dark green
aviator shades.

I fumbled for my wallet, patting two pockets before finding
the correct one. A large shadow swept over me as I pulled out
the license.

"Driver's license, registration and proof of insurance, please."
Voice with the matter-of-fact firmness they must teach at the police academy, Atwood on a nametag above his left chest pocket.

I slipped the registration and insurance cards from the glove
box and handed the documents up to him with a smile. He ex-
amined them and frowned. "Are you aware you were crossing
over the centerline, sir?"

"Ah, no, officer. I must have swung over the line when I was
looking up at that marvelous house up there." I pointed up the
hill. "I'm sorry if I crossed over the line. It won't happen again."

"Oh you crossed over, all right. Did you have business with Mr.
Talbot today, Mr. Brown?"

"No. Not today. Maybe some other day."

"Are you aware that your license plates are expired?"

"They are? No, I wasn't aware of that either. I guess I'm not
too aware today. You caught me unawares." I had a vision of the
registration form lying in the pile of mail on my desk that Jan had
been such a good sport to go through.

"I'm going to write you a ticket for crossing the centerline in
a no-passing zone and a warning ticket on the license tabs. But
I want to make something clear to you, Mr. Brown. I know who
you are. And I also know you just retrieved this vehicle from the
county impound lot. Normally, I'd run your license. But in this
case, I've seen your record and file enough times already to

make me sick of you. What that file tells me is that you stick your big nose into things you've got no business with. And by doing that, you cause trouble for the citizens of my county." He hunched up his shoulders and scowled. "And I want to make it extremely clear that we don't want you or any of your associates bothering Mr. Talbot during his time of grief. We have a quiet little community here, and we want to keep it that way."

He was really laying it on thick. The quiet-little-town speech, for Christ sake.

Atwood's face turned suddenly sour. He took off his sunglasses, bent over to peer in at me. "You say something, Mr. Brown?"

I looked up at his big, overly bright brown eyes, a few freckles on his cheeks, thinking he looked like a pumped-up Ron Howard. Opie tripping on authority and steroids. Seemed like he'd read my thoughts, judging by the pissed-off look, thick red eyebrows all furrowed. *Had I actually mocked him out loud and not realized it? Was I going around the bend?*

"I didn't say anything to you, Atwood. Why don't you just write the tickets so I can get out of here."

The pale skin of his face was turning scarlet when a car came careening around the bend in the northbound lane, tires squealing. Atwood jerked his head toward the sound. His back got stiffer as the driver of the car saw him and let off the gas. The loud blasting of exhaust flashed me back to a night some weeks ago when a Mopar hot rod had squealed away from me in the dark, carrying the guy who'd just rifled my office.

I had the ridiculous urge to give chase but young John Law wasn't having any of that. He turned his steely eyes back to me.

"Aren't you gonna go after that reckless driver, officer?" I said.

"I know who it is. I'll catch up to him in town and give him a little talking to."

"Who is the guy?"

He blinked rapidly three times, put his shades back on. "Would you step out of the car, please, Mr. Brown?" Asking but really telling.

"What for?"

"Please don't resist, Mr. Brown, or I'll be forced to drag you out of the car and handcuff you."

"What are you going to do then, hang me by me pectoral muscles from the nearest tree?"

The skin around his eyes tightened; his jaw muscle flexed.

I slid slowly out of the car.

"Step around the back of the vehicle, please."

"All I want to know is why I need to be out here."

"I believe I detect alcohol on your breath."

"What? Must be the Coney dog smell on my clothes or something. I haven't had a drink since last night."

"Take the sobriety test and prove it."

"Don't I have the right to refuse?"

"You know what, old man? I have the right to have your car impounded. Bring it back to where it belongs. Now you want to close your eyes and stand on one leg and touch your nose with your index finger or do I call the tow truck?"

I passed all the tests with flying colors, except reciting the alphabet backwards. Fucked that one up royally. And by the time we were through with exams it was too late to chase after the muscle car. At least that's what my experiences up here had taught me. Or maybe I was just making excuses.

When Atwood finally gave me the tickets, U-turned and headed north, the sun was hovering low in the sky above the lake and glaring through my window. I drove to the nearest rest stop and sent Burton a text. Never text and drive, you know.

Danboy. Keep an i peeld 4 Mopar hot rod, yellow and blue. Loud pipes. Same one that hit office.

I didn't stop again until my stomach reminded me it was empty. Knife River for smoked fish is a nearly mandatory destination. Even *Bizarre Foods* guru Andrew Zimmern from the Travel Channel stops here on his way north.

The curly-haired kid behind the counter wrapped a hunk of whitefish and a slab of lake trout in newspaper, added a plastic fork and put it all in a brown paper sack. I took them down the road to the edge of the lake. Stratified clouds had moved in and the sky was a gray washboard. Metallic water rolled benevolently onto the gravel shore.

I unwrapped the lake trout, carved off a piece with the plastic fork and was just about to put it in my mouth when my jacket pocket started vibrating. I ate the smoky morsel, set the fork on the newspaper unfolded on the seat next to me, and reached for the phone.

A text message from Burton. Or Tormoen using Burton's phone: A list of names. Men's names. The four owners of Sky Blue Waters Lodge: Byron Barnes, Guy Conklin, Richard Enrico and Dane Moore.

Following that information was Tormoen's idea of letting me know he was working.

Am meetng mystry woman. Xpect results soon. Torm.

I found myself wondering why we just didn't call and talk to each other. Or was that so twentieth century? At least I had something for Tommy to use. Good to know the boys were actually attacking the case. I was kind of surprised.

I looked at the lake and worked on the fish. The whitefish was firm in texture and tangy on the tongue. You could taste the lake in it. The trout was oily in a good way and rich in flavor. I popped the cap on one of the two beers I'd purchased, turned and looked around for cops before knocking down half the bottle.

Daylight began to fade; the sky turned a muted blue on its way to gray.

My mouth tasted of fish oil and beer.

Out on the lake, a saltie was steaming slowly eastward on its journey to the Atlantic, smoke from the big stack curling out behind it like a gigantic black scarf.

Tommy Basilio was in my office when I got there. A cardboard twelve-pack of Miller High Life sat on my desk with three empty bottles standing free next to it. Tommy turned and gave me a nod as he fiddled with my computer. Various electronic parts, wires and a few tools were scattered on the desk.

This was another good sign, Tommy actually using the key I'd given him so he could get started early. Again I was surprised. *Were these guys really buying into this gig?*

"How's it going Tommy?"

He frowned at me, lifted a half-full beer bottle.

"Horseshit, Carter, fucking horseshit. The wife always goes crazy this time of year with the Christmas shit. The presents, the tree... 'Are we gonna have enough money? Should we get the turkey now? Do we still have to go to your sister's? You remember what she said to me last year, don't you honey?'

"I'm tellin' ya, Carter, it's all that shit all the goddamn time. And her fucking dick of a little brother—I gotta cater to his needs or she'll be on my case like stink on shit. Like the twat licker could get hired anywhere else. So today I said fuck it and came over here. Want a beer? Help yourself."

"Yeah, I'll have one. But what I meant was the computer. How's the computer coming along?"

"Oh. It should work."

"Want some smoked fish? Just brought it in from Knife River." I set the two newspaper-wrapped bundles down next to the beer. The desk was starting to look very Minnesota.

"No thanks. I was thinking of hitting the Savannah after I get you set up. That stuff stinks too much for pleasant company."

"Pleasant company? At the Savannah? You can't be serious."

"You wanna go?"

"Yeah. But first let's run some names through your magic box. Kind of a test run."

"Ready to go in a few. Whattaya got?"

"The names of the guys who own Sky Blue Waters Lodge. It's possible that one of them knocked up Rose Talbot. If this is true, the one responsible might know something we can use. It could also be a motive for murder, if the guy had a wife and Rose threatened to take it public or other such considerations. Her being preggers might also increase Billy's desire to see her gone. Besides all that, these guys just seem a little hinky. Who knows what they might be privy to?"

"Hinky?"

"Got that from a James Ellroy novel. Means suspicious or of dubious character."

"How'd you get the names of these hinky guys?"

"Burton's got a new girlfriend works in the restaurant at the lodge. I assume she told him. He and Torm are up there now, digging around."

"I could've plucked those names off the Web from the County Assessor's office, saved you a lot of dough-ray-mi. They'd be list-ed in several different places if they own a lodge. Knowing how to access allegedly confidential databases online pretty much makes the private eye obsolete, the way I see it. At least for find-ing missing persons and digging into personal lives. Two of the major things you dicks do."

I didn't respond to his little dig, just grabbed a beer from the carton and walked over to the window. The sky was dark and Christmas lights were twinkling along the boulevard. Not many shoppers on the sidewalks, though, even with the above-average warmth. Tommy was starting to piss me off, like he always did when he drank. I took a swallow of the High Life and then a deep breath.

"Can you find out if Rose was pregnant?" I said. "Can you use your talent for that? A modern private eye needs a guy like you to help him do the job right." *Honey works better than vinegar, right?*

He snapped a connecting wire into place and straightened up, threw down the rest of his beer and went for another. "That'll be easy if she used her real name. If she didn't, it could get difficult. I'll boot'er up and see what I can find."

He sat down on a metal folding chair in front of the blue iMac. I looked at the skinny son of a bitch in his pipe-stem black jeans and black open collar shirt, the scalp starting to show at the crown of his skull. I had to smile to myself. Here was another aging hipster trying to keep a little excitement in his life, like the rest of us. Maybe, between the four of us, we could keep the fuck-ups to a minimum and get Rose Talbot some deserved justice.

Chapter
11

Tommy couldn't find any record of recent medical visits for Rose Marie Engwar Talbot. He'd scanned every medical facility listed for the State of Minnesota and found nothing of value. A Rose Talbot in Walker had cortisone shots in her knees at a local clinic. And yet another Rose Talbot received treatment for sciatica in Edina. These women were definitely not what we were searching for. And Tommy was getting antsy to hit the bar for some T and A. I had one last thought. Although not brilliant, it got the job done.

"All right, Tommy," I said. "I'll buy the first round if you try just one more thing. Try it under her mother's maiden name. I don't know what it is but I'm sure you can find out, Web wizard that you are."

It took him a while longer than he wanted it to. He pissed and moaned the whole time about his no-good brother-in-law and how he had to carry him at the store and he didn't have the time to carry me, too. But he found it by speed riffing through old marriage and birth records, numbers flying on the computer screen until they popped up the marriage certificate of Harold Engwar and Susan Softich.

Then it was a quick connect to the Fontana Clinic in Eagan, Minnesota, where a Ms. R. Softich, address listed as 3321 Eastview Road, Eagan, Minnesota, had received a prenatal examination and counseling on September 29. Height and weight and age stats seemed to match up. A second visit ten days later was for an ultra-sound. A prescription for prenatal vitamins was issued.

Now we were cooking.

It appeared that Rose had known she was carrying a child. Maybe prenatal vitamins indicated her desire to keep the baby healthy and carry it to term. I wanted to believe that about her. After hearing all the badmouthing from the good citizens of the Minnesota Arrowhead, I was in her corner. Somebody had to believe in her, dead or not.

"This is great, Tommy," I said, looking at the printout. "Now if we can run those four guys' names through real quickly, we should be able to hit the Savannah at least by the time the girls come on."

"Jesus fucking Christ. I wanted to get there before the prices went up. I need something besides this beer. I'm all beered out."

"How about if I write you a check for your services? Say, fifty bucks? You can cash it the club, they always cash my checks."

"A third-party check? I don't think so."

"All right, I'll go with you. Cash one and give you the money. Just run those names and we can go."

No matter what I'd said to Tommy, I'd hoped to avoid the Savannah Club tonight. Place was beginning to feel cheap and tawdry. *Was I becoming enlightened? Coming down with a weird virus?*

Tommy ran the names.

We went to the bar and I got him his cash.

I left him with the strippers and the guys in suits who like to get drunk and insult women. I drove home bathed in the glow of Duluth's Christmas-City-of-the-North splendor. The lights, the big lit-up tree at the intersection of Lake Avenue and Superior Street, the artificial wreaths and the empty stores, it all made me remember how much I hated the holiday. Always an oppressive feeling that begins when the days grow short and the Christmas hype machine cranks up its massive engines.

It was quiet and dim as I turned in the driveway of my apartment on the East hillside. The bulb on the pole was dead but I could still recognize Jan's Audi parked in the dark by the big pine tree. I pulled in close to the concrete wall separating the parking area from the backyard of the house next door. I could see the orange coal of Jan's cigarette flaring in the dark behind her windshield. Then the interior light came on and she was stepping clumsily out wearing a white trench coat and black high heels.

"Jan," I said cleverly, "is everything all right?"

"No," she slurred, "Everything is definitely not fine. I need to sleep at your office again tonight."

"Still got the key?"

"Yes, I've got the key."

I went to my door. "Whatsamatter, Jan? Ricky boy don't want to play with you any more?'

"Asshole wants to put me on an allowance. A strict allowance. No credit cards, no ready-money checking accounts—just what he doles out."

"That's a crying shame, my dear. Would you care to come in my humble abode and talk about it? And most certainly you can crash at the office again tonight if you need to. The bed is yours as long as you need it. But if you're going to be there during the day, you're gonna have to work for your supper. That secretary's job would be perfect for you—with your new situation and everything. Earn some extra money and get some independence from Ricky poo."

I turned the lock, went into the apartment and flipped the wall switch, bathing the room in the dim yellowish light of fluorescent bulbs from the ceiling fixture. Jan followed me in. She was wearing black workout clothes under the coat, tights and-leotard. Very sixties. She flipped her cigarette outside and shut the door.

"You actually have money to pay me?" she said.

"Maybe," I said. "I expect a lot of clients to be lining up, now that I've been cleared of those pesky murder charges."

"And currently, you're working on what? Trying to find the killer of a dead girl with no one to pay you?"

"That's about it. But I've already been paid a lot."

"And your bank accounts are freed up?"

"*Oui, madame.* Or at least soon. Want a beer?"

"I've got some wine in the car."

"Drinking alone tonight?"

"With nobody else. But now I got you, babe."

"Two songs. That's good. You were always good."

It was a game we used to play when we were married and stoned. Using the lyrics of rock songs to have conversations. Again I had to fight back the onslaught of good memories.

"Rick isn't very good at the game. He only listens to Sinatra and Garth Brooks."

Without comment, I went to the fridge and grabbed a cold bottle of LaBatt's. Jan went outside to get her wine.

It seemed I was at low ebb in the murder investigation. Hitting a wall. This was the point in the paperbacks that something big always happened. Something that illuminated important facts or turned the case in a new direction.

For me, that moment was to come later. For the present, it looked like I was stuck in a lose-lose situation with the second of my former wives. And the real funny thing was that I'd been thinking about my first wife lately. The approaching holidays must have brought it on.

First wife Carrie and our daughter Laurie. Laurie away at college, having scratched and clawed and labored to find a means to get away from her mother. And I suppose, me also, to some extent. But I'd always believed Laurie's feelings toward me were closer to indifference than either love or hatred.

Jan came back carrying a half-full bottle of white wine and a pack of American Spirit cigarettes.

"Can't smoke in here, dear. Mrs. Swanson has got the nose of a bloodhound and the temper of a pit bull when it comes to tobacco."

"Isn't she kicking you out, anyway?"

"Yeah, but I want to at least last out the month."

"I'll smoke outside then, if I have to. I bought these after I stomped out of the house. Rick hates cigarettes. One of the things he was constantly ragging me about before I quit the last time."

"I'm afraid I have to support him on that one."

"Oh God, not you, too."

"Sorry dear, but I'm afraid I've jumped on the bandwagon. Fucking coffin nails just make me uncomfortable. But I won't lecture you. I draw the line at that."

"That's a good thing, given your past."

I brushed off the slight and went over to my Sony radio/CD/cassette player, tuned in KUMD, found a clean glass for Jan and settled into my ragged green couch. I tried to relax but half expected lawyer Rick's Benz to come squealing in the driveway at any moment.

A few minutes later, I was headed to the fridge for another beer when my phone buzzed from inside the pocket of my jacket, hanging on the back of a kitchen chair. I lifted it out and discovered another text from Burton:

Update: Petr has left the area. Probably returnd home. Most of lodg staff gon for seasn. Greta leaving aftr New Yrs. Jef and I currently at casino. Quite a gathring. Nearly all players and prsns of intrest here. Bryn Brns here and looks good for baby fthr, altho our grl was known 2 sprd the welth around. Mor updates 2 come.

Although Petr's leaving wasn't the end of the world and Dan had implied promise, I still felt a hole in the pit of my stomach and wasn't sure why. Maybe they could go farther with the father thing. The casino deal sounded intriguing. Maybe the good sheriff could arrange a viewing of the security tapes from the night of Rose's death in the spirit of our cooperation agreement. But the casino was located in a different county and Indian reservations are treated as sovereign nations. Problems give birth to problems.

"What's the matter?" Jan said.

"Just another setback in the case. I was expecting some instant resolution, I guess. Maybe I'm impatient."

"Gosh, Carter, not you."

"Piss off, Jan. You wanna talk about impatience? Maybe we can go back to that time you were waiting for me outside of Jimmy's Lounge in my Olds."

"Forget I said anything."

"You don't want to be reminded that you smashed the car into the bridge abutment?"

"That part was fun. It's that bitch you were with that I don't want to remember. But it's too late now, I'm sorry to say. You really went down in my eyes that night, you know. But I don't want to go there."

"All right then, we won't. I don't know why I brought it up."

The exchange put some ice in the room. Jan finished her wine. There was a tense silence for a few minutes before she said she was going to the office, "Where the TV was better."

"How was the bed?" I said, trying to get things back on an even keel.

"Good enough. At least I can smoke there."

I was going to protest but I knew it would be useless.

* * *

She was still in the office the next morning when I walked in. It was ten a.m. and the couch was back in place. The only way you could tell she'd been there overnight was the tobacco smell and the butts piled inside the wastebasket by my desk.

She was sitting behind the new desk in the immaculate reception area with a proud-of-herself look on her slightly sleepy face. "I just got you another case," she said, beaming.

"Really, someone called?"

"Yup. Poor old lady just had her son-in-law take off with a bunch of her money and she wants to get it back."

"Good luck with that. Sounds like one for the cops."

"She went to the cops but they aren't doing anything. Guy has left the state and she wouldn't press charges. Daughter's husband and everything…."

"How much he get?"

"Thirty K."

"That much? Jesus. What the hell were they up to, buying dope?"

"I didn't ask. It's none of our business. We're just here to serve the client."

"It's we, now?"

"I've decided to take you up on your offer of gainful employment. So are we going to help this poor old lady or not?"

"I could have Tommy run a trace. He says he can find people wherever they are because somewhere they're listed on a computer. DMV. Utility bills. Credit cards—they're gonna leave a trail. Did you tell the lady our fee, or did you leave that up to the actual detective to decide?"

"She'll give you three grand if you find the guy. We don't have to collect for her, just locate the son-in-law."

"That's it? Find him and we get paid? No findy—no get pay?"

"I said we'd help her, and she said she'd give us three thousand if we found him, so yeah, that's it. Nothing carved in stone or written in blood. Get her down here to sign a contract, if you want. You're the hotshot private detective, I'm only the lowly secretary."

"Don't forget receptionist."

"Bite me."

"Where?"

She sighed heavily. "You going to help this woman or not?"

"I'll get Tommy on it. Call her and have her come down. There are some standard contract forms in the file cabinet. There's a place on them to write terms. Fill that in and have her sign it. And uh… about this smoking in the office… There's a no-smoking clause in the lease I signed for this place."

"Not a problem. I just quit again. Only reason I started was to piss off Rick, anyway. But I decided that ruining my lungs was not the best way to get back at him. I've got other ideas."

"I'm sure you do."

Chapter

12

The Farmer's Almanac had predicted a long, cold winter, while the National Weather Service was forecasting el nino winds on the Pacific Ocean leading to a warmer than normal winter in the Midwest. So far, the Weather Service was winning the battle of credibility, at least in northeastern Minnesota. I was all for it.

It was another December el nino day: temperature in the mid-forties with intermittent sun and no wind. I could see fishing boats on the lake trolling the blue-gray surface for Coho and Chinook salmon. Daylight was on the wane and I was at my familiar position at the window of my office, much like a cat that stares out the window when it can't get outside.

I was waiting for Tormoen and Burton. I'd actually tried to call them on the cell phone, but no one picked up. This would definitely be a point of discussion at our next meeting. After failing to make an actual connection with a human voice, I left a text message directing them to my office for said meeting. They were actually due in thirty minutes, but I wasn't betting on their punctuality.

Tommy was already here and working on the trace of our thirty-grand-stealing son-in-law. I'd given Jan a fifty-dollar bill and sent her home to her husband, at least until she got something squared away with regards to her living arrangements. The last thing I needed was a clever, self-infatuated lawyer like Rick Kemp coming after my ass for interfering with his right to consortium or some such shit. I was sure he had ways to make my life even more miserable than it already was without even getting up from his overpriced leather chair.

Tommy uttered a noise that sounded like Yes. He could've been saying Ass; I wasn't sure.

"Found the motherfucker," he said. "Las Vegas fucking Nevada. Electricity service and gas hook-up for 1339 Elm Drive. Customer: Jack Nordling, Minnesota Driver's License #N69872735."

I still wasn't sure whether Tommy had said Yes or Ass but it no longer mattered, we'd just made three grand without leaving the office. Now I was going to have to figure out how much to pay Tommy.

"Thirty big ones would be a nice stake at the tables," I said. "Everybody thinks they can play poker these days—what with the online schools and all the games on TV. This idiot Nordling probably got the bug from watching Texas Hold'em on ESPN. I guess they were right about the evils of television."

"Yeah," Tommy said. "Maybe the dude should sue the network for turning him into a gambling junkie, causing him to steal from his loved ones."

"He could get Richard B. Kemp to represent him."

"Speaking of the Kemps," Tommy said, giving me a serious look. "You think Jan is gonna come here to work? Seems like a stretch to hope for. I mean, if you actually are hoping for it."

"I would like her to work here. And I think she will. Seemed like she was going to stick to her guns this time. I hope she does.

But not for any romantic reasons. I'm through with that shit. Got this new girl I like. She cuts my hair; she's a stylist. That's what they call them now—stylists. You get your haircut the same, but it's not a barber anymore, it's a stylist. Welcome change, though, in this case. Renee is a lot better to have near you than old Mr. Lang, the first barber I ever had. His hands had a weird smell on'em and he used to get the scissors caught in the little hairs on the back of your head. Stung like a sonofabitch. Getting your haircut is an intimate act, y'know. Somebody's coming close to you, rubbing against you, and then they're touching you—cutting your hair—actually removing part of your person. If that isn't intimate, I don't know what is. Kind of like circumcision for your cranium. I'd rather have Renee do the work than some guy. Girl has a pierced nose, two-tone hair, tattoos—and, of course, a great body. She doesn't know I dig her yet, but I'm planning on letting her know real soon."

"Sounds like the makings of a steady thing," Tommy said.

"You think?" I said.

A big turn in the case came tumbling out of left field later that same day. Burton and Tormoen and Tommy were gone and I was alone in the office watching the early evening news on my flat-screen. My guys had returned from Taconite Bay with more information than I'd expected. I was trying to sort it all out.

One compelling bit was the identity of the owner of the hot-rod, a 1978 Dodge Charger. Gloria solved that one for us. Answer: James Sacowski, aka "Middle Sac." The Third Sac, if you will. Allegedly the most stable and straight-laced of the three brothers, James worked as a hunting and fishing guide and jack-of-all-trades and was rumored to be starting a new business in the Taconite Bay area.

If it had been Jim Sacowski driving the night my office was broken into, why had he wanted Petr's letter? With Petr gone, had anything changed? Was "Middle Sac" the father of Rose's unborn child or just working for the father? Was there a third interested party? How had they found out about the letter?

Burton had offered some insight. According to Greta, who was set to go back to Europe herself after the New Year's holiday, Petr didn't know exactly who the father was, only that Rose was pregnant and that someone in the area wanted it kept a secret. Petr had attended some of the wild parties and knew the scene and the players—who had done what to whom.

Greta also told Burt that a change had come over Petr after he'd sent the letter. She implied that he'd lost his nerve. And by the time I arrived to talk to him, he had supposedly changed his mind and no longer wanted any involvement with the investigation.

I'd sensed some reticence in the boy at Palisade Head but also believed he genuinely cared about Rose. He'd seemed to kowtow to Barnes at the restaurant but was willing to talk at the party. Maybe someone got to him. Maybe he was feeding me false information. Or maybe the fact that he knew he was leaving soon—plus a few beers—had emboldened him that night, allowing him to speak the truth.

My assistants had brought back another bombshell, one that pried open a whole new can of nightcrawlers: Rose had a younger sister who'd spent the summer at her parents' vacation home on Lake Superior and had allegedly logged a lot of partying time with Rose. Parties that, according to Greta, "Were very out there—and wild." And exclusive to the high rollers, including at least three of the four owners of Sky Blue Waters Lodge.

Torm and Dan had also picked up on a lot of rumors and bar tales. Evidently some of the townies still believed I was guilty and that my investigation was only a smokescreen. Others weren't so sure, espousing theories that ran from the predictable—Rose was run off the road by a drug dealer from Duluth because of unpaid debts, to the bizarre—she was killed by a traveling band of Canadian gypsies who were trying to kidnap her and sell her into white slavery. The most obviously logical conclusion wasn't even talked about. The locals never mentioned the Sacowskis or Billy Talbot, even in the most drunken soliloquy. At least not in front of my operatives.

Who could blame the humble folk? And who could mock their fear?

Certainly not me.

I was trying to make sense of it all and not having much success when the newsflash came on the tube. I heard the cute blond on WDIO TV mention William "Billy" Talbot, long-time resident of Taconite Bay. She was saying the bereaved widower was missing. Disappeared from his specially equipped boat, which had been discovered run aground with no one aboard near Grand Portage.

I felt the world tilt and shift.

The news lady went on to say that Talbot's boat had been noticed absent from its moorings at the marina some time around the noon hour, but nothing was made of it because of the unseasonably warm weather. Many locals had kept their boats in the water to take advantage of late-season angling. No alarm was raised until the next morning (today) when the boat hadn't returned and Billy's van was still in the same spot in the parking area as the night before. Attempts at radio contact were unsuccessful and a search was begun, culminating in the discovery of the vacated boat.

Rumors of a suicide note were not confirmed by the Creek County Sheriff. He stated that all pertinent matters would be addressed at a joint news conference of the Creek and Cedar County Sheriff Departments, scheduled for the following morning.

Then the screen changed and two men were standing on a large dock, an empty slip behind them—the big lake filling up the background. A reporter held his microphone in front of a reasonably distraught-looking Dick Sacowski.

I grabbed the remote and punched up the volume.

"I brought him to his boat and helped him on around ten o'clock yesterday morning," Dick was saying. "I asked him if he wanted me to go along, but he said he wanted to be alone with his memories. I rigged up a few rods for him and sent him on his way. He was a little down in the dumps, but it was a beautiful day and I thought maybe it would cheer him up to be out there cruisin' around. It's not like he never went out alone. He did it all the time. He could get around pretty good by himself with his special chair and everything. Last thing he said to me was 'Rose would've loved a day like this.'"

Then the camera panned away from Dick's fallen face and stopped on the empty boat slip, lingering momentarily, before sweeping out to the vast and seemingly endless expanse of steel-blue, gently lapping water.

The whole ball of facts and innuendo and assumptions whirled inside my head like a fevered merry-go-round. I could see where this was heading: *Billy committed suicide because he couldn't live without his dead wife. That was the way they were going to spin it.*

Had Talbot really chosen drowning? I didn't for a minute believe the happy horseshit Sacowski had spewed about Billy's feelings for Rose. But then I couldn't be sure. Guilt can be a powerful motivator.

How would Daugherty handle it?

I got my wallet from my jacket and took out the folded matchbook cover the sheriff had given me with his cell phone number written on it. I went to my desk phone and punched the buttons.

Thing buzzed but no one picked up. I didn't leave a message.

Understandable, I thought, probably everyone and their uncle trying to reach him.

I didn't have a clue. Well, I had some clues but I didn't know what to do with them. I was stuck at who had something to gain by Talbot's death. Was there a big insurance policy? A double-indemnity clause? A will? If so, who was due to gain? Was there a suicide note? What did it say?

These were all questions I needed to ask Daugherty. I finally got through to him around nine o'clock. We had a long talk. He said he was going to the press with a statement that Talbot's death was a probable suicide, although at this time, no body had been discovered. A note had been found on the boat that appeared to be in Billy Talbot's shaky handwriting. A note expressing Talbot's despair over the loss of his wife as well as his desire to find peace in the afterlife. These were Daugherty's words, not mine. He wouldn't read me the note, told me he'd be disclosing its contents at the press conference and I'd have to wait, like everyone else.

The thing that stuck in my craw, the thing that both the sheriff and I knew, along with most of Taconite Bay, was that Billy Talbot hadn't been enjoying his wife's company for a long while. Their recent stab at reconciliation, I believed, was merely an attempt by Rose to diffuse any suspicion before she split town for good. Billy must've known she was going to leave eventually, after what he'd done to her. Rose was not the type to forgive or forget attempts at pulling in the reins on her.

Daugherty agreed with me. Said the investigation was going to stay open on both Talbot cases but as far as any public statements, he had to stay with the probable suicide angle until something more concrete came along. Said he'd even considered suggesting that Rose's death was also a suicide and that the evidence of collision on the side and rear of her vehicle was from a parking lot fender bender, echoing my earlier thoughts.

"Think of the headline that would make, Brown," he said. "Husband follows wife's suicide with own. Small town mourns the loss of ill-fated lovers. Tourism Board would eat that one up, don't you think?"

I wasn't sure what I thought. Sounded like Daugherty's strings were pulled too tight. Maybe it was happening to us all.

I stepped aside of his question and inquired about insurance policies and beneficiaries. He said he was checking. I knew there had been a good-sized policy on Rose, which had paid off double for accidental death (murder being the ultimate accident). If her death were suddenly ruled a suicide, the insurance company would save a bundle.

I couldn't remember the exact numbers on the policy but I knew it was low-to-mid six figures. Large, due to Rose's alleged importance as caregiver for Billy. Another concept definitely in question.

How much money would it take for an insurance company to violate the law? Weren't they all run by organized crime? Had Daugherty taken a bribe? Was I just paranoid?

For the answer to these and other questions, tune in—same time, next week.

The Shadow knows.

Cue the mysterious laughter.

And that's about where I was at: needing the help of a pulp-fiction super hero who could stand in the midst of a crowd without being seen.

I didn't feel up to it.

I returned to the couch and stared at the tube and then switched it off. I tried to think about the case but my mind wouldn't let me. In my head, the door to the investigation was spring-loaded and slammed shut every time I tried to enter. In its place, a vague but growing sense of dread was spreading across my brain like a cerebral hemorrhage. I wanted to be someplace else. Years' worth of repressed traumas were rising to the surface.

Along with the dread came inertia.

I decided to stay the night at the office and resigned myself to riding out the misery. I lifted off the couch cushions and pulled out the bed, wished I had a detective story to read. One where the shamus solves the case and beds the pretty girl and everything ends up for the good.

Sadly, the only reading material in the office was the October issue of *American Small Business*, so I stretched out on the bed with my clothes on and gave sleeping a try. It was only eight o'clock and I was strangely exhausted, but after an hour of tossing and turning, I knew sleep wasn't going to come.

I rolled out of bed, threw some water from the bathroom sink on my face, brushed my hair, put on my leather jacket, braced myself for the cold and walked to the Savannah Club. Maybe watching people act out their baser instincts would somehow make me feel better about myself.

What I really wanted was the alcohol.

Leaving the club around midnight in the windy damp, I wasn't feeling any better but I was feeling less pain. Every time my mind returned to the Talbots, I was rewarded with a strong sense of unease and discomfort.

I quit trying, went back to the office and passed out on the sofa bed.

The digital clock on my desk was showing 5:05 A.M. when my eyes popped open. I got up and stumbled in the direction of the bathroom. I could hear the wind screaming and the windows rattling. Swirls of frost coated the inside glass and splatters of thick wet snow were clinging to the storm windows. I peered out into the weird, otherworldly amber glow and discovered about six inches of snow already on the ground and a whole lot more coming in off the lake at a sharp angle with force enough to make a thumping sound when it hit the front of the building. Winter had arrived in a no-doubt, slam-bam-thank-you-ma'am kind of way.

After using the facility, I flopped back into bed and pulled the blankets over my head. It was cold. I knew it wouldn't warm up until the store downstairs opened, the only thermostat in the building being located there.

I drifted in and out of consciousness for a while but the alcohol residue in my system wouldn't let sleep win out. At seven-thirty

I rolled out of bed, turned on ESPN and started up the coffee maker Jan had brought in. The wind was still whining. A couple more inches of white stuff had come down and the plows and sand trucks were chugging back and forth on Lake Avenue like busy dinosaurs. The digital thermometer on the wall said eighteen degrees outside and sixty-two inside. I shivered involuntarily, knowing these storms were usually followed by blasts of Arctic cold air roaring down from places like Yellow Knife, Fort Wilson and Peace River.

Jan walked through the door at ten a.m. She and her hubby were again cohabitating in peaceful coexistence. She'd never officially accepted my offer of employment, just showed up radiating a sense of entitlement. It was all good with me.

The temperature in the office was now a toasty seventy degrees while outside it was a frosty eleven degrees. Jan slipped off her navy blue knee-length wool coat and matching snow-dotted watch cap then pushed through her silvery hair with her hand. She hung the coat on a hook on the wall and set the cap on a radiator, stomped her fur-lined leather boots and looked over at me, the flush on her cheeks making her seem younger than the last time I'd seen her. "We need to get a doormat of some kind," she said, "or this floor is gonna look like a sludge pit." Her eyes went to the still extended sofa bed and then back to me. "Sleep well?"

"Not particularly. My eyes feel like I've been walking in a sandstorm. Have any trouble getting here? I didn't think you'd come in."

"Rick gave me a ride in his new toy. He bought one of those Chevys that look like an old-time delivery truck. Thing is kind of cute. Four-wheel drive, so he just *had* to bring it out today. He's been waiting for the first snowstorm like a kid waiting for Christmas."

"So you and hubby are all reconciled? Had a wonderful forgiveness fuck, did you?"

She sniffed and tossed her head back, her lips bending up on the corner just a tad. "Don't get personal, Brown. Don't forget that we are at the office and should carry ourselves accordingly. With the proper decorum befitting professionals."

"Sorry. Don't know what I was thinking. Actually, I do know what I was thinking, but I shouldn't have let you know. From now on, befitting professionals it is."

"That's better, dear," she said and began to survey the reception area. "We need to get a few things, Carter. Something for the walls... another phone... we need to make it look nice in here. Rick will be sending us a lot of business, so it should look professional."

"Did I miss something? Rick is going to send *us* business?"

"He promised me. He wants me to be working, so the last thing he wants is for you to go out of business. Lawyers are the main source of private detective income, in case you didn't know. At least in the real world."

"I did not know that. But I still think you've got some splainin' to do."

Chapter

13

Christmas came and thankfully went. I spent the big day at home drinking beer and trying to find something worth watching on TV. That proved futile. I popped open a can of sardines for dinner. My new holiday tradition. Getting my calcium. Had a few crackers and more beer. Wished I had a dog. But then I'd have to walk him. Decided I was sad. Rather be sad than depressed. But it still hurt. Every past slight, every moment of disrespect, all my failures and disappointments were playing day and night at my personal cinema. I was the guy wearing the trench coat in the back row of the theater.

And then there was the whole Rose Marie Engwar Talbot situation. I'd gone from being an accused murderer to a—?

I didn't know what.

I'd failed at finding Rose's killer but the whole deal seemed to be fading into the background. Winter had swallowed me up. Staying warm and well fed seemed the only matters of importance.

Much to my surprise, Rick Kemp had, indeed, sent some business my way, paying me to round up witnesses to a car accident case he was working.

I guess you could say I was making it as a detective.

I'd given Tormoen and Burton a Christmas bonus of two hundred dollars each and fifteen hundred to Tommy for his computer expertise. And never being one to skimp on the largesse when I could afford it, I decided to throw an agency party at my apartment on the twenty-ninth of December, two days before I had to vacate. I looked at it as a way to show my gratitude for the fine work of my assistants, thereby ingratiating myself to them in the hope of getting some help with the move.

Carpenters were coming in to make some improvements to the office after the first of the year. Jan had kind of taken over the planning phase. She'd drawn a diagram of the way she thought the place should be and I'd lacked the will to argue. She wanted a walled-in reception area and a small enclosure next to the bathroom so my dresser and clothes and hotplate could be hidden from public view. "It's more professional this way," she'd said.

My pre-New Year's holiday party was a success, more or less. I bought a case of Heineken and a liter of Bacardi and cooked a turkey on the outdoor charcoal grill. All my employees showed up, including Jan. She came without her husband but with some potato salad and two expensive bottles of Chardonnay. Burton brought Greta along. Jan and Greta hit it off from the start. Tormoen came alone, unless you count a bottle of Canadian Club as a companion. There are many among us who would. Despite his solitary situation, Jeff was in good spirits, having just landed the lead role in a local production of Eugene O'Neill's *Moon for the Misbegotten.*

No comment necessary.

We watched college football until the beer ran out and then started on the CC and the rum. Jan begged off the hard stuff and popped the second bottle of wine. After a couple glasses she began to regale Greta with tales of her spiritual searching.

"I've been studying Buddhism and transcendental meditation lately," Jan said.

Burton and Tormoen and I were on the couch facing the TV. Tommy was leaning back in a frayed green easy chair to our right. Upon hearing Jan's statement, the three of us fell silent and turned our attention toward the women, who were to our left at the entrance to the kitchen, sitting side-by-side on red padded chromium-framed chairs.

"How does this transcendental meditation stuff work?" Greta said arching her dark eyebrows. "I have heard of it."

"First you need to empty your mind," Jan said. "And I'm finding out that's pretty easy. My mind seems a lot emptier than I thought. I've been practicing emptying it, but it doesn't seem a whole lot different."

The booze and the moment got to me.

"No surprise there," I said, probably a bit too self-satisfied.

The boys burst out laughing and Greta stared down at the carpet, biting her lip.

Jan snapped her head in my direction, eyes dark with anger and embarrassment. Looked like she was searching for a snappy comeback but couldn't find one.

"Just kidding, Jan darling," I said.

"People always say they're kidding when they really mean exactly what they're saying," she said, her face flushing as she stood.

"Not always," I said. "Sometimes they're just teasing to have themselves some fun."

"Maybe so, Carter." She fluttered her eyes at me as if to say I was a no-good piece of shit. "But I've had enough of your idea of fun for tonight. I should really go home to my husband."

I was thinking the fun was definitely over if that's where she was going. But I didn't say anything. My trusty assistants' eyes once again became locked unwaveringly on the television, jaws held tight.

"But you should stay and finish your wine, honey," Greta said.

"You drink it if you like, I've had enough." Jan grabbed her coat from the back of the couch and put it on. "It was nice meeting you Greta. The rest of you can go to hell."

Then she walked outside, back stiff and eyes trained straight ahead above us all, got in her car and drove away.

Tormoen's head was pulsating, his lips squeezed together. Burton had his hand over his mouth. Tommy was shaking his head in either disbelief or mild disgust, either reaction being a little annoying, considering his own marital situation.

"She'll be fine when she sobers up," I said. "I was married to her, I know."

"I see why you divorce," Greta said.

A high-pitched noise, like air escaping from a pinched balloon, seeped from Tormoen's lips. Finally he couldn't take it anymore and burst out in stomach wrenching laughter, joined by Burton. I laughed weakly, myself.

Eventually the laughter subsided and there we were. The party had come down to four investigators and one femme fatale. A bad ratio if I ever heard one. I'd pledged to myself to keep the conversation off of anything to do with work, thinking that a holiday gathering should be fun, not depressing, and now it seemed we were heading for the latter. The few case-related comments from the others (it was an office party, after all, so something had to slip in) I'd deftly brushed aside.

Staying with the spirit of my pledge, I bypassed Greta's drunken question: "Have you any new leads about Rose? Is that correct word—leads?"

Instead of an answer, I began to spin stories of my first wife and some of her crazy stunts. Like one time in the middle of a binge when she took a scissors to her hair and danced around in front of the fireplace throwing blond tufts into the flames while singing Crosby Stills, Nash and Young's "Almost Cut My Hair."

These tales, of course, triggered nutso-broad stories from Tormoen and Burton, who I think could've gone on all night. But Greta, being one of those drunks who have to do whatever everyone else does, grabbed our attention with a tale about the wife of her boss, Byron Barnes.

Allegedly a "stiff Christian bitch who would have cow if she knew what hubby did when she wasn't there," the woman, on one of her visits, had purportedly drunk a ton of wine and set about berating the lodge employees from afternoon until midnight and beyond, building such animosity that hubby eventually had to send her back home to Illinois. Greta seemed to think this somehow explained Barnes' rep as a pussy hound with unusual appetites. I couldn't necessarily make the connection, myself, but then again, I'd never worked at the lodge.

I'd never suspected there were so many sex freaks in the North Woods. I suppose I was naïve, still holding to the image of a wholesome outdoor people living their lives within the boundaries imposed by the church. I momentarily forgot that the Internet travels to all nooks and crannies of this world, instructing anyone with the ability to operate a computer on the ins and outs, pardon the pun, of kinky sex. And what the hell else is there to do in the winter? Snowshoeing and ice fishing will only take you so far.

Greta prattled on with her story and it might have been total bullshit for all I knew. I looked over at Tommy. He was quiet but his eyes flitted nervously about the room. And then he stood suddenly and announced that he had to go home before he got too loaded, Tormoen loudly interjecting that it was already too late for that. Tommy shot him the one-finger salute and put on his jacket, a new piece of black leather his wife had given him for Christmas. She was a realtor and I think it pissed him off when she made more money than he did. Probably another reason he was working with me.

Tommy dragged a slender hand through his black hair and zipped the jacket over his white dress shirt, brushed the leather down over the top of his signature black jeans.

"Happy New Year," he said, bowing slightly. Then he thanked me for the party and left.

I heard his black Nissan Murano fire up. I went to the window and watched the taillights float away, wondered if he wasn't going to the Savannah Club. Had the feeling he was.

The party atmosphere dissolving, Greta and Dan began making *those kind of eyes* at each other. An awkward silence enveloped the room. At least as awkward as it can get when everyone is liquored up. The communal vibe had broken. Then the CD player kicked out The Killer's "All These Things That I Have Done" and the music suddenly seemed terribly loud and grating.

The lovebirds stood up. I thought about turning down the volume. Tormoen jumped up and beat me to it. Greta hugged me and thanked me before saying, "Goodbye until next year, if we all live that long." I wasn't sure how to take it, but dismissed it as just a problem with the idiom. Burton gave me a quick hug, said he'd see me on moving day, and the lovebirds departed with lust in their hearts.

I looked blearily at the empty bottles on the kitchen counter and the coffee table and the dirty dishes in the sink. Jeff was slouching by the stereo with his hands in his jeans pockets. "Whaddaya say we go downtown for one before close?" I said. "Up for that or do you also have somewhere to go?"

"Only to your side and your bidding, oh wise leader. Leadeth me not into temptation for thou art the power and the glory."

The thermometer on the Northern City Bank sign read ten degrees. We were westbound on Superior Street. Light snow was falling, thin airy flakes that drifted and darted on the wind. We were just drunk enough to go somewhere we wouldn't normally. We debated which saloon might afford us the best chance of picking up women. I lobbied for an upscale place. Torm, always the realist, pointed out that women in those environs tend to be infinitely harder to please than females at a more populist establishment. And with a tone of exasperation in his voice, added that there was a blues band at the Lakewalk Inn, a saloon we frequently frequented.

Thus enlightened, I slowed the Subaru and slid into the left-turn lane with the intent of heading back in the direction of the blues band. I had my turn signal on and was waiting in the intersection for traffic to clear when what should appear in the oncoming lane but a yellow Dodge Charger with a blue racing stripe on the side.

Our heads turned toward the Charger and then back to each other like horn players in a soul revue.

"Was that who I think it was?" I said.

"Couldn't tell for sure with the tinted glass, but that could be the same car. If it ain't Middle Sac, it's at least a person of interest. Follow that car, Kato."

"I thought I was the Green Hornet," I said.

"The Hornet doesn't drive. It's always Kato."

Oncoming traffic cleared and I made a quick U-turn, getting in line three cars behind the Charger, the backs of two heads visible. We followed them east to Lake Avenue where they turned right and rolled down into the Waterfront District. Formerly an area of warehouses, factories, seamen's dives and at least one whorehouse, the district was now the home of big hotels, restaurants, tourist traps and at least one shadowy private detective.

We followed the Charger to the Lakewalk Inn where it turned into the parking lot. Must've been blues fans. I continued down the avenue until we were out of sight, then turned around and entered the lot through the back entrance just in time to see a man with the familiar Sacowski features—curly hair, mongoloid forehead and deep set-eyes—going in Beachcomber's Lounge, another man at his side.

"It's Byron Barnes and Middle Sac," Torm said.

"Either of them going to recognize you?"

"Don't think so. But maybe—I can't say for sure. You and I were both up there at the restaurant… Barnes would probably recognize you before me, though, you being somewhat famous around Taconite Bay and all."

"Nice of you to remind me. I guess we'll just have to skulk around long enough to get a good look at them. There should be enough people inside to hide behind. It's our only play, unless you have the power to cloud men's minds so they can't see us."

"Sadly, the only mind I can cloud is my own. And I think the job has already been done."

We got out of the Subaru and walked across the frozen pavement to the bar. Spotlights in the ground lit up a banner on the brick wall.

Hot blues of Jim Hall and the Squalls

We pushed open the frost-covered doors, kept our heads down. The thud of the bass and the punch of the drums hit me in the chest. I surveyed the room. The band was covering a Buddy Guy tune that I recognized but couldn't recall the title. Once my eyes adjusted to the dim rose-tinted light, I saw our two miscreants at a table in a back corner of the room near the windowed wall separating the lounge from the hotel lobby.

Tormoen and I pushed through the crowd at bar side and were lucky to find two empty stools, one on each side of a reasonably attractive, forty-something brunette in a form-fitting black dress approaching maximum content.

Jeff slid up next to her and placed his cherubic Norwegian face close to her ear so he could be heard over the band. I don't know what he said but it wasn't long before she was standing up looking dreamily into Torm's blue eyes and sliding her nice round butt down one stool. Jeff took the stool nearest the women, who,

I found out shortly, was Kathy, a traveling diamond seller from Minneapolis.

I sat down. Torm tried to introduce me to his new friend. But she couldn't hear very well because the band had just kicked in again. We stayed put for the remainder of the set and she called me Bart three times. I didn't bother to correct her, being more concerned with Sacowski and Barnes, who'd recently been joined at their table by two large, rugged-faced men dressed in high-end outdoor clothing.

Here's where I could have used some kind of hi-tech listening device. I made a mental note to check with Tommy on the latest anti-privacy devices available. Then I instructed Tormoen (while Kathy was on her way to the ladies' room), to request she go with him to one of the tables in the back, where they could get to know each other better. Torm could multi-task with a bit of eavesdropping.

Jeff smirked a little, eyes slipping upward. "Anything for the cause, Boz," he said, reaching out to his empty glass. "I'll have a Jameson, if you please, to honor my Irish mother."

"I didn't know your mother was Irish."

"She had but a wee bit of the blarney in her—but that's enough for me."

I shrugged and gestured to the bartender, who was busy chatting up one of the waitresses. I pretended I didn't care he was ignoring me and let my eyes drift to the band and the tables in front, where to my surprise, I saw a familiar face, the craggy visage and receding hairline of Tim Klein—bookie, hustler, broker of stolen goods and general bon vivant. He wasn't supposed to be in town. I'd heard he'd booked for Vegas, where the gambling was legal and the women were often for sale. I hadn't seen him in at least ten years. Local gossip had it that Tim vacated the Twin Ports to avoid the complications of a substantial gambling debt. Chances for his return had allegedly been scant.

To look at him sitting there with a drink in his hand and gesturing while he spoke, it was almost possible to believe that nothing had changed in those ten years. He was a little heavier, had less hair and a harder look, to be sure, but there he was at a table near the band, as had always been his custom. And the two women and one guy at the table with him wore the same kind of well-heeled hipster look Tim had always cultivated in his associates.

Klein must've sensed me studying him, because he turned his head and looked right at me. I averted his gaze and again beckoned the bartender, this time gaining the tall skinny kid's attention just as Kathy slid back among us.

I ordered Tormoen a Jameson, a gin and tonic for Kathy and a glass of water for myself. I requested a receipt from the bartender. Expenses were adding up. All the booze I'd consumed earlier in the evening was also adding up.

I sipped water while the band roared through a grinding, bluesy version of "Froggy Went a Courtin.'" Out of the corner of my eye I could see Torm working on Kathy, gesturing towards the back of the room and cupping his hand to his ear.

I leaned back and let the music take me. Then without warning there was a hand on my shoulder and another on my upper back. The hand on my shoulder squeezed a tendon and I thought I was being rousted. I squirmed out of the grasp and whipped around, only to discover the bent and twisted grin of Tim Klein, eyes full of mirth and intoxication like a demented man in the moon.

"Brownie, you son of a bitch," Klein said, obviously amused by my momentary panic, "how the hell are you? I thought you'd dried up and blown away—and now look at you."

"No, look at you, Tim." I stuck out my hand. Klein grabbed it and squeezed. "What are you doing in Duluth?" I said. "Heard you moved to Vegas."

"I did. I'm still there, officially. Been back here since August, though. Thinking about moving back. Can't seem to get this town out of my system, you know? Must be the lake. Fucking desert gets to you after awhile. All that flatland, no water, fucking sand blowing around all the time… if I could make a living back here, I'd be back in a flash, ready to stay the course. And that's my half of the story. What you up to these days, man?"

"Trying to make it as a private detective."

He grinned, looked at me knowingly. "I read about you in the paper, man. Getting popped for murder a good advertising gimmick in your line of work?"

"Not the best. But not necessarily bad—as long as you beat the rap."

"Which you have?"

"You didn't see that in the paper?"

"Must've missed it. But good for you. It was hard for me to reconcile the guy I knew with someone who killed a woman. Now I feel better."

"I'm happy for you, Tim."

Kathy was rising from her stool and smiling politely at Jeff. He stretched out his palms toward her and made some half-hearted, last-ditch ploy. She shook her head to the negative and swayed over to the coat rack.

Tormoen turned to me, shrugged and said, "She's married. And faithful, it seems. I tried, Carter, I tried."

"I know you did, Torm, and you're a better man for it. But that doesn't do us much good. You'll have to go it alone. Go outside and come back in through the hotel. Take that table to the left of them, maybe act like a lonely salesman or something. See if you can get in their good graces. Buy 'em a round."

"I could do that. But the chances of Sacowski or Barnes recognizing me go way up if I fly in solo. A bird on the wing always draws the eyes."

"I suppose. But what other option is there?"

"What the fuck are you guys talking about?" Klein said, befuddlement creeping in around the edges of his overly widened eyes.

"See that table in the back underneath the air-conditioning unit?" I said, nodding my head in the direction.

"Yeah," Klein said, squinting.

"Know anybody at it?"

"This about a case you guys are working on?"

"Maybe. I'm not sure yet. Two of the guys there, I know. The smaller ones. Not that they're small, but the great-white-hunter types are some big dudes."

"That they are," Klein said. "I've seen'em around town lately. They drive this big black Suburban with some kind of logo on the door. Outfitters or guiding service or some shit like that. You're right about the great-white-hunter thing. I've seen them in here a couple times this week, and not all the people they were with were the rugged-outdoor type. Some, in fact, appeared to be the wealthy-soft-indoor type. A type of which I am quite familiar."

"Not a lot of hunting going on this time of year," Tormoen interjected.

"As I recall, the sign on the truck had words like *International* and *Worldwide*," Klein said, staring down his nose at Tormoen.

Maybe the men from Taconite Bay were planning a safari. But it didn't seem likely. Maybe they were just meeting old friends for a pre-new-year drink. Maybe they were talking *jihad,* who could be sure?

"So does that make me one of your colorful, street-wise informants, Carter?" Klein said.

"I'm sure it does, Timothy. Do let me buy you a drink for payment."

"That one's on the house. If I find out what it is those behemoths are selling, then you can buy me a drink. Or maybe three. Expensive ones. Johnny Walker Blue."

"You drive a hard bargain. Think you might know someone who knows something?"

"Possibly. I do know some bitches that partied with those dudes. And I do mean bitches. Couple chicks with some mean-ass attitudes. Saw them leaving here with the bwanas last Sunday, it was, I think. Could be the dudes got loaded and shot their mouths off. Braggarts, y'know? Guys like that usually brag and carry on about their manly exploits."

"See what you can find out and let me hear about it. I'll buy you some knock-off Dom Perignon."

"I've had that shit, man, it's not that great. Was a whole lot of it in Vegas over the Fourth. But listen man, what I'm sayin' is—these girls I saw used to have a fondness for the white powder back in the day—how I got to know'em. Two waitresses with great titties. Only work at the best restaurants in town and always rake in mucho gratuitimo. But they must use up all their friendly behavior at work, y'know—fakin' it for the customers and shit—because I'll tell ya right now; they truly are a couple of twats. And you know I'm not one to use that word lightly, being that I hold a deep respect for women of all races and creeds. I'm sure I can find out where they're working. Ain't that many up-scale restaurants in Duluth. Can't be that fucking difficult. Shit, maybe even one of the ladies at my table knows. Which reminds me, I better get back there before any chance of pussy tonight evaporates like piss on a hot sidewalk."

I gave him one of my freshly printed cards and told him to call me.

As Klein wove his way through the too-closely placed tables, Tormoen said, "Piss on a hot sidewalk? Colorful is right. How well you know that guy? Sure he won't blab his mouth to the wrong people? Or go right to those two guys himself and try to sell us out?"

"I don't think Tim is like that. I think he really wants to help, be part of the game. He's always been a player on some level and he's smarter than you might think. I've known him a long time. You can trust him on everything but money."

"Real stand-up guy," Tormoen said, knocking back the last splash of Irish.

I slipped him a fifty and he went out into the cold. A college-age couple smelling of the outdoors with an edge of auto exhaust hopped onto the now-vacant barstools at my side.

A couple minutes later I saw Torm shuffle through the door from the hotel lobby and take a seat at a table next to our friends. I turned back to the band, left him to do his thing.

On the slightly elevated stage, Jim Hall was growling like Howlin' Wolf while the Squalls wailed deep and hard on "Goin' Down Slow." I sipped my water and watched Tim Klein leave his table. He had a cell phone in his hand and was moving in the direction of the men's room, which happened to be on the hotel side of the door Tormoen had just come through.

Klein caught my eye, jabbed at the phone with his stubby finger and moved his lips like he was saying something to me. I couldn't tell what it was. I averted my eyes, not wanting to draw attention. Klein continued on. I scanned the lounge for good-looking women and hoped Klein had enough sense to ignore Tormoen.

The music faded out and the band went on break. The three Squalls joined up with the three remaining unaccompanied women in the room. Jim Hall, a tall, gaunt man with surprisingly dark hair for his age, which I guessed to be about sixty, put on a green down jacket over his green flannel shirt and went out the door, presumably to smoke something.

The bar filled up with voices. Not a dull roar, more like a rising din. Two large-chested platinum blondes in matching leather jackets and sprayed-on jeans came through the frost-covered lounge doors and eyeballed the room. Jim Hall came tumbling after, smoke trailing behind him, and moved to the end of the bar. He beckoned to the tender and put his arm around the shoulders of a cute young waitress.

A new bartender had just come on, redheaded guy with an upright carriage and a pumped-up chest. Reminded me of that deputy from Creek County who'd pulled me over and laid on the harassment boogie. The new guy pointed at my empty water glass, asked with his eyes if I wanted a refill. I was embarrassed to order water. I covered the glass with my hand and shook my head to the negative. I heard a commotion behind me and turned to see Tormoen and Klein approaching, seemingly arguing. Jeff's angry look was burning down on the shorter Klein, who wore his usual shit-eating grin while his hands fluttered like a drunken karate fighter caught halfway between capitulation and retaliation.

Then they were on me and Tormoen was saying something about a douchebag blowing his cover. How Klein, "Just walked right up and asked me what I was doing at a table by myself when you were still up front."

"My bad," Klein said, patting his chest, grin unshakable. "But not to worry."

"Whattaya mean, 'not to worry'?" Tormoen said. "I hear one of the big guys saying, 'The product will be ready tomorrow,' and then you stumble in and they all shut up."

"Not to worry, because I found out what those guys are into. I got a hold of one of the trollops I was tellin' you about. By promising her a little of the white powder—it's meth these days—which I can't understand for the life of me but I'm a slave to the marketplace like everyone else—"

"Get to the fucking point," Tormoen interrupted.

"Hold your water, man, I'm getting there. Impatience is bad for the heart, y'know. So anyway, the chick I'm talking to says the boys are definitely your great-white-hunter types. They do trips in Wisconsin and Minnesota for bear, up in Canada for moose, out West for bighorn sheep and elk and other exotic game— and a couple times a year they go somewhere across the big pond. Could be China, Africa, Asia—anywhere there's wild animals."

"We already know that, don't we?" Tormoen said with an annoyed look.

"Yeah, Tim," I said. "No Johnny Blue for you on that one."

"Both of you gents need to learn how to listen," Klein said. "The kicker is that Jane said the dude was going on about how the japs and the chinks and the gooks and shit will pay big money for the internal organs of bears and mountain lions... the horns of sheep—shit like that—and every other goddamn thing. And it's all fucking illegal. One of the dudes was raving about the government interfering with his right to harvest and sell animal parts any way he saw fit. And get this, there's also a big market for that kind of stuff here in the states and Canada. Old guys want to feel young—they get some eye of newt and powdered bear nuts on their breakfast cereal. Rich broad trying to hold onto her fading beauty might want some pickled rhino nipples in suppository form—who knows? They got books and websites that tell you all the valuable stuff. These gents have the perfect cover."

"White hunters, black hearts," I said.

Tormoen and Klein grew silent. They were facing me, backs to the traffickers. If I cocked my head to the left slightly, I could see around Klein to the back tables.

The two white hunters stood up and stared in our direction before barking a few last words and exiting quickly into the hotel. Sacowski and Barnes looked our way. I slid over so they couldn't see my face.

"We should leave," I said, looking at Tormoen. "Before the fox becomes the hound."

"I agree," Jeff said. "This place is starting to stink." He gave Klein one last dirty look while I turned slowly, ducked behind a newly arriving group of revelers and made for the door.

We hustled across the dirty ice of the parking lot to the car. My dome light had just gone dark when I saw Sacowski come out and stand in the glare of the spotlights at the lounge entrance. I could swear he was sniffing the air like a wolf on the hunt.

We stayed put until Sacowski went back inside. Then I drove Tormoen to his current crashing spot, a small loft above an out-of-business clothing store on Michigan Street. We were lost in thought. As he exited the car, fumbling in his jacket pocket for keys, he grunted something that sounded like "Fun night, let's do it again in about twenty years."

I said, "Keep the remainder of that fifty I gave you, as compensation for your suffering."

He looked my way for an instant then gave me a sheepish shrug before sliding up to a door that had *Baron Knitting Mills* in faded lettering on the glass.

I drove away. My dashboard thermometer read minus one. The radio said we'd be at fourteen below by morning with an extended subzero period settling in. Great weather for moving, I thought to myself, as I tried to shake the despair growing in my solar plexus like kudzu.

Chapter

14

When these arctic cold snaps hit, retreat is the only sensible course of action. Oh sure, you hear the ravings of the fanatics telling you to attack the cold or embrace it or some other nonsense, but believe me, those people are damaged goods. These same folks might tell you that banging your head against a brick wall builds character. Or that waiting on death row for the electric chair is a great lesson in endurance and patience. They do have one good statement to their credit, though: *There is no bad weather, just bad clothing.* Up to a point, this is certainly true.

And so we retreat inside layers of Thinsulate and Holofil, down and wool. Then we retreat indoors. And finally, the mind retreats into itself.

It was this last part I was having trouble with. My head was a swirling morass of seemingly unrelated information, vague unspecified longings, guilt, desire, frustration and general confusion.

All was not darkness, however. To my pleasant surprise, Burton, Tormoen and Tommy Basilio all showed up on the morning of December 29 to help with the move.

We filled Burton's truck and took a load to the storage facility I'd rented. Second run, we hauled necessities to the office, only to be greeted by an unpleasant surprise.

Stuck on the door with an indeterminate adhesive mixture, was a torn hunk of paper hand-scrawled with something resembling blood and feces.

Stay off my back or die.

Short and to the point.

Dents and dirty kick marks marred the surface of the door. At least the new lock had kept them out. Still, my blood began to boil. But an edge of uncertainty was creeping into the mix. Having your place of refuge violated, will do that. Or at least it was doing it to me.

"Looks like someone has donated some environmental art, Carter," Tormoen said, coming up behind me carrying a cardboard box. "I give him a B+ on the medium and a D on the content."

"Penmanship is noteworthy for its flowing attributes," Burton said, also with a box and breathing heavily from the climb up the stairs.

"I wouldn't touch that if I were you," Tommy said.

"This shit pisses me off," I said. I set the box I was holding on the floor, fished my keys from my jacket pocket and went inside for a plastic bag. Using a pencil, I scraped the note into the bag and shoved it in the bottom drawer of the desk. I dropped the pencil in the wastebasket and then went immediately to the bathroom for a paper towel. I cleaned off the smear on the door and washed my hands. My three helpmates looked upon me with poorly hidden concern.

This stuff was getting to me. I tried to shake the feelings by putting on a "That's-life" face. With no further comment, I went back to carrying boxes up the stairs. I was glad the guys were there. They stayed around after the work was done.

I sprung for a case of beer and a sixer of Diet Coke. We discussed the case but didn't get anywhere. Burton was adamant that we do something to derail the trafficking in animal parts. I hemmed and hawed and finally said I'd call Daugherty and tell him what we'd learned. Maybe he could take it further, tighten down on Sacowski and Barnes and alert the proper government agencies. There had to be something we could do.

"There must be government agencies concerned with such things," I said. "Which one would it be?" I was thinking out loud.

"Department of Wildlife?" Burton said.

"Customs?" Tormoen said.

"I'll look it up," Tommy said and pulled out his smart-phone that could do everything but give you head. You had to download an app for that.

He tapped away on that thing and it wasn't too long before he looked up proudly. "Says here it's the Department of Fish and Wildlife."

"I'll tell Daugherty to get in touch with them. But by now he may have decided I'm not worth a steaming pile of moose shit. He might blow it off, you never know."

"You're sounding a bit weary, Cart," Tormoen said.

"Yeah, maybe I am. Must be the cold weather. Or the residue of the fucking Christmas season. Or the simple fact that someone wrote a note with feces and stuck it on my front door. Could be Rose Talbot moaning from her grave that I'm a failure at finding her killer."

"We're not even sure there was a killer," Tommy said.

"You know," I said, "I sense the spin starting somewhere in the universe. I used to feel strongly that it was murder. Now I'm not so sure. There's something twisted going on up there and we all know it, but I'm starting to think a lot of it was only my imagination working overtime. Wanting so badly to justify my time and efforts. Everything that's happened could be coincidence. Intertwined karmic destinies unfolding with no real connection except that they took place near the same small town in the same year. Stuff like that must happen all the time."

"What about the threats and the break-in here and the sweet little note?" Burton said.

"Could be just slightly hinky guys trying to protect their petty scams and indiscretions," I said. "Making money the taxman doesn't see can make a lot of people skittish."

"You really believe that?" Tormoen said. "Or did that note scare you?"

"To some extent," I said.

"To some extent, what?" Tormoen said.

"I really believe what I said, to some extent. And, to some extent, the note scared me. It's not an easy thing for me to deal with, having my home violated. I never figured for this kind of thing when I started with the P.I. gig. I thought it was gonna be a bunch of routine, easy shit like tailing cheating spouses or hunting down witnesses to traffic accidents. The kind of stuff Rockin' Rick sends my way—which, quite frankly, is a lot easier to deal with than this shit."

"So you're content with self-pity?" Tormoen said.

Dan and Tommy looked down at the polished wood floor.

"Not really," I said. "But that's all I can afford right now, emotionally or financially."

"Carter Brown, the sensitive private eye," Tormoen said mockingly.

"Fuck you," I said. "I didn't have to spend any time or money on this. Hunting down Rose's killer was my idea. And my fucking money. You were just along for the ride so don't get holy on me."

"You mean you actually believe Talbot killed himself?" Tormoen said. "I find it hard to accept that he was out there, alone on that boat—let alone he dragged himself overboard in a fit of despair."

"I don't know what I believe. The cops are working on all that. Daugherty's not incompetent."

"The Sacowskis run the town—and he's not incompetent?" Tormoen said, voice rising.

"You wanna go up there and hang out and see what you find?" I said.

"That'd be like trying to break ice with a sewing needle," Torm said. "And besides, I'm doing *Moon* for the next six weeks."

"You've made my point for me. I think we should wait. See if anything turns on the animal-parts scam. Doing nothing has often worked for me. But I've got no intention of giving up. If there's actually anything to give up on that is. I guess I have no feel whatsoever for this case anymore. As far as I see it, waiting is the only tactic. They say good things come to those who wait."

"Tom Petty said waiting is the hardest part," Tormoen said.

"Who wants a beer?" Tommy said.

And so, wait I did.

New Year's went by and the weather stayed cold. Streets and sidewalks were coated with an inch of jagged ice and Duluth was as close to winter hell as it gets. I'd been counting on a stream of jobs from Lawyer Rick to get me through the season. But a week into January, Jan informed me her hubby had sent word that I needed an actual P.I. license or no more work would come my way. Then a few days later the douchebag appointed Jan as his primary investigator, even sent over a notarized letter to that effect. Cases would now go through her until I got my certification. Goes to show you can never trust a lawyer.

Could things get any better?

It depends on how you define better.

I put my nose to the grindstone, my shoulder to the wheel, my eye to the keyhole and all those other good clichés. I started the process of getting the license. The Taconite Bay fiasco faded into the background, only surfacing in dreams or moments of fatigue.

One of these dreams found me on a commercial fishing boat on Lake Superior, working the nets with Rose Talbot. We were both wearing jeans and red and black wool shirts with the sleeves rolled up. The sun sparkled off the blue water and glinted off the sides of the whitefish and herring we pulled from the nets. We looked at each other and smiled. At the sound of an approaching motorboat, I turned away from her smile.

Coming at us fast from out of nowhere was a huge white gunboat, Great-White-North versions of Somali pirates on the deck brandishing automatic weapons.

The Sacowskis.

I heard a splash behind me and turned to find that Rose had somehow gone over the side and was sinking without struggle into the dark depths of the shimmering lake. I reached for her but caught only a handful of icy water. I watched helplessly as she sank slowly, tantalizingly downward, her hands reaching out to me, her face hauntingly beautiful.

Filled with despair, I turned around in time to see the gigantic boat on a ram course, closing in. The murderous Sacowskis were pointing their weapons and raving from the flying bridge, horrific faces engorged with evil pleasure as they braced for the impact.

I woke up with my heart hammering in my chest.

Was this some kind of message from my subconscious? And if it was, did that make it somehow prescient? It was only my subconscious after all, and I don't know everything there is to know. Or are dreams a conduit to a higher intelligence? I had no answers. That was the way my head was working. Spiking my vexation meter. Blame it on winter. Not enough vitamin D. No sunlight. Blame it on the moon.

I was left to consider these and other questions as the dead of winter crawled in like an unwanted pet.

* * *

It was somewhere near the end of January when Sheriff Daugherty called to say he'd made some inquiries on the trafficking in illegal animal parts. The U.S. Department of Fish and Wildlife had confirmed that there was likely a flow of banned meat at the Grand Portage border crossing and promised to follow up on any leads they got. The sheriff also said that Jim Sacowski had apparently come into some money, as he had recently opened a nicely appointed sign painting shop a few miles north of Taconite Bay. Evidently the business did the occasional job across the border in Canada, which could provide a possible cover for a smuggling operation. Daugherty reiterated that no life insurance policy had been written for Billy Talbot. The pre-existing condition of being a paraplegic with spinal damage had evidently disqualified him for coverage.

Another dead end.

I thanked the sheriff for the call and the scuttlebutt and was left with a hollow feeling. Something wasn't right. The new information only added to my confusion. Faced with this jungle of images, feelings, facts and fantasy, my first instinct was ESCAPE. Into alcohol, food, drugs—or what have you. But I'd been through all those things before and they no longer worked for me. So it didn't take long for reality to jump on me like a diseased gargoyle, claws tearing my chest.

Jan running the show at the office had gotten real old, real fast. I was doing the grunt work and she was filing all the papers as the lead investigator. So what choice did I have but splitting the fees with her? This arrangement kept my income slightly above the poverty level and me generally confined to the back rooms at the office. The girls at the Savannah Club were probably pining away for me. I'm sure they suffered in silence.

A welcome relief from the cold arrived when a late January thaw slid in. The sidewalks finally got clear enough of ice to walk on. The office was becoming more and more claustrophobic so

I took full advantage of the break in the weather and added the afternoon stroll to my list of daily activities.

I hardly saw Tormoen or Burton or Tommy Basilio. I felt their absence like a nagging case of lumbago. One day at a time was the watchword but spring was really what I craved. This, of course, made everything all the worse.

Part Two

Into the forest primeval.
Or chip, chip away at whatever ails you.

Chapter

15

I think I know why they call it the dead of winter. The sky gets cemetery gray and it's hard to tell day from night. The snow and ice muffle sound and the outdoor world becomes eerily quiet, only the squawk of the occasional crow, if you're lucky, to break the grave-like silence.

I felt dead inside. Only feeling slightly alive when I was outside walking and the icy wind was slapping my face. Our early-winter warmth had at least kept the lake from freezing all the way across. Having open water in winter is a small blessing, even appreciated by several flocks of ducks I'd seen floating in the calm shoreline pockets. Why haven't these ducks flown south, I wondered? Did they know something I didn't? Had the recession cut into their travel budget?

By mid-February I had a vicious case of cabin fever. Some may think the whole idea of cabin fever is an overblown cliché, but for me, it's quite real. An oppressive physical feeling accompanied by a listless mind and an intense longing for something unobtainable were my status quo. My financial situation didn't allow room for an escape to southern comforts so I had to bite the bullet and grind it out. One of those years when you're forced to find comfort in the fact that your income is low enough to qualify for a large tax refund.

And so it was, that I went to lunch at the Savannah Club on the day my refund check came through the mail slot at the office. I remember it well, because it was February fourteenth, St. Valentine's delight, the magic day for lovers.

Turns out the proprietors of the Savannah were throwing a special Valentine's Day party featuring new dancers. It was this unexpected scenario I walked in on, behind the best mood I'd carried for quite a while. Of course I was going to buy a few drinks for fellow patrons and have a couple myself. Wouldn't you?

I devoured a halfway decent steak sandwich, drank two Heinekens, checked out the new dancers and shot the shit with some of the familiar habitués. They confessed to thinking my prolonged absence from their midst was the result of "taking the cure" or "going on the wagon." I assured them this was not the case. Only an extended bout of the recession blues had kept me from my old habits.

I ended up taking a long lunch and stuffing a few bills in a g-string or two, you know, just to kind of welcome the new girls, and generally had enough cheap thrills to keep me in a decent mood. Walking back to the office, I thought I detected spring in the air, a certain promising freshness you could smell. The sun was bright and the snow was melting, running in the gutters. Brought me back to the great feeling I would get as a kid coming home from school when the winter sun was finally warm enough to melt snow and send it trickling down the streets.

Maybe things were turning around.

I climbed the stairs to my office with renewed confidence. Even Jan acting self-important and pissy wasn't going to get to me today. I went through the door and discovered her standing hands on hips with an unconvincing sternness in her eyes.

I had a hard time suppressing a smirk. A little must've shown through though, because her cheeks grew a light red. But I didn't care, having noticed the beautiful woman in the client's chair in front of my desk.

The newcomer was wearing a tight green dress and black stockings above black leather over-the-calf boots. She had beautiful dark-brown hair and an outstanding figure the clothes showed off nicely. A life-affirming sort of beauty radiated from her. Or maybe it was just the buzz I was carrying.

She turned to face me and the first thing that popped into my head was Claudine Longet.

If you've never heard of Claudine Longet, you're probably under fifty. And you're missing a fascinating piece of pop culture. A beautiful French singer and actress, Claudine gave life and meaning to the term woman-child. I first saw her on a television series called Run For Your Life, starring Ben Gazarra as a man with a terminal illness and only a certain amount of time left in which to chase after life. Claudine, more than likely playing a role close to herself, nailed the part of Gazarra's heartbreakingly unstable true love. A portrayal that still haunts me to this day.

Unfortunately, the thing Claudine is most remembered for is the act of shooting and killing her lover, ski racer Vladimir "Spider" Sabich, in a fit of jealous rage one night in the Aspen, Colorado home the lovers shared.

All this went through my head as I walked towards my desk looking at this beautiful woman standing and extending her hand. I took her soft, smooth white hand in mine and recalled that Claudine had only received thirty days in the Aspen jail for killing Spider, eventually being convicted on the ridiculous charge of reckless endangerment. Three bullet holes certainly constituted endangerment. And also, unbelievably, she was allowed to decorate the interior of her jail cell and actually choose the days on which she would serve out her sentence, eventually settling on the weekends. We've all heard of "weekend warriors," but "weekend jailbird" inches beyond the pale.

During the trial, Hollywood showbiz types had descended on Aspen, en masse, to show their support, including her former husband, "Moon River" singer Andy Williams. But in the end, we all knew it was the spell of Claudine's beauty and charm that had let her walk free. Judge, jury, prosecutorial staff—all were bewitched by her considerable endowments. At least the men. And walk free Claudine did, departing Aspen in the company of her then-married lawyer, whom she eventually wed. Surprisingly, they have stayed together to the present day. Although any thinking person (and anyone close to Spider Sabich) knew the verdict stunk like dead fish in the sun, I'd always looked upon this virtuoso bit of manipulation with a certain amount of awe and curiosity as to the depth of her powers.

"This is Rose Talbot's sister, Lily Engwar," Jan said with an edge of authority that popped my reverie like an old balloon. "She wants to hire you."

So here was the sister I had heard about. "Pleased to meet you Ms. Engwar," gazing into the deep brown of her eyes. Feeling my knees getting weak, I reluctantly released her hand and went around the desk to my chair.

"What is it you want me to do for you?" I said, trying to reel in my composure. I was ready to please.

Lily shared a similarity of features to her sister Rose. But where the curve of Rose's lips, the line of her eyebrow or the width of shoulders might have indicated strength or toughness or the slightest hint of something outdoorsy and rugged, little sister was all sensuality, softness and beauty.

Lily sat back and pressed her dress down with her hands, her bottomless eyes not revealing any opinion of me, something I found myself searching for.

"I'd like you to continue your investigation into my sister's death," she said. "I heard that you've quit the case."

"In my experience, Ms. Engwar, the word on the street is often inaccurate. In this case, I don't think 'quit' is the proper terminology. Taken a sabbatical is more like it."

"I have a checkbook that hopefully will end your sabbatical, Mr. Brown." She crossed her legs, revealing as much shapely thigh as a starlet on Letterman, then lifted a dark green, suede purse from the floor.

Like the fat kid with the chocolate jones in Willy Wonka, I was ready to jump into the warm mass of sweetness gently swirling across the desk from me. Jump right in headfirst with no hesitation. If her little finger wanted me wrapped around it, we should get busy.

"I'm sure we can work something out," I said, trying to act professional. "But tell me, why do you think there's something more to investigate? Sheriff Daugherty believes Rose's death could've been an accident—or even suicide. And truthfully, I haven't found anything to prove differently."

"Daugherty's brain is being poisoned by a backlog of stored ignorance and countless layers of self-justification. Rose had over fifty thousand dollars in cash that vanished into the ozone. I think there's significance in that, don't you?"

"Yes, and I appreciate your candor. But did you ever actually see this money?"

"Not actually." The businesslike mask collapsed for just a flicker and I caught a glimpse of the young girl behind it. "But Rose told me about it. She wasn't one to lie. We were very close. I spent a lot of time up there with her in the summers."

"Did she by any chance tell you what she was planning to do with all that cash?"

"She wanted to bolt. Get away from Billy and Taconite Bay and our parents' influence. The three prongs of the devil's fork, she called them. But then something happened to change her plans. And I think, because of that, the cash ended up in the greasy paws of the Sacowski brothers."

"Something happened, you say?"

"One of the Sacowski boys had come into possession of something Rose wanted badly to acquire. Now Rose is dead, the money is gone and the property is still out there somewhere. That enough for you?"

"May I ask what the property was?"

She uncrossed her legs, brushed a strand of hair from her face, set the purse in her lap and sat up straight in the chair. She looked me directly in the eye with a no-bullshit expression before glancing briefly in Jan's direction.

"I'm going to speak frankly, Mr. Brown, in order to move this discussion along. Telling the truth is part of my therapy. You see, I'm a recovering sex addict, six weeks out of rehab."

Out of the corner of my eye, I saw Jan's head jerk just a tick. I ignored my rising heart rate and kept my gaze on Lily as she looked at me with sincerity and a sort of beatific indifference that I found irresistible.

"What Rose was trying to buy was a remnant from my sordid past, if you will. Sordid—yes indeedy. But at times, a hell of a lot of fun, I have to admit." A streak of pink appeared on her cheek like a forgotten tearstain and then disappeared. "But those days are behind me now. I'm engaged to a successful, rather high profile man. A man who would be ripe picking for any number of scams or extortions the Sacowski family could think of. Not to mention the fire and brimstone my father would raise if he found out. My father, you see, gets his moral guidelines from a rather old-school set of values and religious beliefs."

"Uh-huh." Sounded to me like the old compromising-photo-of-the-future-socialite gambit. A staple of old-time detective fiction. "And this item in question is exactly what?"

"A sex video—Rose and I with various partners. From last summer. Big party over the Fourth of July. A lot of coke and all the booze you could drink. By four in the morning I was a little over the top, I'm afraid, doing my Jenna Jameson bit."

I felt a tingle between my legs and tried not to visualize her Jenna Jameson bit. "That's what I was afraid of," I said.

"What, exactly, were you afraid of?"

"Fate. How do we know that no copies have been made? By now, it could be a big hit on the Internet."

"My plans could be ruined, if that were the case. But then it would no longer have any value as blackmail. Jim Sacowski knows that, he's no dummy. A first-class asshole—but not dumb. He's on the video, by the way."

"I guess I'm assuming you want me to get the original back. Along with some kind of guarantee no copies have been made. I'll have to think about what that might be."

"It's not exactly necessary to get the original back. Although we'd like it back, legal assurance that it won't be released commercially or on the Internet or shared in any way might suffice. My fiancé knows about my past to some extent. We met at a swingers' party—so—we've both put the past behind us and would like it to stay there. That's all. If something else should happen to any of the Sacowski boys, like somehow they all come down with cancer or are struck by a series of hunting accidents—that would be frosting on the cake. Whatever needs to be done, we are willing to pay for." She started to unzip her bag. "I can assure you there are plenty of digits in my checking account balance. If you can put someone away for murdering my sister, all the better. If I have to settle for just the signed statement, I'll try and accept it. I've had my lawyer draw up a sufficient document. My fiancé and I are willing to pay up to ten thousand dollars for the agreement, but hoped you could convince them to settle for less."

I wasn't exactly sure of what kind of deal she was proposing. It seemed there was a lot between the lines. Some of her statements were ambiguous at best. But the way she delivered them and the way she looked—of course I was going to say yes.

"I can certainly give it my best effort, Ms. Engwar."

"Call me Lily. That would be very appreciated, I can assure you, Mr. Brown."

"Call me Carter."

The sharp slam of a desk drawer turned our heads to the reception area. I watched Jan jerk up from her chair and knife across the floor to the file cabinet, her back to us and her neck stiff. In the days when we were married, she often expressed her displeasure with me in a similar fashion, by banging pans together with an extra loudness as she put them away or snapping the cupboard doors shut with a sound like the crack of a rifle.

Lily re-crossed her legs and her dress hiked up even higher than before.

"And what would your fee be for such an enterprise, Carter?"

Something came over me. "It's negotiable, I suppose, Lily. Maybe we should grab a coffee or a drink or something and discuss it." I looked at my watch. "I can see it's past normal office hours—maybe it's time for a little relaxation."

Her face momentarily brightened and then the mask snapped back on. She started to say something when a drawer in the metal file cabinet banged shut with a sound like a truck hitting a bridge abutment.

"I have our standard contract, Ms. Engwar, you should examine it," Jan said, an edge in her voice like a Nazi gym teacher. "Carter is always joking about not working after four o'clock but he knows if he didn't, he'd be out on the street carrying a *Will shirk for food* sign."

I felt a hole pop open in my head and wistfulness come pouring in to fill it. "My faithful secretary—there she is," I said. "Keeping me on task. But Jan is always right. We should do what she says or face the inevitable consequences."

Lily looked like she'd just been released from a chokehold.

Jan brought over the contract and Lily scanned it like it was a Chinese menu. "This seems fine," she said. "But I'm still going to write you a check for five thousand. Think of it as my economic stimulus plan."

Jan walked away and I thought I heard her mumble, "That's not the kind of stimulus he's interested in." But I couldn't be sure, because she always could convincingly disguise her meaningful mumbles.

That little streak of pink appeared on Lily Engwar's cheek again.

Chapter

16

One of the Savannah's new dancers, a blond with oversized blue eyes and undersized everything else, was twisting and gyrating on the stripper pole. She looked a little loaded. I wondered what the market price for a sex video of her might be.

A dollar-three-eighty-nine, said the voice in my head.

I ordered another Heineken from Mabel the orange-haired senior citizen and special-events bartender. They say she once owned the joint but now only comes in on holidays and the like to work the bar, allegedly for old-time's sake.

Lily Engwar wanted the job completed before April fifteenth. That was the only stipulation on my contract. She was getting married near the end of August and wanted everything signed, sealed and delivered before the wedding announcements hit the newspapers and the Internet. Facebook and Twitter, too, no doubt.

I had two months to put it together or lose my chance at a five grand bonus. I was authorized to pay as high as ten grand for the original copy in combination with the signed statement, less for just the document.

Somebody had a lot of money.

Things were starting to come clear in my head. My motivation to find the truth about Rose Talbot's death was rejuvenated. It seemed like some higher power wouldn't let me off the hook. Every time I'd thought I was done with the case, something came along to pull me back in. Here was this Lily person with her raw unapologetic story and big bank balance, sucking me back in for what felt like the final run.

Lily didn't actually hire me to investigate her sister's death, but she did imply that I should reopen my investigation. She had provided me with funding, and a reason to be in the area. She also implied—the way I was reading it, anyway— that I could kill one or more of the Sacowski family and it would be all right with her. I knew what Jan would say: *Do the job you're hired for and get out.* But somehow that would be leaving too much on the platter. Too many opportunities that could haunt me later if I didn't take them.

Mabel brought my Heineken and a toothy red-lipstick smile. Her perfume hit me like a tsunami of lavender. "There you go, private eye," she said, giving her blue-lidded eyes a half roll.

I pulled some bills from my pocket and put them on the bar and looked at the sweating green bottle in front of me. Truly a work of art. Did Warhol ever do a Heineken bottle? If he didn't, he should have.

I picked up the art and took a swallow of the gold inside and watched Dan Burton stride into the club. I'd asked him to meet me here to go over his new assignment. I was sending him back to Taconite Bay as a scout. Every successful military mission throughout history has had scouts or spies. In wartime, it is customary for the military to execute enemy soldiers captured behind the lines and out of uniform, considering them spies. Both sides use spies, but in the rules of war, spying is still considered bad form and deserving of death. One might justifiably wonder if the ever-present act of spying should be considered worse than its context—the ultimate expression of bad form known as war. But since when has anything about war made sense?

I didn't think Dan would face the same fate as wartime spies. I was a little worried, though, if I cared to think deeply about it—which I didn't—as I'd heard a lot of stories while making the rounds of the North Shore bars, including one exceptionally colorful tale concerning the brothers Sac and a local DNR officer.

This incident had allegedly taken place a few years back, when, as usual, times were tough on the northern shore of Lake Superior. The taconite plant was limping along at one-third capacity and not much else was shaking except sporadic construction gigs and hit-and-miss logging jobs. Poaching of wild game and fish was a way of life for many, just to keep food on the table. And it's a safe bet that not an ounce of the illegally procured protein ever went to waste.

One day a local DNR agent got an anonymous tip concerning a pile of nicely dressed-out, out-of-season moose meat waiting to be picked up at a certain spot in the woods. All that the agent needed to do, was stakeout the area until the eventual pick-up transpired and then swoop in and make the arrest.

The DNR guy put in the time and made the bust. But it turns out the arrestee was a friend and associate of the Sacowski boys. A short time thereafter, the story goes, the same DNR officer was out answering a call about a dead moose in an off highway drainage ditch when he was accosted by unidentified assailants and dragged deep into the woods. Within the darkness of the forest, he was stripped naked, staked to the ground and left there. By the time his fellow DNR employees found him, he had severe frostbite in some very sensitive areas, as well as an overwhelming desire to move to Minneapolis—which he soon did.

The more I thought about it, it did seem possible something like that could happen to Burton. But he was a big fellow and could take care of himself, I concluded. And now that I'd paid for his right-to-carry permit he could legally have a firearm on his person. And he needed the work. And if it came down to frozen privates, better him than me.

Tormoen was still interpreting Eugene O'Neill at a local theater and getting rave reviews. He was also spending a lot of time in the saloons after rehearsals and performances. Or so I'd heard, having personally stayed away from drinking establishments since the holidays.

Clearly, Burton was the right man for the job. He'd kept a lower profile in the Taconite Bay area than Jeff and I, and his previously mentioned lack of prominent features helped him blend in. Besides that, I knew he needed the money.

I regretted not getting Lily's check to the bank before close, because Dan was looking pretty lean and hungry as he approached. I would've liked to cut him a check but couldn't afford any more overdrafts.

"Dan the Man," I said as he sat down across from me and gave a cursory look at the big-eyed blond dancer on stage. "Ready to go back up to Taconite Bay and kick some ass?"

"I don't know about the ass-kicking part but I'm willing to go up there and pry around some more, if you need me to."

"And indeed I do, Burto, indeed I do. Now I've got direction. And money. Like I told you on the phone, Rose's little sister wrote me a 5K check for starter money."

"She wants you to find Rose's killer? Why'd she wait so long?"

"It's more of a personal stake for her. That's what this gig is about. The little tart was videotaped doing some improvisational acting. Role-playing, if you will. And the role she was playing was porn star. Now she's getting married to some future senator or some shit and wants assurances the performance won't come back to haunt them."

"We're supposed to get the video back?"

"If we can. But more importantly, she wants a legal document stating that the thing will never be released to the public. All I have to do is get the involved parties to sign it."

"Somebody's actually going to sign something like that? Do we know these people?"

"You could say that we've met."

"Would the name be Sacowski?"

"Well, yeah. But I'm not totally sure who has the thing. Lily Engwar seems sure it's Jim Sacowski, but it could be anywhere by now. That's part of the reason you're going in ahead of me, to root around and see what you can dig up. See if anyone's seen the tape or DVD or whatever it is. See if there are any copies floating around. There's got to be some gossip. You'll be acting as an official representative of Brown Investigations, but I don't want anyone up there to know that. You have to make it seem like you're on your own."

"You get your P.I. license yet?"

"Sometime soon."

Maybe I should've told him my license application was stalled. And I suppose I should've mentioned that you had to post a ten grand surety bond to get a P. I. license in Minnesota and I didn't have the wherewithal. Besides that, you needed a ridiculous amount of training hours. And if you had employees, worse yet, employees that carried firearms, the training requirements and fees shot up like my blood pressure on the day I read the requirements. I did intend to wade through it all one day, so I wasn't really lying to Burton. It hinges on your definition of the word soon. Dan must have known he'd be working as a free agent. I mean, he knew me, didn't he?

Chapter

17

The belly of the beast wasn't half bad. Did seem kind of forced and artificial in some ways but the new wood smelled like the outdoors and it was clean and the lake views were spectacular.

Sky Blue Waters Lodge.

I hadn't planned on staying here. My original mindset involved a cheap motel somewhere out on the highway like the North Star Inn, north of Schroeder, where Burton was encamped. I'd actually been enjoying the drive when I caught sight of the big lodge. Something unseen made me turn in. I went in the office and discovered they'd had a cancellation. It seemed like fate. Even more fateful, I was in the rarefied state of actually having enough money for a place like this.

I was leaning over a gin and tonic and brooding about having to play second fiddle to Jan in my own office. At least out here in the field I was number one. The field, this time, being a square oak bar table overlooking bluer-than-blue Lake Superior. Not a trace of ice to be seen. The way the sun was making diamonds on the endless water, you'd swear you were someplace tropical—if you didn't know the temperature was in the forties outside.

Burton had already been in the area for seven days. A flick of apprehension danced on the edge of my mind when I thought of him. He'd sent several texts his first few days out, ranging from vague to unintelligible, before becoming repetitive. A lot of the same names and basically the same old crapola. Then everything stopped altogether. No texts, no calls, no postcards or email.

As to my other soldiers, I'd run into Tormoen in the sauna at the health center about a week back. He was sweating out a drunk and I was coming off a swim in the pool. Torm expressed his regrets at not being able to join in "the final push for truth," as he called it. His excuse: Moon for the Misbegotten was now entered in a regional competition, which necessitated his being occupied for at least another month and possibly longer, if it achieved any success in the competition.

Tommy Basilio was still pulling his weight, digging out data from the information highway. "The Internet is like a giant invisible pickpocket," he said to me one day, "able to reach out and pick your informational pocket from miles away."

Acting on an unshakable flyspeck of apprehension growing in my solar plexus as the sun sank in the West, I pulled out my phone and sent a text and a voice mail to Burton. One drink later, I had not received a reply. Lack of communication in the Communication Age fed my growing anxiety. I'd expected Dan to meet me in the bar at four-thirty and it was now approaching four forty-five. Not exceptionally late, but definitely not Dan's usual, punctual self.

In his sobriety era, such as it was; he was always on time. Back in his days of swine and hosers, he was always late. When on the sauce, he very seldom returned calls or called in advance of his arrival. Sober, he did those things consistently.

Maybe that's what it was. He'd fallen off the wagon. Isn't that what everybody thinks when a former drunk disappears? In this part of the world it would certainly seem easy enough to do. Easy as falling off a snowbank. *Were the AA meetings up here not satisfying? Were there even any meetings to go to, booze being such a big part of the culture?*

All this worrying made me want a drink. I looked up from my empty glass and searched for a server. Instead, I saw a familiar face coming through the archway.

She scanned the room. She seemed thinner—maybe a few more lines in her face and a little the worse for wear. The softness behind her angular features was fading. Gloria was the type of blond you once might have called brassy. Now there was tarnish on the brass and a fleck of crazy light camped on the edge of her eyes. Her bird's-egg-blue silken jacket with the words *Neon Lion* on the back was torn on the left sleeve and had smudges on the front. Her blue denim shirt fell out over white jeans that fit like the skin of a Polish sausage.

She recognized me and came over, showing a worried look as she sat down across from me at the table.

"Buy a girl a drink, Mr. Brown? I've got some bad news for ya. Your friend Dan is in the hospital."

"Hospital? Jesus. What hospital? What happened to him?"

"Sac brothers pounded on him."

"Is he all right?"

"Says it only hurts when he laughs."

"You've seen him then?"

"No, we communicate telepathically."

"No need for sarcasm. Where the hell is he?"

"I can take you. But first I need a drink. He's about ready to be released, so a few minutes won't do him any harm."

I wasn't sure about her logic. But then a waitress appeared and I gave in and ordered drinks. Gloria had a Jack Daniels straight up and I got a shot of Finlandia vodka. I don't know why.

The hospital was a fading, yellow-brick building located on a state road north of Taconite Bay. I steered the Subaru off the highway and down a small incline, the scent of Gloria's overripe perfume stinging the back of my nose. I took a spot among the parked cars and sent her inside the building. I never go inside hospitals if I can possibly avoid it. The walls start to close in on me and I can't shake the thought that if you aren't sick when you go in, you will be before you leave. Good things rarely happen when you're sitting inside a hospital. Someone's either sick, injured or dying and you can't do much about it. The only good part is when someone gets released. I could wait in the car for that.

On the drive over, a subdued Gloria had informed me that, among numerous traumas, Burton had received a broken nose, a fractured eye socket, a few busted ribs and a severely damaged knee. Three large men wearing snowmobile suits and ski masks had jumped him in the parking lot of his motel and proceeded to wail on him with axe handles. Fortunately for Dan, the motel manager came out to investigate the noise, thus saving Burton from possible death or permanent brain damage. Once interrupted, the three unidentified assailants had jumped on ATVs and disappeared into the woods. The manager said the perpetrators wore masks and it was too dark to get a plate number off the machines—or so Gloria told me.

Burton, as he lay there bleeding, had allegedly talked the motel guy out of calling the sheriff. Dan didn't seem to have much faith in local law enforcement in spite of my assurances of Daugherty's cooperation. Go figure.

The motel manager had taken Burton to the emergency room and agreed to watch over his truck and belongings while he was in the hospital. He even reduced the rate on the motel room. What a guy.

Gloria said she'd caught wind of the beating from the rumor mill, and as a result of that, paid Dan a visit. "Out of a sense of responsibility to Rose," she told me, nervously blowing cigarette smoke out the window.

I watched them coming out through the sliding doors of the hospital. Gloria walked crookedly behind the wheelchair while a rather large female nurse wheeled Burton along. I started up the

Subaru and drove over to the ramp. Dan looked like he'd inhaled some beach stones and they'd come to rest beneath his eyes. His knee was elevated in some kind of brace or cast and he didn't look all that happy to see me.

Gloria helped him into the back seat where he struggled to find room for his damaged left leg and his crutches. After a few grunts and groans he looked me in the eyes. "Another fine mess you've gotten me into, Brown," he said, with just enough humor in there to make me relax a little and feel a little less guilty. Maybe it was too easy for me.

"How ya doin', Dan Boy," I said, "Hear you've been fighting again."

"Not exactly fighting," he said with some difficulty, the slight slur of pain medication coating his words. "Mostly playing punching bag for your friends named Sacowski."

"You sure it was them? Gloria said your assailants were wearing masks."

"Come on man, goddamn it. Who the fuck else would it be, smelling like cigarettes, cheap beer and exhaust?"

"Just about everybody and anybody up here," I said.

"Fuck you. Three guys: one giant and two other muscular fucks. Told me I should mind my own business and proceeded to add some motivation."

"I guess it makes sense, but why didn't you call me? I've been worried about you for days."

"I called the office before I went in for surgery, but the machine wasn't on. After I came out, I was just too fucked up. Once I started getting better, I didn't want to be accused of whining or malingering, so I figured I'd wait until I got out. Besides that, my phone was damaged in the fight and I lost your cell phone number."

"Could be you need to rethink the underpinnings of your macho persona. Get in any good shots on those assholes?"

"A few. Not many."

Gloria climbed in the front seat and looked over at me, her face twisted up like a painted croissant.

I asked Burton if he recognized the voices of his attackers.

"One sounded like your gray-haired old buddy. The other one I heard was the successful Sacowski. Jim. Man Mountain didn't say anything at all. Probably thought he was being clever."

"What makes you think it was Jimmy Sac?"

"I'd just talked to him that day—out at his new shop. Voice was fresh in my mind."

"You paid him a visit?"

"I couldn't stop thinking about the senseless killing of those animals, just so a bunch of Chinese broads could look younger. I guess I lost it. Went over to the prick's store and told him I was going to see him punished for what he was doing to animals."

"What'd he have to say to that?"

"Said he didn't know what the fuck I was talking about. Look on his face said different. Then he told me to get out of his store or he'd call the cops. That made me laugh. I called him a coward and started to go for him but then this couple walked in and I left."

"Think that was wise, in retrospect?"

"Leaving?"

"Going there in the first place."

"In retrospect, no. At the time, it was worth it to see the look of fear cross his face."

"Ah, my good English lad," I said. "You can take the boy out of the bottle but you can't take the bottle out of the boy. You didn't, by any chance, ask him about the sex video, did you?"

"Nah," his eyes glassed over and moved downward. "I aready told you I lost it. The implications of that statement are obvious."

"And did you forget, then, the purpose of your visit?"

"Of course, asshole. Lay the fuck off, would you? I took a god-damn beating for your fucking investigation."

"Seems to me you volunteered for the job, this time around."

"Yeah, I did. But that doesn't make it hurt any less. Or give you an excuse to be an asshole."

"Sorry."

"What kind of pain pills did they give you?" Gloria said.

"Vicodin."

"I can get you oxies if you want them," she said.

I stared at her. Tried to give her my best outraged-Puritan stare. "Dan has what is called, by some, an addictive personality, Gloria. I don't think it's wise to—"

"I'm capable of speaking for myself, Carter, goddamn it. But, unfortunately, you're right. I think it was the Adderol that made me freak on Jimmy Sac like that. I'd been taking too many, I guess. Oxycodone might be good to have around, though, should the pain get any worse during the healing process. You know how it is when something's healing... there's a period you go through when everything hurts more than it did when the shit first happened."

"See how your mind works, man?" I said. "You're trying to convince yourself that you need stronger shit than the doctors gave you."

"Ain't that always the way it is?" Gloria said, putting a cigarette between her red lips.

"Can you not light that, please?" I said.

"The Great Oz has spoken," Burton said.

Gloria huffed and sneered and then her face went blank and she put the cig back in the pack like a kid responding to a parent. I looked at her, tried to get a read. "So Gloria," I said. "What do you know about an alleged sex video starring Rose's sister Lily?"

"Everybody in town has heard about it," she said. "I've never seen it, myself. Some people claim they have. Others claim to be in it. I heard Jim Sacowski has it."

"I have a client who wants to buy it back. This client is also financing a renewal of my investigation into Rose Talbot's murder."

Gloria, sinking into the car seat, said, "You met the sister then?"

In the rearview, I could see interest growing in Burton's sallow face. "I'm not at liberty to reveal the identity of my client," I said.

"I'll take that as a yes," she said. "Quite a number, that one."

I pulled the floor shift to D and drove out of the lot. "I'll take you back to your car," I said.

I dropped her by the Malibu before going to the North Star Inn. I paid Burton's bill and put his stuff in my car. His working days were over for a while. The motel manager said he could arrange for Dan's truck to be delivered to Duluth for a fee of fifty dollars, plus gas. I paid him, thanked him and headed down Highway 61. Burton quickly nodded off in the backseat. I brooded and fumed and planned my next move.

Chapter

18

It was after ten before I got back to Sky Blue Waters. I stepped out of the car and looked around, surveyed the shadowed areas of the parking lot for lingering thugs. I had a Yale padlock tied to a red bandana in the back pocket of my corduroys and a recently purchased eighteen-inch police-style flashlight in my left hand. Sighting no thugs, I hurried into the bar for a nightcap. The six other people in the room all stared at me. Must've been the flashlight. I settled down onto a heavy oak stool at the bar. An NBA game between the Celtics and The Heat was flashing on the flat screen on the wall.

No wonder the local hockey teams struggle to win games, I thought to myself, *they watch the NBA up here.* I ordered a Bacardi and grapefruit juice, my new health drink. I sipped and glanced up at the basketball game, knowing you had to wait for the middle of the fourth quarter before the overpaid ballers started giving maximum effort.

I'd been trying to formulate a plan. Nothing of substance had come my way. In the comfort of the bar, the alcohol was going to my legs but not pushing any creative buttons. I needed to get the sex video situation resolved or I wouldn't get paid. So that was priority one. The trick was getting the deal done while still being able to exact some revenge on the Sacs. The situation had become somewhat personal.

I got a second drink and let my mind drift. It drifted right up to the TV where former Minnesota Timberwolf Kevin Garnett was blocking a lay up attempt by Miami Heat superstar Duane Wade. Instantly bored, I got out my phone and searched for the home number of Jim Sacowski. Sometimes these douchebags have wives who don't know the dirty business hubby is up to and wouldn't tolerate it if they did. It was possible Jimmy Sac was more afraid of his old lady than he was of the sheriff's department. At least it was worth a try.

I found a listing and punched it out. The signal was there, and sure enough, a woman answered. "Is Jim there?" I said.

"Who should I say is calling, please?" the no-nonsense voice responded.

"This is Carter Brown."

"Honey, someone named Carter Brown is on the phone for you." She paused. "It's kind of late for a business call, don't you think, Mr. Brown?"

"I am sorry, but I'm afraid it couldn't wait."

I heard a cough and some mumbling in the background and then the rustling of the phone as it changed hands.

"Hello, who is this? Who's calling?"

"This is Carter Brown of Brown Investigations."

"The bogus detective that's been digging around in other people's business, right? What the hell you calling me for?" Sounded like he was biting down on rocks, his voice a scratchy hiss.

"I've a business proposition for you Jimmy. One that stands to put some cash in your pocket."

There was a long silence on his end. "Stay on the line, Brown," he said, "I'm gonna go somewhere where I can speak more freely." His voice moved away from the phone: "I'm gonna take this into the workshop, honey," his tones now oval and unstressed.

In a couple minutes he was back. About the length of time it would take to get on his cell phone and call his brothers, tell them I was in the area in need of a beating.

"You've got one minute to convince me you're not talking shit, Brown."

"What I'm proposing is a very simple, straight-forward deal, Jimmy. I have it on good authority that you are in the possession of a video that was made without the permission of the participants. Amateur porn—from what I hear. I have a client who's interested in paying cash money to make sure this video never meets the public eye. In exchange for written assurance, viable in a court of law, my client is willing to line your pockets with silver, Jimmy boy."

"I don't have this alleged video, Brown, but I may know who does. But I can't talk here. Come to my place of business tomorrow morning and I'll have more information for you. And just exactly what kind of money are we talking? I'd like to make it clear, you know, so I can tell the guy and get a feel for what he thinks about it."

"My client is prepared to pay five thousand dollars for the original copy together with a signed agreement to the terms I mentioned."

"The guy has to sign something saying he made the film? I don't know if he's gonna go for that."

"He needs to swear that he's in control of the vid and that it's the only copy and he hasn't exploited it commercially. What's the big deal? No laws were broken. All the participants were legal adults above the age of consent, I assume."

"Damn straight. Or so I heard."

"Then as long as there's been no reproduction, sales or distribution, there shouldn't be a problem. No threat of prosecution exists, Jimmy. No sweat, as the sauna haters say."

"Stop calling me Jimmy, you crazy fucking freak. Just because I'm doing business with you doesn't mean I like you or that you get a pass on all the shit you've pulled."

I started to say something about the shit he's pulled but the line went dead and the tone buzzed loud and hollow.

*   *   *

Sacowski's place of business was a boxy, wood and cinderblock building on the upper side of Highway 61, a few miles north of Taconite Bay. Fresh white paint and birds-egg blue trim at the roofline and around the windows radiated a crisp, efficient vibe. What had once been an antique or agate shop was now Border Country Guide Service and Sign Emporium, as the green letters on the large white placard at the mouth of the driveway had proclaimed. At the bottom of the sign it said Engraving done here, in fine gold script.

The sun was up over the lake and shining through my passenger window as I turned the Subaru onto the gravel driveway. A black pickup loomed large at the back of the building and a Dodge mini-van was nosed in perpendicular to the west wall. I parked next to the van and stepped out to an icy wind blowing off the lake, reminding me that winter wasn't quite ready to loosen its frigid grip on my balls.

As I was going through the front door, I heard the crunch of tires on gravel and turned to see a green and white sheriff's department SUV rolling into the parking lot. I acted like I didn't care and went inside to a clean, knotty pine room with fish and deer mounts on the walls. The right side was given over to a service counter with a long workbench behind it cluttered with assorted signs, painting and engraving tools and various accessories. The left side of the room contained a large oak desk holding stacks of brochures. Behind it, photos of smiling hunters and fishermen holding game and fish dotted the walls.

Jim Sacowski was standing behind the service counter showing engraving samples to an older couple. Jim had the family resemblance but his complexion was slightly darker than that of his two brothers. His hair was youthful and dark except for a smattering of gray at the temples. There were more wrinkles and creases on his face than I remembered from the blues bar. His chest was still big and broad.

He gave me a slight nod of acknowledgement and then went back to his demo cards. I walked over to the guide desk and picked up a glossy brochure titled *Backcountry Fishing Trips,* a picture of a grinning man holding a glittering gold walleye on the front. I leafed through the pamphlet and gazed out the side window at Deputy Atwood sitting nonchalantly in the SUV at the back of the lot.

I was going for a second brochure—*Lake Superior Trout and Salmon*—when the elderly man and his wife thanked Sacowski and exited via the front door. Sacowski was frowning as he patted together a small pile of cards and looked at me. Then his eyes went past me to the window.

"Bring your friend out there along with you?" he said accusingly.

"Dude just followed me in here. I can't seem to go anywhere around here without a police escort these days. And I don't think that kid likes me very much anyway."

"That one don't like very many around here, from what I've heard," Sacowski said. "You come here to talk business or what?"

"I came here to talk business. You able to locate the man with the video?"

"Come on in the backroom. We can talk there."

There were two knotty pine doors on the back wall. We went through the one on the right and came into an office area that filled the rear third of the building. There was a scuffed black metal desk cluttered with papers, catalogs, more brochures and a computer. A huge lake trout and a moose head looked glassily down at us from the wall and a couple of straight-backed wooden chairs sat in front of the desk. Rising up from one of them like a swamp grizzly was my favorite Sacowski.

The monster had a smile on his lips but his eyes had cold fire at the edges. He looked like he was going to say something but he just kept staring at me and smiling in that twisted way of his.

I got a bit uneasy.

"Relax, Brown," Jim Sacowski said smugly, going around to the back of the desk. "My brother is only here to insure that there's no trouble."

"Funny you should say that, Jimmy, because, coincidentally, that's why the deputy is out in the lot. All I have to do is punch redial on my phone here—" I pulled it from the pocket of my leather jacket and waved it at him. "And Deputy Atwood will come running to my aid. You see, James, Sheriff Daugherty and I are real good buddies now. We've been discussing ways of bringing you boys down, if you want to know. I think you and I have a lot we need to talk about."

Little Sac glowered.

Jim took a short breath and squinted at me. "I'm still going to have David check you for a wire," he said. "Dave…"

Like a dog on command, the behemoth lumbered close to me. I could smell stale coffee and poorly digested meat on his breath. His body odor reminded me of the coyote urine a friend of mine had once used to ward off deer from his marijuana plants. Those were the days.

Little Sac gazed down on me. For a second I thought he was going to throw me through a window. Instead, he said, "Lift up your shirt, little man."

"And I always thought I was too skinny for you, Dave-o. Maybe there's a future for us after all." His hands made fists as I lifted up my black fleece pullover and the gray T-shirt underneath. "See, boys, no wire."

Dave-o moved faster than I imagined he could. Before I knew it, his ham-like appendages were clapped around my right thigh and moving downward. He patted down one leg and up the other, not stopping until the side of his hand smacked me in the nuts just hard enough to make it difficult to talk or see or breathe.

"That's enough, David," Jim said. "You can go now. I'll handle it from here. Bring me the truck back at five."

Man Mountain mumbled and stumbled out the back door.

Trying to hide my discomfort, I eyed big Jim. He had on L.L. Bean khakis and a green chamois shirt. The great white hunter's face was tan with a big crease running down above the jaw line on both sides, pancakes for cheeks.

"Now that we can talk freely," I said, "what have you got to say? Are we going to do business? Get a hold of your friend?"

"I have the video in my possession. But this signed agreement shit sticks in my craw like a fishbone."

"I promised you there would to be no problems with the cops."

"As if your promise is supposed to mean something to me. And then you bring Sir Lancelot out there as a bodyguard and tell me you and Daugherty are working together to bring me and my brothers down?" He smiled bitterly and shook his head in disgust. "What kind of shit is that? Am I supposed to just grin and bear it? Enjoy your cleverness? It changes things, Brown. Makes me think twice about selling you the video. Give me some fucking credit, man. You may think I'm a backcountry bumpkin, but I didn't just fall off the turnip truck."

"My working in concert with the sheriff can be used to your advantage if you play it right," I said. "What if I told you Daugherty has known about your little animal parts smuggling thing for some time now. That he believes you're hooked up with one or more of the owners of Sky Blue Waters Lodge in the deal. They also know you're moving the shit across international borders. That kind of info, do you any good?"

Some of the color went out of his skin and his eyes momentarily lost confidence. He sat down in his chair and leaned back on the rear legs, fingers intertwined behind his head.

"How is that supposed to help me?"

I sat down in one of the chairs in front of the desk.

"Maybe it will keep you from—I don't know—getting caught? Seems to me if one knows he's being watched, he could change his habits in some significant way."

"Your man was in here the other day raving about exploiting animals and all that fag shit. Everybody and their fucking uncle know about this?"

"Pretty much. And you and your bros put my assistant in the hospital for his knowledge."

"We didn't have anything to do with that. Asshole must've been banging someone else's woman or something. Lot of jealous guys up here."

"Uh huh. And birds fly north for the winter. But that's neither here nor there to me. I suspect Burton will attempt to deal with the situation after his recuperation period is completed. My main concern is the video. In exchange for it and the signed agreement—let's say that in addition to the cash, I can provide you information as to what the cops are doing concerning your little side business. Last we talked, they were contemplating calling the feds in. But I think Daugherty now sees the chance for a big bust that could clean off some of the tarnish from the two recent unexplained deaths in his county. I think he's reluctant to bring in the feds if he can help it, wants all the glory for himself. One thing for damn sure, the good sheriff most certainly has a hard-on for you and yours."

He rocked forward in the chair and rested his forearms on the desktop. "Let's pretend I know what you're talking about, Brown," he said, his features growing feral. "Why wouldn't I just quit trafficking in illegal stuff, if what you say is true?"

"You could do that, I suppose. But I think you've gotten used to the income. Winter vacations, new businesses, new trucks,clothes… those boots you're wearing must've set you back at least three bills. Why give that up? Sell me the vid, sign the paper and I keep the sheriff off your ass. At least for as long as it takes me to find Rose Talbot's killer."

I watched for his reaction. He had none. He was staring at a spot on the desktop, rubbing his chin. His eyes were blank and cloudy like those of the creatures on the walls.

He looked up and his eyes softened, fake friendly. "Problem with the vid is that I didn't do the filming. I mean, I admit I was in it—quite prominently—but the camera was just set up in the room and running. And it wasn't even my camera or house."

"I'm aware it was a rented cabin and the camera belonged to Byron Barnes, but in this case, I believe possession is considered nine tenths of the law. We can have the lawyer fine tune the wording. Lawyers are good at that kind of thing. But the video has to be the only one of its kind. Any Internet leaks or copies coming out or things of that sort, and the deal is void. And you'll be liable for any cash received. So what do you say, should we set an appointment to get you your five K?"

"Only now it's going to cost you ten, asshole. Since I'm losing all that alleged income and everything, y'know. Speaking hypothetically, of course."

"Of course."

He was nibbling at the bait and about to swallow the hook. If I pulled it away from him, I might never get another chance.

"I'll have to see if the client will agree to that," I said with as much humility as I could muster. The prospect of losing five grand was hitting me like a punch to the solar plexus. "Why don't you give me your cell number and I'll get back to you on that. Unless you prefer I call you at home."

He made a face like he had a sour stomach, grabbed a pen from a white plastic mug with images of ducks on it, tore a slip of paper from a notepad and wrote down a number. He handed it across the desk, giving me the hard eye, like I, somehow, was the villain in this deal.

I took the paper and stood up without a word. He rose simultaneously, puffing out his chest and strutting past me like a big red rooster. Reminded me of myself trying to impress a good-looking woman.

We went into the front room. I stopped and lingered at the service counter, picked up a sheet of glossy paper displaying various engraving styles.

"You do all this fancy work?" I asked.

"Yeah," he said, giving me the fisheye.

"Where'd you pick up a skill like that?"

"I was a gifted child."

Chapter

19

The sheriff's department vehicle was gone by the time the lake breeze hit my face. Truth was, Deputy Atwood had followed me here on his own accord, having seen me roll by from his perch in the parking lot of the Superior Inn Motel just north of Taconite Bay. And if I had actually punched the redial on my cellular, the phone at the Chinese take-out place in Duluth's Plaza Shopping Center would've started ringing. But you've got to play to your strengths, and being that I didn't have any, I had to make shit up.

I drove back to the lodge. In spite of the nagging loss of five grand, I was feeling optimistic. At least I would get my fee. And if I was lucky, exact some revenge on the Sacs. Or justice. I wasn't sure which one I wanted. One thing I was sure of, Jimmy Sac was as greasy as cheap hair oil and about as trustworthy as a rabid skunk.

I'm sure he felt the same about me.

I went straight to the front desk at the lodge to see if I could extend my stay for one more night. The petite brunette informed me that management had comped the room. It seemed I was getting my first perk from the wrong side of the law. I'd been shotgunning when I accused Sacowski of complicity with the lodge owners, scattering shot in the hope of hitting something. The free room seemed to confirm that I had at least put a few pellets on target, as the tactics had switched from scaring me off to buying me off.

I confirmed I was staying another night. As I turned away from the desk, I saw the back of Gloria's head going out the front entrance. I'm no expert on body language, but the girl seemed like all the steam had gone out of her, like going outside was taking all she could muster.

I started toward the bar to use the phone. Had calls to make I didn't want a record of. I saw Barnes standing at the dining room entrance projecting a plastic smile. Our eyes met and he turned away.

The bar was empty of customers, the tender readying the place for the lunch crowd. I went to the payphone next to the coat racks and called Daugherty, filled him in. Then I dialed up Jan and instructed her to get in touch with Lily Engwar's legal counsel.

Communications completed, I went out to the Subaru, drove north through the forest to Zup's market in Ely, where I bought some smoked whitefish and a small box of soda crackers. I ate in my car in the parking lot of the Mesabi Hiking Trail. It was warmer here away from the lake and I put my window down.

After my extravagant lunch, I motored off to rendezvous with Daugherty at a wayside off Highway 2. Even with the nice weather, traffic was pretty light. We sat there and discussed things. Although he wasn't too happy with the liberties I'd taken, he agreed to go along with my plan. It was a good plan and he knew it.

Daugherty drove away. As the Creek County SUV faded into the distance, I put in a call to Jim Sacowski, told him the law was set to raid his house in a search for illegal animal parts. His voice went up an octave. I listened to him swallow and clear his throat and get his voice back down.

"How do you know this?" he snapped.

"Heard it from the horse's mouth," I said.

An informant had allegedly seen banned items in Jimmy Sac's house. At least this was what Daugherty told the judge responsible for the warrant. In this neck of the woods, merely the name Sacowski was often enough to convince local judges that a warrant was viable. Jim was well aware of that.

Daugherty knew it was risky. Knew there was a chance he wouldn't find anything. Knew he could end up taking a lot of gas. He was going out on a limb for my plan. I guess he was a gambling man. Or desperate. Or both.

I had my own way to play it.

Jimmy growled a few curse words. "Goddamn it, Brown, you better be right on this or I'll make you wish you'd never been born," he said.

"I often do already, Sacowski."

After he switched off, I took my time and enjoyed the sunshine. I came back into Taconite Bay from the north side and cruised through the small residential area until I found a spot a block away and slightly uphill from Jim Sacowski's dwelling. I parked and took my trusty binoculars out of the glove compartment. I watched. Nothing moved at the house.

Soon the red ball sun was kissing the tops of the pine trees.

Darkness seeped in and took over.

Shortly thereafter, an outside light blinked on above a side door of the modest white bungalow, putting a bright yellow circle on the blacktop driveway. About ten minutes later a ratty, camo-painted Bronco pulled in and stopped short of the light. I watched Big Sac and Little Sac exit the Bronco, walk through the yellow ring and enter the side door of the house. Then the light went out and the circle disappeared.

A few minutes later the door reopened. In the dim glow of the streetlights, I could see the brothers carrying what looked like plastic coolers of the type you'd use for camping or a picnic. They put them in the back of the Bronco, went back in the house and came out with two more. Then they drove away and I followed at a safe distance. All the way to Sky Blue Waters Lodge, where the Bronco rolled around back and out of my line of sight. Not wanting to be discovered, I gave up the surveillance, parked and went in the lodge to the bar.

I sat over a drink and ruminated. Ruminating was my thing.

I could assume the coolers contained contraband of some sort. Most likely bear paws, moose testes and other assorted animal organs and brain parts. Whatever it was the rich and decaying were buying these days.

I also assumed that bringing the contraband to the lodge meant someone here was involved in the racket, as I had previously guessed. That they didn't just destroy the stuff, probably meant the value was high enough to warrant taking a risk. And someone involved was smart enough to know that if the search of Sacowski's house came up empty, a separate warrant for a luxury hotel that was a major local business would have a very low chance of approval. Thus, the risk was a worthy one.

But now what were they going to do with the contents of those coolers?

I had another drink and then one more. I got my answer as I was going out to the car to get my phone. Glittering in the Management Only parking slot was a new-looking, black mini-van bearing Illinois plates.

I jumped in the Subaru, found my phone and texted the plate number of the van to Tommy Basilio. When I pressed Send, a feeling of foreboding passed through me like a bank of cold fog.

I went back inside the lodge. While ascending the stairs to my room I noticed Barnes and a dark-haired guy in a blue down jacket standing together near the entrance to the bar. Their eyes followed my direction but their heads stayed still.

Once inside the room, I turned on The Daily Show, hoping for a few laughs. All I got was a few smiles but that was good enough. My brain was going in circles but my stomach was set on dinner. Then the cell phone dinged on the bedside table. Tommy's text identified the van as a rental, recently leased to Christopher Enrico of Chicago, Illinois, owner of Chris's Shooters Emporium and likely relative of Richard Enrico, co-owner of Sky Blue Waters Lodge.

So we had a match. I made a mental note to think about giving Tommy more money when this thing was over and went downstairs to eat.

The broiled walleye in the Falling Waters dining room was mediocre. Instead of this frozen Canadian import, I should have ordered the lake trout or the whitefish, two fish that actually come fresh from Lake Superior. Fortunately for me, the booze they were serving was effective. Barnes and the guy I believed to be Enrico were nowhere to be seen.

I got a decent buzz on. Trying hard to celebrate because I'd made the deal for the sex video. I couldn't quite get to it. Something was tugging on me and I didn't know what.

My phone vibrated in my pants pocket. I took it out to discover a string of long and rambling texts from Dan Burton, the gist of which was that he had a lot of time on his hands and a lot of prescription opiate in his system. He was using the resultant creative energy to work on the puzzle of Rose Talbot's death. A lot of gibberish and random revenge fantasies followed. Occasional moments of lucidity brought the focus around to the security video from the Big Trail Casino on the night of Rose's fatal crash. Twice he wrote: U MUST VIEW SECURITY TAPE. LAST TIME ROSE WAS SEEN ALIVE.

It seemed he had a point. A twinge of anxiety hit me, followed by a brief sensation of being squeezed in a vice. I looked around the half-full dining room, hoping to change my head. The voices were as loud as a parade. I got up, left a ten-dollar tip, paid my bill at the cashier and walked foggily up the stairs. I was strangely fatigued and slightly feverish, like I was coming down with something.

I turned the television on in my room and lay down on the bed, thinking I could do some phone work. But the atmosphere had shifted or something, and I couldn't get a signal. Dead zone. I grabbed the TV remote and flipped through the channels. One of those reality-cop shows caught my eye. Normally I would flip on by, but this time I stopped and watched. Two cops in a cruiser were pulling over some poor slob with a broken taillight. The offender, of course, would inevitably be discovered in the possession of some form of illicit substance and carted off to the slammer, adding one more chapter of misery to the miscreant's pathos-ridden life story.

Thinking it was a sick world indeed; I switched off the TV, put my shoes back on and slipped quietly down the thick-carpeted hallway to the side exit. Once outside, I moved around the side of the building and stopped at the corner with a view of the management parking space. It was empty. I saw the black van in the shadows at the far side of the lot.

I went to the Subaru, climbed in the back seat, reached into the cargo area and pulled out my tool kit. I flipped the switch to keep the interior lights from going on and slid back outside. I crept around the edge of the lot and approached the black van from the rear. I crouched down with a Phillips screwdriver and removed the red plastic taillight cover, took a pliers and pinched the brake light bulb until it cracked, then replaced the cover. It was then I realized how cold it had become. It gets like that up here in late winter and what passes for early spring: clear skies lead to star-filled nights and the bottom drops out of the thermometer. I started to shiver and shake like a man on a Fuzzy Tree. Elvis had nothing on me.

I hurried back to the side entrance, used my key card in the door and slinked to my room with my skin feeling like frozen Melba Toast. My head was pounding as I collapsed on the bed. Ignoring the murmurings in my brain about semen residue on hotel bedclothes, I wrapped myself up in the spread. After a few minutes, I warmed enough to kick off my sneakers and crawl under the blanket. I tossed and turned and eventually fell asleep.

The next thing I remember, I was sitting at a long and narrow wooden table in a dark, Victorian-era room. In front of me was a large silver platter heaped with strange-looking cuts of steaming meat. Candles burned in heavy silver holders. Various brass and earthen pitchers held thick red wine. Bunches of grapes and assorted other fruits were stacked to overflow on several ornate silver platters. Rose Talbot was sitting to my right, dressed in a leather tunic and orange flowing scarves, an unearthly glow in her eyes. She smiled sweetly and offered me a crisply cooked hunk of meat steaming on the tines of a large silver fork. "Have some leopard gallbladder, Carter," she said, her eyes shining with lust and her mouth smeared with grease and meat juice. "It helps with the potency, you know."

I wanted to tell her that Viagra would do the same trick but instead, I leaned forward and allowed her to feed me. The meat tasted strange but not altogether unpleasant. Rose watched me curiously, with a hint of lust, as I chewed and swallowed. Feeling her gaze burning on me, I grabbed for a silver sugar bowl filled with coarsely ground yellowish powder, which somehow I knew was powdered rhino horn. I poured some in my wine goblet, took a large swill and looked around the room.

Jim Sacowski was sitting at the head of the table in a high-backed, throne-like chair made of wood and leather. His head and torso were tilted downward as if he was looking at the floor or on the verge of passing out. His eyes were slits. Gloria was to my left, stretched out on her back on a wooden bench dressed like Barbra Eden in *I Dream of Jeannie*. She was reaching her bare arm across the table with a hunting knife in her hand and offering meat skewered on the tip to Byron Barnes. He leaned in and savagely bit into the offering.

I turned away from them and discovered that the room was an old-time surgical theater, where observers could sit in the rising circular rows of wooden seats and watch the procedures, live and in living color.

Looking down upon us from a large opening in the ceiling, like the Greek gods at a tribunal, Sheriff Daugherty and Deputy Atwood held their hats in their hands and frowned disapprovingly. Across from them, at the other side of the hole, Little Sac and Big Sac leaned against a railing gripping large cigars and chatting with Barnes' three partners in Sky Blue Waters Lodge. Occasionally they would all gesture in my direction.

Those of us on display were then joined by strangers.

Rolling into the room on wheelchairs came skinny gray-skinned, white-haired old men and aging women wearing expensive clothes and excessive make-up. Close behind them, third-world leaders with epaulets on their military-style jackets marched in together with grizzled, snaggle-toothed, turbaned sheiks.

I tried to get up from my chair but couldn't move. The undigested meat knotted my gut. Nausea crawled up my throat. I searched frantically for a way out. Then I saw Tormoen walking confidently into the room with Jan hooked on one arm and Lily Engwar on the other, all three of them clad in garish, white fur coats.

"Hope were not late for the party," Tormoen said, "I'm sure looking forward to some braised wolf liver and a good bottle of Beaujolais." In response, the girls gazed up at him like he was a rock star and ground their crotches against his thighs.

My frustration was growing as Dan Burton appeared in a wheelchair beneath a red, glowing EXIT sign, a scolding but wasted look on his pale face. Sweat ran down my forehead like ice melting on a rooftop. Panic was coming on like a familiar enemy. At the far end of the table, Jimmy Sac looked up and shook his head from side to side. His short respectable hair had become long and greasy and flew out like Medusa's serpents as he rose from the throne.

"ARE WE HAVING FUN YET?" Jimmy roared, hunks of meat spewing from his twisted mouth. "ABOUT TIME WE ALL HAD SOME FUCKING FUN, DON'T YOU THINK, BROWN?"

All eyes turned on me. The glowing orbs were filled with expectation and demand and resentment. Sacowski began to pound his tankard on the table: Bang, bang, bang—rhythmically—growing louder with each downward stroke. I felt my legs kick and my hands flail, trying to push it all away.

My eyes popped open to the darkened hotel room. First thing I remember was the sound of a car door slamming from somewhere below me. I struggled weakly from the bed and went to the window in a confused haze. I peeled back a corner of the curtain and put my face to the glass.

Below on a narrow utility road, the thin amber glow of sodium-vapor lamps illuminated the black van backed up next to the hotel. I tried to rub the film from my eyes and focus. Best as I could tell, the van's engine wasn't running. There were no signs of movement. But there could've been someone inside that I couldn't see.

I let the curtain swing shut and looked at the bedside clock: 5:45 A.M. I flipped on the lamp on the wall above the bed and grabbed my cell phone, hoping that Sheriff Daugherty was awake enough to take my call. He had, after all, been busy at three A.M., raiding Jimmy Sac's abode. I punched out the numbers before I saw the no signal designation.

No bars, you hopeless bastard.

I went against my caution and dialed from the room phone. Daugherty picked up on the second ring, voice throaty with a hint of sinus congestion. I filled him in on the details. He assured me he'd have somebody waiting out on the road, as per our plan, which so far seemed to be working just fine.

As long as I had him on the line, I figured I might as well pump him for information. He beat me to the punch by offering that the raid on Sacowski's house hadn't turned up anything illegal. But he seemed cool with the possibility of heat from the media or any overpriced, big-city lawyer Sacowski might bring in. And if the deputies found any contraband in the Illinois van, we would be "in like Flynn." His words, not mine.

If I hadn't felt so shitty, I would've given myself a self-congratulatory pat on the back. Instead, I fell back on the bed and tried to burrow down into some much needed sleep.

But you know what they say about the best-laid plans of mice and men.

I did a toss and a turn or two and finally gave up on the chase for oblivion at 6:32 on the digital clock. I went into the shower and tried to steam my illness away.

By seven, gray light was creeping into the room. I pulled the curtain aside. The van was gone. Leafless trees and dark conifers stretching out in the muddled distance painted a desolate tableau. Loneliness clawed at my insides like a rabid lynx and I felt empty.

I dressed slowly and went downstairs to see how angry the hornets in the nest were getting.

Barnes was lingering in the restaurant, standing by the stainless-steel double doors to the kitchen, looking like he hadn't slept much. Seemed like he was always there when I came into a room. It appeared he'd grown extremely tired of my presence.

Would my room still be comped? I pondered this and took a table by the window.

Clouds had moved in. The sky was a pale gray, the lake a shade darker with whitecaps skidding across the roiling surface. On the shore, naked tree branches reached for the heavens, shaking and shimmying in the heavy wind as if trying to call spring back from the dead.

I stared out at the gloom and felt Barnes' gaze like two laser beams to the back of my head. Heaviness around the eyes and a burning in the sinuses gripped my face. The server plodded up to the table—a fifty-something woman with thinning dyed-brown, medium-length hair and plenty of midriff bulge.

I ordered steak and eggs and hash browns and hit the coffee like it was the secret to life. Last night's dream was still lingering.

I didn't know if I was hungry or just thought I should be. I was operating on the feed-a-cold-starve-a-fever belief system, hoping belief would win out.

The coffee provided momentary relief and cleared my head some. I was yawning and stretching my arms when the cashier, a tall, thin young man in a white shirt and black trousers, black hair like a horse brush, moved from behind his counter and came in my direction. At first I thought he was going to throw me the fuck out of there but instead he smiled politely.

"Are you Mr. Brown," he asked, softly.

I wondered how he knew my name but a quick survey of the dining room told me I was the only single male in there. Or maybe everybody in the goddamn hotel knew who I was and my life story, besides.

"Yes I am," I said, looking up into his soupy eyes.

"There's a phone call for you sir, at the front desk."

I didn't like the sound of that for some reason I couldn't quite discern.

"My food's about to come out," I said, my voice breaking in my scratchy throat and sounding like a whine.

"I can have the cook keep your breakfast warm while you're gone, sir. Or I can have the desk inform the caller that you're unavailable at the moment. Whatever you wish."

"I'll take the call," I said.

Behind the blond-wood front desk stood a businesslike, forty-ish woman. She pointed to a yellow phone on the end of the counter. I picked it up and said Hello.

"I've got some good news, Brown." I recognized Daugherty's tired baritone.

"That's nice to hear," I said. "Should we be celebrating?"

"Not quite yet. I need to meet with you. Can you get to that same roadside by one o'clock? I think our prisoner will be all settled in by then."

"That sounds promising. I'll check out of here and see you later."

He buzzed off and I set the receiver in its cradle. I turned back toward the dining room and caught sight of Barnes lingering in the hallway by the restrooms. He gave me the evil eye, turned and moved briskly in the direction of the swimming pool.

I returned to my table and the food followed close behind. I discovered after a few bites that I didn't have much of an appetite. The coffee was starting to churn up my stomach but I drank more anyway. I grew anxious and decided to leave. I left a five for a tip and paid my bill, giving the cashier a weak smile.

I went to the room and took a sizeable dump before throwing my things into a canvas carry bag. Caffeine was driving me onward like a team of acid-crazed horses and a little bird was telling me I better get the hell out of here while I still could.

As I tried to check out, the stern desk clerk informed me that I owed for a pay-per-view porn movie. I didn't remember ordering it, let alone watching. I attributed this to illness-onset delirium and paid the tab without much dissent. I didn't linger gracefully but strode quickly outside.

"Just like a rat," said the voice. "Scurrying away like the cowardly scum he is."

I turned toward the sound and discovered Barnes on the sidewalk behind me, looking like he'd already heard the bad news. "Excuse me," I said. "Do I know you?" I kept backing slowly in the direction of the car and watching for any sign of random thugs.

"I think you do," he said, coming closer, rubbing his right fist with the palm of the left hand. "I'm the guy who comped your room. I think you know a hell of a lot more than you let on."

"Like that you exploit foreign labor and rip them off like they're on a company farm?"

"Those kids love it here. Not one of them ever complained to the cops."

"Probably because they're afraid of getting hurt bad, maybe run off the road like Rose Talbot."

"You saying I had something to do with Rose's death? I liked Rose. We were friends. Why would I want to hurt her?"

"Because you knocked her up and she threatened to tell your wife back in Illinois about how you pass the winter days when she's not around."

"You got a vivid imagination and a diarrhea mouth, Brown. Not a pleasant combination. You've been warned before, but you're evidently too stupid to heed the warning. Trouble seems to come to anybody you're involved with, including Rose Talbot. Don't come back to my hotel. If you've got any brains at all, you won't as much as slow down your car in this part of the world, ever again."

"Believe me, I'd like nothing better. But unfortunately for you and me, I've got some unfinished business to attend to. And as much as I'd like to continue our chat, I've got to hurry off to a doctor's appointment for my bedbug bites. I suggest you check my room; you may need a new bed in there. I may have picked the little critters up somewhere down the road."

His face started to swell like an over-filled water balloon. He balled his fists against his hips and his skin reddened. The wind pushed a hunk of his black hair strait up in the air like the comb on a rooster and lifted the coat of his expensive suit until it flapped beside him like a gray wing. For a moment, he reminded me of the statue of the giant rooster on the western edge of Two Harbors. I was about to say something to that effect but a twinge in my gut shut me up. I turned my back and be-bopped to the Forester, trying not to move too fast, hoping Barnes wasn't sneaking up behind me with a rock in his hand.

He wasn't.

I drove out. Barnes was still standing in the wind doing the funky chicken. I headed north into the woods and let the excitement and anticipation flow through me. Adrenaline seemed to have chased out the virus. I'd become as popular as roadkill at a wild-game banquet but it felt like things were happening. We had at least shaken the bad guys complacency, removed a few bricks from their perceived secure foundation. I knew my comment about Rose carrying Barnes' kid had shaken the man; I'd seen the way his head twitched.

My hopes were up. Maybe we'd get lucky and Chris Enrico would start talking. Could be he knew about more than just the smuggling and animal parts trafficking. Maybe, to save his own ass, he'd give us some info on Rose's killer or insight into the demise of Billy Talbot.

I drove aimlessly through the forest for hours, the dark sky and darker trees a dull counterpoint to my racing brain. Time moved slowly. Eventually, with my gas tank reading near empty, I was turning into the wayside. It was 12:45.

I parked. Reddish brown vines and yellow weeds swayed and shook in the breeze. Kind of like my thoughts. I could see some kind of monument up on a small rise but I was too tired to get out and read it. I sat back in the overly stiff front seat and admired two gulls circling and diving above me in the muddy sky. As they glided below the tree tops, a large crow burst out of a tall pine, black wings spreading wide. A red squirrel zipped up the side of a nearby birch tree chattering at the crow. We were all doing our thing.

Daugherty rolled up at exactly one o'clock, a prompt and conscientious public servant always. Instead of coming into the wayside, he pulled across the entrance and gestured for me to follow him. I hit the ignition, clicked the floor shifter into D and turned the Forester loose. Daugherty cut across the highway and headed north. I stayed behind him. Ten miles up the road he turned right at a State Forest Picnic Area and I followed him in. We stopped next to some green wooden picnic tables chained to pipes in the ground. A dark brown wooden outhouse stood behind the asphalt parking area and a long narrow patch of wrinkled snow snaked along the edge of the tree line.

Daugherty got out of the green and white SUV and leaned against the driver's door. His belly sagged over his belt and his face was haggard under his wide-brimmed hat.

I stepped out and approached him. It didn't feel as positive as I'd expected. In fact, it felt quite negative. The trees slowed the wind gusts but it was still cold. I started to shiver and made an effort to rein it in.

"Whatsamatter Sheriff, you don't like putting away the bad guys?" I gritted my teeth to keep them from chattering. "Or did the bust somehow fall through?"

"No, it went okay. The Fish and Wildlife boys are there now, working on Mr. Enrico. We got enough to make a case on him, but it's possible he won't implicate anyone else. Lawyered up, straight away. Some sharpie from the Twin Cities has already called, e-mailed and faxed the department, warning us of the negative possibilities should we try to interrogate the prisoner before he arrives. Somebody is looking after our man real good."

"That's what I've been saying, Sheriff, there's more to this thing than we can see. Can't you offer Enrico some kind of deal? Suspended sentence in exchange for implicating Barnes or Sacowski? Something, like that?"

"It's in the hands of the federal boys now. They must've heard Atwood on the radio, because they were at the jail waiting before he even got back with Enrico. Somehow they knew about the bust almost before it happened. More of your great work, Brown?"

"Not me, Sheriff. I've been riding around in the forest primeval. Cell phones don't even work up here. Besides, what would I have to gain from that?"

"Feds give a reward for that kind of thing. T.I.P. Turn in poachers. As if you didn't know. Sleazy private dicks are always looking out for themselves, right? If you hadn't warned Sacowski about the raid, at least we'd have him now."

"But this was a chance to get all of them—Barnes, Sacowski and the rest of those assholes at Sky Blue Waters Lodge—a bust that would have resonated. And maybe the guy will still roll over. Enough time and enough threats might make him come around."

"I doubt it. Looks like the penalty for what was in that van only amounts to a fine and suspension of hunting and guiding licenses, things of that nature. Something that might have hurt Sacowski, but this guy Enrico—it's gonna bounce off him like water off a duck. He owns a gun shop outside of Chicago. I 'magine the gun business is brisk in Chi-Town."

"He could still give us Sacowski—given the right incentive."

"Nobody has ever rolled on Jim Sacowski. I thought I had him a half-dozen times over the years. The locals are afraid of him and the Chicago guys must be, too. Mighty easy to get hit by a stray rifle bullet around here, y'know. You need to understand something about the Sacowskis, Brown. They're jackpine savages—lived off the land for so long they're part of the geography. Whether it's hauling logs, poaching—selling weed, steroids, speed or what have you, they've become entrenched. Face it, Brown; you fucked up. You might want to think about finding a new occupation. The private eye crap is wearing as thin as April ice."

"Come on, Sheriff, we can't give up, now. We've got them stirred up. Keep applying the pressure and maybe they'll slip up. Who knows, Enrico could get a conscience and decide to unburden his soul."

"That's about as likely as me screwing Hillary Clinton. And how do you propose I put the pressure on them—got another one of your ingenious plans?"

"What about Billy Talbot? Can't you pin that on anyone? Got enough circumstantial evidence to pull in someone like Dick Sacowski and give him the rubber hose treatment?"

"Coroner says Talbot drowned. No signs of struggle. And no motive for anyone wanting him killed, far as I can see. I'm about to close the case just to have some good news to tell the press. Reporters from Duluth and Minneapolis are sniffing up my ass. That's all I need."

I was at a loss for words and stared foggily through the pines at a truck stacked with fresh cut logs rattling by out on the highway.

"Look Brown," Daugherty said, "I know you mean well and I know you want to see justice done for Rose Talbot. But I also know you just brokered a deal with Jim Sacowski that's putting ten K in the son of a bitches' pocket. Sometimes I wonder what you're really all about. You could be a pathetic pissant with low self-esteem, trying to puff himself up. Or you could be a seriously dangerous incompetent bringing trouble down upon everything you touch. Either one, I'm thinking, I don't really want messing around in my district. I'll continue to look the other way for a while, if you're planning on continuing to meddle, but from here on you're on your own. Don't come to me unless you got something locked up as tight as a nun's snatch. Otherwise you could find yourself back in your old room at the jail for interfering with a police investigation."

"You mean interfering with the lack of a police investigation."

His eyes grew sharp and cold. Then he shook his head from side to side and grinned knowingly, like I was an untrained dog who'd just pissed on the carpet. He opened his door and got in. The engine roared and gravel sprayed my shins as the SUV jerked away.

Daugherty was still playing good-sheriff-bad-sheriff, all wrapped up in one sagging package.

It was time to get some petrol in the tank, return home and reconnoiter.

Chapter
20

After the Sheriff was long enough gone that it was unlikely I'd run into him on the road, I pointed the Forester in the direction of Lake Superior and got rolling.

I was back at square one. I knew I'd have to return to Taconite Bay but I had no idea what to do when I got there. I still had to meet with Lily Engwar's attorney and set up a time and place for the video exchange. That is, providing Jimmy Sac was still bullish on the deal. I hoped ten grand would be too hard for him to pass up. And there was still a chance, however slight, that he didn't associate me with the bust. If he believed the line of bull I'd fed him, it follows that he thought Daugherty had been watching him, so it was possible I was out of the radius of suspicion. Maybe it was too much too ask.

I'd get a read on that soon enough.

Back on Highway 61, I let the road and the trees and the lake hypnotize me. I put a Tom Petty disk in the player and caught a groove. Guitars soared and tires whined.

I couldn't help but think how different it was up here when you looked deeper into things. How the people in the mining towns are, for the most part, a breed apart from the folks the tourists come in contact with during the warmer months. Sure, you've got your artists, contemplative types and the granola bunch running the antique shops and agate emporiums, but those idealistic, friendly, environmentally-conscience citizens are about as few and far between up here as are the days that it's actually comfortable near Lake Superior.

On a relentlessly dark afternoon like today, you might get a feel for the prevailing reality. Just dip a little under the surface and you'll find the hardscrabble hustlers and the mean drunks and the lonely women ready to do anything to feel a tingle of affection. How the years and the boredom and the struggle against nature wear away at these people, causing many to become bitter, hardened and suspicious with a marked propensity for backstabbing and maliciousness. Meth and prescription painkillers have hit them hard and alcoholism is as common as wood ticks on a field mouse.

Let the tourist associations put that in their brochures, I thought to myself as I came around a bend and dipped down to lake level. And then majestic Lake Superior was stretching out endlessly to my left, waves crashing and breaking on the rocks, spray flying wildly and I was reminded why we stayed here at all and why we came back. The lake was like a magnet to the soul, strong enough to work its power on all of us: the bourgeois, the bad, the bureaucrat and the sleazy private eye, et al.

You might say I was in a mood.

I guess I needed some sunshine.

Jan was still in the office when I walked in. The overwhelming smell of some kind of cheap deodorizing spray put me on edge from the get-go. I have a low tolerance for artificial scents.

"What's that stink in here?" I said.

"It's that new Cloreze scent," Jan said. "There was a sour odor coming from your living area."

"So you sprayed that shit in there?"

"Yes—a little."

"I can forget about sleeping in there tonight. Don't do that anymore, please."

"Well, the smell of your dirty clothes didn't seem very welcoming to clients."

"I suppose not. But that is predicated on the concept that clients might actually walk in here. A definite unlikelihood."

"For your information, Rick sent someone over today. Lady going through a divorce wants you to tail her husband."

"You're joking, right? You tell her I was currently otherwise engaged and would be unable—no, make that unwilling—to take her case?"

"I'm afraid I didn't."

"What *did* you say to her?"

"I told her you were an expert at such things and would probably be glad to help her."

"You're going to have to get back to her and explain that I'm too busy— and growing too sane—to take her case. You reach Livingston, yet? We still have to schedule our meeting. I'll be in the back room putting my laundry in a bag."

I basked in the glow of telling my ex what to do and retired to the anteroom.

Then the cold or flu or whatever it was started coming back on me like a missed mortgage payment. I stuffed my dirty clothes in a canvas duffel bag and fought the urge to collapse on the couch. The flowery, artificial stink in the air was searing and insistent and provoking my fight-or-flight response.

I chose flight.

Thinking that the Savannah Club might provide refuge, I headed for the door. "I'll be at the Savannah," I said in response to an all-too-familiar look from Jan. She was mumbling something as I went by but thankfully, I couldn't make it out. The gist, of course, was more than clear.

Someone wise once said that the only thing you can be sure of finding in a bar is alcohol. For the moment, that was good enough for me. The barkeep at the Savannah set me up with a bottle of Molson Golden and a shot of Finlandia and I got ready to brood.

The crowd was decent for the afternoon and judging by the frequent glances my way and resultant murmurings, many of them knew who I was. I'd become a minor celebrity. Which was easy, of course, all you had to do was give them something to keep their minds off their own doomed lives.

I knocked down the shot and started on the beer, felt the buzz float down to my legs. Halfway through the beer, an image of Burton sitting alone in his apartment racked with pain took center stage in my head and wouldn't move out. It quickly became clear that there was going to be no afternoon of peaceful numbness for me. At least not here.

Burton's small house was on East Fifth Street in a neighborhood of duplexes, modest family homes and brick apartment buildings. I knocked on the scuffed wooden door inside the closed-in porch. He yelled for me to come in. He was stretched out on a sagging brown couch with the TV on, the leg with the cast elevated by a folded-up pillow. Two aluminum crutches leaned against the arm of the sofa. He turned in my direction but his eyes didn't light up with joy. The bruises on his face were turning yellow, giving him a decidedly leper-like look.

"Hey, man," he said, voice low and subdued.

Guilt filled me up. "How's it going, Burt?" I said.

"Just great, Carter, just great. Afternoon TV is so uplifting. And Vicodin is truly a wonder drug." He grimaced, grabbed the broken leg at the thigh and gingerly slid himself around until he was sitting upright and facing me. "Sit down, if you want," he said. "What brings you to the recovery room? More important sleuthing stuff?"

I crossed the room and sat in a frayed maroon, padded rocking chair facing the couch. "Nah, nothing like that. I just came to tell you I'd be covering all your medical bills—in case you were wondering. And as soon as I get this sex video deal taken care of, I can give you some money to tide you over 'til you're back on your feet."

He nodded and his eyes opened a little more. "Please tell me you're not giving money to Jim Sacowski," he said.

"I'm afraid I can't. Given the situation, I thought it best to take care of the interests of my client first and go after Sacowski, second."

"After he's 10 K richer."

"Yeah. It's a pisser, I know. I didn't know what else to do."

He shook his head slowly; my guilt level increased. "Anything turn on the animal parts deal?"

"I thought we had him. But now it looks like he could skate. The deputy sheriff picked up the brother of one of the lodge owners in possession of banned meat, but so far it doesn't look like he's going to roll on anyone. Daugherty insists that everybody's scared of the Sacowskis."

"I'd like to get those bastards in the sights of my deer rifle, see how scary they are then. What, exactly, happened?"

I proceeded to tell him the story, leaving out the part about watching the brothers carry the coolers out of Jimmy Sac's house.

"Your story makes me need another pain pill," Burton said, smiling half-heartedly. "How did you know the stuff they were putting in the van was contraband?"

"Instinct, I guess. I don't know; it all seemed to fit. Guy from Illinois… coolers loaded in the dark at the lodge… guy owned a gun shop…"

"Just as easily could have been legal stuff," Burton said. "Fish fillets, venison steaks, you know…"

"Yeah, maybe. What did I have to lose? Pinching the guys tail-light bulb seemed easy enough."

"They pick up on that, they could scream illegal search and seizure."

"Cops didn't do it, so Daugherty's conscience is clear. I suppose a sharp lawyer could make a stink if they checked out the broken bulb—but I can't worry about that. I've got other beasts to broil."

"What about the security tapes from the casino?"

"I'll have to kiss Daugherty's ass long and hard for that one. I seem to have fallen out of favor with the good sheriff. And the casino is in another county, besides."

"You better swallow your pride and do it, Carter, because that's where the answer lies. I can feel it in my bones."

"The broken ones or the non-broken?"

"Piss off."

"Heard anything from our boy Torm, lately?" I said.

"Talked to him today. His play didn't win the competition, so he's on the loose. Said he was coming over to cook me dinner."

"What are we having?"

"He's bringing over some burger. We're gonna fire up the grill."

"I'll go to the store and get more burger. Anything else you need? Should I call Tommy?"

"The more the merrier. Sometimes this place gets like a mausoleum when nobody's around. Pick up some cheese, would ya?"

I drove the ten blocks to the Whole Foods Co-op. In keeping with my newfound dedication to health and fitness, I purchased two pounds of grass-fed ground beef, a roll of organic Colby cheese, three organic tomatoes and a box of frozen organic fries. On the return route, I stopped at a liquor store and picked up a twelve-pack of beer and a six of diet soda, neither of which were labeled organic.

When I returned, a rusty, champagne colored Acura Legend was parked behind Burton's truck. A faded sticker on the rear bumper said *Theatre People Do Lines*. I pulled in behind it as Tommy's Murano came around the corner.

We had a good time preparing the meal. Tormoen was in good form, keeping up the banter. I could tell Burton was enjoying himself by his shit-eating grin and the returning light in his eyes. It felt like we were back in college again, those heady, party-filled days when the four of us shared one side of a brick duplex while attempting to balance weed, women and beer drinking with school work, not always to the best of results.

Many years later, here we were, a little heavier in some cases and a little less hair in others (mostly mine), trying to balance weed, no women and beer drinking with the demands of our quasi-adult take on modern life.

Tommy was still married. I'd been divorced twice and Burton and Tormoen had crashed and burned through one marriage apiece. I think Dan missed having a wife while Tormoen was thankful to be single. Tommy and I were ambivalent.

Tommy had his own business, so he had that aspect covered, at least for the present—all you could expect in the current economy. The rest of us, were a little less financially stable. Burton was unemployed and possibly handicapped for life; Tormoen was a part-time bartender, thespian and occasional late-night radio voice. I, of course, was the private dick with an "income."

Gathering together like this, we could easily be mistaken for younger men. Well preserved. Basically healthy and strong, except for Dan, who at least used to be that way, and, with luck, would be again.

Jeff did a great job with the burgers. The cheese was delicious and the tomatoes crisp, carrying much more flavor than your average supermarket tomato. The frozen fries were a lot better than expected. After we ate, Tommy and I cleaned the kitchen, which made Burton even happier. Then we sat around the living room smoking cheap cigars. Camaraderie ran high. We talked about the old days and fishing and motorcycles and the local hockey teams. Tormoen even got in a few theater stories, all associated with excessive drinking. Dan hesitantly relived the story of his beating. You could sense his desire for revenge riding just below the surface.

Tommy shuffled out of there about ten. Burton was snoring on the couch. Neither Tormoen nor I could decide if we should wake him. We left him alone and took our leave. The outside air was still unseasonably warm. For some reason it made me uneasy.

"Later dude," Tormoen said as he opened the door of the rusty Acura. "Just let me know when you want to go back up to Tacky Town. I'll be ready. Seeing what they did to Burto really got my blood boiling. And the prospect of a reunion with fair Gloria brings on salivation and tumescence."

"Fair Gloria is aging fast without you, Torm. Maybe even fallen below your standards."

"And what is that supposed to imply, oh surly one?"

"Nothing. I'll be in touch. Phone still working?"

"So far."

Driving home, I was dead tired and feverish. The virus seemed to have waited until I was most vulnerable and then struck like a squadron of stealth bombers. As I sunk into the pain and fever, my thoughts did a one-eighty. I was seeing Brown Investigations as a make-believe enterprise peopled by arrested adolescents and fronted by a deluded loser.

I parked in the lot kitty-corner from my building and walked slowly across the faux-cobblestone street, feeling old and vulnerable. The air was still surprisingly mild. Traffic was heavy for this hour. I struggled up the stairs to my office like it was Pike's fucking Peak, half expecting a thug or a cop or some other unwanted thing to jump out of the shadows.

No bogeys showed themselves.

Chapter
21

The next morning I was feeling a little better. The noxious scent still lingered, but at a tolerable level. After orange juice, toast and a banana, I went to the fitness center for a light workout and a sauna.

When I returned at ten, Jan was sitting at her desk in a crisp blue suit and a ruffled white shirt, her eyes clear and sharp.

I avoided her inquiring glances.

"I got the porn star's lawyer on the phone when you were out," she said pointing her nose up at me. "He says he can come up at anytime but will need a week's notice."

"Porn star?"

"Your darling, Lily Engwar."

"My darling? The girl's engaged to one of societies' favorite sons for Christ sake. Put nails in your coffee this morning?"

She ignored me and looked down at her desk. "And the woman Rick sent over called, too. She seemed really anxious to hire you."

"Would you stop with the divorce-business shit? I'm in no mood to do anything but what I've been working on. This thing is starting to grate at me again and I can't think of anything but my desire to have it over. As much as I hate the word closure, I guess that's what I crave."

She looked up at me, her eyes clicking into that semi-accusatory stare that must've been part of her DNA. "Tie one on last night? You're looking kind of rough this morning."

"If I'm looking rough it's from that poisonous chemical you sprayed in my room yesterday. That shit brings disgusting to a whole new level."

"Get a skin, Carter," she said, tapping on her keyboard and leaving me hanging like an empty clothesline. "I'll print out these requirements for getting your license, so you can study them," she said, as I turned away.

"Fuck that. I'm thinking of quitting the business as soon as the Talbot case is finished."

"Oh my god," she said, shaking her head and scrunching up her face.

I went into the back room, closed the door and sank into my stained blue easy chair. Somehow Jan was able to make the computer keyboard sound like a hammer on a tin roof.

I must have fallen asleep, because the next thing I remember, the phone was ringing in the outer office and no one was picking up. I stumbled out to find an empty desk and the phone jangling. Jan was gone and she hadn't hooked up the answering machine. Her little payback.

The phone kept going. I picked it up. "Brown Investigations," I said.

It was a woman's voice: "Mr. Brown?"

"No, Mr. Brown is not in at the moment. This is the janitor, I thought you were my wife calling to nag."

"I beg your pardon?"

"Don't beg my pardon, lady, I got no pardon to give."

She sniffed and hmmed and then hung up, hopefully to never call back.

I sat down at the desk and rubbed my forehead and eyes. The digital clock said 3:07. Jan had left early and without so much as a note. Another fence I would need to mend.

I went to the window and looked out at the sunshine. I thought something was off kilter when the thermometer read 65 degrees. I noticed I was feeling better. At least until I realized I would have to work the phones myself. I needed to call Jim Sacowski, Sheriff Daugherty, David Livingston (Lily's lawyer) and Tommy Basilio, as well as touch base with Tormoen and Burton.

I sat at my desk and fidgeted. Sixty-five degrees in March and I was stuck inside. Something wasn't right. A day like this should be spent on the banks of one of the heavily flowing North Shore streams, soaking up sun and the positive ions from the rushing water while forgetting about my obligation to Rose Talbot or the trio of backwoods miscreants currently making my life miserable.

I said *Fuck it* and started going through my list of phone numbers.

Three hours later, I'd set up Tommy with some new research projects, pleaded, begged and cajoled Sheriff Daugherty about the surveillance videos from the casino and arranged a meeting between the parties involved in the amateur porno negotiations.

Daugherty finally relented to my pleadings but only after a long battle. He dragged me through the ringer until I did the oral equivalent of getting down on my knees and swearing eternal undying allegiance to him and his department. My manly pride will not allow me to release the details of my supplication. Suffice to say that it worked.

After a few calls back and forth between Taconite Bay and Minneapolis, I was able to set up a meeting with Jim Sacowski and David Livingston. Sacowski insisted it should take place at his lawyer's office outside of Taconite Bay, and held fast to that requirement. Livingston wasn't particularly pleased, having hoped to meet in Duluth or somewhere else closer to his office, but eventually relented and gave me a date for two weeks down the calendar. Jimmy Sac agreed on the date, although I thought I detected impatience in his tone.

By the time I finished, it was nearly five-thirty. The shadows outside my window were getting long. I called Torm and gave it the two-rings-and-hang-up-and-then-call-again routine. To my pleasant surprise, Jeff picked up and agreed to meet me at the Savannah—after I promised to buy him a beer.

Walking down the sidewalk to the club, the unseasonably warm air felt good on the bones. I got to the club entrance and saw Torm ambling across the railroad tracks in my direction. I waited beneath a neon sign of a naked girl and a martini glass. The evening light on the sign revealed chipped paint and corroded metal, things the night disguised.

We got a table against the wall to the right of the stage and I began to fill him in. Halfway through the second beer, I had a flash of déjà vu. Seemed like I was stuck in some form of circular reality, forced to do the same things over and over until they came out right. My first instinct was to try and break the circle. But then I realized the only way out was by staying in until the unbreakable chain was broken. If that makes sense to you, good luck.

Torm and I were determined to go back to Creek County and stay until we found something we could use or ran out of money, whichever came first. We finished our beers, left the club and drove to Burton's in my Subaru. Dan was up and moving around on his crutches and looked noticeably better.

We put down three lawn chairs at the edge of the front steps and let the evening come to us. To our right, two squirrels were chasing each other up and down a big leafless maple tree at warp speed. A college kid was revving the pipes on his crotch rocket in front of the white house to our left. Down the block, three little kids were scooting around on tricycles and screaming with glee. A middle-aged guy across the street had the hood up on his sixty-nine Chevy Super Sport, peering at the engine while gripping a beer can.

We sat out there without saying much until the sun was totally gone behind the hill and the sky was filled with red ink. The heat seeped out of the day real fast. We went inside and ordered a pizza and watched high school hockey on the tube.

Chapter

22

Ten days later, heading northward on Highway 61, I was feeling like a commuter, just one of the hundreds who plied this road daily going to and from work. I'd spent the recent downtime working out and even studying some of the requirements for a P.I. license. Boring, monotonous shit that only served to reinforce my desire to end my sleuthing career after this case was finally resolved.

Torm was behind me in his Acura. Upon reaching our destination, we would be moving in separate directions. He was going after Ned Fifield, the crank freak who'd tried to implicate me, and I was stalking Dick Sacowski. It was a desperate move on my part but I hoped applying pressure and hurling accusations would get things rolling towards a conclusion. I was fully aware it could end up with Torm and me in the hospital or the morgue while the Sacowskis still roamed free to rape and pillage.

C'est la vie.

C'est la guerre.

Torm had been in communication with Gloria. She said Dick and Dave Sacowski were spending their days in the woods logging now that the frost ban on the dirt roads had been lifted. This surprised me. I'd assumed the brothers were living high with the money extorted from Rose Talbot. This was a big part of my theory. If they were out harvesting logs—hard physical work—chances were good their wallets were leaner than I'd theorized. Little Sac was evidently daylighting from his chef's job, logging likely a good way to work off excess testosterone from steroid abuse.

Concerning Ned Fifield, the rejected witness for my prosecution, Gloria said he was living in an old RV on the outskirts of Taconite Bay, having recently completed a county-mandated rehab program and a moderate sentence at the Northeast Regional Corrections Center.

I'd reserved a cabin at the Whitefish Point Lodge, a quaint, old-time motor court updated enough to be booked solid from May through October every year. It normally wasn't open in March but the absence of snow and unseasonably warm weather had coaxed the owners from their winter dens. I'd seen their ad on a North Shore tourism website and snagged a lakeside cabin for a week with the option of staying longer.

Driving in tandem, Torm and I took the expressway to Two Harbors, crawled through main-street traffic and hooked up with Scenic 61 on the north end of town. Fog was rolling in off the water, making the going slow. Temps were in the forties by the lake and the sixties inland. You could sense the sun trying to break through the mist but not quite making it.

We continued to weave northward, past Sky Blue Waters Lodge, Betty's Pies, Gooseberry Falls, Split Rock Lighthouse and Beaver Bay. Coming up on Palisade Head, some wayward spirit was evidently beckoning me, because I made an unplanned turn into the lot at Tettegouche State Park and watched Torm roll in behind me.

We both deplaned and walked down the road to the footbridge spanning the river. Below us, tea-colored water rushed and

and foamed over huge gnarled rocks, thin spray bouncing up to join the fog in a gray dance. I breathed deeply and tasted the North Woods.

"Looking for clues, Carter?"

"Clues for the clueless, Torm. That's why I brought you along."

"To guide you through difficult and perilous times?"

"Yeah, that's it. This is the Baptism River, man. A wash of this holy water might change your heathen ways."

"Good luck with that. I'm afraid I'm a pagan for the duration. But I bow to your righteousness, oh great spiritual dick."

"You should. I've been to church at least twice in the last decade."

"Let me guess. Once for your wedding and the second time for your mother's funeral."

"You nailed it. Let's take a walk down to the lake." I put the collar up on my black leather jacket and started walking.

"Whatever you say, boss."

We made our way down a wooden staircase to a meandering path of mud and rock leading to a beach of gray stones and gravel. A few feet offshore a serpentine rush of tannin-stained river swirled and mixed with crystal-clear lake water. You couldn't see the sky for the fog. It didn't feel windy but two foot waves were breaking white against the rocks, making a sound caught somewhere between a roar and a sigh. Soothing, like a horsehair brush to the soul.

We took it all in, not saying a word. Minutes ticked away as I let my senses run free. The more I listened, the more I heard. As the waves washed over the gravel, they seemed to be whispering to me: *Rose... Rose... Rose....*

I tried to shut it out, bring back the neutral sound of water hitting rock. I knew I was going crazy so I turned and started up the path. Torm watched me studiously, zipped up his blue nylon windbreaker and followed.

We got back on the highway.

Turning in at the freshly painted sign, I wondered if Jimmy Sac had done the handiwork. I followed the winding gravel across the railroad tracks and down toward the lake, Tormoen close behind. I came upon a skinny guy in black wool pants and dark green wool jacket pushing a broom across the asphalt in front of a rectangular, one-story, dark-red shingled building with nailed-on plastic letters spelling OFFICE running vertically alongside the door. He had close-cropped gray hair and a sharply creased, weathered but friendly face. He looked at us with a mixture of curiosity, anticipation and wariness. The default look for these parts.

One of the best features of Whitefish Point Cabins was that you couldn't see them from the road. Highway 61 is the only artery connecting the towns of the North Shore and I was concerned about being spotted. But I also knew we would eventually be noticed and the word would spread across the Taconite Telegraph at the speed of sound. I hoped to put off the inevitable for as long as I could. I'd stressed the need for secrecy to Torm, hoping he'd at least keep our location away from Gloria's ears.

I parked in front of the office and Tormoen pulled in next to me. I got out and smiled at the man holding the broom. He smiled back.

"Hello," I said, putting my hand out. "Carter Brown. I called about a reservation."

He shook my hand. "Been expecting you, Mr. Brown. I'm Paul Ottinger, owner, manager and maintenance man of Whitefish Point Cabins. Welcome."

"Nice to meet you, Paul. This is my partner, Jeff Tormoen," nodding in Torm's direction as he leaned against the Acura with a peculiar grin spreading across his lips.

Ottinger hesitated for an instant, looked at me and then back at Tormoen, who was mincing toward him, holding out a slightly bent wrist.

Then it hit me. I'd used the word "partner," a word encumbered by new meaning in our modern world. It was still a generally homophobic world this far north and Ottinger looked uneasy as Jeff laid on his best gay hustler schtick, shaking hands loosely and cocking his hip jauntily. I didn't know whether to be angry or burst out laughing. I stayed stuck somewhere between the two, my face feeling heated even in the damp forty-four degree air.

Ottinger cleared his throat and regained his composure. "I got you set up in cabin number one. First one on the left down there," he said, pointing a thick finger down the gravel drive. "Real cozy little place. Only got one other guest right now, a couple from Iowa, over in number three. So you'll have plenty of peace and quiet. We're not usually open this time of the year, but with the early spring weather and all, it seemed like the right thing to do. You gotta jump at any chance you get to make a buck up here, especially in this economy."

"I hear that," I said, looking him in the eye. "We'll be working in the area ourselves." I instantly knew I shouldn't have said that. My discomfort had come out my mouth.

"What kind of work you fellas do?"

"I'm a freelance writer and Jeff is my photographer. We're doing a story for *Minnesota Monthly* on the unseasonable spring and the beauty of the changing seasons. I'll make sure to mention your lodge."

"That would be great, Mr. Brown, we can always use the publicity. And by the way, someone called for you earlier this morning wondering if you'd arrived yet."

"They leave a name."

"No—told the wife they'd call back."

"Male or female?"

"Male, I s'pose. Wife didn't specify. Wait a minute—maybe she did say a man called. I can check with her if you want."

"No, that's all right. He'll call back if it's important."

I looked at Tormoen. He smiled sickly.

"Let's go get cozy, Carter," he said.

I wanted to strangle him.

"Hold on while I get your key," Ottinger said, face reddening "You probably want to put your feet up."

"That's not all we'd like to put up," Tormoen said, before flouncing into the Acura.

Ottinger turned away quickly, like he was fighting back a mental image, and went inside the red building.

The Acura's window slid down. "I'll be waiting for you, sugar buns," Tormoen said, deadpan.

"Would you shut the fuck up," I said, trying hard to be stern. "You want the Reverend Phelps coming in here after us?"

He put it in gear and drove down the road. I could see his shoulders shaking with laughter. Funny guy. Theater humor.

It was a cozy little place. Knotty-pine walls, a small clean kitchen with a newer fridge and microwave and a modest wooden table and chairs. Against the wall adjacent to the kitchen were a propane space heater and the doors to the bathroom and bedroom. There was a queen-size bed with beige spread in the bedroom. In the central living area, there was a brown plaid sleeper sofa facing the lake. Across from the sofa, a small television set rested on a black wood table to the left of the bay window. There was a stuffed chair matching the couch on the right side of the glass.

"I'll take the bedroom," I said after Ottinger left.

"You mean we're not sharing?" Tormoen said, giving one last mincing pose.

"Fuck you."

"Is that what you had in mind, sweet cheeks?"

"For fucking Christ sake, it stopped being funny ten minutes ago. Your audience has left the building. Time to start taking this seriously. This cabin didn't come cheap."

"All right then, boss. Buy me lunch and I promise I'll get to work."

"Were you able to find a weapon to bring along?" I asked, reminding him of an earlier request.

He went to the couch, unzipped his bag and pulled out a strange-looking handgun.

"What the fuck is that?" I said.

"Prop gun I borrowed from the theater company."

"Does it work?"

"Shoots blanks okay."

"So what good is it then?"

"Might scare someone."

"Scare them enough to go get their own real hand cannon. That's how people get killed."

"I'm aware of that. Wasn't really planning on using it. I wasn't boxing champion at Mankato State for nothing."

"How many years ago was that? I've got a genuine weapon in my car, in case we need it."

"Cattle prod?"

"Three-eighty, semi-auto."

"Registered?"

"I took the carry-permit course in January, in anticipation of just such an occasion," I lied.

We took lunch at a roadside restaurant that had a *Fresh Fish* sign out front. I selected the broiled lake trout and Tormoen, being a true Norwegian, (half, anyway) ordered the pan-fried herring. I was nervous about being seen. But since somebody had called asking after me, it was possible the secret was already floating on the wind with the seagulls. I relaxed with the inevitability. And it could've been Tommy or Dan who'd called. They were the only ones I'd told of our destination. But I couldn't be sure, secrets turned to rumors real fast around here.

I got nervous again.

Following an excellent repast, Torm went off to find Ned Fifield's RV. As for me, I knew the Sacs were somewhere out in the woods but didn't know exactly where. I could have made the rounds of the bars, asking questions, but that tactic, besides being time and gasoline consuming, had led to trouble in the past.

Time for something from my detective's bag of tricks.

I flipped on my cell phone and called directory assistance, got the number for the Sacowski's parents' residence. Being that there were only two Sacowski's listed and one was James, it was easy to find.

A woman I assumed was Ma Sac answered. "Is this Mrs. Sacowski?" I said.

"It sure is."

"My name is Frank Mehle, Mrs. Sacowski. I'm an old buddy of Dick's from a long-ago construction job. I'm in town for a visit and wanted to get together with Dick to pay him back the fifty bucks he loaned me way back then."

Mrs. Sac got talkative after that, telling me how Dick hadn't worked a construction job in ten years because he kept flunking the urine tests. I remarked how it must have been at least fifteen years since I'd been back this way.

"You gonna pay him back after that long a time, son?" she said incredulously. "You must be some kind of good Samaritan."

"Not really," I said, "I just remember how Dick helped me out. My wife was sick back in St. Paul and I needed to get down there. I was broke, but Dick lent me the money for gas and stuff. I never came back here, and I've been thinking about it all that time."

"Sure it was Dick Sacowski, mister? Dick usually borrows a lot more than he lends. What was your name again? I'll be sure and tell Dicky you called, next time I see him. Which'll be tonight, I imagine, if I'm still awake when he comes sneaking in here smellin' like the bottom of a beer can."

"Frank Mehle," I said. "But I've only got a short time here, so I hoped you could tell me how to find him today"

"What you do for a living these days, Mr. Mehle?"

"I'm a carpenter. Down in St. Paul."

"That's a good occupation. Well, believe it or not, Dicky and his little brother are out logging, working for Bill Miller. I think he said they were out on the Hustad Road."

"Thank you very much, Mrs. Sacowski," I said. "I'm sure Dick will be happy to see me. Nice talking to you."

"Okay, Mr. Samaritan."

I clicked off and got my Creek County map out of the glove compartment. After much searching and turning the map to catch the dim light of the cloudy sky, I located a Hustad Road about ten miles north of Taconite Bay that ran roughly east to west through the forest.

I opened the glove compartment, took out my pistol and replaced the map. I racked a cartridge into the chamber and slid the pistol underneath the driver's seat. I headed north. Memories of the beat down Dick had given me at Palisade Head kept popping into my thoughts like an evil jack-in-the-box. Every time I pushed them back, they came springing back harder.

I was determined it would be different this time around. If I had to use the gun to ward off Man Mountain, so be it.

Ten miles on a dirt road always takes longer than you'd think it would. During the drive, my resolve waxed and waned like the moon in time-lapse photography. What the hell was my plan, anyway, beat Dick into submission until he told the truth?

I guess that was the core of it. But what chance was there of that happening with Little Sac standing in the wings like a pet gorilla, ready to tear my arms off and use them for fly swatters?

I had my padlock on a red bandana in my back pocket and I had the gun and the big flashlight. The farther along I went the more these things seemed senseless. And then I saw dust rising off a dirt road coming up on my right, green sign at the intersection announcing Hustad Road. A beat-up dark green flatbed truck stacked to the max with logs was turning in my direction. I made the right and passed alongside it. Didn't recognize the guy behind the wheel but it said Miller's Logging in faded white paint on the driver's door.

I followed the dirt until the dust was thick in my nostrils and tasted bitter and acrid. I was thinking if I had any sense at all I'd turn around and head back the way I came. But if I had any sense at all, would I have come this far?

My mind waged war with the pros and cons of the endeavor while my hands gripped the wheel. Ten minutes went by in what seemed like thirty seconds and my bladder was suddenly full. Eventually I came abreast of an opening in the thick roadside foliage where I could see a long strip of cleared land with deep furrows running through the torn-up dirt. Loose branches and debris from trees were scattered everywhere. About a quarter mile further down the Hustad, a familiar camo-painted Bronco was nosed up against the pine trees.

I slowed to a crawl and sighted along the deep gouges of the skidder tracks. Clumps of fog rolled across the broken ground like ghostly gray tumbleweeds. About a hundred yards down, two tan coverall-clad bodies—one large and one industrial size—were chopping at big logs with brush axes. A rusty, faded yellow log skidder loomed behind them like a dormant prehistoric beast.

Well here it is, I thought to myself—go time. My make or break moment. I pulled to the shoulder of the narrow road and shut off the ignition. I looked toward the Sacowskis. They were staring back at me, brush axes cradled in front of them in the manner of rifles on a soldier. The bros probably couldn't tell who I was through the murk. I reached down beneath the seat and squeezed the pebbled pistol grip, lifted out the weapon.

For some unknown reason—just a feeling, I guess—I slid the gun back under the seat, yanked the padlock out of my pocket by the bandana and tossed it to the passenger side floor. I was going in naked, so to speak, some spark of macho lunacy reverberating from my DNA to my conscious mind like a bugle call to a defeated army.

I walked across the road, stepped over some standing water in the ditch and popped through low pines and leafless birch trees into the cleared area. The fog was getting thicker and the Sacs now seemed vague and distant, peering in my direction, maybe wondering about the approaching leather jacket and jeans-clad figure. Exchanging quick words and glances, maybe deciding what they were going to do with my body.

I kept going; heart hammering in my chest and head getting light while my feet grew heavy and my gut did flip-flops like I'd swallowed a live rabbit. I stuck my hands in the pockets of my jacket and started up a small rise. Twenty-five yards ahead of me the Sac brothers stood stiffly, now aware of who was entering their workplace without an invitation.

I came within ten feet and stared into Dick Sacowski's eyes. Held his gaze, saw the confusion and the rage simmering beneath the surface as his thick, gnarled hands kneaded the polished handle of the brush axe. Man Mountain Dave didn't seem as big as I remembered. He had a look of puzzled disbelief but wasn't vibing flat-out hostile like you might expect. His head appeared smaller and his signature meanness seemed diluted, washed out. As I got closer, a half smile crossed his lips,.

"What the fuck you doing here, Brown?" Dick said.

"That any way to treat an old friend, Sac? That how you practice Minnesota Nice around here?"

He hesitated; the anger left his eyes for a flash and then returned. "You forget what happened the last time I caught you meddling, Brown?"

"Haven't forgotten, Sac. That's part of the reason I'm here. Hoping for a rematch. Only I'm afraid I forgot my brush hook."

"I don't need this to kick your ass, fag boy." He threw the axe to the side and stepped to me. I backed up.

"You see Richie," I said, "the way I figure it, all the murdering and stealing and assaulting you've been doing has got to be weighing you down. I remember when you were a pretty nice guy, ready to help a friend move or jump his car or help with a little carpentry work. Nice guys like that don't have what it takes to stay bad. They got a conscience and it doesn't stop working on them, day or night, night or day."

I was praying I was right.

He squinted at me, suddenly looking old and tired. His nose was red-veined and swollen and the skin under his eyes hung down like wet teabags.

I put up my fists in a boxer's posture. "So come on, old man," I said, "let's see what you got left in you. Let's see what happens when righteousness is your opponent." I knew that one was way over the top.

He lunged and threw a roundhouse right. I ducked and side-stepped and caught him with a glancing left hook to the side of his head. He spun around and came at me again. I jabbed a left into his mouth and threw a hard right cross to his ribcage that made him wince. But instead of fading, he ducked and charged and came on like Joe Frazier in Carhartt.

He rammed his shoulder into my hip and tried to wrap me up with his ape-like arms. I danced, stiff-armed him and spun out of the attempted tackle like I was back on the high school football field. Sac stumbled and fell to his knees. I moved in quickly and kicked him in the ribs. Damn near broke my toe. Running shoes are not made for kicking ribs.

I hopped away in pain as Dick struggled to his feet, putting himself back together like the fucking Terminator. He charged once more, this time staying high. I put up my forearms to block but he caught me square in the ear with a right hand that sent flames through my skull. I danced away again, thankful for those hours in the gym.

I set my feet and raised my fists. Adrenaline put me up on my toes. Sac was breathing hard and heavy, wheezing slightly. He coughed and then coughed some more. The skin on his face was tight and red with streaks of white running down it.

"You see, Sac, what I said? That's the weight of murder dragging you down. You can't fight me, and your guilt both. First Rose—and then Billy.... You killed your friend just so you could keep the money your brother squeezed out of Rose. Billy's credit card money. Was it worth it? Worth spending the rest of your days in Hell?"

His facial muscles went slack and his hands dropped. I stuck a left jab on his nose and moved quickly, trying to keep Little Sac in sight. Big man was just standing there, hands on his hips, watching the whole thing, seemingly amused and strangely detached.

Dick made one final desperate lunge in my direction but I was ready for him. I feinted to the right, sidestepped his charge and stomped the side of his knee as he went by. I heard a hollow popping sound. He howled like a dog in a bear trap, spun to the ground in a beaten heap, gripping his knee with both hands.

"There you go, Dick," I said. Tough guy like you and you can't even take a citified cake-eater like me. That's what evil does to a good man."

Dick's eyes were sunk back in his head, burning with pain and hatred. "You're fucking nuts," he said. Then he turned his glower on his brother. "Why didn't you do something, David?" he growled "Why'd you let this asshole fuck me up."

The big guy's face almost looked kindly. But many years of learned indifference and sibling resentment couldn't be hidden. "Looked like a fair fight to me, Dicky," he said, his voice surprisingly soft. "I'm sick of being you and Jimmy's enforcer. Now that I'm off the juice, I don't have the taste for fighting. I don't want to hurt anyone anymore. Just want to be left alone. All this mess is you and Jimmy's fault." He turned his back to us and resumed chopping branches off the one-foot diameter log at his feet.

"It's over, Sac," I said. "You ain't going anywhere on that knee for awhile. Turn yourself in and the state will fix it for you."

"You really are fucking crazy, Brown. You got no proof of anything—and I didn't kill anyone. Me and my brothers were at the casino the night Rose went off the road. I do feel guilty about Billy, but only because I let him go out alone that day. I never knew how much he was hurting. I thought he hated Rose. But after she died, he put her on a pedestal. All of a sudden she was his precious Rose Marie, the love of his life."

"Oh c'mon, man, someone tried to set me up. And someone also ended up with a shit load of money from Rose's credit card excursions."

"Not me. You were trying to do Billy right, I knew that. But when you kept fucking up, Billy flipped out. He was gobbling handfuls of pills. Blamed himself for hiring you. Then Jim comes up with this idea to forge your handwriting on that note to make it seem like you were threatening Rose. Billy was a mess, for God sake. He convinced me you were a chronic loser and a sociopath. Said his condition made him super sensitive to people's souls."

I was looking down at him and thinking about stomping the other knee. "What a crock of shit that is. And I suppose the money she charged is hidden out in the woods and nobody knows where. And you say I'm fucking crazy. Who else but you guys would hit my car?"

Dick sat up, gripping his bent-up knee, the left leg stretched out in front of him on the dirt. I stomped down on the left knee. He howled some more. Louder this time. Dave stared at me. Was his mood swinging?

"Tell him the truth, Dicky," Little Sac said. Tell him how Jim blackmailed Rose about the sex tape they made the night they wouldn't let you and me in the party. Tell him how Billy would get so goofy behind all that dope he didn't even know what Jim was doin' behind his back. How he'd get so twisted up inside he'd ask us to kill her. How he paid you and I to smack into Brown's car. Tell him and the man will leave you alone. Won't you, Mr. Brown?"

I didn't have an answer for that so I just continued looking down at Dick, nodding slightly, trying not to incite the big guy, who was starting to pace around in the dirt, soft on his feet.

"It's all true, Brown," Dick said, wincing. "But we never killed her. We were all at the casino, I swear to God. Everyone knew Billy would change his mind eventually, once the drugs swung the other way. He was a good guy. His accident and his wife and everything fucked him up royally. Mix that with all them pills and…. It wasn't us, man, I swear to God. We weren't even there. We had all the pieces in place and then we just couldn't stop it. Billy was obsessed with nailing you."

"And I suppose you innocent guys have no idea what happened to the money."

"Jim got thirty thousand out of her," Little Sac said, his eyes sad. "He was going to get more the night she died, but Rose changed her mind, said she wasn't giving him any more. They went back and forth about it all night long. Jim kept telling her she'd lose any chance of collecting alimony if the tape got out. And her father would cut her off forever."

"Because her sister was banging the room?"

"They were both on the tape," Little Sac said. "Jimmy called it Sisters in Sin." His eyelids went down to half-mast and he chin nodded at me. "And now, Mr. Brown, I think it's time for you to leave me and my brother alone." Then he set his axe on the ground, leaned down to the log he'd been trimming and jerked it up like a twig. "I've got some work to finish here before I take Dicky to the hospital."

He smiled at me strangely before sending the log sailing in my direction like he was making a two-hand chest pass with a pool cue. Thing flew within a few inches of my head and hit the dirt with a loud thump, shaking the ground beneath my feet.

I got the hell out of there without looking back, hoping I'd make it to the car and the gun before the behemoth's brain switched to the other pole. And he'd said he was off the juice. Makes you think. Makes you wonder.

My heart didn't slow until I got off the dirt and onto the pavement. I could see far enough behind me to know the camo Bronco wasn't on my tail. That's when I started shaking.

I was elated to have kicked Sac's ass, even though he'd been tired from slinging logs and tobacco was sapping his life force.

But ultimately, I was disappointed in what I'd learned. If what Little Sac had said was true, something I might never know for sure without viewing the sex video, the needle on the sordid meter had just hit ten.

But what had I expected? My head had been in the clouds, not in the gutter with the rest of them. I'd wanted to believe Rose was this noble figure trying to save her little sister from shame and ruin. I'd put her on a pedestal, just like Billy had. Maybe nobody belongs on a pedestal. Pedestals fall over easily because they don't have much of a base. Could be a lesson in there, somewhere.

Maybe Rose wasn't either good or bad. Maybe she was just another one of us who sometimes find circumstances overwhelming and do things to stop the hurt that we later regret. And maybe those things snowball and the situation gets a lot worse because we tried to run from the pain. How the hell was I supposed to know the answers? I was just a private dick, not a shrink or a priest or a writer of self-help books. But when you came right down to it, the only thing certain was that someone had run Rose Marie Engwar Talbot off the road that foggy autumn night. And I was the one chosen by the universe to find out who it was. Or so I told myself.

Adrenaline was still buzzing through me. My head was spinning. Who would've guessed Little Sac had a sensitive side? Did he secretly write poetry and dream about puppies? Carve cute little animals out of cedar logs? Was his favorite food quiche?

I pulled off the road somewhere between Taconite Bay and Whitefish Point and tried calling Tormoen, got no response. Called Tommy at his shop with the same result. Punched out the number of my office and nothing happened. Now I knew why they were trying to put a cell phone tower up near the Boundary Waters Canoe Area. Still a bad idea, for sure, but I understood the reasoning.

I had the luxury of driving to a landline. I found a payphone at the Tettegouche State Park ranger station.

I called Torm and he didn't pick up. Tommy was out of the store. The phone kept ringing at Carter Brown Investigations. So there you go, technology saving the world. I found myself wondering if Ned Fifield had a Facebook page. Jim Sacowski? Gloria? Byron Barnes? Did they tweet?

In the paperbacks, when a private eye gets a confession he always has a hidden tape recorder or an associate lurking in a nearby van equipped with recording devices. What did I have? Jack shit. Even if everything the brothers had said was true, what could I do with it?

I could inform the sheriff and he might give me a smile and a pat on the head. I could alert the newspapers and they'd be artificially polite and brush me off like a dead bug. I could tell my partners and they might shake their heads in sad understanding.

I drove along the lakeshore until I came to Larry's Lamprey Inn, a small saloon that never seemed to have many cars out front. I went inside and ordered a shot of Absolut and a tap beer and found a booth in the back by the pool table. Slowly my mind settled down.

In spite of what his brothers had said, I wasn't convinced that Jim Sacowski wasn't Rose's killer. He could have cut a separate deal with Talbot or maybe Rose had threatened to go to the police or her father about the extortion. Jim could've killed her to keep her quiet. And thousands of dollars were still unaccounted for, if you believed the Sacowski boys. Where was it?

I needed Tommy to do a trace on Jim Sacowski's recent financial transactions. Above all, I needed to see the security tapes from the casino. And I hoped against hope that Torm had somehow convinced Fifield to go to the law and implicate Jimmy Sac.

I was a pulsating hive of hope and anticipated disappointment. I knew of extortion, bribery, illegal trafficking in animal parts and bad taste in clothes.

But what could I prove?

Chapter

23

I spent the rest of the afternoon inside cabin number one. A newer Buick was parked in front of cabin number three. It never moved while I was there. Could be they were honeymooners or illicit lovers in the throes of an affair. Or too old to go anywhere.

I was alternately pacing, sitting at the table, looking out at the lake or watching television. There was cable. I wrestled with the idea of calling Sheriff Daugherty. I was skillful in my evasion tactics. I couldn't stay in one place for long and sorely wished I'd picked up some liquor.

Outside, the light was fading. I was getting hungry and anxious. In the middle of a pacing session, I saw Torm's Acura rolling up. I watched him climb out of the car. Looked like he was whistling. Ned Fifield wasn't at his side wearing a look of contrition. Detective's assistants weren't supposed to whistle.

He came through the cabin door. He was still whistling. Sounded like "Wind of Change."

"What are you so happy about," I said, letting my irritability come through. "Get Fifield to sign a confession?"

"Not yet. But we are becoming friends. I suspect he'll be ready to roll over when you and I pay him a visit tomorrow." His eyes narrowed as he studied my face. "What the hell happened to you, man, run into a door?"

"My old pal Dicky Sac and I had a little discussion about social ethics."

"You kick the geezer's ass?"

"Sort of. Mostly his knee."

"Learn anything pertinent?"

"Time will tell. But let's get back to Fifield. What makes you think he's gonna roll our way? You actually see him?"

"Of course I did. I found him at his humble abode in the boonies—and I do mean humble. Rusty old RV makes my apartment look like the fucking Taj Mahal. Anyway, I explained to the skinny wasted bastard that I was a representative of a nationally published true-crime magazine researching a story on the deaths of Rose and Bill Talbot and that we were interested in the stories of anyone involved in the case. And since his name was listed in the initial case files, now accessed through the Freedom of Information Act, we were prepared to pay him a nice fee for his signed and recorded story."

"He went for that?"

"Not without reservation, oh hirsute shamus. But Ned and I did form a bond over a mutual affection for the illegal stimulant. We know his tastes obviously run toward the methamphetamine. Crank, crystal, ice, shards—whatever you call it, it's a substance way too strong for human consumption. I merely tried to manipulate his damaged brain toward a less malevo-lent substance."

"You don't do crank, do you?"

"Please. What do you take me for? My body is a temple."

"A temple with a distillery in the basement."

"Point taken. But remember that I am an actor, *mein herr.*

An actor who just spent months playing the role of a whiskey pig. All junkies, either on the stuff or off, share a deep fascination with their substance of choice. I, through fantasy and illusion, brought Mr. Fifield's romance with meth to the surface. That, and I promised him some cocaine if he'd spill his guts on tape."

"You promised him coke."

"I did. As a form of payment for his sordid tale."

"So you promised an obviously unstable drug addict an illegal substance."

"And the dude beamed like an eight-year-old on the day before Christmas."

"And how do you propose we produce this coke?"

"Bath salts."

"Bath salts."

"Is there an echo in the room? I know of some bath salts you can buy that look just like real coke. Supposedly get you high, too."

"That synthetic garbage I read about in the paper, right? So now we're going to give bath salts that get you high to a recovering addict—and he's going to tell us what we want to know. That, pretty much it?"

"That's the gist of it, boss man. Slick, don't you think?

"Slick as snot on a raincoat, Torm. Except it might be tough to find those particular bath products up here in the sticks."

"I can always make a run to Duluth in the morning. I know some people order it off the Internet. We don't have to meet him until one."

"And how exactly is it you know so much about these psychoactive bath salts?"

"Theater folk know about all kinds of weird shit. And, like you said—it was in the newspaper."

"Uh-huh. And they just made the shit illegal, if I recall correctly. Ah, hell." I fought back a sigh. "You and Mr. Fifield discuss any other subjects?"

"Some. I gave him a ride to the county hospital—Burto's home away from home—for his court-mandated rehab session. We talked a bit. Mostly about how hard it was to kick the stuff and whether it was worth all the suffering."

"So you're going to give the guy something to reignite his addiction?"

"We don't have to actually give him the stuff, just hold it in front of his nose like the proverbial carrot before the horse."

"That sounds peachy. You didn't, by any chance, discuss his role in my arrest—like you were going to do?"

"By the time I dropped him off at the hospital, we were getting along famously—a real junky-to-junky thing. I brought the case up more than once and he never backed off from his initial statement that he saw another vehicle trying to run Rose's car off the road. He freely admits he was high as a blimp—drinking, smoking, tweaking—the whole smorgasbord—but he insists he knows what he saw."

"Maybe a couple lines of bath salts will get him to change his tune, eh?"

"It could."

"And what good would it do us?" I said. "His story carries about as much weight around here as a dead fly."

"We don't have to go back there tomorrow, if you think it's an exercise in futility. Remember, it was your idea that I go there in the first place."

"I still want to hear his story, watch him when he's telling it. I know meth freaks can be skilled liars, but I think we can learn something from hearing him out." I looked at my watch. "It's almost seven o'clock, man. What the hell have you been up to since you dropped him off?"

"You know my life philosophy, Cart. All a man needs for happiness is good sex, loose shoes and a warm place to shit. And two out of three ain't bad, you know. I'm assuming the crapper in here is warm. But since I had some time to spare, I hooked up with Gloria for a little of the old in and out."

"What a surprise that is. I thought I detected the scent of fallen woman on you. And how is dear Lady Gloria these days?"

"She ain't no lady, Bwana. Truthfully, I found her less enthusiastic in our coupling than in the past. But she's skinnier now, kind of got that heroin-chic look going—and it kind of turns me on. Helped to make up for the lack of enthusiasm on her part."

"Glad you could endure and persevere."

"You know me, always willing to sacrifice for a good cause. But I'm afraid all this toil has made me hungry. What is the agency going to buy me for dinner?"

"I'll run over to Beaver Bay and grab some frozen pizza at the Holiday Station."

"You sure know how to treat a guy, sweet cheeks."

I flipped him the bird and walked out to the car.

Chapter

24

The next day dawned a little earlier than the day before, as is normal this time of year. *El nino* must have been on sabbatical because the wind was coming hard off the lake and little clumps of snow were slanting down from a pewter sky. My hands, back and knees were stiff and sore from yesterday's fight, there was a throbbing bruise on my cheekbone and my left ear was red and swollen. As I loaded the packet into the coffeemaker and looked out the window at the bending and bobbing trees, I wondered if Ottinger was still glad he'd opened up his cabins early.

Tormoen was sprawled across the sofa bed. He opened his eyes when I rattled some cups. "Getting an early start on it, eh, Cart," he said, his voice husky with sleep. "What the fuck time is it, anyway?"

"Eight o'clock. Sun's been up for almost an hour."

"Thought so. I could tell by the blinding grayness pouring in the window." He rolled off the mattress and stumbled toward the bathroom, running his hand through his matted blond hair.

A few minutes later he was sliding into his jeans and pulling one of his many fisherman's sweaters (a dark blue one) out of a duffel bag. He slipped it over his head and moved a little stiffly into the kitchen where he filled a white porcelain cup with coffee.

"Nice day for a drive to Duluth," I said. "You better hope the temperature stays up so the snow doesn't stick to the road."

"Lake always keeps it melting this time of year. With all the ice gone this early, the water must be a blistering thirty-eight degrees or more."

"Just the same, take it easy. Don't want to get in an accident while in the possession of psychoactive bath salts."

"Definitely not," he said, blowing on his coffee.

"I'm gonna try and get a look at those casino tapes today," I said. "Suppose I'll call Daugherty and see if he's amenable to that. I don't know how else to play it."

"You could get yourself arrested—then you'd have an excuse to be at the jail."

"That'd work. I could throw animal blood around inside Jim Sacowski's store and stage a sit-in in the parking lot. Burton would approve."

"Now you're cooking with gas, big mon."

We drove in tandem to Two Harbors, *les Harbors Deux*, as Tormoen called it, and had breakfast at a small café on the main drag. I used the payphone to call Daugherty. Something about those mobile phones still makes me nervous.

"You are just the man I want to see," Daugherty said after I identified myself. For some reason, I didn't like the sound of that. "You owe Creek County money for storage fees, Brown. If you don't pay up, I'll have to put a warrant out on you."

"Storage fees for what?"

"For when your Subaru Forester, blue four-door, license number MN-787, was in the impound lot. Being a cash-strapped county, we take our fees very seriously—and yours is long overdue."

"I never got a bill for that."

"Says here one was mailed out on January 8."

I wanted to argue more but quickly realized the error of my ways. "If I come in today and pay the fee," I said, "would there be an opportunity to view the security tapes from the casino?"

"I might be able to arrange a viewing."

"How much do I owe?"

"Two hundred and eighty dollars—plus a fifty-dollar late fee."

"Jesus Christ."

"Lay off the profanity, Brown, and you'll feel better at the end of the day."

Mr. Bad Sex Jokes was lecturing me. "Feel a hell of a lot broker, too," I said.

"Doing one's civic duty is good for the soul."

"If you say so, Sheriff. I can be there by ten-thirty. That work for you?"

"I'll have everything waiting. And Brown…"

"Yeah?"

"Bring some popcorn for the movie." He laughed a little too uproariously and hung up.

Everyone's a comedian these days. His belt must have been too tight. Cut off the blood supply to his pinhead. But he had me by the short and curlies so what else could I do but buy a bag of popcorn and head for the hoosegow?

Chapter

25

I wish I could say it was good to be back at the Creek County Jail. I take that back. I have no wish to say anything good about the place. Or any jail, for that matter. They all give me the crawls. Sure, it's a dangerous world full of bad people—but most of the really bad ones aren't in jail. Your average county jail inmate is a pathos-ridden, clueless miscreant with a penchant for losing and failure. Rarely a candidate for Public Enemy Number One.

I know, because I had been one.

I had my checkbook in my hand. A forty-something woman in a too-tight grey dress of somewhat stretchy material was sitting in front of a computer at a metal desk behind the counter. She too, looked unhappy to be there. She asked could she help me. I said I was there to pay an overdue impound lot fee. She started to tell me I was in the wrong place but then Daugherty strode into the room and took charge like a sheriff should.

"It's all right, Helen," Daugherty said. "We can do it. I asked Mr. Brown to come here. Use the receipt book under the counter there and put his payment in the cash box. I'll take care of the rest later."

Daugherty waited with his hands on his hips, looming there like a plastic-eating bear. I wrote out a check for three hundred and thirty dollars and gave it to Helen, who was standing at the counter impatiently, studying me with dark-ringed, accusing eyes.

I entered the check amount in my account balance and put an X next to it to represent a business expense. This was going to be written off whether the IRS approved or not. When I looked up, Daugherty was smiling smugly.

"Come on back here, Brown," he said, sweeping his hand towards the hallway. "I've got a few things to say to you." His tone was neutral and I was wondering which sheriff I was going to get—white hat or black hat.

I followed him back to his office. It looked the same inside as before.

"Sit down," he said, "I've got everything ready to go," gesturing towards a combination TV, VCR and DVD player on a two-tiered, metal-framed shelf wheeled up to his desk. No multi-screen monitor here, like the big city departments. "Keep in mind that the picture quality ain't that good. It's an old system and the folks at the casino use the slowest speed to record... or is it the fastest? Never could get that stuff straight. Anyway, they use the speed they can get the most time out of on each individual tape, trying to save money, you know, so the resolution ain't what you'd call high-def. You'd think, with all the dough they rake in, they could afford a few videotapes."

"You'd think." I was getting the corn-pone sheriff.

We both sat down.

"I've watched the tapes a few times," Daugherty said. "And two things stand out to me. One: All the players are present that night, including the three Sacowskis—unusual in itself. Those boys don't normally have money for gambling, and if they want to tie one on, they're gonna be at the muni or the Safe Harbor or sitting in a truck someplace. Here you can clearly see them playing the slots and buying a crap load of drinks. Number two:

Barnes from Sky Blue Waters Lodge is there—as well as the two girls—and they all interact at one point or another."

"Two girls?"

"Rose Talbot and Gloria Salminnen."

"Really. Should we get started? You've fueled my interest."

He opened the top drawer of his desk and lifted out three videocassettes. "Which one you want to start with?"

"Why are there three?"

"Three different cameras. It's a long narrow room. Each one covers a different part of the room. Haven't you been there?"

"No."

"You'd think you'd have been up there asking questions by now."

"I'll do that after I see the tapes. You go ahead and pick the one with the most dramatic impact for our viewing pleasure. You look more like Orson Welles than I do."

"Is that a putdown cleverly disguised as a putdown?"

"Not at all. I only implied that your level of maturity was higher than mine."

"You got that part right." He snatched the tape marked Front Entrance, 10/29, and slid it in the VCR, lifted a remote from his desk and flicked on the entertainment. I took the bag of popcorn from my inside jacket pocket and set it on his desk.

Daugherty looked at the Old Dutch bag and then at me. His eyes smiled and his mouth wrinkled slightly. "Good man, Brown. You brought the corn. The wife's got me on Weight Watchers for Men and popcorn makes a good snack. Not too many points."

"Have at it, Sheriff; I just had breakfast."

And then the screen was flickering and I was watching Dick and Dave Sacowski walking into the casino, dressed in the same Carhartt coveralls they were wearing at the logging site. On the tape, the coarse brown cloth looked cleaner and new-er. The boys went immediately to the bar, directly below the camera location.

"Jim Sacowski and Barnes are there already," Daugherty said. "On another tape you can see them plugging video poker machines."

"What about the women?"

"They'll be coming in pretty soon now. Watch for the reaction from the Sac boys."

A few minutes later, Rose walked into the room. Noticing the Sacs at the bar, she sneered and turned away, started down an aisle between rows of slot machines until she was out of the picture. The Sacs poked and elbowed each other and made mock snooty faces as she stormed off.

"Where's Gloria?" I said.

"Just wait, she'll be along."

"I was expecting them to be together."

"Oh no, they came separate. They get together later, though. You'll see."

Another twenty minutes of the Sacs getting drunker and flashing money at the bar went by before Gloria walked in. She was a little unsteady on her feet and her face looked pinched. Could have been pain or anger. The picture quality wasn't that great, as Daugherty had warned. When she caught the Sacs in her sight she went right to them, sliding up next to Dick at the bar. He saw her and laughed and put his arm around her shoulders, which she promptly shoved off. Then it looked like Dick was offering to buy her a drink and she was shaking her head to the negative. Dick looked at her, feigned great surprise. In response, she put her hand in the pocket of her satin-look jacket and came out with a pack of cigs and a plastic lighter, which she deftly manipulated until a cigarette was stuck in her mouth and fire was put to it.

She blew a cloud of smoke in Dick's face. This stopped his laughing but made his brother start up. Gloria then began to harangue at the two of them for a brief spell before Dick lit a cigarette of his own and blew the smoke in her face. She formed an expression that seemed to say, "That's cute!" and went back to haranging. Dick, his shoulders slumping, said something to her and gestured toward the back of the room before turning and looking at his brother, who was grinning like a shit-faced gorilla.

Gloria put her hand around the purse hanging from her shoulder and went off in a huff, swaying away from the camera until she could no longer be seen.

"That was entertaining," I said. "Anything else interesting on this tape?"

"Not unless you find the Sacowski boys getting hammered and buying half the bar drinks interesting."

"No more woman sightings?"

"Gloria comes back there pretty soon, ignores the boys while she gets herself a shot and a beer. Downs the shot at the bar before she leaves, then comes back in ten minutes and does the same thing all over again. She does that maybe four times in the next hour and a half."

"Anymore interaction with the brothers?"

"She shoots them the bird after the fourth shot. Sacs think it's hilarious. Which just makes her madder. At one point you think she's gonna throw an ashtray across the bar at them—got the thing in her hand like she's ready to toss it—but this broad next to her grabs her hand and talks her down. Then Gloria goes to the back of the room and starts in on Barnes."

"What do you suppose that's about?"

"Can't be sure without a sound track. Hard to read lips on those tapes, not enough focus. Low on the pixels, you know. But if I were to make a guess, I'd say it might have something to do with the fact that Rose Talbot was sitting next to Barnes when Gloria first went back there. Those two looked to be involved in a deep discussion and Gloria obviously had issues with that. Jim Sacowski had to intercept her and keep her at bay."

"He restrained her?"

"Not so much physically. Just stood in her way and talked to her and put his hand on her arm and kind of steered her over to a row of slot machines. That's about when she goes back to the bar the first time. She gets her beer and goes back to where Jim is, and he gets her to sit down. They talk and she knocks down the beer in about three gulps and goes back to the bar for more."

"What is Rose doing through all this?"

"Still talking to Barnes."

"Look like they're arguing?"

"Not arguing, maybe, but a serious discussion, I'd say. No smiling or flirting going on. Shall we watch? I think I'll have some of this popcorn."

He ejected the first tape and put in another, sat back down and ripped open the popcorn bag, grabbed a handful and stuffed it in his mouth.

I listened to him crunching while the tape started up.

We saw all the things he'd said and more. We watched Rose get up from the chair next to Barnes and go directly to where Jim Sacowski was sitting, Gloria squinting at her crookedly. Jim and Rose then walk out of the picture while Gloria rises unsteadily from her chair, weaves across the aisle and plants herself next to Barnes, who puts his hands up in a stop position, points at his watch, says something, then gets up and walks toward the front of the casino and out of the picture.

"He leaves," Daugherty said.

"Gets in his car and drives away?"

"Don't know. Only got him leaving the building."

"Do they have a tape of the parking lot?"

"Manager never mentioned one. He did say that they recorded over all the tapes every couple of days or so. If they did have one of the lot, it's probably been erased by now."

I wanted to call him an idiot. How could he not check for a parking lot tape? Instead, I tried diplomacy. "Would you consider asking the manager if there's a lot tape for this night?"

He shook the last of the popcorn into his hand, tilted his head back and dropped it in his mouth. When he finished crunching he crinkled up the bag and deposited it in the wastebasket at the side of the desk. He rubbed his hands on his pants and nodded at me. "Since you were nice enough to bring me that corn, Brown,

I will make a call to the casino and see what I can find out. Wouldn't hold my breath, though. The casino is considered part of a sovereign nation, y'know. Normally you need a federal warrant to get anything from them. Only reason they've cooperated so far is because I once let the manager slide on a DWI. Besides, what could be on there? Probably just cars going and coming."

"Could be a lot of things on there. Maybe Barnes waits in his car until Rose leaves and then follows her and runs her off the road. Rumors had it that she was pregnant with his child."

"More rumors."

"Yeah, but what if it's true? That would give Barnes a motive for killing Rose. And besides that, there could be other meetings in the parking lot that we don't know about. Like where do Rose and Jim Sacowski go after they leave the picture? What about the other tape?"

"They ain't on it. If you wait a minute, they come back in the picture here. Coulda been out in the hall. Here they come now, take a look."

Rose stormed in first; her head held high and her chin and chest thrust out. Had the look of someone who'd just stood up to a bully. Or maybe I was reading too much into it. Low pixels, remember.

Jim Sacowski followed a few seconds behind Rose. Looked like he was saying something to her back as she strode away. He had a little sneer on his face and he stood there with his hands on his hips watching her go. Then he shook his head and lit a cigarette and looked around for a waitress.

"Rose goes up front to the bar," Daugherty said. "Has a few words for the other two and then goes over by the waitress station and strikes up a conversation with the bartender. Little Sac and Big Sac are totally wasted at this point and whatever she said to them seems to douse their party spirit, because they leave shortly after."

"And Gloria?"

"She gets up in Jimmy Sac's face for a bit. That should be coming up real soon. Then he leaves the room and presumably goes to the lounge in the back of the building, where there ain't any security cameras. You don't see him again for a good hour, but he never left the place. Gloria goes up front and sits next to Rose and they have a quiet *tete a tete* which you can't see much of because there's some tall people getting in the way of the camera. They sit there for a half an hour, give or take, and then Rose leaves. Gloria stumbles out a bit later, and, judging by the way she was walking, should've been stopped for DWI."

"What was Rose's condition?"

"She looks all right. I think you only see her have a few glasses of wine the whole night. Want to see the other tape?"

"Here comes Gloria. As soon as I take a look at this, you can switch tapes."

"I'll let you handle the machines, Brown, you're a smart guy. I gotta go up front and see about some lunch, that popcorn only got me started."

"Watch what you eat, Sheriff."

"Watch what you say, Brown."

He left and I and watched it unfold the way he had said. After Gloria weaved out of view on her way to the parking lot, I changed the tape. I watched until my eyes glazed over. Glancing at my watch, I saw it was quarter to one.

I only had a few minutes to rendezvous with Tormoen and his psychoactive bath salts. I punched out his number. Nothing happened. I went to the payphone in the hall and rang Whitefish Point. Ottinger picked up after a couple rings. He said Tormoen's car was in front of the cabin. He was good enough to take a walk down in the foul weather and get him on the line for me. He would get a nice tip when our stay was over.

Chapter
26

Ned Fifield's RV brought to mind a plate of congealed spaghetti, the reddish streaks of rust on the fading yellow paint resembling rotting tomato sauce. The tires had long ago given way to concrete blocks and there was a skirt made of cut-up cardboard boxes duct taped around the bottom of the camper to serve as a windbreak. About twenty yards to one side sat a sagging, flat-tired Dodge sedan from the era when all cars were the size of Donald Trump's ego. The once green paint was slowly taking on the hue of its colorless surroundings.

Fifield's residence was planted in the corner of a big open field alongside the highway. A dirt road running perpendicular to the two-lane asphalt got you to the mud-and-rock entrance path. Across the dirt road from the RV was the Mueller Tree Farm, so designated by little green signs tacked to the gray wooden fencing.

We were far enough away from the lake that the snow was coming down in thick wet flakes and starting to stick on the ground and in the branches of the uniformly sized pines of the tree farm.

I turned onto the dirt and had to hit the brakes at a large muddy, water-filled dip at the mouth of the makeshift entryway. After traversing the water, I eased up in front of the decaying RV that once, at least in theory, had held a pack of happy campers. No more.

My head was spinning with too much information. The Sacowski confessions, the scenes on the videotape, thoughts of bath salts, the upcoming sex video meeting and general destructive impulses were all grinding away between my ears like a blender full of screws.

Tormoen had a small glassine bag of bath salts in the pocket of his blue down jacket and the stuff did, frankly, look illegal. Having had my own battles with illicit stimulants, I was a little uneasy about using this alleged "designer drug" to persuade Mr. Ned.

"I'm having second thoughts about this plan, Torm," I said, shutting off the ignition. "It's not right to take advantage of this guy's addiction for our own personal gain."

"Dude tried to put you away for murder, man. Don't forget that."

"He never said anything about me, personally. I saw his statement in Daugherty's file. All he said was that he saw a small SUV trying to run Rose's little red car off the road that night. He said they were 'dicing' or 'dueling' or something like that."

"Just so happens to be what you drive and what the Sacowski bunch smacked into to frame you."

"Yeah, that's true. But Fifield was admittedly tweaked out, and it was foggy that night. There are plenty of other small SUVs on the market besides Subarus. I mean, what if what he's saying is true? Dick and Dave Sacowski told me they'd backed out of the scheme by then, they—"

"Ah, those pillars of truth, freedom and the American way. Of course you should believe what they tell you."

"I did believe them. You weren't there."

"Forgive me if I don't think everyone has a good side just waiting to come out when doing the right thing is called for."

I was searching for a witty comeback when the trailer door squeaked open and a bearded man, skinny as a zipper, appeared there like an apparition.

"Jesus fucking Christ," I said.

"Kind of looks like him, doesn't it," Jeff said. "A little the worse for wear...."

"Only things missing are hair dye and a cross."

"I suspect he carries the cross around with him," Jeff said.

Fifield came down the steps slowly and I could see his body shaking. By the time he got to us, Torm was out of the car saying, "Hi, Ned. It's Jeff, man. Remember me from yesterday? We're here to get your story about the night Rose Talbot went off the road. Remember what I said I'd pay you with?" He pulled the tiny bag out of his jacket and wiggled it in the air.

Fifield immediately tensed up like someone was pulling a wire affixed to both ends of him. His eyes bobbed from left to right and back again, searching the surroundings with paranoiac fervor.

I stepped out and walked around the front of the car. "Or we can give you cash," I said. "If you'd rather have cash."

"I been thinkin'," he said, moving cautiously around me toward the rear of the Subaru. He peered in the back window, then straightened himself and squinted up and down the road. "As much as I appreciate the offer of coke—I'm tellin' you the thought kept me tossing and turning all night— but I been thinking that maybe it ain't such a good idea to be doin' any shit right now. Money would be fine, though. But I ain't gonna say nothin' I ain't already said to the law."

"You still insist a small SUV drove Rose's car off the road?" I said.

He looked at me. The skin around his eyes twitched as he jerked his hand through his stringy, shoulder-length gray hair.

"Never said I saw her go off the road. Place she went over was farther along—past where I was. What I saw was two vehicles goin' down the road, filling up both lanes. Scared the shit out of me, thought the blue one was gonna hit me. They went by swerving at each other, horns honking. I heard metal on metal. Then they were around the bend and I couldn't see 'em anymore and I had to stand there and wait for my heart to stop hammerin' before I could get goin' again."

"What were you doing out there on that stretch of highway?" I said.

"Comin' back from a buddy's place. Been tweaking and drinking Windsor all day." His eyes seemed to gain focus and he took a long look at my Subaru. "This rice burner here looks a lot like the one I saw that night, y'know. Even got the dents." His head snapped to the side like an invisible hand had boxed his ear. "Say, who the hell are you, anyway? You the one who drove her off the road?"

"C'mon, Ned, relax," Tormoen said in a reassuring monotone. "This is my editor. The guy who's going to pay you for your recorded statement, just like I told you. Maybe we should go inside and get busy. It ain't getting any warmer out here." He laughed a friendly laugh.

"You really think my vehicle is like the one you saw?" I said, looking him in the eye.

"Yours looks shinier, but I can't say for sure. Newer, maybe. Kinda like the one I saw, though, but I think that one had a chrome roof rack."

"You were fucked out of your gourd, it was foggy and dark, and you think you saw a chrome roof rack?" I said. "Seems to me that's a little too detailed for the conditions."

"Crank makes your eyes as sharp as an owl's, mister. Cuts right through the fog."

"Well, okay, then," I said. "Maybe we should go in and finish this thing. I've got a tape recorder in the car, let me get it."

"Yeah, Ned, let's go inside and get comfortable," Tormoen said.

"Ain't been comfortable in a real long time, Jeff. That really would be somethin."

They started up the steps. Fifield was inching toward the entrance when a sound like a steel hammer hitting sheet metal slammed the RV, sending little bits of insulation flying in the air. The loud thud of a high-powered rifle reverberated from the woods.

I froze. Fifield got stiff with fear and his head jerked in the direction of the shot, a tree-lined bluff four hundred yards down the dirt road. Tormoen lifted Fifield over his shoulder like a sack of flour, charged up the steps and dove through the portal. They hit the floor in a tangle as two more shots banged the RV. I rolled behind the front tire of the Forester and another shot clanged high on the fender as the camper door slammed shut.

All I could hear was my heart pounding like a bass drum and Fifield screaming, "I knew they were coming for me. I knew it. Oh God and Jesus, help me."

After ten minutes went by with no more shots, I saw the RV door slide slowly open. Torm came slipping down next to me. "You got that pistol with you, Carter?" he said, voice up an octave.

"In the glove compartment," I said.

"I'm going in after him," Torm said. "I'd say he was shooting from that hill back there in the tree farm."

I cautiously peered around the front tire and tried to focus on a gray stand of pines and leafless deciduous trees in the blurry distance.

"That's insane, Jeff, he's got a rifle. You'll be a sitting duck if you walk back there."

"That's why I'm driving this thing."

"Are you shitting me, it already took one bullet. Thing is solid but it's not a tank."

"We got to go after him, dude."

"Wait a fucking second. Whoever was shooting had to get there some way. Must be a road on the other side of those trees. Ask Ned."

"I should go back in the line of fire to ask a hysterical tweaker having a meltdown if there's a road?"

"You move better than I do."

He frowned at me but then burst out from behind the Subaru and up the steps and inside. It took longer than I'd hoped but no shots came. I crab-walked backwards, opened the car door and slunk into the passenger seat. I kept my head down, got my pistol from the glove compartment and pulled myself over the counsel into the driver's seat. Slinking down as low as I could, I turned the ignition. Still keeping my head below the window, which wasn't easy, I moved the floor shifter into D and rolled up to the camper at an angle, blocking the line of fire.

An eternity later, Torm emerged from the RV, jumped to the ground beside the Subaru and slid inside.

"Fifield says there's a road about a quarter mile down that cuts across and joins another one on the other side of the tree farm. That's got to be where he is."

I cut the wheel hard to the left and bounced along the dirt until we hit the gravel road. I sat up a little higher, turned left and hammered the gas, hoping to throw up enough dust to obscure any sight lines. But the snow was keeping the gravel moist and only a pitiful, thin mist rose from the spinning tires. I turned right at the asphalt and flew down the highway until we came to the Mueller Road, where I made a perfect, sliding dirt-track turn. Three-quarters of a mile down I made another right turn onto the pavement at the Berman Road.

Everything was quiet and empty. The dark forest seemed to pulsate around us. We were coming up on what I thought was the hill behind Fifield's place. "There it is," Tormoen snapped. "There it is." He pointed at tire tracks on the shoulder.

I pulled in behind the tracks and stopped. We got out slowly and looked up into the trees. Objects in the distance blurred and blended. Nothing moved.

"There's the footprints," Tormoen said. "Gimme the gun and I'll follow them in."

"Why should you have the gun?"

"Because I move better, remember?"

"All the more reason that I should have the weapon."

"Give me the gun and I'll go in first. If there's anyone still in there—which I doubt—I'll drive them out toward you."

"And I would do what, grab a stick and pretend it's a rifle?"

"You could hide behind a tree and poleax them as they run by."

"I think I'll keep the gun. Being I'm the official investigator on this case, it's probably better—for legal reasons."

"Of course," he said, giving me the fisheye.

Then he started running toward the tree line—about thirty yards up a small incline—glancing down at the faint imprints in the trace snow. I racked the slide on the .380 and followed dutifully.

Torm got to the tree line and slid up sideways against the trunk of a large maple. He scanned the ground around him before slipping into the forest. Three steps in and he was gone from my sight, part of the gray darkness. I picked up the pace and followed his tracks as best I could.

Inside the woods, everything changed. Sightlines were muddled and fuzzy. Instead of leafless hardwoods, we had six-foot, tree-farm conifers, all of which looked like a human, if I let my imagination run free. I thought I saw Torm moving slowly about thirty yards ahead, but I couldn't be sure. I squeezed the pebbled grip on the pistol and crept along. The snow was thicker in there and I could make out three sets of tracks, two going in and one coming out.

Torm shouted. "Here it is, Carter! Come on, man! Son of a bitch! This is where the bastard was."

I followed Tormoen's boot prints toward the sound of his voice, pushed my way through the sea of green-needled humanoids to a small clearing at the top of a hill. Jeff was peering through an opening between two spruce trees. I put the pistol in my jacket pocket and joined him.

"This is where the bastard shot from," Jeff said. "You got a straight shot from here to the camper. You can see where he was lying on the ground using that log for a gun rest."

I looked down at the scuffed area, couldn't see any shell casings. "You find any bullet shells?"

"Not a one. Must've been a pro or a big CSI fan."

"I'd vote for the latter." I took out my phone and snapped a couple close-ups on the boot prints leading to and from the spot. "Who in hell knew we were coming here today?"

"Just me and Ned, far as I know."

"And anyone he decided to tell about the big-time magazine people here to interview him."

"That's a possibility. But hospital staff? Rehab counselors? Who could he tell?"

"Maybe they have a group. Support-group thing of other addicts. That's usually how those deals work. After the session is over, they're having coffee and a cig, get to shooting the shit, and Ned tells the story of this big blond-haired guy offering him drugs in exchange for his story. Makes him feel important."

"No smoking in the hospitals anymore."

I shot him a look. "All right, no cigs. So they're having coffee with lots of sugar and he gets a meek little buzz and feels momentarily important because these big-city journalists want to hear his story. He tells it to the guys hanging around the coffee pot and one of them happens to be a friend of one of the Sacowski brothers. The guy makes a call and this is what you get."

"It could happen that way, I suppose. Seems like a lot of trouble to go through to scare a guy who already freaks at the sight of his own shadow."

"Maybe the message was meant for the two journalists. Given this vantage point and that nice log to rest the rifle on, any experienced hunter could have put us down if he wanted to."

The snowfall was getting heavier. I could feel it melting on my hair and dripping on my scalp, sliding down the back of my neck in icy rivulets. I was cold and beginning to shiver. I stuffed my hands in my jacket pockets and tried to brace up. "Let's get out of here," I said. "We better go back and check on Fifield, make sure he didn't have a stroke."

We followed the shooter's tracks out. Looked to be about a size-twelve boot print. Snow was filling in the impressions, the toe section already becoming indistinguishable from its surroundings.

We got back to the RV and found it locked. Tormoen banged on the door. "Ned, this is Jeff. You all right in there? We found the spot where the shooter was. He's gone. Nothing more to worry about. Let us in and we can talk. We still intend to pay you, you know."

In a weak, shaky voice that sounded a million miles away: "Nothing more to worry about? I got plenty to worry about as long as you fuckers are around. Never should have let you devils in. You don't got to live around here like I do. Go the hell away and leave me alone."

Tormoen started to say something. I put my hand on his shoulder and squeezed, motioned toward the Forester with my thumb. He nodded.

I wedged a fifty-dollar bill in the space between the RV's door and the frame and we left Fifield to wrestle with his demons, figuring we'd done enough damage for the day.

I jacked up the car heater and fought off the shakes. My nerves were approaching the breaking point. The tires whirred along and the sky kept spitting snow. I found myself wondering if I had what it takes to see this thing through. Up and down, up and down, like a kid on a teeter-totter. All that energy expended, just to stay in the same place. Up and down, up and down. Not getting anywhere or solving anything. Bringing trouble and misfortune to everything I touched—isn't that what the sheriff had said?

Maybe he was right.

And now I was losing my nerve. I'd conquered Dick Sacows-ki but maybe that was as far as I could take it. I'd been scared back there in those woods. Tormoen had run at the trouble like a fireman into a burning building while I'd lingered behind like a pussy. I was waking up from a lifelong dream and not liking what I saw in the mirror.

"I think we could use a drink," Tormoen said, breaking the long thick silence.

I started to answer him but my vocal chords were locked. I coughed and cleared my throat and tried again. "I second that motion," I said. "But I don't feel much like hitting a bar. Someone around here seems to know our every move."

Jeff looked at me with concern. "I don't think it's that bad. Someone wanted us dead we'd probably already be there. Look at it this way; if the long rifles are out, we must be getting close to something. Maybe you should tell Daugherty about this. He can have a ballistics guy pull the slugs out of the RV."

"So they can find out they came from a deer rifle? Like everyone and their mother owns up here?"

"You got different calibers and different types of bullets. Maybe this is a unique slug that only a few people use."

"I'm afraid I've burned all my goodwill with Daugherty. He'd probably think it was my fault someone shot at us. Lock me up for causing a disturbance of the rural peace."

"Well, let's pick up a jug and take it back to the cabin, instead," Tormoen said, smiling weakly. "It is approaching the cocktail hour. And my nerves could use a little bracing. We'll see if demon rum will break down the barriers to the truth."

"You do have a way with words."

Chapter
27

By the time we arrived at Whitefish Point, the dampness was all the way inside me. The snow had stopped but a good wind off the lake was licking me all over like Old Man Winter's tongue. I hurried inside the cabin and turned up the space heater. Tormoen followed carrying a paper bag containing our packaged goods.

I searched the cupboards for some suitable glasses and found none, settling on the white porcelain cups we'd used for morning coffee. A good drinking vessel has to have substance. Plastic, thin glass or metal containers relegate the act of alcohol consumption to a level uncomfortably close to addiction. A proper drinking container feels good and solid in the grip and makes a meaningful thump when placed down on a tabletop.

I put a little water and dish soap in the sink and washed out the cups, wiping the insides with paper towels. They weren't the most ideal vessels but clearly the best we had. "You want ice, Torm?" I said, pulling a plastic cube tray from the freezer compartment of the Amana refrigerator. In lieu of an answer, I heard the short pop and hiss of a beer can opening.

"Three rocks for me, sir," Tormoen said, following the satisfied "ahh" of a swig of brew. "Another beer for you, oh benevolent one?"

We both had knocked back a beer in the car on the way here; the cans of LaBatt's Blue breached only seconds removed from the liquor outlet. Although illegal, I suspect an open beer container in a motor vehicle remains an inherent part of the culture of northern Minnesota. I'm perfectly willing to go along with tradition.

"Well, maybe one more," I said as I set the cups on the kitchen table.

Tormoen slid a sweating can from the twelve-pack box my way before cracking the seal on the Bacardi and pouring rum into each of the cups. My nerves were beginning to quiet down and my feet were nearing the ground.

"So what do you think, Torm?" I said, sitting and sipping. "Think we're crazy for staying involved?"

"Mos def. But crazy always attracted me. Especially in March in Minnesota, when you're already half nuts from being trapped indoors all winter. A little controlled madness is good for the head, I find. Risk is the spice of life, after all."

"I'm not sure how controlled this is. And a bullet from a deer rifle is definitely not good for the head."

"I hear that," he said, lifting a cup to his lips. "But in spite of everything, I have a positive feeling about all this. Like a solution or resolution is not far away."

"If I'd gotten a recording of the boy's confessions, at least I'd have something to take to Daugherty that might tighten the skin on Jimmy Sacowski's nut sack."

"That has a ring to it. And speaking of rings, why didn't you use your cell phone recording app?"

"My what?"

"Most of those smart phones have an app for making recordings. If you can take pictures with it, you can probably make voice recordings."

"Are you shitting me?"

"It's true. A picture of a microphone shows on the screen. Let me see your phone."

I still had my leather jacket on. I took the phone from the pocket and handed it over. He set to work punching buttons.

"Yeah," he said. "You got it. See the microphone?"

I did.

"God fucking damn it," I said. "What a loser I am."

"Cut yourself some slack, dude. Technology can be a little overwhelming for a guy your age. You'll get'em next time."

"If there is a next time. Maybe I should call Dick and Dave and see if I can have a do-over. They can repeat their soul cleansing revelations into my phone in exchange for a piece of pie at Betty's." I took a pull of beer and a sip of rum and stood up. I needed to pace. Frustration wouldn't let me stay down.

"That's good pie," Tormoen said. "I'm not sure if it's that good."

I walked into the front room, white cup in hand, and stared out the window, hitting on the rum. The sky was deathly gray, the lake raw and surly. The Buick was still in front of Cabin Three.

"Maybe I should cut my losses while I still can," I said. "Go through the exchange of the video, collect my fee and get the hell out of here for good. Call the whole thing off."

He was just about to say something when his phone chimed inside his jacket on the back of his chair. He snatched out the phone and looked at the screen. "Missy Pulchritude," he said.

I continued pacing. Torm went over by the small window above the kitchen sink and talked softly into the phone. After about a minute, he severed the connection and returned to the table.

"She wants to hook up," he said. "Can't seem to get enough of my Scandinavian love."

"What's the deal with you two, anyway? Just sex? Just a piece of ass? You ever talk?"

"I'm not planning on proposing marriage, I can tell you that much. And fucking is what we usually do. But we have talked some."

"What's her story? I've been involved up here all this time and I don't even know what she does for money. She work?"

"She used to waitress, I guess. One of the restaurants on the shore. She's currently collecting unemployment. And I think there's something coming in from another source."

"What? Ex-husband? Inheritance? Trust fund?"

"I'm not exactly sure what. There is an ex-husband—Gloria is living in the former honeymoon cottage. I think maybe she mentioned something about him being in Texas."

"Any kids?"

"None around here. I guess she gave one up for adoption when she was a teenager. Kid is in Ohio or Illinois or something."

"So you *are* getting to know her. I was beginning to think you were just using her for sex. The old keep-your-legs-open-and-your-mouth-shut thing, y'know—"

"She's using me as much as I'm using her. Could be more on her part. But you know how it is, you're drinking and you gotta do something to fill in the down times—so things come out. She's not dumb. Just a sad lonely girl who drinks too much. Not given to much deep thinking, maybe, but definitely not dumb. Seems like she could get pretty attached if the situation was right. Like if I lived up here in close proximity."

"You've been out to her house?"

"Yeah, little bungalow outside of town. Dead cars in the yard… woodpile…old sagging garage. Pretty typical local real estate."

"Going out there tonight?"

"She wants me to. Says I make her happy. I told her you might have something for me to do. Said I'd call her back."

"I've got nothing. I don't know what else to do except wait until the meeting with Jimmy Sac and the lawyers. That's in two days. Daugherty was checking on another video from the casino, but he hasn't gotten back to me. Maybe tomorrow. I need to call Tommy and have him research a couple things for me, but I can do that unassisted."

"So I'm free to indulge myself?"

"Knock yourself out. Just don't miss curfew. But I must confess my mystification. Gloria just doesn't seem your type. You being a theater guy and all. I'd think you'd have your pick of theater gals."

"Theater Guy. Sounds like one of those bogus super heroes that are all the rage in the movies these days. Can't you see me in gold Spandex with a big TG on my chest? Maybe an ascot? As for the self-consciously high-minded, overly earnest, neurotic species you refer to as Theater Gals, I'm afraid most of them have too much of an overblown sense of self worth for my taste. I guess I prefer my women a little wounded."

"I won't even comment on the implications of that."

"Good."

I nuked another frozen pizza for dinner and then Tormoen went on his merry way, answering the call of the flesh. Once again alone, I turned on the television and caught the last half of Justified, followed by the ten o'clock news.

My mind was still racing. But after flipping back and forth between Letterman and Leno in a vain attempt at diversion, I went into the bedroom, took off my jeans and crawled into the sagging bed. I tossed and turned for a while but eventually drifted off into a night of animal attacks, rapidly approaching enemies, spinning bullets coming at me in slow motion and even a semi-erotic scene with a naked Gloria telling me I was the one she really wanted.

I awoke to a noise in the front room and reached for my pistol on the bedside table but it was only Torm coming in. The clock said one-thirty. Torm wasn't stumbling. I fell back asleep smiling, concentrating on my breathing.

The next morning the sun was out and the wind was down. The temperature on the outside thermometer by the lakeside window showed forty-two degrees, a good ten digits above the high temperature for the previous day. Tormoen was still in bed, the green-flowered spread wrapped around his head to keep out the light.

I made coffee, waited until eight o'clock and then got on the phone. Tommy was at the shop and seemed genuinely glad to hear from me. Go figure. I gave him a short list of research requests, which he accepted with grace and no smart remarks. I wish I could say the same for Jan, who, after answering the phone at the office—a pleasant surprise—proceeded to harangue me with numerous repetitions of *Be sure you, You'd better* and *Don't forget to.*

Just like old times.

After I assured her I could take care of things on my end, she apologized for her petulant behavior in the recent past. I accepted her apology and refrained from asking if the apology was retroactive to the years when we were joined in holy matrimony. Jan went on to say there was a message from Lily Engwar's attorney (nearly spitting out the lady's name). Livingston wanted me to join him at Jimmy Sac's lawyer's office for the exchange. Jan thought he was possibly a little intimidated by the north woods environment and wanted me for muscular support. I suggested he was obviously quite desperate if that were the case. Jan had no further comment.

When I hung up, Tormoen was stirring. He soon rose like a phoenix and stumbled into the head. Something about being close to the big lake that gets me thinking in nautical terms. The sun was streaming in. My mood rose higher when Tormoen emerged from the water closet (no explaining the British reference) and offered to cook breakfast, saying Gloria had made a gift of venison tenderloin that would go well with the eggs he'd purchased at the Beaver Bay Holiday Station on his return trip last night.

The food was surprisingly good—always better when somebody else cooks. I was momentarily content. Then my phone buzzed.

"Stayin' out of trouble, Brown?" Daugherty's booming baritone gave me a shot of electricity.

Wondering what he'd heard, I played innocent. "Doing the best I can, Sheriff, you know me."

"That's what worries me," he chuckled. "But I've got some good news and some bad news for ya. First of all, the parking lot video for the night in question has already been erased."

"Shit. And the good news?"

"There've been some new developments in the animal trafficking case."

"Such as?"

"Too much to say over the phone. You'll have to come in here."

"One o'clock soon enough?"

"That'll work."

"Need any popcorn?"

"Not today."

"How about peanuts?"

"I prefer cashews."

"You got it."

He clicked off.

"Good news?" Tormoen said, yawning and scratching his head with both hands.

"Maybe. No casino parking lot video, but Daugherty alluded to some new developments on the animal trafficking."

"Anything you need me for?"

"You can do the dishes."

"Ah, the important stuff."

"Someone's got to do it. And every task is important. The world turns on the mundane as well as the sensational."

"Thank you for your words of wisdom, great sage."

"And thank you for your great venison steak. Where'd Gloria score that?"

"Said her brother shot it. I guess he stays at her place during deer season and gives her a rasher of meat as payment for the lodging."

"Nice deal, I suppose. Going to see her today?"

"She wants to take me to Grand Marais for lunch. I was hoping you would have some sleuthing shit for me to do so I'd have an excuse to back out."

"Can't you lie to her?"

"I'm trying to stop lying to women. Call it a step toward a greater maturity."

"How noble."

"That's me in a nutshell."

"Why don't you go? You'll have the whole day to get to know her better."

"Bile is rising in my esophagus."

"She ever say anything about Rose?"

"Not much. Not since last fall."

"Ever mention Byron Barnes?"

"Narry a word. Has plenty to say about the Sac boys, though."

"She ever say anything about me?"

"Just what a stud you are."

"Uh-huh. If you spend the day with her, you might be able to squeeze a little more out of her. Information, I mean."

"Is that an order?"

"I think so."

"I may have to spend some money."

"Get receipts."

* * *

The woman behind the counter still didn't look very happy to be there. She waved me on through, saying, "Sheriff Daugherty is expecting you, Mr. Brown, just go on back."

The big man was behind his desk leaning back in the chair, both hands resting on his still ample belly. Weight Watchers for Men had evidently not yet taken hold. President Obama smiled benevolently down on us from the wall as I placed the bag of roasted cashews on the desktop and settled into the middle chair.

"Why thank you, Brown," Daugherty said. "You're too kind."

"I look at it as a cheap bribe, Sheriff."

"Watch what you're saying, Brown."

"I kid, Sheriff, I kid."

"You and Don Rickles, eh? I'll tell you one thing for sure, that cue-ball- headed son of a bitch ever talk to me the way he does his audience, I wouldn't take it smiling like those schmucks do."

"Sorry. Just my weak attempt at humor. Forget I said anything."

"Pretty feeble. But I do love cashews. The champagne of nuts." He grabbed the bag and tore away the top, grinning all the while.

I took in a deep breath and let it out slowly, waited until he had some cashews down before I said anything. "So what exactly are these new developments you mentioned?"

He chewed and swallowed, brushed his palms together and grinned some more. "I got a call from the Fish and Wildlife boys. Said they had Chris Enrico's nuts in a vice. Seems this kind of trafficking is getting a high priority in the courts these days. Evidently a conviction can get your license to deal in firearms revoked. Quite a blow to someone who makes a living with a gun shop, wouldn't you say?"

"I would. Enrico is rolling over then?"

"Looks like he might, but nothing's final yet. This Officer Wilkins tells me that Enrico is claiming he knows a big-time trafficker in Thailand, a guy the powers that be have a strong desire to see behind bars. Looks like Enrico's gonna set the jerk up to save his own butt."

"What about our boys here in Minnesota?"

"I let it be known that we sure would like to have Mr. Sacowski and Mr. Barnes be part of the package. Some testimony implicating them, at the very least. Shouldn't be too much to expect, I'd say. And these federal boys seem willing to help out whenever they can."

"What about the other guys—Moore, Conklin and Richard Enrico?"

"Looks like their involvement was minimal. More than likely they knew what was going on but never actually took part. The feds've got travel records for Sacowski and Barnes and Chris

Enrico showing trips to places that are known distribution cen-
ters for banned animal parts as well as exotic pets like tigers and
leopards and the like."

"Travel records are enough to convict?"

"No, not necessarily, but it is enough to get the IRS involved.
So at the very least, the fancy-pants bastards at Sky Blue Waters
Lodge are gonna get a visit from the taxman. And if we're real
lucky and say our prayers at night, maybe the immigration folks
will take a long look at the lodge's foreign-employee situation."

"I like the sound of that."

"Thought you would. How about you, been able to dig anything up?"

I told him the story about my confrontation with Dick and
Dave Sacowski and the subsequent revelations. He perked up
when I got to the part about Jim Sacowski extorting money from
Rose over the video. He frowned and sighed when I admitted the
lack of a recording. Trying to end on a positive note and leave
the good sheriff in an upbeat headspace, I finished with Little
Sac's words of contrition and his desire to refrain from any future
violent actions.

"If that's true, Brown," Daugherty said, "It will certainly make
my job easier. But I'll believe it when I see it. But anyway, you did
good. Shook those boys up a bit. Got a next move?"

"Not really. I'm thinking maybe I should quit while I'm ahead.
Finish the exchange of the sex tape and call it a wrap."

"This ain't no movie, Brown. And I still don't like the idea of
putting dough in Sacowski's pocket. Maybe you oughtta leave now,
before I get sour." He stared at me like a Buddha with a bite.

"I haven't thrown in the towel, yet. I'm just saying, you know.
The meeting with Sacowski and his lawyer is set for tomorrow.
You wouldn't happen to know where the lawyer's house is lo-
cated, would you?"

"Sacowski uses a guy name of Thomas Rilling, moved up here
from Duluth. Lives in a house on the lake, north of town. Place

used to belong to a Rourke Mining executive. Back in the day, after the taconite-tailings fiasco shut the plant down, most of the execs left the area. Some damn fine homes went dirt cheap, including this one. Rilling picked it up from the second owner, client he defended on a smuggling charge. Got the guy off, but took his house as a fee. How's that for slick?"

"What was the guy smuggling?"

"Minoxidil. From Canada. Stuff they make Rogaine with, y'know. Crap that makes your hair grow back."

"I didn't know it was illegal."

"It's not. The feds claimed he wasn't paying the duty on it. Treated it like he was running heroin or coke. After Rilling got him off, the guy went on to make millions off the crap and didn't give two hoots about losing the house. Or so I heard. Rilling has his office there. Address is in the phone book. I tell you this much, I'd have all my ducks in a row before I went there if I were you. The man is slippery as a leech in a bucket of snot."

"Any suggestions? I mean—there *will* be another lawyer there. An over-priced Twin Cities lawyer, to boot."

He didn't say anything, just shook his head to the negative and stood, a non-verbal communication stating that our time was up. He turned and walked out of the office, headed down the hall towards the back of the building. I was left behind with a mouthful of wise-ass remarks and no one to hear them.

I went outside to sunshine and mild air. The thermometer in the Subaru said fifty-two degrees and the forecaster on the radio predicted a high in the mid-sixties. I had nothing to do but wait. I drove back toward Whitefish Point, felt the heat of the sun coming through the windows. My ambition was evaporating like the condensation on the windshield. Maybe I'd done all I could. Maybe it was enough that the feds were investigating Sacowski and Barnes. When those government boys come after you, they usually find something. And if they can't find anything concrete, they often try very hard to mix their own cement.

But things still felt unsettled. Something was buzzing on the edge of my consciousness like a lazy black fly. Unlike a fly, I couldn't lay a hand on it. Winter fatigue was coming at me. Northern Minnesota was enjoying the closest thing to a real spring in years and I was stuck in a morass of confusion and contradiction and sordid sexuality. Like walking through knee-deep mud in a lead veil and cement boots. Who could blame me if I took the money and ran Venezuela? Or Florida or Texas or Southern California. And God help me, maybe even Louisiana.

Sometimes you have to jump ship to keep from drowning.

*　*　*

I rolled in to Whitefish Point and saw Ottinger standing with his back to the bright sun, brushing green paint on cabin number two. Tormoen's Acura was still in front of number one. The Buick was gone from number three. I pulled in front of our cabin and shut off the ignition.

"Nice day for painting," I said, exiting the car.

"Yessir," Ottinger said, smiling. "Warm enough so it might even dry today."

"Can't complain about that."

"Nosir, sure can't."

"Looks like my par—photographer decided to stay in today," I said, eyeing the Acura.

"Not exactly," Ottinger said. "Blonde honey picked him up just after I started painting."

"Must be showing him some good spots for photos."

"Could be, I suppose. Didn't see any cameras, though." Ottinger grinned and turned back to his painting, dipping the brush into a roller pan.

Hoping the manager's homophobic thoughts of us were now dispelled, I went inside the cabin. Tormoen was indeed gone. The dishes were done and the sofa bed was back in place.

I was hungry. I took the last piece of venison from the fridge and put it in the microwave. There were four beers left and I popped one. Had a second one after I ate, then put in a call to Tommy and arranged to meet him for happy hour at the Savannah. I needed to get out of the cabin and move. A drive on the North Shore on a sunny day is always a good idea. And I had to pick up some clothes for the meeting with the legal eagles. Livingston had let it be known that I should "dress appropriately."

I looked at the clock on the stove and noticed it was almost three o'clock. I could make it to my office by four and maybe catch Jan. Didn't want to call her in advance. I guess I was playing games.

Chapter
28

The next morning started off gray. Last night's Eyewitness News weather guesser had forecast another sunny day, but at Whitefish Point, thick fog was rolling in off the lake. Maybe it was sunny somewhere away from the consistently frigid water. Tormoen was snoring on the sofa bed. I hadn't heard him come in. The aroma of oxidizing alcohol with undertones of perfume and Old Spice rose from his body.

I was to meet Livingston at noon in Two Harbors at the Holiday station at the bottom of Highway 2. Jan had made the arrangements. By the time the details got to me, it was too late to change anything. Not that I needed to change anything, but because Jan was the one made the arrangements, I automatically rebelled. At least in my mind. In the physical world I just went along with it. Charlie Chan say, "Not good to rock floundering ship, may get in over head."

I punched the TV remote, tuned in Sports Center, went into the kitchen and fixed up the coffeemaker. Tormoen groaned and stirred. I had the feeling I'd overlooked something. It took me about halfway through the first cup of coffee before I figured out what it was.

I should have checked out Rilling's place on the shore, done some reconnaissance. Reconnoiter. Daugherty had warned me in his own subtle way but it had slipped by me. But what the hell could happen? Everybody involved had their own agenda and all agendas would be served if the deal went down smoothly. Sacowski would get his payment and his lawyer would get his fee. Livingston and I would get our money and Lily Engwar would get the tape and be free to pursue marital bliss with the future congressman or senator or whatever the hell he was.

But still, it bothered me. I had let my natural tendency toward irresponsibility take over and instead of doing some advance surveillance I'd gone on a pleasure drive. But my core beliefs hold that good weather this far north is a precious commodity that should be taken advantage of whenever possible. You hate to go against your core beliefs. And besides, I had learned some interesting things from Tommy's computer searches.

I couldn't deny it, though, Livingston wanted me to lead the way to the meeting and I had never been to the house before. I would have to act like I knew where I was going and hope Rilling's place was easy to find.

"You gotta cup for me, detective?" Tormoen said, yawning and stretching.

"In the kitchen. What time you get in last night? I didn't hear a sound."

"White man walk soft, like feather in wind. Must've been about one."

"Early night for you two. Shine worn off the jewel?"

"Whatever the hell that means. Actually, I fell asleep on her couch watching TV and woke up to her shaking me. She was drunk as a monk and twice as pissy. Started yelling at me, crazy neurotic shit. I was half asleep and I started yelling back at her and she took a swing at me. Took me fucking twenty minutes to get her calmed down enough to drive me back here."

"She must've been in great shape for driving."

"She's a veteran at driving half-loaded, like pretty much everyone around here, so I wasn't worried."

"A cultural thing."

He arched his blond eyebrows, got out of bed and went into the kitchen in his red flannel boxers and black R.E.M. tee shirt.

"I need you to go with me today, Torm. Livingston wants some muscle behind him. You know how those Twin City guys are—get nervous around all the barbarians up here."

Tormoen flexed his right bicep. "Muscle I got," he said. "Just don't ask me to think. Ol' Gloria done sucked all the thoughts right out of me."

"What'd you do to piss her off?"

"Nothing. Actually, it was your fault."

"My fault. How's that work?"

"You're the one wanted me to ask her questions about Rose and Barnes."

"That's why she flipped out?"

"She really didn't have anything to say when I posed the questions. But later she was screaming shit about me using her. Like the only reason I hung around was because of your investigation. Said I was just like all the rest—take advantage of her and then throw her away like a used Kleenex."

"Aren't you?"

"I certainly never looked at it quite like that. Well, maybe in the beginning, I did. But I never made any promises. She's a needy person but I did enjoy her company on occasion."

"Good. Because I want you to call her. See if she knows where Sacowski's lawyer's house is located. I'm supposed to lead Livingston to the place and I don't want it to look like I'm scratching in the dark. If I do this right, maybe down the line he'll send some business my way."

"I thought you were quitting the P.I. business."

"If I should decide not to."

The fog was not quite pea soup, more like a light clam chowder. We had to drive slowly, somewhere between a snail's pace and the speed of a three-legged dog. You couldn't see the tops of the trees and every now and then you'd come around a curve and a cloud would be lying on the road and the visibility would go down to a few yards.

As a result of our slower-than-expected pace, we didn't hit the Holiday station in Two Harbors until 11:58. Not late, but not as professionally early as I'd hoped. I could almost hear Jan's scathing comments rattling in the back of my head.

There was a black Mercedes sedan parked facing out at the north end of the lot. I pulled alongside and stepped out. The driver's window on the Benz slid down and a well-groomed, gray-haired gentleman in a dark wool topcoat looked up at me. I wanted to say *Mr. Livingston, I presume,* but held off.

"Mr. Brown, I presume," he said, wrinkling his lips to represent a smile. "Tom Livingston." He stretched out a light brown calf-skin-gloved hand. I took it and he pulled back without squeezing much, as if he might catch something through the leather.

"Nice to meet you, Mr. Livingston. I'm Carter Brown and that's my assistant, Jeff Tormoen, in the car."

"I only require one person to accompany me."

"Mr. Tormoen can wait in the car while we do the business, if that's your preference."

He blinked rapidly. "Has everything else been arranged to my specifications?"

"Yes. But I'm sure you already checked on that with Mr. Rilling."

He wrinkled his lips and glanced away. "Yes I have. We should get on the road."

"Have you had lunch yet? If you need to, we can stop for a quick bite."

"I'll be fine until after the meeting, Mr. Brown. It shouldn't take very long once we get there."

The window went back up and the engine started. I got in the Subaru and looked down at the Mercedes and had to smile at the contrast in our respective vehicles. I backed out and got the wagons heading northward.

Livingston rode my ass for the first few miles but after a couple blind curves and a deer running across the foggy pavement in front of me, he backed off and kept his distance. It took us about forty-five minutes to reach Taconite Bay. The fog was still rolling in, heavier now. The in-dash thermometer said forty-eight degrees.

"According to Gloria, Rilling's place is quite easy to find?" I said to Tormoen, who had been dozing off intermittently, head lolling forward.

"Yup, about ten minutes north of town, she said. Big stone pillars at the driveway with a railroad lantern on top of each pillar. Should be easy enough to spot."

"In this weather? Hard enough just seeing the road. You keep looking."

"Go slow. I keep eyes peeled, Kemo Sabe."

I continued on at forty mph. I could see the dim yellow glow of the Benz' fog lights in the rearview. The digital clock on my dash was up to 12:50 and we hadn't found the house yet. I was getting anxious. I imagined Livingston mumbling to himself about incompetence and provincial morons. Then, as luck would have it, I spotted a big black pickup truck in the on-coming lane; left turn signal blinking.

"I think that's Sacowski's truck," I said. "He's turning in."

"A truck that size is a sign of feelings of sexual inadequacy," Tormoen said.

"Then we must be at the right place."

I followed the truck between the gray stone pillars, green-lens railroad lantern on top of the left pillar and red lens on the right one. The Mercedes rolled in behind me. The meandering drive was lined on both sides by pine trees of various sizes and shapes. Fog hung low and thick. About fifty yards in, we came to a partially cleared area. At the far end of the clearing, near the lakeside cliff, a large, boxy, well-built two-story white house with a sprawling redwood deck and a shitload of windows rose from the mist. In front of the deck, a gray Lexus sedan was parked inside a square, gravel-covered area. About twenty yards to my right, a rusty Volkswagen camper bus rested on concrete blocks between two giant pine trees. Rilling's before-and-after vehicles, I assumed.

Sacowski slid his truck in beside the Lexus.

"I ever tell you about the Ford Motor company psychological evaluation test for the prospective SUV buyer?" Tormoen said.

"No," I said. "But it'll have to wait."

"You'll be missing a lot of insight into the psyches of guys who buy those huge vehicles," Tormoen said.

"Save it for after we're done here," I said. "I might need a laugh."

I pulled behind the pickup and started a new row at the rear of the gravel. Livingston slid in alongside me, shut off the Benz and fiddled with the knot of his tie. I was wearing the jacket from my only suit, a gray one, but no tie, so I fiddled with the collar on my black pinstriped shirt.

The backdoor of the house swung open and a medium-sized man with tousled black hair, black sport coat and white dress shirt open at the collar above designer blue jeans and brown leather boat shoes came out to the deck wearing the smile of someone about to make some easy money.

Sacowski stepped down from the cab of the truck and nodded in his lawyer's direction before turning toward Livingston and me. The smirk on his face provoked my urge to pummel. Instead, I stepped next to Livingston and put on a serious face.

Sacowski kept smiling arrogantly as Livingston and I moved forward in tandem, nearly shoulder-to-shoulder. Feeling like I was in the procession at a gay wedding, I glanced up at Rilling on the deck. His eyes were focused on something behind me and the satisfied smile had vanished, replaced by a bewildered, shocked expression. My first thought was that Tormoen was doing something rude, maybe pissing on the ground or openly smoking pot.

As Livingston stretched out his hand to Sacowski, Jimmy Sac's head jerked in the direction of the VW bus.

"FORNICATOR," roared an oddly reedy voice. "PORNOG-RAPHER!"

For an instant, I still thought it was Tormoen. But then Livingston and I turned simultaneously toward the sound and saw a tall thin man in camouflage gear resembling tree bark and leaves coming out from behind the VW and limping toward us through the fog.

"PEDOPHILE! BABY RAPER! SATAN'S SPAWN!"

I stared in disbelief as a handgun rose from the hip of the camouflaged one. He straightened out his arm and the muzzle flashed three times in rapid succession, explosions muffled by the fog and the trees.

Sacowski toppled backwards to the ground, bleeding, feet twitching. Livingston scurried back behind the Mercedes and I leapt forward to Jimmy Sac's truck.

The air was eerily still as I reached out from behind the massive truck tire, grabbed the shoulders of Sacowski's deerskin jacket and dragged him behind the rear wheel.

"IDOLATORS! LIBERTINES! YOU SHALL BURN IN THE LAKE OF FIRE!

I stayed in a crouch as two more shots banged into the pickup, then watched in disbelief as Tormoen came streaking out of the Subaru, flew across the mist like a blond Bronco Nagurski and tackled the shooter to the pine-needle-covered ground, knocking the pistol free.

Livingston was on his feet yelling, "Hold him down. Keep him there. I'll get the gun."

I heard heavy footsteps on the deck and turned in time to see Rilling escape inside the house. Screams and shouts and the sound of fists hitting flesh came from the yard as Torm continued to struggle with the shooter.

I am not a doctor. Nor have I ever taken a course in emergency medical training or any such thing. But when a person isn't breathing, has no heartbeat, blank eyes, two blood-gushing bullet holes in the chest and one just below the Adam's Apple, I feel safe in assuming the person is dead. Such was the case for Jim Sacowski.

A voice in the back of my head was urging me to search for the videocassette the recently deceased had allegedly labeled Sisters in Sin. I ran my hands through the dead man's pockets, being careful to avoid the blood, which wasn't easy. I found a little card-like object resembling a shrunk-down floppy disk. Ah, technology. I lifted out the disk gently, dropped it in the inside pocket of my suit coat and stood up just as Rilling returned to the deck with a green bottle of Cutty Sark clutched in his trembling hand. His skin was the color of dried bone.

"Everybody all right here?" Rilling said weakly. "I called 911. They're sending and ambulance."

"I think everybody's fine except your client," I said. "I'm afraid he didn't make it."

"Oh no," Rilling said. "Jim's dead? Goddamn fuck." His shoulders sagged.

Torm and Livingston each had a hand under an armpit of the shooter and were half-dragging, half-carrying him toward the deck. The tips of the old man's hunting boots scraped a jagged trail through the pine needles. His thin gray head hung loosely forward on a gaunt, loose-skinned neck. Blood and saliva dripped from a slack mouth.

"That's fucking old man Engwar," Rilling said, wiping the excess scotch from his lips with the back of his hand. "The crazy bastard killed Jim. I can't believe it. Fucking geezer has always been a whack job, but I never thought he was this crazy."

Engwar groaned as they set him down against the steps of the deck. In the distance, sirens were beginning to howl.

Chapter
29

Fifteen minutes later, there were so many red and blue and yellow shafts of light bouncing around in the gloom of Rilling's yard, you'd have thought it was the last night of the State Fair. Sheriff Daugherty was there. Deputy Atwood was there. Even my old pal Monty Marshall put in an appearance. The Cedar County Sheriff and one deputy had seen fit to show up, as well. There was an ambulance, the local fire rescue unit and a game warden. I guess there wasn't much else to do around there.

The EMTs patched up old man Engwar's face and Monty Marshall hauled him off to the jail. Deputy Atwood discovered the codger's black Cadillac Escalade parked among the trees on an old power company trail, about a hundred yards west of Rilling's property line.

I asked Livingston what he thought would happen to the old boy.

"They'll probably try to plead insanity in some form," he said. "But that seldom works, so they'll offer a plea bargain and hope to get him locked up in a cushy mental hospital. A man like that can afford some expensive and effective legal counsel."

"More expensive than you?"

"Just slightly," he said.

Sheriff Daugherty, who hadn't looked this alive since I'd known him, was snapping off orders and making sure Atwood got photos of the body and properly measured off the distances according to our re-creation of the incident. A Cedar County Sheriff's Deputy helped with the proceedings.

Daugherty put Livingston and me into his SUV and took our stories. By the time he got to Tormoen and Rilling, a swarm of reporters was already shoving microphones in their faces. The scotch had loosened the boys up to a point where they were competing to spin the most entertaining version of the events. The two of them were swaying back and forth on the deck like a vaudevillian comedy team, describing what they'd seen in the most artful manner they could devise. I gave Torm the edge in drama, pacing and language but Rilling was better at the details. I don't think Daugherty enjoyed the show very much.

Having had the foresight to move my Subaru out to the highway before all the emergency vehicles arrived, I slipped away in the midst of the chaos. I knew I'd have to go in and give an official statement at some point, but I had the disk in my pocket and wanted to get out of there before anyone noticed it was missing. I needed it for one more thing.

I had an offer for Mr. Byron Barnes that would be hard to refuse.

I swung into the Sky Blue Waters parking lot with a head full of ideas about man and God and law. Me and Bobby Dylan. We weren't going to work on Maggie's Farm no more. At least Dylan wasn't. Economic conditions could possibly force me into considering a supervisory position.

As I went through the entrance, my heart was thumping in my chest. I fought against the impatience trying to pull me along by the lips, hoping the news about Sacowski hadn't traveled this far yet.

The stern-looking lady was behind the front desk again. Her

nose lifted up an inch when she saw me. I was well known in these parts.

"I'm here to see Byron Barnes," I said. "Tell him Carter Brown is here."

"Do you have an appointment, Mr. Brown?" the lady said, still looking like she had something foul on her upper lip and was trying to get away from the smell.

"I don't. But he'll want to see me."

She scrunched up her face and gave me a look that said I was obviously a nutcase worthy of pity. Maybe she was right.

Lady Stern picked up the phone and punched a few buttons, turned her back to me and spoke softly into the receiver. I heard her mention my name and watched her neck muscles tighten. When she turned around, I pretended I wasn't paying attention, just gazing out the front door at the scenic asphalt.

"I'm afraid Mr. Barnes is busy at the moment, Mr. Brown."

"Tell him it's about a movie deal," I said. "I understand he's quite an actor."

Her expression changed to one of a nurse at a mental hospital trying to deal with an unruly patient. She relayed my message. Her eyes snapped a little wider open.

"Mr. Barnes says he can squeeze you in, but only briefly. His office is down the hall and to the right."

She pointed.

I went in the direction of her point, trying hard to slow myself down so I didn't stammer when I talked. I reached the elegant door marked *Management* and my upbringing took over. I knocked politely.

A growled, "Yeah," came from behind the thick, polished wood. I turned the knob and stepped in.

"What the hell do you want, Brown?" Barnes snarled as he stood up behind a large blond-wood desk. He was wearing a dark blue blazer with brass buttons. His shirt was white and his maroon tie had thin blue horizontal stripes. He smoothed down the front of his khaki chinos and gave me the evil eye. It looked plenty evil but what did I care.

"I thought I told you never to come back here, asshole," Barnes said.

"I guess I just don't listen well. My teachers used to think I had a learning disability but the reality was that I never listened well in class. Always thinking about something else. That's not one of your textbook learning disabilities—but I'm sure you can see how it could prove a hindrance to the recollection of educational material."

"Cut the fucking wiseass crap, dickhead. What's this shit about a movie deal? More of your brain-damaged rambling?"

"I was just responding positively to your role in a locally produced video I currently have in my possession. Thought your wife might appreciate the performance as much as I did. See all that she was missing and everything...."

The cocksure look on his face fell away, leaving beet-red skin and a grimace of violent rage.

"You fucking twerp. What is this, a shakedown? Fucking Sacowski give you the tape?"

I just stood there staring at him.

"You're bluffing. Jim wouldn't give it to you. He said he was selling it back to..." He trailed off.

I gave him one of my self-satisfied smirks, brought the disk out and waved it in his face.

"All right, slimeball, how much do you want for it?" he said, struggling to regain his composure.

"Money can't buy my love, Byron, buddy. What I want is your ass in jail for the murder of Rose Talbot. The way I figure it, Rose got tired of paying Sacowski the blackmail and told him to buzz off. Then she threatened to inform your wife about the little bun in the oven, unless you reimbursed her for the money she'd given Mr. Sac. It was your kid she was carrying. And mama might not like what papa had been up to in her absence. You know what they say: absence makes the dick grow harder. And from what I've heard, you proved the validity of that maxim on numerous occasions."

"You've been standing too long under the power lines, Brown. I've been over all this with the Sheriff. I was at the casino when Rose went off the road."

"I've seen the tape. You left before she did. Probably waited out there on a side road until she came by."

"I came straight back here that night. You want to check my vehicle for dents?"

"Your blue Acura MDX?"

His eyebrows went up a notch. "So you know what I drive. It's not a big secret. It's black, by the way. And immaculate. Never had a scratch on it. Check the body shops if you want."

Tommy had already tried that and found nothing. I could feel Barnes' confidence growing.

"So you paid one of the Sacowskis to run her off the road with that camouflaged junker Bronco of theirs."

"You're grasping at straws, douchebag. Give me your price for the tape and at least you can crawl out of here with some money in your pocket."

"Still not for sale." I could feel the straws slipping through my fingers.

"Maybe I'll just take it from you then."

He started around the desk, seemingly bigger, somehow. I had no weapons but I stood my ground. He made a fist of his right hand.

"Jim Sacowski is dead, Barnes."

His face went blank. He kept his fist clenched but didn't throw it. "What are you fucking talking about? I just talked to him this morning. This bullshit ain't gonna keep me from kicking your skinny ass." He started to cock his arm.

"Old man Engwar ventilated Jimmy's chest with hollow points a couple of hours ago, Byron. Right in front of Rilling's house. Seems the old man took issue with some of Sacowski's lifestyle choices. Got a police scanner in the building? I'm sure there's quite a buzz going on it."

He lowered his hand and stared at me. The color drained out of his face and his shoulders sagged. He sat shakily back down behind the desk and rubbed his forehead with the fingertips of both hands. "Are you fucking serious, Brown? If this is a trick, I'll gut you and jam your intestines in your lying mouth."

"And I'm sure you'd be good at it, Byron. But this is no joke. Won't be long before everyone knows about it. Don't you think there's been enough death around here? Don't you think it's about time to clear the air?"

He leaned back in his chair and sneered; a wrinkle crossed his upper lip. I could see the pain behind it.

"Goddamn Jim," he said, "he always pushed things too far. I told him that video was a bad idea."

"And hindsight is twenty-twenty. How much of the buy-back was going in your pocket?"

He blinked. The hatred came back for a second. Then he sniffed and turned his head toward the window, stared out at the fog over the lake. "We were going to share the take. All I wanted was to recoup what I gave Rose for an abortion. She took my money and then changed her mind. Said she was keeping the kid. Threatened to tell my wife. That's when I went to Jimmy. He got together with Talbot and came up with the plan."

"And a lame plan it was, boyo."

He winced. "It actually might've worked. We knew Rose was coming to the casino that night, supposedly to pay off Jimmy and get the tape. Dicky Sacowski had a spot all picked out to send her off the road into the lake. But she changed her mind. She was always changing her mind. Decided she was through getting pushed around, I suppose. Said she was done paying. That did it for me. I saw how crazy it all was. Told Jim I was out of it. As much trouble, as a kid would've caused me—it was still my own flesh and blood. I told Jim to call it off."

"But the Sacowski's weren't about to let it go that easy?"

"Little Sac didn't want to do go through with it either. Said

Rose was nice to him. Then after Rose said she was leaving town, Jim called it off."

"Quite a story, Barnes. Convenient how it lets you off the hook. Except, of course, for a charge of conspiracy to commit murder."

"If you think I, or the Sacowskis are going to repeat this to the cops, you're dumber than you look."

Not too dumb though, to use the record function on my smartphone.

"So now you know the story, Brown," Barnes said. "What are you going to do with the video? My wife is a devout Christian and that thing will kill her."

"The thought of all the money she can drag out of you in a divorce settlement might just bring her back from the dead. But you just relax and go with the pain. I'm going to give the tape to Lily Engwar like I was hired to do. Your transgressions are safe with me. Except of course any dealings you might've had with illegal animal parts. I suspect a few warm-and-fuzzy government agencies are going to be contacting you quite soon in that regard. If you're really lucky, and supplicate yourself to the gods above, maybe the feds will stay at the lodge here and run up a nice tab while they investigate and interrogate. Should be a fun spring. Enjoy."

I turned and walked out of the office, leaving Barnes there to stew. I would've liked to be a fly on the wall in there. Thing of it was, I believed Barnes' story for the most part. It seemed to make sense. What a tangled web we weave. The jackpine savages had conspired and connived, but in the end something had pulled them back from the breech. Call it Minnesota Nice or conscience or fear of getting caught. And now it seemed we might never know why Rose left the road that night. One of the Sacs had probably disabled her airbags—and deserved justice for that— but I was feeling drained and empty and ready to turn what I had over to Sheriff Daugherty. I was due a big check from Lily Engwar and summer was on the horizon.

As I left the lodge parking lot, my phone was buzzing in my pocket like a baggie full of bees. I shut off the phone and drove to Whitefish Point. As I went by the office, Ottinger came out the door and waved at me. I waved back and kept on going down the gravel toward the cabin.

I parked and got out and noticed Ottinger jogging down the road in my direction. "Mr. Brown," he said, a worried look in his eyes. "Mr. Brown. The county sheriff is looking for you. He called three times. Says it's urgent that you contact him. Your photographer, Mr. Tormoen, also called three times. Said to tell you he's at the jail and needs you to pick him up."

As much as I would've liked to, I couldn't avoid my responsibility any longer. I apologized to Ottinger for the trouble, got back in the Forester and drove down to the jailhouse.

Chapter

30

They were all waiting for me: Tormoen, Daugherty, Livingston, Rilling, assorted deputies and a handful of reporters in cheap suits. Torm was still half in the bag, holding court in the waiting area of the jail. Everyone wanted a piece of him and he was glad to oblige. He mentioned Brown Investigations twice that I heard, and made sure to smile for the cameras.

Daugherty was pissed off at me for vacating the crime scene. He thawed slightly after I played him the recording of Byron Barnes fessing up. He took possession of my cell phone, visions of positive headlines dancing in his head.

It took me the rest of the day and part of the night to get out of there. When I finally departed, Daugherty was settling in for a one-on-one with the county attorney. I had denied taking the videodisk off Sacowski's body. I'm not sure if the sheriff believed me. I know damn well the CA didn't. He threatened to have me arrested and searched but Daugherty convinced him I would be more help to them if they let me slide.

And slide I did, right out the door and into Livingston's Benz, where I gave him the disk in exchange for a rather large check. Mission accomplished. All I needed was a leather codpiece and an aircraft carrier to prance around on.

Tormoen and I hit the road to Duluth like conquering heroes. The scotch was pretty much out of Jeff's system. His flowery elocution had turned to minimalist prose. We hadn't caught Rose's killer but it looked like we'd caused a whole lot of trouble for those who'd conspired against her. I felt good about that but something still nagged at me. Torm philosophized that some secrets are never revealed and we just had to accept it. I acknowledged the truth in his pronouncement but still couldn't shake the edge of dissatisfaction. It was like winning a game by forfeit, you're left wondering if you could've won it the hard way.

We made a stop in Two Harbors and I picked up a twelve-pack of Heineken. Torm accused me of trying to get him sick. "You know the saying, Carter," he said. "Whiskey on beer, never fear. Beer on whiskey, mighty risky."

"But I know you're a risk-taking guy, Torm," I said, lifting out a frosty green bottle.

"And you know me well, private dick," he said, taking the bottle from my hand.

The next morning I made it in to the office at ten a.m. I hadn't slept much and you could probably smell alcohol on my breath, but the adrenaline was still pushing me along and I didn't feel that bad. Jan was positively beaming at her desk.

"Lily Engwar called for you," Jan said. "You just missed her."

An involuntary pang hit me and I was doused with wistfulness at having missed the call. I thought I hid it well from Jan but she did give me a kind of Mother Superior stare for a brief moment.

"What did she say?"

"Wanted to thank you for your diligence. She seemed a little subdued. Having your father facing murder charges will have that effect, I 'magine."

"Probably would. I don't think the girls got along that well with the old boy, but you never can tell about such things—power of the blood and all that."

"As long as her check is good," Jan said, returning to her typing.

I had intended to stay at the office and catch up with other business but now I was buzzing too much to concentrate. A trip to the bank to deposit the check kept the buzz going. A trip to the Savannah for lunch somehow got extended to happy hour. Tormoen and Burton joined me. Dan was getting around much better. I no longer had a mobile phone so I called Tommy from the house payphone. Drinks were on me.

The four of us were gathered at the bar when the six o'clock news came on. The lead story, of course, concerned the murder on the North Shore. The young lady behind the news desk read her lead-in over footage of old man Engwar being led into the jail. Then the picture switched to a bleary-eyed Jeff Tormoen describing in detail how he subdued the assailant.

We patted Torm on the back and hooted.

Identified as a Duluth actor and employee of Brown Investigations, Jeff was hailed as a hero. I ordered another round to celebrate. Then Sheriff Daugherty came on the screen with a joy that was hard to conceal. He did his best to remain serious as he described the day's events and the resultant charges. The piece closed with footage of the two remaining Sacowski boys and Byron Barnes doing the perp walk. We all cheered and stomped our feet. The other patrons in the bar clapped, as well. I'm not sure they knew what they were clapping for, but at least they got their blood flowing for a moment.

———————

The local news ended, the national news began and the bottom dropped out of me. Adrenaline had worn off and the booze was taking me somewhere I didn't want to go. I left a fifty on the bar and went back to the office with a hole in me I couldn't explain or think away.

The silence in the office was deafening. Felt like a mausoleum. Jan was gone and the reality that this was my home dropped over me like a shroud. I was supposed to be savoring my success but it wouldn't take hold. Around eight o'clock, I drove to the Super One at the Plaza shopping center, bought a rotisserie chicken and found a paperback copy of *Moonlight Mile,* Denis Lehane's final installment in the Patrick Kensey detective series, named after a Rolling Stones' song Mick Jagger wrote while on cocaine.

Thinking of Jagger naturally moved me along the thought highway to my recent purchase of the remastered CD of the Rolling Stones' classic album "Some Girls." I stuck it in the Forester's player and cued up the often-bootlegged-but-never-before-released song "Claudine," a barrelhouse-boogie retelling of the night the French chanteuse blew her ski-racing lover away. *Blood on her hands, blood in the snow.*

The song led me down a mental path to Lily Engwar and stoked the passion within me. Maybe gratitude could turn to romance, I thought. Who knew for sure?

A fool and his mind are soon parted, they say.

I drove back to the office, ate chicken and read until my eyes would no longer stay open.

A week went by before things at Brown Investigations returned to what passed for normal. It was a week of sunny skies and temps in the mid to upper sixties. Hadn't been so much as a flake of snow since the day Tormoen and I were shot at. The idea of work seemed impossibly gray. After paying Burton's medical bills and bonuses to Torm and Tommy, I was quickly returning to indigence. But what the hell, I thought, summer will soon be here and the first of the month is coming along with my inheritance check. Why not throw a party? And what better place to have a spring fling than the North Shore of Lake Superior?

Sky Blue Waters Lodge no longer seemed an appropriate location for our celebration but I desired a similar environment. I searched the Internet and found a place called Scenic Shores. Located between Two Harbors and Taconite Bay, I'd driven past it on numerous occasions. I booked a party room. There was a pool and sauna and a woodsy-look bar, all photographed for the website. And best of all, they offered full catering. What more could we need?

Chapter
31

The day of the party dawned gray and cold with sporadic wet snow showers, reminding everyone that the North Shore of Lake Superior was definitely not South Beach. I'd checked in at Scenic Shores the previous day and set everything up for what I was calling The Vernal Equinox Celebration, even though we were already past the date. I had selected various hors d'oeuvres from the list of catering options. There was a choice of rib-eye steak or lake trout for the main course and blueberry or apple pie for dessert. Libations included a pony keg of La Batts Blue, champagne and red and white wine. For serious imbibers, hard liquor was available at the hotel bar.

The long, rectangular party room had a big fireplace on one end with the head of a large stag mounted above it. At the opposite end, a moose head mount stood watch over a ping-pong table and one of those old-time bowling machines where you sail a metal disk down a sawdust-covered lane at plastic, electronically controlled pins. A bank of tall windows ran along the lakeside wall. Graphite replicas of trout and salmon dotted the freshly milled wood paneling. A flat-screen TV rested on a dark wood table to the right of the fireplace. Music floated in from wall speakers. I had requested KUMD FM, for its mix of country, new rock, world music and classic rock. Today's college students are an eclectic bunch.

I had invited Sheriff Daugherty and his deputies but doubted they'd show. Probably held compunctions about spending leisure time with former jail tenants. My lawyer, Sam Frederickson, was also on the guest list. Ron Rilling wasn't. In a moment of hormonal weakness, I had considered sending an invite to Lily Engwar, but the whole situation with her father seemed to have rendered that incongruous.

Along about five o'clock on the night of the scheduled gathering, I was in the party room on a brown leather couch, staring out the windows at the brooding gray water. Snow was beginning to stick on the ground. Out of the corner of my eye I saw Burton and Tormoen walk in with Burton's Romanian twist in tow.

Dan and Greta had been corresponding over the winter. When the young lady learned of her man's injuries and the subsequent arrest of the Sacowskis and Byron Barnes, she'd jumped on a plane and rushed to her lover's aid. Wet nurse would be an appropriate term, I think.

The four of us hugged like old war veterans before going to work on running the foam out of the beer keg. After that fearsome task was completed we had to sample the remains for quality.

A little later, I was loitering by the hors d'oeuvres table, about halfway through my first official glass of beer, when Gloria straggled in looking like Old Man Winter had kicked her around a bit. She was wearing a light-blue ski jacket above jeans and half-calf suede boots rimmed with fur. Her hair was longer and darker than I remembered. She held a package wrapped in white butcher paper. Torm was over by the fireplace. I glanced at him and he winked, as if to imply that he'd known she was coming. It was fine with me.

"I brought some venison sausage for the party, Carter," Gloria said, shuffling up, the scent of alcohol following her words. She lifted the package. "Jeff said you liked venison."

"I do like it, thanks a lot. That meat you gave Torm was great. Need anything to prepare it? We can get things from the kitchen."

"Got any paper plates?"

"Right on the table. Knives and forks, too."

Gloria sliced up a couple tubes of sausage and set them on the table near the crackers and cheese. I tried some. It was tangy and seductive. In my youth I could eat an entire roll of the stuff in one sitting. My youth was long gone.

Gloria hovered near me. Torm was, conspicuously, still lingering by the fire, conversing with Dan and Greta.

"You're not having any?" I said.

"No," Gloria said, her voice soft and subdued. "I've been kinda living on it this winter. I'm pretty sick of venison, honestly. I'm saving room for the steak."

"Good plan. Had a lot of deer meat this year, did you?"

"More than I could eat by myself, that's for sure."

"Jeff told me your brother gives it to you."

"He does," she said. "But this year we both got a deer."

"You're a hunter, eh?"

"Oh yeah. And I've got a lot of meat in the freezer. If you want more, just tell me, I can bring it over tomorrow. Chops, steaks, hamburger— whatever."

"Thanks for the offer, but I'm afraid I don't have any place to store it. Not much freezer space in my office."

She looked at me like she didn't know what I was talking about, nodded, smiled nervously and let her eyes wander over to where Tormoen stood. I slapped a couple more of the silver dollar-sized slices of sausage on some Ritz crackers and shoved them in my mouth. Gloria wandered over to the fireplace. Torm put his arm around her narrow shoulders and she looked up at him. Sadly, I thought.

I joined the group. The five of us sat around the fire and experienced the communal conviviality we had once known, even though nobody sang "Kumbaya" or "We Shall Overcome." Our blissful state was broken when Jan and her husband Rick sauntered in. Tommy Basilio and his wife Irene showed up ten minutes after them. Now we had the makings of a party.

I looked around at all the couples paired off and reality gave me a hard slap. I was the only unattached person in the room. It hit home. My brain had been so occupied with everything Rose that my own romantic needs had taken a backseat. Time for that to change. If only Lily Engwar would realize she was made for me. Didn't seem like she'd had the realization yet.

Folks were getting a buzz on, frequently sampling the venison, smoked fish and cheese. When Sheriff Daugherty appeared in full uniform, some of the guests tensed up. Mainly Burton and Tormoen. But the good sheriff smiled jovially and nodded greetings to the group. I went up to say hello and convey hospitality and he motioned me to follow him into the hallway.

I closed the party room door behind us and leaned against the dark red, floral patterned wallpaper in the hall. Down the way, two little girls emerged from the pool area, squealing and dripping water on the earth-toned carpeting. "Thanks for coming, Sheriff," I said. "Sure you don't want something to eat? Stay for dinner, why don't you. We've got steak and lake trout."

"I appreciate the invite, Brown, but I can't stay. I'm on duty. Besides, I'm not sure socializing with your outfit sends the right message to my constituents."

"And what message would that be, Sheriff?"

"That the Creek County Sheriff's Department fraternizes with scofflaws and ner-do-wells."

"Scofflaws and ner-do-wells. That is pretty horrible."

"Don't get me wrong, Brown, I'm grateful for your effort. All the hoopla made everyone forget that we still don't know what exactly happened to Rose Talbot."

"Putting the Sacowskis in jail and busting up the animal parts smuggling ring seems to me like a real positive for the community."

"That's what I wanted to talk to you about," he scowled. "That recording of Barnes on your phone somehow got erased. County Attorney Burnside was unsure of the validity of such a recording from the get-go, and now that it's gone, he's going to drop the conspiracy-to-commit-murder charges."

"Are you fucking shitting me? How did the goddamn thing get erased?"

"We're not sure. We had a tech guy come in to extract the recording from the phone and there was nothing there. You know how this high-tech stuff is, seems like something is always malfunctioning. My computer at the office is constantly freezing on me. Maybe the phone erased itself, I really don't know how those things work."

"Sounds kinda funny to me. What'd the tech guy say?"

"Said he could try and retrieve it. Hasn't got it yet. Meanwhile, Barnes is doing a good job of stirring up public outrage. After Jimmy Sac's funeral, there was a whole bunch of 'em raving about invasion of privacy and entrapment and a bunch of shit they evidently learned from Mr. Rilling."

"And after they sobered up?"

"Their outrage was noticeably decreased, I'll admit. But where the beverages ferment, rage can foment."

"Ferment… foment… did somebody buy you a thesaurus for your birthday?"

"Long winters up here are ripe for introspection. And I practice the ancient lost art known as reading."

"Whodda thunk it. Federal investigation still moving along?"

"Still all ahead full, far as I know. Indictments are reportedly on the way. Scuttlebutt has it that the lodge is going on the market real soon. I imagine the feds will be swooping in along with the return of the songbirds."

"At least something is going right. Any other news?"

"Just that it's getting slippery outside. Your guests had better practice moderation with the booze and with their driving on the way home."

"I hear that. But I think everyone is staying here tonight."

"That's good. Caution is the watchword, Brown. Caution is the watchword. Now I have to get back to work." He nodded to me, turned and started down the hall.

"Thanks for coming, Sheriff. You sure you don't want to take some food along with you? We got plenty. Maybe Monty Marshall could use something to eat. Destroying evidence must be draining work."

I saw Daugherty's shoulders stiffen. He stopped and turned back toward me, jaw set. Gave me a hard look. It was a good one. I flashed a hard stare of my own. His face relaxed and he shrugged. A grin crossed his lips. He formed a gun with the thumb and forefinger of his right hand and shot me one. "See ya around, Brown," he said. "Don't take any wooden nickels."

I watched him walk away and felt my enthusiasm for the party go with him. I decided not to tell my guests the news for fear of killing their buzz. I'd spent all this money and at least someone should enjoy it. I opened the door to the party room and went back in.

Nobody seemed to have missed me. There was an NHL game on the tube with the sound off and a Wilco song drifting in the background. Outside the windows the ground was turning white and the sky was fading to black.

I made a brief tour of the room, greeting Tommy and Irene. Burton started to ask me what the sheriff had to say. I blew him off and skulked upstairs to the hotel bar. Some situations demand the hard stuff. I pounded two shots of Finlandia and looked in vain for available women. Sighting none, I returned to the party.

I wandered around the periphery of several conversations until a waitress came in to take our dinner orders. My guests seemed pretty loose. Probably headed for a group sing. Maybe we'd get to "Kumbaya" yet. Everyone was getting along famously. I couldn't figure it out.

I ordered the rib eye, medium rare. The rest of the men also requested steak. All the women, except Gloria, asked for trout. The steak wasn't bad but I'd had better.

Once the food was cleared away the serious drinking started. Burton maintained his sobriety like a good boy but his gal pal had made no such pledge. Greta and I got involved in a deep discussion about something I quickly forgot. Kindred spirits. We sat on the couch in front of the fire and got sloshed together. Then Dan limped over with his cane and whisked her away from me. They went outside to smoke weed and I stared out the windows. The snowfall was slowing down.

I went for the wine. I was feeling surly and frustrated. Jan and Rick approached me with their coats in their arms. Jan gave me a hug and a thank you. Rick extended his hand. I shook it. "Thanks for the great time, Carter," he said. "Good food, good drink and good people. But I'm afraid us old folks are going to retire to our room and enjoy the local ambience."

"Thanks for coming, you two," I said. "It's been fun." No more words came to me so I just smiled stupidly until they got the message and left. I watched them walk away and realized I no longer cared what Jan did. She and Rick. Rick and her. It didn't matter anymore. Maybe Rick wasn't such a bad guy after all. He'd cracked down on Jan's runaway spending habits and I had to give him credit for that.

After the door closed behind them, I looked around the room. Tommy and Irene were still on the couch in front of the fire. I noticed how similar their features were. Both had black hair and dark eyes and olive skin. I wanted to quiz Tommy about cell phone voice recordings but held back. This wasn't the time to talk shop. Tormoen was at the windows looking out at the white lawn sparkling in the floodlights with Gloria at his side as if attached by a short rope.

Still angry and frustrated, I homed in on the last bottle of red wine on the table. Picked it up and found it empty. "Goddamn it," I muttered.

"What's the problem, boss man?" Tormoen said from behind my back, startling me.

I turned and the two of them were standing there. I thought I detected an air of annoyance in Torm. Gloria seemed somnambulistic, heavy lidded eyes looking up at me from somewhere far away.

"The fucking red wine is all gone," I said.

"I'm sure the hotel bar has some," Torm said.

"At this stage of the evening, I can no longer afford their prices," I said.

"I can run down to the muni in Taconite Bay and pick some up," Gloria said, sounding more alert than she looked.

I looked up at the clock on the wall. 9:30. "Thirty minutes until close," I said. "But the road must be pretty slippery by now."

"That's no problem for me," Gloria said proudly, standing erect and smiling crookedly. "The party must go on. I've got these Finnish snow-and-ice tires that grip the road like frozen turds."

I looked at Tormoen. He raised his eyebrows and smiled slightly.

"Nah," I said. "I can get by with what we have. No sense in risking an accident just for a little vino. I could take my Subaru, anyway, all-wheel drive, y'know."

"No risk, Carter," Gloria said, puffing out her ample chest. "I drive these roads in all kinds of conditions. I want to go. Give me the chance to have a ciggy butt."

"You sure?" I said.

"I can vouch for her all-conditions driving ability," Torm said.

"Well, okay," I said. "But let's all go along. Just in case you slide into the ditch."

"Oh goody, an outing," Tormoen said.

I told Tommy and Irene where we were going and they took the opportunity to thank me and retire to their room. Burton and Greta returned just as we were putting our jackets on. Their faces were sagging and I could smell the weed on them like a layer of ash.

"Looks like you two have got the place to yourselves for a little while," I said. "We're making a wine run to Taconite Bay."

"Looks pretty greasy out there," Dan said, as Greta stumbled over to the couch.

"We'll be fine," I said.

There looked to be nearly four inches of wet snow on the road. Wavy tire tracks ran through the traffic lanes but the shoulders and ditch were pure white. "Pure as the driven snow," went on repeat cycle in my head.

Gloria's Chevy seemed to handle it well, as much as I could tell from the backseat. We were all three on the far side of sober so were probably underestimating the dangers. I had taken a look at the alleged magic tires before we left and determined that yes, the tread design looked unusual and efficient. If the Finns didn't know about driving on ice, who the hell did?

Intrepid adventurers all, we motored through the darkness to the shining oasis of the Taconite Bay Municipal Liquor Store and Lounge. Brought to mind my futile attempts at following Rose.

Gloria swung in by the front door of the bottle shop. I went in, glad to escape the stink of Marlboro Lights. We'd made it with ten minutes to spare. I bought two bottles of Berenger Rosé. It's pronounced roh-zay but it's still rose. Either a ghost or my subconscious was trying to tell me something.

Illuminated by the spotlight on the wall of the liquor store I returned to the Chev, looked down at the tire tracks in the snow. Something popped in my head. I crawled into the backseat, set the bag with the wine on the seat and the thoughts came flooding in.

Gloria skillfully maneuvered us into the southbound lane of Highway 61 and pointed the Chevy toward from whence we came. She was going faster than I liked but the tires seemed to sit heavy on the pavement and grab like a thousand little fingers. There wasn't much going on. Darkness ruled the highway while the forest was wearing white. Tormoen fiddled with the radio, found mostly static.

"That venison sausage sure was good, Gloria," I said. "Was that from a buck or a doe?"

"I don't know," she said. "My brother shot a doe and I got a spike buck. I think the butcher mixed the two of them together."

"Did you know Gloria bagged a deer this year, Torm? She tells me she and her brother both got one."

"I did not know that," Torm said.

"I told you that, Jeff," Gloria said, before putting flame to another Marlboro Light.

"It must've slipped my mind. I guess I had better things to think about when I was with you, Glory girl."

Glory girl? Jesus.

"What kind of gun do you use?" I said.

"I don't know," she said curtly. "Just one of Jamey's guns."

"Jamey's your brother?" I said.

"Yeah."

"Where's he live?"

"Down in the Twin Cities."

"Come up here often?"

"Deer season. Duck season. Few times in the summer for fishing. Maybe the salmon run in the fall...."

"Must be nice for him to have a free place to stay up here."

"It ain't exactly free, he helps me with the rent when he's here."

"But still, it must be nice. He's got his gear stored here and that saves time on the packing. And he's got you to cook and clean for him."

"That's a laugh," she said, loosing a cloud of smoke at the windshield, which floated back to my unwilling nostrils. "I don't cook shit. Me and my brother were raised to take care of ourselves.

We were alone most of the time growing up. He can cook. I can hunt. We're survivors."

"Parents divorced?"

"My father drowned in a duck hunting accident when I was eleven. My mother was always working—at least until the cancer got her."

Tormoen turned his head and shot me a what-the-fuck? look. The dashboard lights coated his Nordic features in soft green light.

"Sorry about your parents," I said.

"Yeah," she said, shrugging her shoulders.

Then we fell silent and Tormoen found a radio station. Neil Young came out wailing "Down by the River."

I sat back in the seat and watched the back of Gloria's head as she drove. The muscles in her alabaster neck seemed tight. Driving on ice will do that to you. A few minutes later we were turning in at Scenic Shores. There weren't many cars in the lot.

Tommy's black SUV and lawyer Rick's weird Chevy. Burton's truck was up in the handicapped slot by the front door. Snow covering made them all look new.

Gloria pulled up near the entrance and shut off the ignition. Tormoen opened the passenger door and stepped out. He pulled the seat back up and I crawled out with the sack of wine.

Torm," I said, "ever see a tire track like that before?" I pointed down at the fresh prints in the snow. He looked at them and then at me and then at Gloria, who was taking the last puffs off a cigarette. "Unusual tread design, wouldn't you say?"

He looked back down at the tracks and I saw the realization crawl across his face like a biting insect. He seemed to be struggling internally, caught up in a tug of war with himself. "They do look familiar," he said, turning sheepish.

Gloria pushed open the driver's door and put one boot on the ground.

"They look familiar to me, too," I said.

Gloria put her other boot on the snow and stood up, caught in the glowing ring of the interior lights. She flipped the cigarette butt away and eyed me pensively as I came around the front of the Malibu.

"How long you had this car, Gloria?" I said, moving around the opened front door and facing her.

"Oh, I don't know. Few months, I guess."

"You must like it. Those tires are pretty slick. Thing that bothers me though, is that the tread marks are just like the ones Torm and I found out by Fifield's camper, the day we got shot at. Tracks were right where the shooter came out of the woods."

"They do look the same," Tormoen said, coming around next to me. "But I imagine there's more than one set of those around here, given the climate."

"You buy them locally, Gloria?" I said.

She seemed to be shrinking right in front of me. She crossed her arms and gave her self a hug. "They came off one of my brother's vehicles."

"Would that be the blue Toyota RAV4 originally registered to James Harold Alseth that you traded in on your Malibu at Dave's Chevrolet in Eveleth?"

Tormoen's head snapped in my direction. Gloria seemed to freeze, standing statue-like except for the recently commenced shivering. She didn't respond, just chewed her lower lip and stared at me. Her face was stark, like someone caught unexpectedly in the flash of a camera.

"I talked to Dave Glowacki at Dave's Chevrolet," I said. "He told me he had to do quite a bit of bodywork on the RAV4 you traded in. Said it had quite a few dents on the front and passenger side. Is that what you were driving when you ran Rose Talbot off the road?"

"Yes. I mean no. I...I... that's what I was driving back then but I never ran Rose off the road." The shivers had become shakes now. She reached in her jacket pocket for her pack of cigs and her hand was fluttering like a flag in the wind. She tried to reach inside the pack but her fingers wouldn't settle down.

"I've seen the security tapes from that night at the casino, dar-lin'. You and Rose had a less-than-friendly conversation. When she left, you staggered out shortly after. You'd just found out she was having Byron Barnes' kid. Your former lover's child. And there he was, waving you away like a pesty horsefly. You decided to confront Rose and she didn't deny anything. You were at the breaking point and couldn't take it anymore. Another man us-ing you while your supposed friend was fucking him right under your nose. You followed her down the highway and somewhere along the way you completely lost it. Knocked her little Ford Fo-cus right into the trees. Seeing her smashed up like that shocked you to your senses and you went down to take a look. Rose was dead when you got there and there was thousands of dollars of cash in the car. There was nothing you could do for her. The li-quor in you was screaming to take the money and run. Didn't you deserve it, after all the heartache you'd suffered? About time the world paid you back, right? Then a few weeks later you've got a shiny new car and I'm in jail for what you've done."

A snarl took her lips and her eyes seemed to bug out of the sockets. "Rose and her little slut sister were fucking everybody. I wasn't even invited to the goddamn party. The high rollers kept us peons out. You're right; I couldn't take it anymore. But I didn't mean to kill her. I just came up behind her and gave her a little bump. Nothing serious. I was only trying to scare her. I thought she'd pull over, but she flipped me off and sped up. I came along-side her and she gave me the bird again and swerved into me. I was drunk. I blew up, lost my mind. I swear I didn't mean to kill her. I was bumping her and she was bumping me. There was so much fog. Then we came to that curve in the road and she kept going straight, right into the ravine."

She seemed to be collapsing in on herself, sinking down like a building imploding, tears and sobs rushing out in a torrent.

Human voices wake us, and we drown.

Out of the corner of my eye, I saw Tormoen inching toward her, on his way to keep her from falling to the pavement. But when I looked back at her she was standing straight as a hunk of hard leather, tears still erupting from her twisted face. It was like a dream sequence in a movie.

At this point a man and a woman came out the hotel door, stopped and stared in our direction. I stared back at them. The look on my face must've been intense because they both turned their backs and quickly shuffled off to their car.

Before I could stop her, Gloria was back in the driver's seat of the Malibu, spinning out of the parking lot.

"We've got to go after her, Torm. Watch which way she turns." I dropped the bag with the wine bottles to the ground, heard one break, and ran toward the Subaru. I pressed the button on the key fob and Torm and I jumped in.

"She's headed north," Tormoen shouted

I hit the highway and cautiously gave it some gas. Went around a bend and came up behind a sand truck, warning lights flashing as it dropped the salt and sand mixture that keeps our vehicles rusty and the roads from being more of a deathtrap than they already are. The wide-carriage county truck blocked my sight lines. We were losing her. Part of me wanted to pull over and call the sheriff or the Highway Patrol. Go back inside where it was warm and drink myself to oblivion. Another part of me was calling that part a cowardly asshole.

I pulled out to pass the truck and felt the tires sliding. I tried to walk the line between safety and haste. There had been just enough traffic on the road to tamp down the snow to an icy glaze. I gently pushed down the throttle and skated by the sand truck. As I moved tentatively back into my lane the truck driver blinked his headlights at me. Up ahead was inky blackness. Where was she?

"She's probably in a ditch somewhere," I said. "I can barely go forty-five without fishtailing."

"The girl can fucking drive," Tormoen said. "You saw it. Those tires work. When did you figure it out?"

"At the liquor store. I looked at the tire tracks and I knew they were the same pattern as the ones from the sniper. She's the one shot at us. Probably wore a pair of her brother's boots to disguise the footprints. She's smarter than she lets on."

"A wily coyote, that one. I always sensed something hidden in her."

"Sure you did. Where do you think she's headed?"

"She ain't going to Canada. And she ain't going across the lake. I don't know—home, maybe? Hole up and barricade in with a stash of guns and ammo? Go out scorching her name on the wall? Real North Woods standoff?"

"Highly unlikely. She was crushed. She's been trying to get far away from this reality ever since the night Rose died.

Maybe she would have succeeded, eventually, if we hadn't come along. But still, I think she's full to bursting with regret."

"She could be hiding at a side road, waiting for us to go by. Soon as she sees us, she heads south to Duluth and points beyond. Maybe we should call in the Highway Patrol."

We were approaching a long curve to the left. I could feel the ditch devils pulling at the tires, sucking us toward them. I let off the gas and feathered the brakes, shimmied slightly but held the road. As we came around to the dark straightaway, a big semi-trailer roared by in the opposite lane, kicked up a cloud of snow and threw a blast of hard wind that shook the Subaru. I gripped the wheel and saw them up ahead: two little red dots. Taillights.

"That's her," Torm said. "I recognize those taillights."

"It's two little dots, Torm. No way you can—"

"I know it's her, man. Trust me on this. She's going to Palisade Head, we're almost there."

"Then we've got her. It's a narrow road. We'll block it with the Forester and she'll be trapped up there."

"She's going over the top, Carter. She used to talk about it when she was in the lachrymose phase of a drinking bout. People are always jumping off that cliff. Doomed love. Fatalistic romance. Shame. Failure. Emotional breakdown. And now, crushing, unbearable guilt."

I watched the red dots disappear into the hillside. Tormoen was probably right. He knew her better than I did. As my headlights illuminated the entrance road, I eased up on the speed and got ready for the turn. You can't get very far in the ditch.

I made the turn. There was only one set of tracks going up into the darkness. The Subaru scaled the incline without any trouble. At the first curve in the road her tracks veered close to the edge. I could see her lights above us, sawing through the stately pines. I took the corner cautiously; the tires barely held purchase.

"Hurry up," Tormoen snapped.

"I'm doing the best I can," I snapped back.

Halfway to the top, the road becomes a series of mountain-style switchbacks. Gloria's tracks zigged and zagged ahead of us. Tormoen was tense, leaning forward in his seat, squinting into the dark. I took a hard right and straightened out, then a hard left and soon, another right. Gradually, we approached the summit. My lights raked a small storage shed and a barren oak tree as I took the final left.

Gloria's Chevy was nose in to the stone retaining wall, snowflakes drifting in the headlight beams like frozen gypsy moths. The driver's door was open and warm light bathed the white ground. Exhaust smoke swirled in the air, enveloping the car. Gloria was on top of the wall, lit up like the last of the Flying Walendas, hugging herself and looking down into the abyss.

Her head turned as we slid to a stop. Her makeup was smeared, running down her cheeks.

Torm and I burst out of the Subaru.

"Don't try and stop me. I should've done this a long time ago."

"Come on, Gloria," I said. "This is no way to end it. Come on in with us and tell your story to Sheriff Daugherty. There was no intent on your part. The whole thing was just a horrible accident. Don't lay another tragedy on top of the first one."

"I don't deserve to live. I'm just a loser. A lame, dumb loser that can't hold her men or her liquor. I stole from a dead person. God wants me dead."

"You're talking crazy, honey," Tormoen said. "You're as good a woman as I have ever known. You've got a good soul, sweetie. Now come down here and let me take your chill away."

"Listen to you, Jeff. You're as full of shit as the rest of them. I'm not so dumb that I can't read the signs. My life ain't gonna change, and you and I both know it."

I could hear the rolling surf way down below us, calling out an invitation to wayward souls. The damp, biting wind found its way beneath my clothes.

Jeff and I inched closer to the wall.

"Don't come any closer," Gloria shouted. "I'm going over, I swear I will. Don't waste your time on me."

I saw her lean forward, knees shaking.

"You've got too much guts to go that way," Tormoen said, his voice soothing and resonant like it was coming from some other world, a world that was safe and warm and free from turmoil. "Choose life, honey, and I'll make sure you get a good lawyer. It was an accident. There was fog. Rose was smashing into you. Things happened that nobody planned. Come on, darling, save yourself. I promise I'll stay by your side the whole way."

Her head turned slowly back in Torm's direction, a strange detached smile on her lips. It seemed for a second like she was going to come down to us. But then she said, "Fuck it," turned her back to us and spread her arms like she was going to fly.

He who hesitates is lost, goes the old saying. In this case, it became she who hesitates is saved. I'd snuck in closer while she was staring at Torm, my legs tingling like I was the one on the ledge. As she teetered forward, I lunged and grabbed her around the waist, set my feet against the wall and pulled with everything I had. My weight canceled her momentum and she fell backward, tumbling on top of me to the pavement in a tangle. Her body went limp like a cried-out baby. She was a mess but we had her.

Tormoen bent down and gently lifted her up to a standing position, brushed the snow out of her hair. She buried her head against his chest and sobbed. He circled his arms around her. I went to the Chevy, shut off the ignition and the lights and closed the door. Torm put her in the back of the Subaru and got in with her.

I drove slowly back down the hill, hoping never to return.

We went straight to the sheriff's office. Daugherty gave us a look like it was a new episode of *Punked*. Then he got a better view of Gloria's deathly countenance and brought us back to his office. The girl was shaking uncontrollably. Daugherty got blankets and coffee. She wouldn't take any java but Torm and I did.

Daugherty wrapped her in a blanket, set her in a chair and we told our story, leaving out the part about the sniper attack and neglecting the detail of thousands of dollars gone missing from Rose Talbot's car. Gloria didn't say anything but maybe she was listening well. Daugherty brought out a pad of writing paper and put it in front of her. She stared blankly at the wall. We left the room. Torm started pacing like a tiger in a cage. I called Burton at the hotel and filled him in. He asked if he should come to the jail. I told him no.

Chapter

32

Three days later, Tormoen and I were at my office debating the merits of attending happy hour at the Savannah Club. The sun was out and spring had returned to Lake Superior. Jan wasgone for the day. Jeff circled around my desk like a dog preparing to lie down. "So, Carter," he said. "I bet you're hoping to hear something from Lily Engwar. Like maybe your white knight bit got to her and she's feeling the type of gratitude that leads to sexual intercourse."

"Will you please fuck off? Her father is going on trial jail for murder for Christ sake. Hardly the ideal conditions for new romance."

"Somehow I got the impression that the old gaffer didn't generate much love from his daughters."

"Don't jump to conclusions about shit like that. You never can tell about blood."

"That's gospel, but come on, man, tell the truth. She's still got you hung up, am I right? Even after all you've heard about her."

"I wouldn't say hung up. More like—not turned off."

He smirked the smirk of the imbecile. I knew it was an act. "Sounds like she really loves to ball," he said.

"She was a sex addict. You obviously don't understand addiction."

"Oh, I understand addiction, alright. It means you can't stop from doing something. Like the way I'm addicted to breaking your balls."

"And you obviously need rehab. A ninety-day vow of silence while you haul firewood for cloistered monks might straighten you out."

"Me and Leonard Cohen, eh?"

"That's right," I said. "You and Lenny. Two birds on a wire."

Outside my window, the blue lake was sparkling. Gulls were again circling in the exhaust from Burger King. "Let's go to the Savannah," I said. "I hear they've got a new dancer, goes by the name of I.R.S. She doesn't take off her clothes but everyone in the audience loses their shirt."

"I can get behind that," Tormoen said, and we left.

An hour later, we were at the bar when the early news came on the tube. Breaking news from Taconite Bay: Gloria Salminnen had been charged with driving under the influence and— here's the kicker— reckless endangerment.

I looked at Torm and we both grinned.

Somewhere on the planet, Claudine Longet was dancing.

And singing a happy tune.

ABOUT THE AUTHOR

T.K. O'Neill is the author of several novels and short stories including his Northwoods *Noir* trilogy, written under the name
Thomas Sparrow and set in the vast darkness of the north
woods—a chilling backdrop and powerful force for the lives of
the ill-fated men and women within the pages of *Northwoods
Pulp, Fatally Flawed* and *Northwoods Standoff.*

.... AND HIS PREVIOUS 2012 NOVEL

T.K. O'Neill introduces former boxer Johnny Beam in *Fly in the
Milk*, a crime novel set in northern Minnesota and a provocative
tale of death, betrayal and hypocrisy spanning three generations.
Following is an excerpt from Chapter One.

I

March 1978, Zenith, Minnesota

One of the harshest winters on record didn't leave without a struggle, but the cold snap had finally broken, the temperature rising during the night to above the freezing mark for the first time in three weeks. At six a.m. the mercury hovered in the mid-thirties at the airport and slightly warmer downtown by the big lake.

Officer Adams of the Zenith Police Department wondered how the steaming wreck in front of him—a late model Olds with the crumpled body of a black man slumped against the steering wheel—had ended up a battered and broken mess at the bottom of a fifty-foot embankment. There was no ice on the streets, only a little ground fog in the low spots. Shouldn't have any trouble stopping on that.

The location and condition of the auto suggested that it had blown through the railing at the top of the cliff and bounced down along the jagged rocks to the street where it now rested uneasily, crushed in upon itself like a four-door squeezebox, the front end dented and shattered and all four tires flat.

Poor bastard's brakes must have given out, Adams thought. Pretty new vehicle, though, to have the brakes go out like that and pick up enough speed to rip through the guardrail.

Adams bent over and looked through the empty hole where the driver's window had been. Chunks of glass lay on the broad but lifeless back of the man in the seat. His head rested at a crazy angle against the steering wheel, blank eyes facing the passenger window. There was a large bloody dent above his right temple.

A flare of recognition hit Adam's gut and his heart got heavy in his chest. Something familiar about the shoulders and the dark wool overcoat and the shape of the head.

Adams bent in and peered at the bruised and bloodied face. Then he straightened up and filled his lungs with the damp air and squinted up at the top of the cliff again.

Once more he bent down and stuck his head inside the Olds. He was pretty sure now. The face was swollen and distorted but who else could it be? He heard Patrolman Hayes coming up behind him. Adams took another long look inside the wreck.

It was Johnny Beam, without a doubt.

Johnny Beam looking like he'd lost his last fight.

Adams stepped back and fought away the sick feeling as he watched Hayes bend over and study the body, hands in the pockets of his uniform like he was window shopping.

"Looks like there's one less nigger on the planet," Hayes said, snapping his gum.

"Don't let me hear that kind of shit again, Dennis," Adams growled, balling his fists. "I knew this man. Used to watch him play football when I was a kid. He may not have been the most responsible guy you'll ever meet, but he wasn't a nigger, and I won't tolerate that shit."

"Hey, I didn't mean anything, you know—I was just saying…"

Adams stared down at the body, eyes narrowed. "This is Johnny Beam, used to be the state light-heavyweight boxing champion. Great athlete. And a good guy."

"Ain't he the one they brought in on that weapons sting back in January?"

"Yeah, that was him. He'd fallen on some hard times, made some bad decisions."

"Well, it looks like he's fallen on even harder times now," Hayes said, the corners of his mouth rising into a smirk. "You might say he finally hit bottom." He spit his gum on the pavement, hitched his shoulders and gave Adams a stare.

Adams returned the stare. "You really are an enlightened guy, Hayes. For a fucking cretin."

A siren wailed in the distance as steam smelling of antifreeze, brake fluid and burnt motor oil drifted across the chunks of broken rock, shards of glass and colored plastic littering the pavement. Hayes kicked at a jagged hunk of metal and stared blankly at the wreck. "You sure pick some funny guys to defend, Adams," he said. "Wasn't this guy a bookie and a pimp and every other goddamn thing?"

"Fuck you, Hayes. I knew the guy, okay? It ain't easy to see someone you know, dead."

A few blocks to the east, an ambulance careened onto Superior Street and roared toward them with the siren screaming. Further back a tow truck and another squad car were also rolling toward the body of Johnny Beam.

"I got a question for you, Adams." Hayes said, squinting at the approaching ambulance. "How do you think your friend went off that cliff? Think he was drunk—at six o'clock in the goddamn morning? Stinks like booze in there, but still—couldn't the son of a bitch use the brakes?"

"That's a good question, Dennis. A question I'm sure somebody is gonna want answered."

"You never know, the brakes coulda failed," Hayes said. "You know how them niggers are, never fixing anything."

Adams swallowed hard. Was about to respond in kind when the ambulance came careening to a stop and the paramedics jumped out. Swirling red lights sliced through the steam and the fog and the grayness.

Like some kind of horror show, Adams thought. "We got a dead man in there, boys," he said. "Go easy on him."

The ambulance jockeys looked at the body with wide caffeinated eyes, searched for a pulse and grimly nodded to Adams.

Who's gonna care about a dead nigger in this town? Patrolman Hayes thought. Sure, there'll be a few like Adams who'll moan about it long enough to make sure everyone knows they feel real bad. And then they'll forget about it just like everyone else.

The tow truck rumbled up alongside Adams, who was scratching his head and trying to reign in his emotions. The gnarled-faced driver leaned out the window, cigarette smoke seeping from his nose and mouth. "You want us to drag that thing out of the way, officer?"

"You bet, Jack," Hayes snapped, stepping between Adams and the tow truck. "We got traffic that's got to get through here."

Adams bristled. "We're gonna have to leave it where it is until the chief and a medical examiner get a look at it. This could be a crime scene, Hayes. You go up to the top of the hill where he came through and look around." He pointed at the arriving squad car. "Bring McNally and Ledyard with you. Put some tape around the area and make sure the tracks and everything are left intact. I'll wait here for the brass."

Hayes blinked and thought about saying something but instead launched a gob of spit on the damp pavement and strutted toward the patrol car. He leaned a hand on the driver's door and filled in the inhabitants.

As the squad car pulled away, the chief of police and the chief of detectives arrived from the opposite direction in separate Ford Crown Victoria sedans, one blue and one brown.

Chief of Detectives Harvey Green was a friendly, heavyset man who was smarter than he looked and well liked by most. His personal motto was *Do a good job but take care of you and yours first.* He seldom thought or felt too deeply about anything and as long as the larder was full, life was good.

Police Chief Ira Bjorkman was old and tired and had been on the job for too long. Everyone on the force knew it and so did he.

A recent increase in local crime coupled with the intrusion of the national press covering the Norville murder trial into his previously serene existence had stoked his growing desire for retirement. There was just too much bullshit going on these days for someone who was raised on Live and let live.

Harvey Green let the chief walk slightly ahead of him as they approached the wreck.

Adams watched them come, waited for the slow-moving pair.

"What have we got here, officer?" Chief Bjorkman asked, bending over and peering into the car.

"What appears to be a dead man, sir, who I believe is Johnny Beam, the boxer. But I didn't look for I.D. I haven't touched anything."

"Very good," Bjorkman said. "Looks like we got another one for the coroner. That fat son of a bitch hasn't worked this much in his whole goddamn career." He turned around and looked east along Superior Street. "And the asshole better get here in a hurry."

Chief of Detectives Harvey Green bent over and peered inside the Olds.

"Looks like this could be the end of the line on the ATF boys' case, eh, Harvey?" Bjorkman said, pawing at the damp pavement with his worn wingtip.

"Maybe so, Ira, maybe so. You think someone got to Beam here? He's pretty battered. Nobody ever hit him that much in the ring."

"Driving off a cliff will do that to ya."

Green pulled a clean white handkerchief from his trouser pocket, draped it over his left hand and reached inside the dead man's coat. He came out with a long wallet that he placed on the roof of the car then leaned back in and sifted the outside coat pockets.

"Here's a winner for you," he said, holding up a set of keys. "Still got his keys in his pocket. Look at the little gold boxing gloves. Must be a spare set there in the ignition, just got a plain chain. That's a little off, wouldn't you say?"

"A man gets older, starts hitting the sauce, there are times he'll forget just about anything. You telling me you never thought you lost your keys and then found them later?"

"No... but not like this. This is a heavy set of keys. Man's gotta know it's in his pocket."

"Yes and no. If a man has been up all night hitting the sauce and the foo-foo dust, he might not know much at all. He may be stumbling out the door in a hurry and not know his ass from a tuna sandwich."

"Yeah, s'pose that's a possibility," Green said. "And it is March...."

"That it is, Harvey, that it is."

Green straightened up and scratched his chin. Scowl lines formed deep furrows above his eyes. "I think we need to call in a professional accident guy on this one," he said, turning to gaze at the frozen bay and the hazy outline of the grain terminals in the distance. "Someone whose expertise will override ours. The way the media is jacked up these days, with that goddamn Paul Richards sticking his beak in everything, I think we need someone out front on this."

"You're right. I agree," Bjorkman said. "Your wisdom suits that of the next police chief. But Jesus, what the hell happened to this poor son of a bitch Beam? How did it ever come down to this? I remember when he was really something."

"Me too, Ira. Me too."

* * * *

Enjoy the rest of Fly in the Milk,
a T.K. O'Neill crime/noir ebook
available at all major online book stores

CPSIA information can be obtained
at www.ICGtesting.com
Printed in the USA
BVHW030205290220
573687BV00001B/19

9 780967 200668